Light Reading:

A Collection of Novellas

By

Sydney Canyon

2014

Light Reading: A Collection of Novellas © 2014 Sydney Canyon
Triplicity Publishing, LLC

Igniting Temptation © 2013 Sydney Canyon
One Night © 2013 Sydney Canyon
Fine © 2014 Sydney Canyon
Shadow's Eyes © 2014 Sydney Canyon
Triplicity Publishing, LLC

ISBN-13: 978-0990471608
ISBN-10: 0990471608

Printed in the United States of America
First Edition – 2014
Cover Design: Triplicity Publishing, LLC
Interior Design: Triplicity Publishing, LLC

Acknowledgements

Special thanks to thank C.J. for catching the little things that seem to slip past everyone else.

Dedication

This book is dedicated to the special people in my life that motivate me every single day and to my fans. Without you, I'd have no reason to tell my stories.

And for those of you who enjoy holding a good book in their hands as much as I do, this collection is for you!

Sydney Canyon

Table of Contents

Igniting Temptation

By

Sydney Canyon

Sydney Canyon

Chapter 1

Mac finished suturing the eyebrow of her six year old patient. Brushing his sandy colored hair back with her palm, she applied a small Sponge Bob bandage over the tiny blue threads above his right eye.

"There you go, Scottie, all fixed up. Try not to jump anymore ramps with your bike. Okay?"

"Yes, ma'am," The young boy answered back with a lisp.

"Thank you, Doctor," his Mom said before escorting the boy out of the emergency room.

Dr. Mackenzie Trotter walked out of the exam room yawning. She was five foot six with an athletic, slender build, lightly tanned skin, short blond hair, and astonishing green eyes. She was also the Head of Pediatrics at Hilton Head Medical Center, in Hilton Head Island, South Carolina. Everyone in the hospital knew her. She was beautiful, vibrant, highly intelligent, and a workaholic.

"Mac, what are you doing working down here tonight?" A short, black man in pale green scrubs spoke as he handed her a cup of coffee.

"Hey, Lyle. It's slow in Pediatrics tonight, so I thought I'd help out in the ER for a bit. Thanks for the coffee. I was just about to come get some myself."

"I see. Is Loren out of town again?" he asked.

"Yeah. How'd you know?" she grimaced.

"Because you're heading into your eighteenth hour on shift. You're killing yourself working like this. But, it's none of my business."

"Thanks." She smiled and made a rational decision to finally go home.

Mac parked her dark blue Mini Cooper in the empty parking spot next to the black BMW. She grabbed her backpack and briefcase and head up the stairs to her condo. She tossed everything aside as she walked through the door. A tan and white Chihuahua came running towards her from around the corner.

"Hey, Stimpy!" She bent down and picked up the little girl who couldn't wait to lick her Mom's face.

"You're home early. I wasn't expecting you until tomorrow," Mac said with a touch of surprise as she made her way to the kitchen holding the small dog. An olive skinned woman with long, straight, black hair was standing at the kitchen counter. She was similar to Mac in build and height, but appeared to be a little bit older, definitely closer to forty.

"Why? Does it bother you? Were you expecting someone else?" The woman said dryly.

"No, Loren. My God, do you really think I have someone waiting in the wings for me every time you go out of town on business? At this rate I wish I did, hell I'd probably see her more than I see you." Mac ran a hand through her hair and swung open the refrigerator. She grabbed a cold beer and set Stimpy on the floor as she went to change out of her scrubs and take a hot shower. Stimpy followed her and curled up on the rug by the sink. *What an asshole. Welcome home Cruella! Hope you missed me while you were in hell. Sorry they sent you*

4

back!

Halfway through her shower the glass door opened behind Mac.

"I'm sorry baby. I had a long week and I'm glad your home. I know you must've been working double and triple shifts at the hospital while I was gone. I know you're tired."

"Yes, you know I work a lot while you're away. But, I really don't need you jumping down my throat constantly, Loren. You're the one that is gone two weeks out of the month. At least, I try to work my hospital rounds away from our time together."

Loren went to butt in and Mac cut her off. "Look, I really don't want to fight with you. I haven't seen you in a couple weeks and I miss you."

"Good, I miss you too." Loren quickly took off her clothes and helped Mac finish the rest of her shower, making sure to wash *all* of her parts.

The next morning Mac was standing at the bathroom sink brushing her teeth when Loren was leaving for work.

"Hey Loren, make sure...you...vote today, don't…forget. Can you…feed…Stimpy for me?" Mac said between brushes.

"I know. I'm going to do it on my way to the office. Come on, Stimpy. I don't have all day," Loren said snagging a quick kiss before headed out the door. The little dog hesitated before following slowly. Mac could swear she saw the dog roll her eyes.

~

"Morning, Neil, ready for the voters to take over? I

saw the line starting to form at six this morning," Captain Smith said. He was a balding man, in his late forties with a thin mustache.

"I could care less as long as they don't touch anything. I worked all day yesterday cleaning this place. If nothing else we can people watch today. I have five dollars that says we won't get a call until eleven o'clock this morning," A short, athletic looking, young woman with shoulder length, naturally curly black hair pulled back in a pony tail and piercing blue eyes answered him. She was sitting at the table eating a bowl of cereal and a banana. She quickly downed the glass of chocolate milk in front of her.

"Really, that late, huh. Okay, you're on," he said shaking her hand.

"Wait, wait, I want in on this bet," a young guy said as he walked into the room.

"Harris, you're too late my son, we already shook. Go bet with Brown, I'm sure you can sucker him out of five dollars."

"Damn it, Neil, you two always get away with it before anyone can join in."

"Seniority baby, seniority," she said. They all laughed.

"It's all good. Keep eating your Wheaties, Neil. You'll need them since you're on the hose today," Harris said.

"The hell I am. Since when do you tell me what to do rookie? And they're not Wheaties thank you very much. You should try them, you might actually grow some…never mind, I might crucify your virgin ears, baby boy!" she said sarcastically.

"Ha, Neil, you're too fucking funny!" A voice was heard in the distance as a young guy named, Thomas Brown, snuck into the kitchen grabbing a banana from the stalk and a glass of orange juice. He and Daniel Harris were both very young and rookies in the department.

"Can't we all get along?" Smith and Neil laughed together.

"Hey look guys, here comes another wave of voters. Woohoo!!" Brown and Harris slid down the pole next to the fire truck and ambulance trying to impress the voter ladies.

Neil and Smith shook their heads as they walked down the stairs to make sure the truck was stocked and ready to go. The four of them always rode on the fire truck together and Lawson and Vincent, who were already down stairs rode on the ambulance on their shift. Eleven more fire fighters and EMT's worked out of the same station on a three days on and two days off rotation schedule.

~

Mac parked her Mini Cooper on the edge of the road behind all of the other voters and walked towards the Hilton Head Island Airport Fire Station. *How the hell does a fire station become a voting precinct? No wonder this government is so ass backwards.* She thought stopping inside the bay out of the sun and in a line of at least twenty people. She was about thirty minutes behind Loren. She had already come and gone.

She noticed all of the fire fighters and EMT's were in a group staring at the people in line waiting to vote. The only female in the group seemed to be looking directly at her so Mac smiled. Immediately, the woman winked and smiled back. Mac turned her head quickly following the line as it moved forward.

~

"Man these people are serious about voting. Why the hell would you drive over here, and wait in line, just to punch some numbers in a machine?" Brown stated wryly.

"It's called being patriotic, dip shit." Neil growled at him.

"Hey now, she's a cutie. I wonder where she's headed after this? I bet she works in…"

"Wait? Are you talking about the blond over there in the khaki pants, white shirt, and sneakers?" Neil asked quizzically as she interrupted him.

"Yeah, why?"

"I have to hear this Brown, where does she work?" She asked as she slid her hands into the pockets of her dark blue pants. Her dark blue button down oxford shirt was still tucked in perfectly along with the white tee shirt underneath it.

"She works in a restaurant," Brown said.

"Ha-ha, you're kidding me right?"

"Well where do you think she works miss high and mighty?" Harris said.

"I don't have a clue, but I can ask her," Neil said.

"That won't be necessary," Smith chimed in. "She's a doctor."

"How the hell do you know?" They all questioned.

"I've seen her at Hilton Head Medical. I think she's an attending in the ER."

"Hmm…I've never seen her," Brown said. "What do you think, Harris?"

"I think Smith is lying through his teeth. He likes her and doesn't want any of us to talk to her first. Anyway, look at that guy over there in the shorts, he's got to be a mailman, wearing shorts that short…gross. The woman behind him is definitely a housewife. She still has curlers in her hair," he chuckled.

"Oh, this game is fun!" Brown climbed up on the fire truck and sat above Smith and Neil who sat down on the back bumper. Harris followed him up.

As the blond woman came out of the voting booth Neil smiled at her again and nodded for her to come over to where they all were gathered around the truck. She jumped to her feet and walked a few feet away from earshot of the arrogant men she worked with and was astounded at how cute the woman was up close.

"I'm Kylie, but everyone around here calls me Neil." She pointed at her last name stitched above the right breast pocket of her shirt as she stuck her hand out.

"Hi, I'm Mac...uh...Mackenzie," Mac said shaking Neil's hand. She looked shyly into the woman's blue eyes as her hand was squeezed.

"It's nice to meet you," Neil said."I know you're busy, probably heading to work."

"Yes, that would be correct," Mac laughed.

"Can I call you sometime?" Neil asked blatantly.

Mac stopped breathing for a second. *Wow, she's definitely straight forward.* "Uh...uh...yeah sure," Mac said giving Kylie her cell number.

"Sounds good. Have a good day at work. It was nice meeting you, Mackenzie." Neil said grinning at the woman standing in front of her.

"It was nice to meet you too." Mac made her way to her car and drove off. *Holy shit, Mackenzie! What the hell were you thinking boldly giving your number to a stranger? An absolutely adorable stranger!* "She could be a friend, a new friend, *just* a friend!"

Sydney Canyon

Chapter 2

"Dr. Mackenzie Trotter, please call extension one, two, one." The loud speaker announced. Mac grabbed the phone at the pediatric nurse's station and dialed the number.

"This is Dr. Trotter."

"Hi, this is Dr. Thorp in Neo-natal. Excuse me for paging you over the intercom. I don't have your number in my phone."

"That's not a problem, what do you need?"

"I have a newborn down here that we may need to send down to Savannah Children's Hospital by helicopter. She was born this morning at thirty weeks and is just over three pounds."

"Okay. I'm on my way."

~

Kylie Neil took a hot shower, then grabbed her cell phone dialing the number on the scrunched up piece of paper in her wallet. The phone rang twice before going to voicemail.

"Hi, this is Dr. Trotter. Please leave a message at the tone. If this is an emergency please press one to send me a page. Thank you," The voice on the message was

11

definitely the same woman she met earlier that morning.

Doctor...hmm...so maybe Smith was *right.* "Hi, this is Kylie, we met at the fire station. You can call me back at your convenience," she said leaving her number.

Just as she hung up the phone the station bell rang loudly as an emergency call came out for an auto accident. Kylie jumped up and ran over to the pole sliding down to the truck. Smith tossed her the keys to the ambulance.

"Lieutenant Neil, I need you to drive the ambulance. I'm going to need two in the back on this one."

"Yes, Sir." She was the smallest person, but second in command to Captain Smith and everyone else in that station house was under her command when that bell rang.

~

"Hi, Samantha." Two tiny brown eyes glared back at Mac as she rubbed the fingers of the little baby. She quickly analyzed the chart with Dr. Thorp. Her cell phone went off and she immediately sent the call to voicemail.

"Her vitals look good. What did cardiology say?"

"The tear is so small they think it may heal on its own. We're going to give it twenty-four hours before flying her down to Savannah in case it closes on its own. "

"She has very strong vitals, maybe she won't need surgery. Fortunately, they are set up for that sort of treatment down there."

"I definitely agree."

"Keep me in the loop," Mac said rubbing the baby girl's fingers as she stared up at her.

~

Neil parked the ambulance twenty feet from the crash scene next to the fire truck that she was following. She jumped out rushing over with the orange EMT bags.

"What have we got here?"

"This man's car pulled out in front of that woman's car over there and she hit this one between the driver's side front and rear doors." The arrogant cop spoke in monotone.

Neil immediately went to work on the young boy that had been sitting behind his father. When the other car hit their car the impact from the door crushing in caused a large gash on the child's head and his breathing was very slow. She worked with Lawson to move the boy onto the backboard and get a bandage on his head to try and stop the bleeding. The woman was alone in her car. She had minor cuts and bruises and didn't want to go to the hospital. The boy's father had cuts and bruises from the seatbelt and shattered glass and was going to be transported with his son since he could sit up on the seat in the back with the guys.

"He's out, let's move!" Neil shouted to her team. "Smith, we're out of here!"

~

Just as Mac was listening to her voicemail, her cell phone went off again.

"Dr. Trotter?"

"This is Doctor Kenny in Emergency. We have a trauma coming in involving pediatrics."

"I'm on the way." Mac said running to the nearest stairwell taking the stairs two at a time. She walked briskly through the ER in her green scrubs and white lab coat as the stretcher came through the double doors. She was extremely focused on the small child and didn't notice Kylie pushing the stretcher. Mac shed her lab coat at the nurse's station on her way into trauma room two.

"MVA, involving two cars. This boy was in the driver's side passenger seat and the car was t-boned at his door. He has a four inch laceration on the left side of his head just above his temple and shallow breathing. We didn't need the call for intubation on scene," Kylie spoke calmly.

"What's his name?" Mac asked as she shined the light and lifted his eye lids to check his pupils.

"Tommy."

"How old is he?" She spoke again as she held the stethoscope to his chest. She heard a tiny wheeze as he struggled to breath.

"Eight."

"Hi Tommy, I'm Dr. Trotter. If you can hear me squeeze my finger." He squeezed gently. "Good, now that we know each other you can call me Mac, how's that?"

He squeezed again. "Okay buddy, I know it hurts, I'm going to take care of you. Do you have asthma, Tommy?" He squeezed her finger softly. "Okay, We'll fix this little cut you have and then send you for some quick tests okay?" He squeezed again.

"Get me a number three suture kit please. Call x-ray, tell them we have a priority one coming their way for a complete chest scan. ETA, five minutes." She spoke to the attending ER nurse and the resident doctor that wcrc working with her. "Let's go ahead and get an Albuterol nebulizer ready for a breathing treatment as well."

Kylie stood back and watched the magnificent woman work as she rapidly stitched the young child's head closed like it was second nature to her and as easy as tying a shoe. He never even flinched as she gave him two shots of Novocain.

"Okay, he's ready," Mac said with two minutes to spare as she sent him down the hall. She tossed her gloves in the trash and ran over to the next room to see if Dr. Kenny needed any help with the father.

"How are we doing here?"

"Good, a few stitches and a splint, then he'll be out of here. How's the boy?" Dr. Kenny said.

"Doctor, how's my son?"

"He's okay. I closed the laceration on his head and he's on the way to get some x-rays to rule out broken bones. I heard a slight wheeze in his chest. He said he has asthma. Is that correct?"

"Yes, Ma'am."

"Okay, the wheezing is probably asthma related, but I'm running the tests to make sure. We're going to give him a breathing treatment as soon as he is finished with his x-rays."

"Thanks," the man said.

Mac stepped out into the hall to sign the boys chart and wait for the test results. Kylie walked up to her.

"Hey there," Kylie said.

"Hi." The shyness in Mac started to creep up as a tiny blush on her cheeks.

"You're amazing, I had no idea you were a doctor."

"Yeah, I'm actually the Head of Pediatrics. I'm only down here when it's a Pediatric Emergency or I have free time on my hands to help out. I spent my entire residency in the ER," Mac said.

"Wow, that's crazy."

"Life's definitely more settled now. I spend most of

my time up on the fourth floor with the children and generally behind a desk."

"You're very good with kids," Kylie said.

"Thanks."

"Do you have any?"

"No, maybe one day, but I'm in no way ready for children. I barely have time for my dog, besides she's my baby so she'd freak out." She smiled and Kylie laughed.

"What kind of dog is she?"

"She's a five pound, tan and white Chihuahua." Mac smiled from ear to ear.

"How cute. What's her name?"

"Stimpy," Mac said proudly.

Kylie looked at her awkwardly for a second. "Did I hear that right?"

"Yes, Stimpy."

"That's interesting. I bet she's cute."

"Most of the time. Until she tears something up," Mac said. They both laughed.

"So how bad is the boy? Do you think he's bleeding internally?"

"I don't think he is. I believe he inhaled a lot of blood and that coats the wind pipe and he has asthma so that doesn't help his breathing. If it's all clear we'll give him a breathing treatment to open his lungs when he gets back over here."

"I don't see much in the way of hurt children. I'm a fire fighter, so I'm not on the ambulance much and accident scenes are usually rescue or recovery situations and our EMT's take over."

"Really? I figured you were an EMT."

"Nope. I know I'm short, but I'm the station Lieutenant." She smiled. "And driver of the engine. I'm usually inside fires. That's my real job. Our Captain works the outside and I work the inside. I'm only on the ambulance when we need three EMT's because I have to be EMT certified to be a lieutenant. The rest of the firemen only have to have EMS training which is basic," Kylie explained.

"Wow, that's interesting. Hey by the way, I'm sorry I missed your call. I was with a patient," Mac said.

"It's no problem."

"Not what you were expecting when you saw me this morning, huh?" Mac said.

"You can say that again." Kylie laughed.

"So, will you go to dinner with me Friday night?"

Oh shit! Shit! Shit! Shit! "I…uh…I…look, I think you're a nice person and everything, but I'm not looking for anything more than a friendship. I'm sorry," Mac said.

"No, don't be. You're straight?"

Mac laughed. "No, in a relationship."

"Ah…I see. I totally understand." Kylie nodded.

"Thanks."

"We can still hang out as friends. I promise not to flirt with you…too much."

They both laughed. "All right, it's a deal. My girlfriend's working this weekend so I'm free after work Friday night I guess."

"Cool…" Kylie said as Mac's phone rang.

"Dr. Trotter."

"Great, that's excellent news. Thanks." She hung up the phone. "He'll be ok. He has a hairline crack in two ribs, and some internal bruising from the seatbelt, but no bleeding."

"That's great!"

"Yeah, so…I need to get ready he's coming back and I

17

need to speak to his father."

"No problem. My shift ends at six Friday, call me."

"Sure thing." *Mackenzie what the hell are you getting yourself into?*

Chapter 3

"Let's go to dinner tonight," Mac said when she walked in the door.

"Why?" Loren raised an eyebrow.

"You're leaving again tomorrow so..."

"Yeah, so that's an occasion to go spend money? Damn it Stimpy get off of the couch!"

"Never mind, Loren, we can cook and stay here. I just thought we'd do something different for a change," Mac stated sharply.

"Don't get testy with me because you want to go, go, go," Loren growled.

"What are you talking about?"

"All you ever want to do is go here, go there."

"I just wanted to spend time with you before you leave. My God, Loren, you're gone every two weeks."

"So my job bothers you now?"

"God damn it, Loren, I'm not fighting with you about your job."

"What's the big deal then?"

"I know you have to travel, just like I'm on call twenty four/seven. That's not the point. The point is, when you're here you never want to spend time together. We never make love anymore and I see you coming and going these days. I'd like to spend a little fucking time with my girlfriend, is that asking too much?"

"Whatever, Mac, you're never here either. Then when you are, all you want to do is go places."

"Fine, I said we can stay home, it's not that big of a deal. You always have to fight with me over the stupidest things just to make a point, of what, I don't know," Mac flopped down on the couch with Stimpy in her lap.

~

"You're rushing out of here on time, since when?" Dr. Foley, who was one of the Resident Pediatricians asked.

"I have plans tonight. Besides, I work eighty hours a week, hell sometimes more. I think I can leave 'on time' one night if I want." Mac laughed.

"Yeah, I guess you can. So where are you and Loren going?" he asked.

"She left this morning for Washington to cover the new congressman story. I'm actually hanging out with a friend tonight."

"Friend? I didn't know you had friends, Mac."

"Ha, ha," Mac said sarcastically.

"Have a drink for me. I'm here until two am."

"Good luck. Call me if you need anything," she said.

"Yes, Ma'am."

Mac got into her Mini Cooper and drove towards the condo. She scrolled through the phone book on her cell phone and pressed the call button.

"Neil."

"Hey, it's Mackenzie."

"Ah, the good doctor. What's up?"

"I'm on my way home from the hospital."

"And where's home?"

20

"We have a condo out in Shelter Cove."

"Nice. I actually live on the mainland so I'm leaving from the station house. Where do you want to go?"

"I don't care. You decide."

"All right, want me to pick you up or do you want to meet me?"

"I'll meet you." Mac pulled into the parking lot next to the empty spot that was usually occupied by Loren's black BMW.

"Meet me at Salty Sam's. You do like seafood, right?"

"Of course!"

"Cool, meet me there in…uh…is a half hour long enough?"

"Yeah, I'll take a quick shower and go."

"See you there."

Mac ended the call and stepped from her car. *Behave Mackenzie she's just a friend. A very attractive...friend.*

~

Kylie took the fastest shower ever and towel-dried her hair. She threw on a pair of jeans, a light yellow colored polo shirt and flip flops, barely saying bye to the guys as she practically ran to her Jeep.

Mac showed up right behind Kylie and parked next to her.

"Cute car."

Mac smiled. "Thanks. I wanted something easy to maneuver in the parking garage at the hospital."

"I see, and a large four wheel drive truck just wouldn't fit, huh," Kylie teased.

"Yeah, something like that." Mac chuckled.

They walked inside and were immediately seated in a

21

booth by the window.

"I like your Jeep by the way."

"It's my baby."

"I almost bought one, I wanted to use it to drive up and down the coast and ride with the top off, but my girlfriend, Loren, doesn't like them, so I didn't buy it."

"Oh, what does she, uh…Loren…what does she do?"

"She's a journalist for the Hilton Head Times and Channel Three News."

"Cool, is she on TV?" The conversation stopped long enough for them to order two beers and an appetizer from the waitress.

"No, she's not an anchor, just a journalist. But, she's guaranteed front page and almost always cover story for the paper. She's also a correspondent for the news channel which is why she is gone so much. She's on TV with them here when there is breaking news."

"Wow, how often is she gone?"

"Every two weeks and for a week each time. Sometimes, if it's a really big story that breaks she leaves right away or is gone longer if she's already in the field. The news is twenty-four/seven just like medicine I guess."

"Man that sucks."

"It takes a while, but you get use to it," Mac sighed.

"How long have you been together?"

"Five years."

"Wow."

"I met her at the end of my residency. I became an attending a few months later and she went from writing in the paper to being a news correspondent that travels all over not long after that. Now, five years later, I'm the Head of Pediatrics and she's the number one journalist in the State."

"Wow, time flies."

"Yeah, before you know it, you stop and think what the hell has happened? It's like life flashes before your eyes," Mac sipped the beer the waitress set in front of her.

"I went straight from high school to the fire department. I completed my Bachelor's at the local college and then transferred out here to the Island. I'm originally from Goose Creek, outside of Charleston."

"That's cool. My family is in Charleston."

"Wow. Really? Where did you go to school?"

"I went to Duke for my undergrad and medical degrees. They offered me a nice scholarship and I really liked the program so I left home for eight years. I returned and did my internship at Charleston General Hospital, then I applied for residency at Hilton Head Medical Center and here I am," Mac said.

"Nice. So what made you become a doctor and a pediatrician at that?" Kylie asked.

"I had a younger brother that came down with Kawasaki Disease and the doctors did everything they could up until the end. He died a few weeks later. I was ten and he was seven. I made it my duty to help kids with their pain. Those doctors knew they couldn't fix my brother once his organs started shutting down, but they did everything they could do to keep him comfortable and in good spirits. He died happy, even though he was very sick. I love making kids feel better and seeing the smiles on their faces reminds me of him."

"You're an amazing woman," Kylie said.

Mac blushed. "Thank you. So miss big bad fire fighter, what made you decide to do that?"

"Well, it's not as exciting as your story. I'm an only child and my Grandfather and Father are both fire fighters.

23

My father is a Chief in Goose Creek and my Grandfather retired as a Chief in Lexington. I guess it was my destiny. I love it though, whether I'm fighting a fire or helping someone, it's an adrenaline rush."

"I know exactly what that is."

Their meal came and went. Both women enjoyed each other's company so much that they lost track of time, until Mac looked down at her watch and realized it was almost midnight. They said quick goodbyes and shook hands, vowing to hang out again soon.

Kylie walked into her two bedroom townhouse and sat on the couch. "Mackenzie, you're one captivating woman, too bad you're with someone. I only hope she treats you the way you deserve to be treated. If not, move over Loren." On that note Kylie got up and walked up the stairs to go to bed.

~

Kylie finished the paperwork on a fire victim that she transported to Hilton Head Medical. She decided to mosey up to the fourth floor and see if she could find the sexy doctor. She walked up to the nurse's station when she stepped off of the elevator.

"May I help you?" one of the nurses asked.

"I'm looking for Dr. Trotter's office."

"Is she expecting you?"

"No, Ma'am, I'm a friend and just wanted to say hey if she was in her office."

"I believe she is." The woman pointed. "It's the fifth door on the right down that hallway."

"Thank you." Kylie strolled down the hall and stopped at the door with 'Head of Pediatrics, Mackenzie L. Trotter

M.D.' stamped in large black letters. She knocked softly.

"Come in," Mac said.

"Hi, how's it going?" Kylie asked popping her head in.

"Hey, not too bad, you?" Mac said waving her inside.

"I just came from a small fire. We brought an elderly man in for minor smoke inhalation."

"Oh."

Kylie sat down in a brown leather chair in front of the large Mahogany desk. She quickly noticed all of the awards and diplomas on the wall, along with the picture of a beautiful woman next to another picture of a tiny little tan and white dog on the desk in front of her. If she had to guess she'd say the woman was a few years older than Mac and definitely had Latin or Italian blood going by her exquisite features. The dog appeared to be queen of the house. Mac noticed Kylie eyeballing the pictures in front of her.

"That's Loren and Stimpy," Mac said signing another chart in the pile of paperwork in front of her.

"She's beautiful and she's cute."

"Thank you."

"Where is she from?" Kylie asked.

"Loren's Brazilian, her mother and father are both from there. She was born here in the States while they were vacationing. She spent the first twelve years of her life in Brazil, then her parents moved to the states to let her follow her dreams. They moved back to Brazil when she graduated from college."

"That's interesting. Is she back home yet?"

"Nope, I should see her tomorrow evening when I get home," Mac said flatly.

"Well, I should let you get back to work. I just wanted to stop and say hi since I was in the building."

"Sure, anytime." Mac looked up at the blue eyes staring down at her and smiled. "I enjoy seeing you." *You're adorable and every time I see you I feel a little flutter that I haven't felt in a long time. You're going to be trouble for me, but I just can't say no.*

"Likewise," Kylie said with a wink. She left the room walking straight to the elevator and riding down to the ER.

"Let's go, Lawson," she said when she found him leaning on the wall.

"Where did you disappear to?"

"I went to see a friend."

"That wouldn't be 'doctor heartbreaker' would it?"

"As a matter of fact we're friends. Get your ass in the ambulance before I leave you here and tell them you need a colonoscopy."

"That's great, Lieutenant," he said rolling his eyes.

"Don't tempt me." She started the ambulance and drove off.

Chapter 4

"Welcome home, baby." Mac went to the door when she heard Loren coming in. Stimpy sat on the couch without a care in the world.

"Hey. How was your week?" Loren kissed her lips and went to the bedroom to put away her luggage.

"Hectic, but not too bad. I was only in the ER once, which is a rarity I took advantage of. How was your week? Did you get the story?" Mac followed her.

"Don't I always?" Loren said arrogantly as she emptied her suitcase.

"Well yeah, I guess. So I take it you had a good week, then."

"Not bad."

"Oh." Mac went up behind Loren and took the clothes out of her hand. She spun her around and kissed her softly at first, then passionately. Both women were lost in the moment, until Loren stopped and continued to unpack.

"What was that for? You must've missed me?" Loren said.

"Of course I did. Did you not miss me?"

"Honey, I always miss you." She pressed her lips to Mac's and Mac slowly pushed her out of the closet towards the bed.

Their love making was quick and to the point, both

27

women got what they wanted, and then Mac jumped in the shower. Loren finished unpacking and took her shower afterwards.

"A few people are going to Daisy's Bar tonight. I was hoping you'd want to go. I have a friend I want you to meet," Mac said as Loren stepped from the shower.

"Isn't that the small bar on the tip of the mainland?"

"Yeah."

"I guess we can go, I don't want to be out late though. I have to be in my office at six am. This story has to go to print tomorrow night."

"Sure, we can go say hi and have a drink or two then go. I have to be up early too, I have a full schedule tomorrow."

~

Kylie threw on jeans a tight black polo shirt and flip flops. She met up with Harris and another friend who were riding with her to Daisy's Bar.

"So is the doc going to be here?" Harris teased.

"Yes she is, and we're just friends. Don't start, Harris. I'm not in the mood, besides her girlfriend will be with her."

"That sucks."

"It's not like that," Kylie said.

"If you say so."

She stopped the jeep in its tracks. "Would you like to walk smartass?"

"No, Ma'am."

"Okay then." She continued on.

Kylie didn't think Mac was there yet since she didn't see the Mini Cooper in the parking lot. "Come on guys let's go meet up with DJ and Jennie since Mackenzie isn't here yet."

"Yes she is. She's over there with a gorgeous woman," he said point at the bar.

"That woman is her girlfriend." Kylie rolled her eyes.

"Damn. She's a lesbian?"

Kylie shook her head rounding up her friends as she made her way over to the bar.

"Hey," Mac said with a smile when Kylie put her hand on her shoulder.

"I didn't see your car so I wasn't sure if you were here yet."

"We're in Loren's car, the black BMW."

"Oh."

"Kylie, this is Loren. Loren this is Kylie and a bunch of people from the local fire station that I see all the time and Jennie is an ER nurse at the hospital." Loren shook everyone's hand politely making a mental note to keep a watchful eye on the young woman smiling at her lover.

"So, what's everyone drinking? First round's on me." Mac waved at the bartender.

The look on Loren's face let on that she wasn't thrilled about Mac buying the drinks. Kylie noticed the piercing dagger eyes that Loren shot Mac.

Less than an hour later Loren looked bored.

"We should go, I have to get up early. I told you I didn't want to be out late."

"Sure, I know you're tired. We can go." Mac said closing out the tab. She quickly said bye to everyone and she and Loren left the bar.

~

29

Mac finished her shift, thankful the last of her meetings was over at five. She'd finally get some daylight time away from the hospital while it was still warm out. She drove down to the Windmill Harbor Marina and parked in one of the front spots.

"Afternoon Mac. How've you been?" The Dock Master always took the time to learn the locals, especially since he was paid to watch their boats. Most of them were worth more than he could make in an entire lifetime.

"Hi, Roland, how's my girl?" She spoke back to the old bald man. He had a thick gray mustache and always wore a fishing cap to keep his bald head from burning in the hot summer sun.

"I think she's lonely," he said.

"Me too," Mac said wondering if she was still talking about her boat.

She walked past him towards the end of the dock. Her prize possession was tied up in the second to last slip on the left, bobbing softly in the blue water. It was a thirty eight foot Beneteau Sailboat. The beautiful white sloop had a dark blue water line, stainless rigging, and dark oiled Teak trim. The inside was magnificent, with a moderately large forward v-berth, a stunning aft cabin complete with dressers, a closet, and an enclosed sink, shower, and head. The entire middle of the boat was the salon living quarters and the galley. A nice sized TV with a satellite receiver was attached to the wall directly across from the L-shaped sofa. The galley was all stainless appliances with Teak cabinets and counter tops. Baby blue curtains covered all of the portholes.

Mac stepped aboard *'Rin'* and kicked her sneakers off before going below deck. Happy to feel the small AC kicking, she grabbed a cold beer from the refrigerator and turned the TV on before lounging on the couch. She had the electrical panel set on a timer to cycle the air conditioner on and off every day to keep the temperature inside the cabin tolerable in the summer heat. She did the same thing with the heater in the winter thanks to shore power. Mac's cell phone rang just as she finished her beer. She saw the name on the caller ID and smiled. *Kylie.*

"Hey, what's up?"

"Hi, not a whole lot, just sitting on my boat."

"Your what?" Kylie questioned.

"My sailboat, come down to the Windmill Harbor Marina and I'll give you the Grand Tour."

"You're full of surprises! I'm still on shift for another half hour, unless we get a call. Will you still be there?"

"Yeah, I'm just doing some cleaning, that is if I ever get my lazy ass off the couch."

"I see. Okay so I'll call you when I get there."

"Sounds good," Mac hung up and stretched her tired body. She missed sitting in that same spot every night. As much as she liked the spacious condo, she always held a special place in her heart for her boat.

An hour later Mac's phone rang again.

"I was beginning to give up on you," Mac teased.

"Me? Ugh, that's terrible…grouch!"

"Yeah yeah, go through the gate and down dock B, I'm the second to last boat on the left. I'll come out."

"Okay."

Mac stepped out onto the top deck in time to see Kylie making her way down the dock, still dressed in her uniform and receiving interesting stares as she stopped and stepped aboard *'Rin'*.

"Rin? Ah, I get it, Rin and Stimpy. How cute."

"Watch your step so you don't slip and fall in. I'd hate

to have to toss you floaties," Mac said reaching for her hand.

"Shut up." Kylie playfully smacked her hand away and stepped past her. Mac pointed past her towards the cabin entrance.

"Go ahead."

Kylie stepped down into the living area and took a look around. "Mackenzie, this is amazing."

"Thanks. She's my home away from home. As a matter of fact me and Stimpy lived on her for a few years until I first met Loren."

"Oh, where is she, by the way?"

"Out of town. She hates boats, so I come down here and spend time cleaning her and taking her out when Loren's gone. Usually Stimpy's with me, but I came from the hospital."

"Cool. I still need to meet this dog."

"Stimpy's my baby. I'd take her with me to work if I could. I bet the kids would love her."

"Probably. I bet she's a chick magnet."

"It depends. Loren's not too fond of her."

What is *she fond of?* Kylie thought to herself. "So, are you taking her out anytime soon?"

"Tomorrow, that's why I stopped by tonight. I need to make sure she's all cleaned up and ready to go. Hey, would you like to go with us?"

"Us? You and Stimpy, I gotcha. I'm actually off this whole weekend, that never happens so I'm definitely going to take advantage of it." Kylie shrugged. "Sure, where are we going?"

"I usually go out about twenty miles and tack back and forth up and down the coast. Sometimes I go just off of the beach and anchor out. Whatever you want."

"Sounds like fun. Do you need any help getting her ready?"

"Considering I'm still on my ass that would be a yes. But, only if you want to, I mean you don't have to. I do this all the time."

"No, I'd like to stay and hang out."

"Cool, there's beer in the fridge if you want one."

"Most definitely! Thank you. So why the fondness for a cartoon?"

"Huh?" Mac shot her a questioning look.

"Rin and Stimpy? Isn't that a cartoon?"

"Oh, yeah." Mac smiled from ear to ear before a small shadow washed over her face. "Rin and Stimpy was mine and my brother's favorite cartoon. Every morning we would get up at six to watch it no matter what day of the week it was. We always tried to act out the quirky things they did."

Kylie smiled at the endearing sound of Mac's voice as she spoke of her brother.

~

Kylie appeared right on time the next morning just before the sun was completely above the horizon. She had a few bags of groceries she picked up from the store and a nice bottle of Chardonnay.

"Morning," she yawned.

Hey." Mac nodded to her guest. Stimpy heard the unfamiliar voice and came running up the stairs and out onto the deck. She growled at first before walking over sniffing Kylie's ankles. "Don't worry, she won't bite you. This is her boat and she's checking you out."

"Oh really, is that what it's called these days?" Kylie

laughed bending down to pet the tiny dog. "You're too cute, running around here like you own the place. I can definitely tell your Mommy spoils you rotten."

By the time Kylie finally sat on the couch Stimpy was in her lap demanding to be petted. Mac shook her head.

"Now you've done it. Once you give in to the lap petting you're toast. You will become her pet slave. But, you will also become top priority to her."

"I see. You can definitely tell she loves you though. She follows you everywhere you go."

"Yeah, that's why she wears this." Mac pulled out a doggy life jacket with an attached lanyard. Kylie broke out in a fit of laughter.

"What the hell?"

"Trust me, she likes to wear this. You would too if you flew off of the deck and into deep cold water on more than one occasion. I had to jump in after her when she was a puppy. Now she wears this thing and goes all over the boat. If she falls over the edge the she's suspended in mid air and I can grab her with no problem," Mac explained.

"Neat."

Later that afternoon they were making their second pass on Hilton Head Island. Mac was at the helm with Kylie standing next to her in awe.

"This boat is fascinating. I've never been on a boat like this before." *She has no idea how fascinating she is either. Loren you're one stupid woman.*

"First time for everything." Mac smiled shyly.

"So shall I start the steaks?" Kylie asked.

"Sure. I'm going to drop the anchor here anyway."

~

"Kylie you're a great cook." Mac said after clearing her plate.

"Thanks, but I think the wine helped you with that decision."

"Nah."

"Hey I brought my bathing suit, do you think the water's cold?"

"No not in August. Want me to go with you?" Mac said.

"Sure, if you want."

A few minutes later Mac emerged from the aft cabin in a baby blue string bikini top that left little to the imagination and matching shorts-style bottoms that were very low-cut and very short. Kylie had changed into a black bikini that covered her nicely in the right places.

Both women quickly dove into the warm, almost tropical water. Kylie was thankful her top stayed up and Mac was kicking herself for offering to go, hoping Kylie didn't noticed how small her swimsuit was.

"That's a cute bathing suit, I like it." Kylie couldn't stop the blood rushing between her legs, thankful she was in the water cooling off.

Too late Mac. "Thanks, I've had it for a while. I keep clothes here on the boat so I don't have to drag things back and forth. I also have scrubs incase I get a call and need to go to work, but this is the only bathing suit I had aboard. It's a little skimpier than I would like, but it was free so I kept it and threw it on here. I guess my other one is at the condo."

"Don't worry, I won't stare at your semi-nakedness...too much," Kylie teased.

"Gee thanks," Mac said splashing her with water.

"I'm sorry, I know you're shy."

They both smiled. Mac climbed back up the ladder and put Stimpy in to let her swim a little bit.

"So you had Stimpy before you and Loren got together?" Kylie asked, still treading water a few yards from the boat.

"Yeah, she was a puppy." Mac lifted Stimpy back onto the deck. "Loren wanted me to give her away and sell the boat, but she gave in quickly and asked me to move in with her. I told her Stimpy was coming with me, so we went looking the next day and found a condo big enough for the three of us," Mac said floating on her back nearby.

"Do they get along now?"

"They tolerate each other. It's quite funny actually. When Loren's not home Stimpy is fine, but when Loren's home she gets in the bathroom trash and gets on the furniture because Loren doesn't like her up there."

"That sucks."

"It's not so bad. I guess I'm use to it. Stimpy is mine and always will be. She was jealous at first, hell they both were, of each other. But, like I said, they get along for my sake."

" I'm starting to look like a prune. Are you ready to get out?" Kylie asked. She was tired of fighting the desire to look at Mac's scantily clad body on display. Talking about her girlfriend only made it that much more of a mistake. No matter how bad she wanted Mac she couldn't have her.

"Sure," Mac said. Both women climbed up the ladder wrapping in towels as soon as they were aboard. Mac found it hard to look away when Kylie had her back to her. She had almost forgotten what it was like to feel her body want another and it felt good. Too damn good.

"Yuck, now I'm all sticky from the saltwater."

"You can shower if you want. I'm about to anyway."

~

They each showered one at a time and sat on the couch. Mac started the generator so they could run the AC and watch TV. Soon after, the sun began to set.

"What time do you want to head back? I mean, I can handle the boat in the dark, it's not a problem."

"It's up to you. I could stay out here all night," Kylie sounded so relaxed and so at home on the boat.

"Well I use to live on this thing so I'm completely comfortable. I'll take you back whenever you're ready."

"Mackenzie, we can stay out here tonight. I'm totally fine with that."

"Okay, you can have my cabin and I'll sleep in the V berth."

"Don't be silly, you can have your bedroom. I'll be fine," Kylie glanced at Mac with a raised eyebrow.

"If you say so, I won't argue with you."

Two hours later they called it a night and went to sleep in their separate areas. Mac was extremely tired from the long day including the eighty-hour work week she had just completed.

Mac was sound asleep listening to the waves with Stimpy curled up next to her under the sheet. They both jumped up when they heard a loud bang, followed by yelling. Stimpy barked at first, but Mac calmed her down.

"Ouch, son of a bitch!" Kylie was rubbing the knot that was quickly forming on her forehead. Mac found her in the moonlight shining through the curtains on the windows.

"Are you okay?" Mac asked going to her side.

"Yeah, my head hurts like hell."

"Here sit down, I'll get some ice."

"I didn't mean to wake you I'm sorry. I was dreaming I was at work and the bell went off. I jumped up to go and hit my head."

"Ouch." Mac grimaced.

"You think so!" Kylie shot her a vicious glare.

"Sorry."

Mac turned on the light to check Kylie's vitals and make sure she didn't have a concussion and helped her sit on the couch. A few minutes later Kylie was asleep with her head on Mac's shoulder where she had been holding the ice for her. *I guess I'm spending the rest of the night out here.* Mac grabbed the throw blanket from the edge of the couch and tossed it over them.

Kylie woke up first, noticing that she was in Mac's arms on the couch with the blanket wrapped around them. *I didn't hit my head that hard!* Mac woke up when Kylie stirred.

"Good Morning. How's your head?"

Kylie reached up rubbing the knot. "It hurts."

"I bet it does." She looked down at the way they were positioned. "Sorry, I didn't mean for us to end up like this. You fell asleep on me and I didn't want to wake you so I stayed out here with you."

"Thanks. You're such a sweet person."

Mac blushed and turned away.

"Aww, look at you!"

"What?" Mac stood up and stretched nervously on her way to the galley. "Are you hungry or something?"

"Don't try to change the subject. Look at you blushing, that is so cute."

"To you maybe. Anyway, I'm hungry, we should eat."

~

Back at the dock Kylie hugged Mac quickly and backed away. The simple gesture sent her body all the wrong signals. She cursed herself for falling asleep in the woman's arms to begin with.

"Thank you for a wonderful weekend. I had a great time."

"You're welcome. I enjoyed the company and I know Stimpy did too. She seems to like you."

Kylie bent down and picked up the little dog to give her a hug and kiss bye.

Chapter 5

"Hey Neil, is the doc coming to see you today?" Brown joked as he finished tying his tie. Kylie refrained from slapping him in the back of the head as she walked by.

"I'm sure she will be there, but she's not going as my date, asshole. Everyone knows we're just friends."

"Well you've been spending a lot of your days off with her over the past month and a half. It sure looks like you're dating to me."

"You hang out with your friends too, besides you've been out with us a few times. It's really not a big deal."

"It sounds like he's just jealous, Neil."

She turned towards the voice. Smith was standing there, also finishing his tie.

"How do I look?" She ran her hands down the front of her Navy blue dress uniform. The Gold buttons down the front meshed perfectly with all of her decorations and metals on the left side of her chest. Her rank insignia was up on her collar.

"You look spiffy, Lieutenant." He winked and smiled.

"Thanks Captain, you don't look bad yourself."

The entire Station had to wear their dress blue uniforms to march in the Annual Veteran's Day Parade held downtown every November eleventh. Most of them didn't mind, but a few complained the whole day. Once they arrived at the starting point, one of the rookies drove the fire truck and another rookie drove the ambulance while the rest of the group marched behind the trucks carrying their station flag. Kylie was in the front left spot and Smith was in the front right. They walked along waving to the crowd that lined the streets. As they turned the final corner Kylie saw Mac standing with a few of the hospital staff members. Loren wasn't with her. Mac smiled and waved and Kylie smiled and waved back.

~

"I missed you at the parade today," Mac said as she pet Stimpy on the top of her head and walked into the living room.

"I was stuck in the office. I had a deadline to meet," Loren stated flatly.

"I figured as much when you didn't call. I went down there with Louise and Hannah."

"Oh."

"Do you want to do something this weekend?"

"Like what?" Loren looked up at her.

"I don't know, maybe go sailing."

"Mac it's November, and sixty degrees outside, I'm *not* going sailing," she hissed.

"Okay, is there something else you would like to do? We haven't played golf in a while."

Loren shook her head no.

"I'm trying to make plans with you for the weekend, Loren. Would you care to contribute?" Mac tried to keep the agitation out of her voice.

"I have to start prepping for my trip next week. I have a huge story to cover in New York."

"So you want to sit here all weekend and start your work for next week instead of spending time with me before you take off again."

"Don't get mad at me for working, Mac, sometimes you don't even come home from that god damn hospital for two days."

"Yeah, but I don't leave for weeks at a time. Twice a year I go away to conferences. Not every other week."

"My career has never bothered you before. What's the deal now?"

"Forget it, Loren." Mac stood up and went into their room to take a shower.

When Mac opened the glass door to get out of the shower a few minutes later Loren was standing there holding her towel.

"Can I have my towel please?" Mac asked dryly.

Loren handed over the towel slowly with a seductive look on her face. Mac didn't buy into it. She snatched the towel, dried off and walked past her into the bedroom. Loren followed her putting her arms around the blond from behind. She began kissing the back of her neck at her hairline. Mac pulled away from her.

"Don't start this, Loren."

"Don't start what? I can't make love to my girlfriend?"

"No, not after you were just fighting with her."

"Baby, making up is the best part of fighting." She stepped closer to her, stealing a kiss.

"Loren,…" Mac kissed her back then turned to go put clothes on. "I really don't feel like it okay."

"Whatever." Loren stormed off pissed that she didn't get her way for once.

~

The fire station was fairly quiet for a Tuesday morning, until the bell rang loudly. Neil, Smith, Harris, and Brown slid down the pole. Connor and Harris were already getting into the ambulance. The fire team was on scene within two minutes of the call. The two story wood and brick framed house was almost completely engulfed in flames. Screams were heard from the second story window as they prepared the hoses.

"Neil, take Harris and Brown in with you." The captain said.

"Yes, Sir," she said. They were already dressed in their Kevlar turn-out gear. She quickly checked her oxygen tank, checked the radio, dashed into the burning house with her respirator on and the two guys behind her.

They could barely see through the smoke. Neil led them up the staircase towards the screams. At the end of the hall was a small bedroom with a young woman crouched in the corner. Neil took off her mask and gave it to the woman to breath fresh air just before she picked her up and carried her all the way downstairs and outside, as the guys blocked the flames from getting to them. As soon as they hit fresh air Neil began coughing and handed the woman to Connor and Lawson, who were waiting with the stretcher.

"Neil, come with me. You need oxygen." Smith said taking her straight to the ambulance. The coughing persisted and her vitals were slowing down.

"Connor, get this thing going. Take Neil with you, she needs to be checked out."

"Yes, Sir." He strapped her into the jump seat and

gave the call for Lawson to take off.

~

Mac was close to finishing her shift and decided to take a walk through the ER to see if her assistance was needed.

"Mac, it's great to see you. We have a young woman and a fire fighter coming in with smoke inhalation. We could probably use your help," Lyle said. He had been friends with her the entire time she worked for HHMC and she always enjoyed working with him.

"Sure. Do you know the name of the fire fighter?" She questioned.

"No, sorry." He shrugged.

Just as she turned around the first stretcher came through the doors with a young woman lying on it breathing through an oxygen mask. She was quickly followed by the second stretcher. Neil was still in her yellow turn-out gear and was holding a mask to her face. Mac immediately ran over to her. *Oh no...Kylie!*

"Put her in number three!" Mac grabbed her stethoscope and began listening to Kylie's lungs. Kylie pulled the mask away and tried to sit up and talk. Mac put her hand on Kylie's chest and pushed her back down.

"Put this back on your face and breath. I know what I'm doing!" Mac went back to checking all of Kylie's vitals as the moved her over to the hospital gurney from the stretcher.

"Go ahead and get a complete chest work up. Let's also get her blood down to the lab and do an ECG," Mac said. The nurse nodded and walked out of the room. The young girl Kylie saved was already on her way to x-ray.

"What a mess," Lyle said as Mac walked up next to him at the nurse's station outside of Kylie's room.

"Yeah you're telling me. That is so painful," Mac said.

"Hey that was our local girl wasn't it? I see her here and there. I didn't know she was a fire fighter though."

"Uh huh, she's actually the Lieutenant."

"Wow."

"Excuse me, Doctor, there's a call on line one about the fire fighter." The nurse at the desk said.

"Thanks." Mac ran over to the phone.

"This is Dr. Trotter."

"Hi this is Captain Smith. One of my fire fighters, Lt. Kylie Neil was just sent there for smoke inhalation. Can you give me an update on her condition?"

"Yes, she's in x-ray right now. It doesn't sound too bad. She's able to breathe on her own and pending the results, she will probably be released this evening or tomorrow morning. The other girl was far worse and will require admittance for a few days."

"Thank you, Ma'am. I know she's in good hands with you."

Mac wasn't sure what he was talking about so she just said 'thanks' and hung up.

~

"You're coming home with me tonight," Mac said two hours later. Kylie tests results showed that her lungs weren't damaged and the CO2 level in her blood wasn't extremely high, but she still needed to be looked after. The effects of smoke inhalation could easily cause the tests to be present normal at first and worsen as time passed.

"No I'm not, Mackenzie I'm fine."

"Kylie damn it you're hurt and do not need to be alone tonight. I'm only letting you go home because I know how pig-headed you are!"

"This isn't the first time that I inhaled smoke. I'm a fire fighter for god's sake! I'm fine!"

"Okay, you won't listen then I'm admitting you!" Mac grabbed the chart and stormed out of trauma room number three. Kylie jumped off of the bed and ran after her pushing the IV pole with one hand while the other held the back of her hospital gown closed.

"Damn it, Mackenzie, this isn't funny!" Kylie growled.

"Get your ass back in that bed before I give you two days!"

"Look, can we talk please?"

Mac followed her back into the room. "I'm listening."

"I don't want to impose on you. Besides, I'm at the station until tomorrow night anyway. Then I'm off for two days. I'll recuperate then."

"First of all, you're not imposing. Second, you are not working for the next two days at all anyway. I've already talked to Captain Smith. I told him I'd get you home tonight and that you needed to be on bed rest for at least three days."

"What about Loren?"

"She's out of town as usual." Mac huffed.

"Fine, but I'm not going to your house. You can stay with me."

"On the mainland?"

"Why not?"

"Compromise, we'll run by my house and get Stimpy and stay on the boat. I'm off tomorrow anyway."

"Fine."

46

~

"Here let me help you." Mac grabbed Kylie's waist and helped her climb aboard the boat. Stimpy passed both of them and was already waiting at the cabin door. "Patience is a virtue Stimpy, pretend you have some!" Mac yelled at the tiny dog that was barking at them to hurry up.

"She's just excited. I can't believe she loves this boat so much," Kylie said walking down the steps to get into the cabin with Mac standing in front of her offering assistance.

"I know it's crazy. Here, I have some clothes you can change into." Mac threw a small pair of cotton shorts and a small tee shirt at Kylie.

"Can I shower first? I smell like fire."

"Yeah, can you hold yourself up?"

"I'm fine."

"Okay, call me if you need me."

Mac was in the galley making the box of soup that she grabbed from her house when Kylie emerged freshly showered. Her naturally tan skin looked pale. "Here, eat this and drink this Gatorade. They'll make you feel better. You need to stay hydrated. You can sleep in the aft cabin and I'll sleep in the V berth."

"Yes, doctor." Kylie said shaking her head. She'd been through this before, although not as bad, but she still knew what signs to watch for and how to recover. It was still nice having Mac take care of her.

A few hours later both women had gone to bed after Mac insisted on listening to her lungs two more times. Mac was sound asleep until she heard Kylie coughing and fumbling in the galley.

"What are you looking for?"

"Water, my throat's dry as a bone." Kylie sounded very hoarse.

"Here," Mac said pouring her a cold glass from the fridge. She unconsciously rubbed Kylie's back as she swallowed the liquid. The coughing stopped abruptly. Kylie turned towards Mac, not realizing how close they were standing to begin with. Their breast were now touching.

"Thank you, for everything. You're such a passionate person and an amazing doctor." *I wish you would wake up and see what's right in front of you. You deserve so much better.*

Mac blushed. Luckily it was dark and Kylie didn't notice, but she was well aware of the heat stirring between them. Kylie leaned forward and Mac slowly backed away.

"I...uh...I'm..." Kylie fumbled to find some kind of words.

"Kylie, not like this. You're hurt and we're both tired. There's no need to apologize." Mac reached out and pulled Kylie into a friendly embrace. "Goodnight." *I have to keep reminding myself that I'm with Loren and you're just a friend.*

Chapter 6

"It's good to have you back, Neil." Smith spoke softly between bites of his banana.

"I've been back for three weeks, Captain. Where have you been?" Kylie finished the last bite of cereal and put the dish in the sink.

"I know you were here, but you weren't a hundred percent. You're just too damn stubborn to take time off to heal. All I'm saying is you're starting to get back to your old routine. I noticed you finally stopped coughing and taking your medicated inhaler a few days ago. Are you running again?"

"Yeah, my lungs feel a lot better. I guess I didn't realize how bad it was until I still couldn't breathe a week later," she said.

"I know what you mean. I went through that right before you joined this station. I had to stay in the hospital for a few days and I swore my lungs were burnt to a crisp. At least you had 'Doctor Love' taking care of you."

"Come on, I get shit from the guys about her all day long. Do I really need to hear it from you too?"

"I'm only pulling your leg, Neil. She seems to be a great friend and she genially cares about you. I'm glad you have someone to spend time with. Whether you're sleeping with her or not, that's none of my business."

"Of course I'm not sleeping with her! She's in a relationship in case you guys haven't noticed." The agitation was starting to show in her voice.

"Calm down before your eyes pop out of your head. You're starting to look like a cartoon. I'm really not trying to piss you off. We've been pretty close for a long time and I just wanted to let you know that I'm glad you have her as a friend, that's all."

"Well, thank you, I guess. I'm going to make the new rookie wash the truck today."

"Ha ha, that should be fun to watch. It's freezing outside."

"It'll be even better if Harris and Brown crack jokes with me about Mackenzie, I'll make them help him."

"Perfect!"

~

"I bought the airline tickets today so we can go see my family for Christmas," Loren said as Mac walked into the kitchen.

"You did what? Without talking to me first?"

"Well, we saw your family last year so we're going to see my family this year."

"Thanks for telling me that you decided this three days before Christmas. Loren, you know I can't just take time off at the last minute to fly to Brazil. I run part of the damn hospital!" Mac was furious.

"Exactly, you run the place. How hard can it be to adjust your schedule for two weeks? You never take any vacation time anyway."

"You are so selfish! I swear, Loren, one of these days

I'm not going to be here when you come home."

"What's that suppose to mean? You're going to leave me because I want to take you home with me for the holidays? That's ridiculous, Mac."

"Fine, Loren, if that's the way you want it to be. You obviously don't hear what I'm saying or you just don't give a shit. Either way, I'm not changing my schedule for you, not anymore. I'm tired of this, I'm tired of us...I won't be here when you get home. Your Christmas present is under the tree. Take it with you and open it there. I'm moving back onto the boat," Mac said walking out of the room.

"So that's it? You're just going to throw it all away because you won't take time off?" Loren questioned.

Mac spun back around. "No, Loren! Don't you fucking get it? I'm done, finished, it's over...we're over. I'm so sick of fighting with you and doing everything that you want to do. I'm tired of being the third most important thing in your life next to your career and your god damn ego." Mac went into the bedroom and tossed a bunch of clothes into her gym bag along with her toiletries. She stopped long enough to grab Stimpy and all of her dog stuff and stormed out of the condo, looking back only once. Loren never came out after her.

~

"Hey, Merry Christmas," Kylie said when Mac answered her cell phone.

"You too." Mac smiled.

"Are you at the hospital?"

"Yeah, my shift ends in a few minutes, then I'm driving to Charleston to see my family."

"Cool, where's Loren?" Kylie asked, trying to show

compassion.

"Brazil I guess."

"Oh."

"I'm staying on the boat," Mac sighed.

"What?"

"I moved out. Well not completely but I'll be gone by the time she comes back."

"Oh, Mackenzie, what happened?"

"I don't really want to talk about it right now."

"I understand. Hey, I'm driving back to Goose Creek to see my family. We should car pool."

"I don't mind, but I may need to come back in a hurry if there is a problem at the hospital."

After the two and a half hour drive Kylie dropped Mac off in front of her parents home and continued on to see her family. Mac had a great time visiting with her own family, especially her uncle, whom she missed dearly. Still not ready for it to be real, she told everyone Loren had to work during the holidays. Their visit was short and sweet and she promised to see them again soon.

Eventually, Mac told Kylie the story on their drive home. She explained how much they actually fought and how Loren was in charge of every decision they made. Kylie was happy to see Mackenzie finally realizing that she didn't have to take Loren's shit anymore. Kylie wondered why the hell she had hung on for so long. She deserved so much more than some halfwit talking to her like a piece of shit and treating her like a dog. Kylie decided now was not the time to rant and rave to her about it.

~

"How was your New Year's, Mac?" One of the young Resident Pediatricians was always fascinated with Mac's life. She never could figure out why, but she was use to being idolized by the young newcomers. She wondered if maybe he was in the closet. Either that or he was attracted to Loren since he always asked about her.

"Fine, I took my sailboat out and stayed on it all weekend."

"Oh, I bet Loren liked that."

"Actually, she was out of the country. I was with my dog." *Alone.*

"I see."

~

"Welcome back, Neil, Happy New Year." Smith gave her a hug.

"Thanks, you too. Were you guys busy?"

"No, not too bad. A few close calls with some homemade fireworks, but that's about it. I still can't believe how quiet the Island is this time of year."

"I know, the tourists are all gone, I love it," she said.

"So what did you wind up doing?"

"I actually cleaned my apartment and read a book. It was nice and peaceful."

"Cool, did you see the doc?"

"No. She took her boat out for the weekend, alone."

"I take it she's still not talking to her girlfriend."

"No, they're broken up. Mackenzie packed all of her stuff and moved out last week. I think Loren comes home this week so we'll see what happens. They were together for a while so it's a lot to deal with and a lot of ties to sever. Thanks for not telling the guys."

"It's your business, Neil. I would never have known if you hadn't accidentally mentioned it after Christmas. Besides, I'm sure she needs a friend right now and you make a pretty good one." He smiled.

"Thanks." She smacked him on the back. "Let's go see what our 'kids' have gotten into. It's too quiet around here."

~

Mac sat at her desk signing papers and typing on her laptop. It was no surprise to hear a knock at the door. Most of her staff would pop their heads in from time to time if they hadn't seen her on the floor.

"Come in," she called out.

Kylie appeared in the doorway with her hair pulled back in a pony tail and her ice blue eyes twinkling.

"Hey busy bee. What's up?"

"Not much, just catching up on some of my desk duties. What brings you here?" *She has the prettiest eyes* Mac thought.

"MVA, nothing major, just cuts and bruises. One of our guys is on vacation so I'm filling in on the ambulance this week."

"Oh. Is it busy down there?"

"No, this is our third trip today. I haven't seen more than three or four people in trauma at a time. Nothing life threatening so far."

"That's good then."

"Yeah, so what are you doing for Valentine's Day?" Kylie asked.

"Uh…working…why?"

"I was hoping you and Stimpy would come to the townhouse for dinner."

"Sure, I guess."

"You don't have to. I'm not really doing anything and I figured you'd be alone so…"

"Of course we'll be there. At least let me buy the wine if you're cooking dinner."

"Sounds good."

"Are you sure it's okay for Stimpy to come too?"

"Absolutely, I love that dog, she's a trip!"

"Okay, see you about six thirty." Mac smiled.

~

A few days later, Mac walked into the two story townhouse. She set Stimpy down on the floor and proceeded to follow Kylie around on the Grand Tour. Kylie was dressed in jeans and a white polo shirt. Her hair was down just past her shoulders with loose wavy curls. Her deep blue eyes were glistening in the light. Mac was sure her heart skipped a beat. She was attracted to Kylie the first time she saw her and the idea of acting on that attraction wasn't something she let herself fantasize about because of her relationship with Loren. Now, she was starting to wonder what that might be like.

"It's probably not as big as your place was, but it's perfect for me." Kylie implied as she showed Mac her bedroom, complete with a queen sized sleigh bed and surprisingly large bathroom. Then, they moved into the spare room which was set up with a full sized bed and dresser set. Downstairs, Kylie showed her the kitchen which had an eat-in dining room. The table was already arranged with a flower centerpiece and candles burning on either side.

"This is nice, and something smells wonderful, what

is it?" Mac sniffed the air. Stimpy had taken her own tour and was already in the kitchen pacing in front of the stove.

"A surprise, sit down."

Mac sat while Kylie opened the bottle of Chardonnay and poured two glasses. She slid the bottle into the chiller then turned back towards the stove.

"Here we go." Kylie set two large plates of her special mixed seafood pasta.

"Wow, this looks as good as it smells."

"It's fettuccine noodles with lobster, crab, mussels, and scallops in white wine clam sauce." Kylie smiled.

"And you made this from scratch?" Mac's eyes were bulging.

"Yes, Ma'am. Eat before it gets cold."

"This is delicious," Mac said between bites.

Kylie smiled.

Both women finished their pasta and moved to the couch to eat the chocolate covered strawberries that Kylie prepared.

"Wow, you're an amazing cook."

"Thanks, I only cook on special occasions, meaning when I have company. Otherwise, I usually eat some kind of frozen dinners when I'm here. We all take turns cooking at the station and I think that's what got me so into cooking. The guys go crazy when it's my night to cook."

"I can see why! It's fantastic!" Kylie shoved a strawberry into Mac's mouth as she finished her sentence. Her finger grazed the side of Mac's lips.

"Mmm…what was that for?"

"You're embarrassing me, just eat."

"I see, so you do get embarrassed too!"

"Yeah but not as easy as you do."

Mac stood up and took the empty plate into the

kitchen. She turned to find Kylie standing right behind her. Their breasts and thighs were close to touching. Mac saw the desire burning in Kylie's blue eyes as she bent her head slightly. As their lips touched Kylie backed away.

"I...I'm sor...Kylie I'm sorry." Mac didn't know what to say. She was caught up in the moment, the heat was rolling between them like electricity and she knew she wanted to feel Kylie. She had wanted to touch every inch of her for months. Now she was free, no longer able to hold back due to attachment and dedication to a relationship that was impossible.

"Don't be...I...I just want this to be what you want, Mackenzie."

"This *is* what I want."

Kylie pushed Mac into the counter threading her arms around the blonde's neck as their lips met passionately. Mac slid her arms around Kylie's waist and pulled the smaller woman against her as tightly as she could. The kiss was slow and intense, their bodies yearning to be closer. Mac moved her hands under Kylie's shirt running them up her back, feeling every muscle clinch and release under her soft touch. Kylie pulled Mac away from the counter walking her backwards towards the couch. She followed her down lying on top of her slowly with her tongue tracing the edge of Mac's lips daring her to beg for more. Mac couldn't take it any longer. She grabbed Kylie pulling her down tightly.

Mac kissed Kylie playfully biting her lip and sucking her tongue as her hands massaged the soft skin of her back under her shirt until Kylie sat up and straddled Mac.

Kylie exposed her stomach and breasts as she took her shirt off tossing it on the floor. Mac inspected the small, taut body in front of her, covered with silky tanned skin.

Kylie's perky breasts fit in her hands as she squeezed them teasing her brown nipples to perfect peaks. She watched Kylie's eyes glaze over and she continued massaging her breasts stroking her nipples with her thumbs. Kylie moaned pulling Mac up into another deep kiss. She quickly released Mac's bra as she pulled her shirt up over her head throwing it on the floor next to her own.

Mac pulled Kylie against her once again pressing their nude upper bodies together as she kissed her neck on the soft skin below her ear. Kylie shivered in her arms. The wetness pooling between her legs was starting to soak her pants. Mac couldn't remember ever wanting another woman so much. She moved her hands between them unbuttoning Kylie's jeans and looking into her eyes. Kylie nodded and stood up to take her jeans off. Mac stood next, adding her own pants and underwear to the pile.

Kylie lay back on the couch and Mac gently moved on top of her. She pressed her lips to Kylie's teasing her with her tongue as she ran her hand down her stomach to her thigh tracing the edge of her thin hairline. Moving her head lower she sucked one taut nipple between her lips lightly as she pressed her fingers into the wet folds rubbing in slowly circles. Kylie spread her legs further pushing her hips up asking for more and causing her thigh to rub against Mac's wet center.

As Mac entered her, Kylie took a quick breath and let it out slowly. Mac moved her fingers in and out of her in a slow motion, pressing deeper with every stroke. She continued kissing Kylie's mouth, then her neck, finishing with her breasts as Kylie thrust against her digging her short nails into her back. Mac pushed her fingers as deep as they would go swirling in circles before pulling almost out. She repeated the motion faster and harder until she felt the muscles around her fingers tighten and quiver. Kylie moaned gasping for air. She wrapped her arms and legs tightly around Mac looking deeply in her eyes as the orgasm passed through her body.

Immediately, Kylie maneuvered under Mac carefully pushing her onto her back as she crawled on top of her. Wasting no time, Kylie moved her hand down to the wet center that she had already felt on her leg. Mac gasped as Kylie's fingers slid easily inside of her. She pulled the smaller woman against her begging her to give her everything she could until she could feel her insides explode. Kylie pushed her fingers deep and harder with each thrust as Mac moaned. She pulled her fingers out stroking her clit lazily before pushing back inside. Kylie kissed Mac tenderly as her hand continued the same movements over and over.

Mac pulled away from her mouth breathless, gasping for air and clawing at the couch as her body tightened. Kylie felt the wet muscles quiver and clinch her fingers as Mac's orgasm tore through her. She pulled her fingers when Mac relaxed.

"Happy Valentine's Day," Kylie said with a smile kissing her lips softly.

"You can say that again." Mac struggled to regain her composure.

Kylie tucked her head under Mac's chin, still lying half on top of her.

Mac woke up three hours later with Kylie in her arms and the throw blanket from the back of the couch over them. *This is a seriously comfortable couch. What am I saying? Look at the position I'm in...what the hell have I done? Look at her, she's beautiful.*

Sydney Canyon

Chapter 7

"You're really upbeat today, Neil. Who did you bring home for Valentine's Day?"

"Harris, it's confidential and if you knew I'd have to kick your ass. Therefore, I'm going to save you the despair and not tell you," she said. His mouth fell to the floor. "I was alone jackass!" She laughed shaking her head.

The Captain came in just in time to catch Harris walk away sulking.

"What's with him?"

"I don't know, his ego just got deflated." She smirked.

"I see. Way to go, Lieutenant."

"Thank you, Captain." They both walked out of the bay laughing.

"The doctor?" He questioned quietly.

"Yeah." She smiled.

He smiled back as they climbed into the truck.

~

"You seem really chipper lately, Mac. What's up? Did you join the gym or something?" Lyle continued to write on the chart in his hand as he spoke.

"No, Lyle, just a change of pace I guess."

"Oh. I noticed you haven't been working a hundred

61

hours a week either. Loren must be working closer to home."

"As a matter of fact, Loren and I broke up before Christmas." Mac said without skipping a beat.

"Oh my, I'm sorry. I guess news doesn't travel as fast as it use to," he said.

"Nah, it's not a big deal. It was three months ago. I've moved on. Besides, no one at the hospital knew except Jennie."

"How did she know before me? I've worked with you longer than most of the people here? I'm deeply saddened." He smiled.

"She only knows because I'm dating someone new and she's friends with her."

"Ah, I see, so dish it out. Who is she? What does she look like? Do I know her?"

"Actually, that's her right there." Kylie walked through the main doors of the ER with Harris.

"Hey I know her, she's a sweetheart. A damn good looking one I might add."

Kylie walked up to Mac and Lyle. Harris was practically up her butt at her side.

"Hey you." Kylie winked at Mac.

"Hey yourself. What brings you guys here?" Mac said smiling at her.

"Harris is here to have his annual immunization updated." The young man at her side winced. "He's a big baby, so I decided to come down here with him for my own guilty pleasure." She laughed.

"I didn't know we did those in the ER," Lyle said.

"You don't. We have an appointment upstairs. We just always use this entrance."

"Oh."

"I was planning on making my way to your office, but this is even better," Kylie said to Mac.

"Excuse me and my bad manners, Lyle this is Kylie Neil, she's the Lieutenant for the Airport Fire Station, and this is..."

Kylie jumped in. "This is Joe Harris, he's a weenie...I mean a rookie fire fighter."

The black man reached his hand out to Kylie. "It's nice to formally meet you. I'm Dr. Lyle Ferguson, Assistant Emergency Room Director."

"It's nice to meet you too. I know I've seen you a hundred times." She smiled. Her eyes twinkled when she looked over at Mac.

"We've known each other for a little over six years. We met back when we were both ER residents. Lyle stayed down here and I branched out," Mac said.

Lyle was called away to attend to a demanding patient. Kylie refrained from kissing Mac, although she was dying to do so.

"Will I see you later?" Kylie questioned.

"Sure, I'm headed home when I finish my paperwork. Why don't you come over when your shift ends," Mac said.

"Sounds good. Oh, I almost forgot, you need to get me a key for the gate at the Marina so I don't have to go track down Fred, or whatever his name is. It takes him twenty minutes to get to the gate to let me in."

Mac laughed. "Here take mine, I have another one on the boat and it'll be daylight still when I get home." Mac removed the key from the key ring in her pocket.

"Thanks."

"See you soon." Mac winked.

"Not soon enough." Kylie called out over her shoulder

as they stepped into the elevator.

~

"Aww, Neil has a girlfriend…finally!" Harris teased.

"Cut it out, Harris." She growled.

"Oh please."

"At least I'm getting it, that's more than I can say for you," she said as the elevator doors opened. "Come on before I leave you here by yourself you big baby. You're lucky I didn't tell them how you whined and pouted until I agreed to go with you. And you damn well know I only came to see her. So now that I have, well I guess you're on your own hot shot!" She turned to walk away.

"No! Neil, please…come on I was only kidding…please stay with me…"

"Harris you're pathetic. Let's go." She gave in shaking her head.

~

Mac was standing at the stern of the boat talking to her dock neighbor when she saw Kylie coming her way. She was still dressed in her dark blue fire station uniform. Her dark curly hair was down around her shoulders and blowing in the breeze as she smiled from ear to ear. Mac swore she felt her heart skip a beat.

"Hey there." Kylie walked up giving Mac a soft kiss on her lips.

"Hey yourself."

"Harry, this is Kylie. Kylie, this is Harry, he lives on the twenty-five foot Islander next door." She pointed towards a light green colored, smaller, and slightly older sail boat in the slip next to her own.

"Hi, it's nice to meet you."

"You too," The older, bald man said smiling.

Kylie followed Mac below deck when they said goodbye to the neighbor.

"Hey!" Kylie called to Stimpy as she bolted towards her. Kylie quickly bent down picking up the excited little dog. "Thanks for the kisses. Yes…I missed you too!"

"I think she likes you almost as much as she loves me. Hmm…note to self, separate the Chihuahua and the girlfriend," Mac said laughing. Kylie rolled her eyes laughing with her.

"Honey, do you really think I'm going to take your dog from you?"

"I'm a little worried. I mean she could be getting bored with me." Mac acted as serious as she could, then burst into laughter. "She'd never leave me!"

"Of course not, she loves you!"

"Oh really?"

"Yeah, she just told me she does."

"Is that a fact?" Mac grabbed Kylie by her waist sliding her arms around her, pulling the smaller woman against her. She quickly pressed her lips to Kylie's teasing with her tongue as her lips parted. The passionate kiss continued until Stimpy became jealous and began barking at them.

"Not now Stimpy, can't you see I'm busy!" Mac said as she slowly pushed Kylie up against the galley sink. She kissed her again. Kylie lips parted slowly allowing a deep intimate kiss to be exchanged between the women. Mac pulled Kylie's shirt loose sliding her hand under and running it along her bare back. She stopped briefly to release the bra strap in the middle. Kylie threaded her fingers in Mac's short hair pulling her down into the kiss as it continued.

Seconds later, Mac walked Kylie backwards to the aft cabin peeling pieces of clothing off with every step. Both women were nude by the time they hit the sheets. Kylie bit Mac's ear softly crawling on top of her.

"Mmm, I bet you taste that good everywhere," Kylie said with a growl.

"Why don't you see for yourself, tiger!" Mac winked and licked her lips.

Less than a second later Kylie was between her legs licking her clit in lazy circles sucking the swollen nub into her mouth with her tongue and biting teasingly here and there.

"Yeah, you do tas…"

"Oh my god! Don't stop!" Mac yelped when Kylie paused to speak. Kylie smiled kissing her way back down Mac's thighs.

Kylie put her mouth back where Mac wanted it. She licked back and forth sucking her clit with each pass.

Mac moaned loudly thrashing around under Kylie as the orgasm washed over her like a monsoon bringing rain to the desert. She grabbed Kylie and pulled the smaller woman up against her and kissed her, tasting herself on Kylie's mouth sent her body over again. She shuttered from the unexpected second orgasm.

Kylie sat up straddling her. Mac sat up with her fondling Kylie's body until she found the moist spot that she was lazily searching for. Kylie practically forced Mac's fingers inside of her. Mac stayed still as Kylie moved slowly at first riding up and down on Mac's fingers progressing fast and deeper with each thrust of her hips. Mac held Kylie in her arms kissing her affectionately from her neck and chest to her lips as Kylie drove herself down on her hand over and over gasping and moaning. Mac felt the rush of climax pass through Kylie as she tightened around her fingers pushing them as deep as they would go. She finally relaxed settling against Mac as she slipped her hand free.

Mac looked into the most beautiful ice blue eyes that she'd ever seen. "You're like a drug addiction. It's like I can't get enough of you," Mac said softly.

"I know what you mean. I feel like I can't breathe unless you're inside of me." Kylie's eyes twinkled in the moonlight peeking between the curtains.

"Mmm, I like the sound of that."

"Yeah, I think I'm having trouble breathing, doctor, you might need to help me," Kylie said seductively.

"I think I can prescribe some drugs." Mac laughed and rolled Kylie onto her back.

Chapter 8

A week later, Mac was sound asleep in Kylie's bed with Kylie curled up next to her. The rattle of her cell phone vibrating on the nightstand woke Mac instantly. She realized it was her cell phone when the ringing tone started. Kylie jumped up thinking it was the fire bell.

"Who is calling you at three a.m.?" Kylie said sleepily.

Mac looked at her phone. "The hospital."

"Hello, this is Dr. Trotter," Mac answered.

"I'm sorry to wake you, Mac, I have an emergency that needs your attention."

"It's ok, Lyle. What happened, is it a baby or a child?" Mac got out of bed looking for her clothes.

"It's not a child…"

"Then why are you calling me?"

"It's Loren…"

Mac's heart stopped, she felt the breath escape her lungs.

"She was in an auto accident," he said. "I didn't know who else to call."

Mac still wasn't speaking.

"Mac?"

"I'm on the way!" She slammed the off button and

68

turned to Kylie.

"What's wrong, honey? You look like you just saw a ghost. What happened?"

"Loren was in a car accident...it's bad...I need to go."

Kylie put her arms around Mac. "I understand, go, she needs you."

~

Mac walked into the trauma room and couldn't look past the doctor in her to see her ex-lover lying in shambles in front of her. Instead, she started checking Loren's chart and reading the vitals.

"We need to send her for a CT scan of her head and an x-ray of her full chest cavity," Lyle said talking to the nurse. "Are you sure you can handle this, Mac?" he said when he saw her.

"I'm fine, Lyle. Send her to radiology. Did you talk to the police?"

"Yeah, she was heading east on 278, probably on her way home. The other car was going west and from the skid marks it looks like that man fell asleep and crossed the double line and hit her head on. They think her car rolled at least twice before stopping on the roof."

Mac took a deep breath and closed her eyes. She could see the bloody face of the woman that she had loved for so many years behind her dark lids. A faint tear rolled down her cheek.

"I think she has a closed head injury. There was some blood coming from her nose, but she seems to be responsive and able to hear me and squeeze my fingers. I listened to her lungs but it's hard to tell until I see an x-ray. I think she definitely has a few broken ribs and bruising in her lungs. Her left lung collapsed at the scene, but I got it re-inflated when she arrived." He paused and put his hand on his friend's shoulder. "I didn't mean for you to come down here to be her doctor. You're still her emergency contact, that's why I called you."

"You did the right thing, Lyle. I know I'm not supposed to treat her. Thanks for allowing me to anyway. I would've done the same if I were in your situation. I'm going to get some coffee, call me when she comes back."

"Will do."

~

Mac grabbed a cup of stale coffee and stepped into the tiny hospital chapel. She crossed her heart as she sat in the last pew.

"You know I don't come in here and bother you unless it's very serious. I believe the last time I was here was last year when I needed help with that baby that had pneumonia and slipped into a coma. You helped me with him and I thank you as often as I remember to." She took a sip of her coffee and winced at the taste. She had to load it up with sugar to make it drinkable.

"This time, it's personal. I'm sure you know what happened to Loren so I won't go into details. This one's out of my hands and I need your help now more than ever. Please give us the power to help her. We can't do it alone, me especially. I'll do anything you ask of me, just help me save Loren. She needs me and I need you. If this is as serious as I think it is, she could be a vegetable, worst of all, she could...die." A few tears rolled down her face. "I know you have your plans, but please consider my request. She's not ready to go, help me save her."

Mac's phone began to vibrate. Mac crossed her chest once more and walked out of the chapel before answering.

"Dr. Trotter."

"Mac, it's Lyle, she's on her way back."

Mac rushed back to the ER and was standing by the doorway when Loren's gurney was wheeled back into her trauma room. She went to work next to Lyle immediately trying to maintain stability until radiology called with the results. She checked Loren's vitals again as the machine breathed through the tube for her. Every time she lifted Loren's eyelids her pupils were different sizes. *Don't think of the signs Mackenzie, they aren't always right.*

"Mac, radiology is on line two."

She practically snatched the phone off of the wall.

"Dr. Trotter, your patient has a contusion on the left frontal lobe of her brain. It's swelling rapidly. She also has some severe bruising on her left lung and three broken ribs on the left side. On a good note everything else is fine. Her neck has some swollen tissue, but nothing extensive. I called neurosurgery and left an urgent message for them to call you."

"Thanks."

Mac hung up the phone and quickly received the call from neurosurgery.

"Dr. Trotter."

"This is Dr. Green, in Neurology."

"I have a MVA victim down here that needs an immediate surgery consult. She has a contusion that is swelling on the left frontal lobe that is swelling."

"I'm on the way, have her sent up to the OR. Number four is prepped and ready to go," he said.

"Green?"

"It's personal, do you think I could…"

71

"Sure. Just don't get in the way."

"I'll bring her myself."

~

Two hours later Doctor Green finished placing the bandage around Loren's head. He had just drilled a small hole into the left front of her head and put in a tiny tube for the blood and excess fluid to drain out of. He stitched the hole closed around the tube and wrapped her head in a bandage. He and his staff put her in a halo-like device to hold her head completely still so that nothing happened to the tube.

"All you can do now is pray, Trotter, it's out of our hands," he said stepping away from the table.

"Thanks," she said shaking his hand.

"I believe she'll recover. We caught the swelling early and her brain activity is high."

~

Mac was sitting behind her desk, staring at the walls when she heard a faint knock on her door. She looked down at her watch. *Nine a.m. already.*

"Come in," she said.

Kylie appeared in the doorway. "Hey."

Mac half smiled at her. "Hi."

"The guys at the station told me about it. How is she?"

"We had to put a tube in her head, her brain's bruised and swelling. She's in a very light coma that the neurologist induced to help her brain handle the swelling. She has some broken ribs and a bruised lung that collapsed at the scene of the accident so she is on a ventilator."

Kylie walked behind the desk and bent down to hug Mac. "I'm so sorry, honey."

"I know. Thanks. She'll be okay, she's tough as nails and pig headed as hell. I'm sure she'll wake up talking about some deadline that she's late for." Mac tried to smile.

"Did you call her family?"

"No, I'm waiting a little bit. It's the middle of the night in Brazil."

~

Three days later Mac was checking on Loren in the Intensive Care Unit when her eyes popped open.

"Hey, don't try to speak, and don't move. I need to check your chest and then I'll pull that tube out okay. Squeeze my finger if you understand what I'm saying." Loren squeezed and a tear rolled down her cheek. "Don't be scared, I'm here with you."

Mac grabbed the phone and dialed the intercom."Dr. Green, you're needed in ICU One immediately."

Dr. Green came rushing though the door. "What's wr…"

"She's awake, her lungs sound okay. You're the doctor in-charge of her chart, so you have to authorize the removal of the ventilator."

He listened to both lungs and nodded. "Yeah, let's go ahead and pull it out. Her lungs sound a lot better. Okay Loren, don't move at all. We need you to try to be as still as possible. Take a deep breath and swallow. We will remove the tube as you exhale," he said to her.

As soon as the tube was out of her throat Loren began coughing. Mac starting massaging her chest softly between her breasts to relax her breathing.

"Mac…" She whispered hoarsely.

"Yes, I'm here."

"What happened? I …"

"You were in a car accident, sweetie. You're going to be fine, you broke some ribs and bruised your lungs so your chest will be sore for a while."

Loren slowly reached up towards her head. Mac quickly grabbed her hand and placed it back on the bed.

"My head…what…Mac…" Loren started crying. Mac bent down and wiped the tears from her face and kissed her cheek.

"You hurt your head pretty bad. Your brain was bruised and swelling. Dr. Green had to put a little tube on the side of your head by your hairline. It's draining excess fluid off of your brain. I don't want you to stress yourself out at all right now. You need to rest your head as much as possible. We'll take the tube out in a few more days when the swelling has gone down," Dr. Green said.

"I'm scared, Mac."

"I know, I'm here for you. I called your job and they all wish you the best and hope you get well soon. That's the last thing you should be thinking about right now, but I know you too well. I also called your Mom and Dad. They flew in last night and are at the hotel right now. They saw you early this morning and went back to get some sleep from the jet lag. I'll call them right now and tell them you're awake."

"Mac…thank you. I know you stayed with me. I kept hearing your voice while I was sleeping."

"Lyle called me when the ambulance brought you in. I was here within a few minutes and I've been at your side pretty much ever since."

"How long have I been here?"

"Almost four days."

"How did it happen?"

"You need to get your rest, Loren. We'll talk about it later. Right now your brain needs to be relaxed so that the bruising can heal."

~

A week later, Loren was released to go home. Mac decided to go stay with her until she was healed enough to take care of herself. Kylie understood that Mac had to go where she was needed most. Loren's parents only stayed for a few days before flying back home.

"Thank you so much for doing this, Mac. You're always there when I need you. You know I still love you."

"I almost lost you, Loren. I still care about you. I always will." Mac sat with Loren on the couch and held her while she slowly went to sleep in Mac's arms.

Mac continued to take care of Loren, waiting on her hand and foot at the condo. She rushed home from work every day to take care of her. Stimpy moped around miserably, growling at Loren when she came near her.

"You're recovering very quickly." Mac said from the kitchen where she was making dinner.

"Really? I guess I don't know what to expect." Loren walked up behind her and kissed the back of her neck. Mac jumped and turned around.

"What ar…"

Loren pressed her lips to Mac's and without thinking Mac threw her arms around the beautiful woman and kissed her back. The tender kiss ended all too soon when Mac realized what she was doing.

"Loren, you're still recovering. You shouldn't stress

yourself."

"I'm not doing anything strenuous...yet." She smiled and leaned in for another kiss. Mac kissed her and pulled away slightly, still holding Loren in her arms.

"You shouldn't be thinking of doing anything like that."

"My physical therapist said I'm as good as new. I'm not supposed to climb a mountain or run a marathon. He didn't say anything about sex. I bet if I was careful not to hit my head on anything it would be fine. I figure as long as we don't use the swing I'll be okay." She smirked.

Mac looked confused. "Excuse me? What swing?"

"It's a joke, Mac, lighten up. I've missed you so much. I'm trying to tell you I want you to make love to me."

"You..."

Loren ran her hands up Mac's back under her shirt and pressed her lips to Mac's.

"Loren, you're recovering from your injuries. You can't do anything strenuous and that includes making love," Mac said.

Loren scrunched her face. "Kissing isn't strenuous is it?"

"No," Mac said wrapping her arms gently around her.

Mac was awake when the sun came up with Loren sound asleep next to her. She quietly snuck out the bed, showered, and grabbed a banana from the kitchen before fixing Stimpy's breakfast.

"Don't look at me like that. What's your problem?" She scolded the dog that was shooting dagger eyes at her. "I know you hate her, that's your problem. Try being nice to her for a change."

Mac drove across the island, parked her Mini Cooper in the 'Reserved for Physicians' area of the garage and walked in through the ER.

"Morning, Mac. How's Loren?" Lyle caught up to Mac as she headed towards the elevator.

"Good, she's almost fully recovered."

"That's great to hear. So how are you doing?"

"I'm fine."

"I take it you broke it off with the firefighter."

"Why do you say that?" Mac stuck her hand out to hold the elevator doors open.

"She was in here last week on the Ambulance. She looked pretty beat. I don't think I've ever seen her not smiling."

"Look, I should get going, Lyle. I have a hundred things to do this morning before I see my patients." Mac stepped into the elevator and leaned her head against the back wall.

Once she was in her office, Mac closed the door and sat down in the swivel chair behind her desk. She picked up her cell phone and hit speed dial.

"Neil."

"Hey," Mac said.

"Mackenzie…how are you?"

"I'm good…sorry I haven't contacted you much."

"I know your busy. How's Loren?"

"She's much better, thanks for asking. Hey…uh…can I see you tonight?"

"Sure, my apartment or the boat?" Kylie questioned.

"Actually, do you think you can meet me down at the pier?"

"Okay? What time?"

"Eight?"

"That's fine, my shift ends at six."

"Hey, I'm glad you're home. I made dinner." Loren went up to Mac and kissed her lips.

"Smells good, what did you make?" Mac asked.

"Chicken with creamed spinach." Loren smiled proudly.

"Sounds good. Hey I need to go run some errands after dinner. I won't be gone long."

"Mac, I sit here all day and stare at the walls. I'm sure another hour or two won't hurt me. It would be nice to spend some time with you though. By the way, you'll need to take a few extra days off next week. My parents are coming to visit and I want you to be with us."

"I'll see what I can do."

~

Mac parked the tiny blue car by the curb and walked up to the Pier. She could see Kylie standing at the end watching the surf. Her curly black hair was down around her shoulders. Kylie turned around and threw her arms around the taller woman when Mac walked up to her.

"Hey, I've missed you." Kylie kissed Mac's soft lips.

"I've missed you too." Mac back away from her when the hug ended.

"When are you moving back to the boat?"

"I'm not," Mac said wryly.

"I thought she was better." Kylie looked quizzically at Mac.

"She is, that's what I wanted to talk to you about."

"No Mackenzie, don't you do this to me."

"Kylie I'm sorry. She…I…we have a history between

us."

"You left her because you weren't happy. What the hell changed?"

"She did. I guess after her accident she realized life's too short to be a bitch to the people she loves."

"Do you love her?" Kylie was fighting back the tears.

"I have always loved her."

"You bitch!"

"Kylie...please...I hoped you would understand. I never meant to hurt you. I...I guess I just belong with her. She needs me."

"What about me...or us? I need you, Mackenzie."

"I'm sorry."

"You're staying with her because you think your leaving her caused this."

"That's not true," Mac growled.

"The hell it isn't. I can see it in your eyes."

Mac didn't say anything. She stared out at the stars. Ironically, the night sky was crystal clear.

"You slept with her didn't you?" Kylie let the tears fall down her cheeks.

"I'm sorry, Kylie. What else do you want me to say?"

"Nothing. Nothing at all." Kylie turned and walked back up the Pier.

Mac felt the warm tears begin to pour from her eyes. *I hope to god you're doing the right thing, Trotter. You just broke that girl's heart.*

Chapter 9

"Neil, you want to talk? You've looked like shit for over a month now." Captain Smith sat down next to Kylie at the breakfast table.

"Is it effecting my job?" She questioned sarcastically.

"Well no, of course not."

"Then butt out," She growled.

"Neil, I've known you for a long time. You wear your emotions on your sleeve. Everyone is worried about you. So I guess you can say it's effecting everyone."

"Smith, come on, my life is of no one's concern except my own. Leave me alone. I have nothing to talk about."

"I thought that friend of the doctor's recovered from her accident."

"She did, two months ago."

"Oh...I'm sorry, Neil."

"Don't be." Kylie stood up and dumped the remaining contents of her cereal into the trash tossing the bowl in the sink. "Have Lawson clean the kitchen. I'm sick of being the maid around here. I'm the damn Lieutenant not some housewife." She stormed off.

~

"I'm sorry I wasn't able to take any more time off this

week." Mac said standing in the kitchen with Loren. They had flown to Brazil to spend a week with her family since Loren was finally healthy enough to travel and would soon be returning work.

"It's okay, I'm sure my parents will understand why we can only stay a week. By the way, I'm glad you dumped that little girlfriend of yours. Frankly, it was making me sick." Loren stated as she helped Mac make drinks for everyone.

"Excuse me?"

"You know what I mean. I'm glad you're here with me...where you belong. I'm sorry it took me nearly dying for you to see where you belonged."

Mac was furious. "Ugh! The nerve of you. You have no idea what I have been through."

"So you had a fling, I'm just saying..."

"No you don't Loren...you're not just saying anything."

"Keep your voice down my parents are in there."

"I don't care. They need to know the truth." Mac raised her voice even higher. "Leaving you was hard enough. I finally started over and then you had your accident. I don't blame you or your accident. I have always loved you and I was there for you when you needed me. It scared me to think I almost lost you. I came home and flew here with you to be with you and your family because I thought you had changed."

"Changed? Why would I change? You're the one that needs to grow up."

"I can definitely see you have not changed at all. And to think I broke that woman's heart because I thought I was meant to be here with you."

"And now?"

"Nothing has changed between us. You're still a bitch, bossing me around left and right."

"Fine, run back to your little girlfriend."

"I'm in love with her, Loren. I pushed everything aside for you, so I could take care of you, and this is how you treat me?"

"Look at the way you treat me. You stand in my parents' home and tell me you're in love with someone else."

"God damn it, Loren, you have no fucking clue." Mac flew through the hallway into the living room. "Mr. and Mrs. Staccia, I'm very sorry you had to hear this. I love you both dearly, and I love you daughter, as I always have. But, I haven't been in love with her for a long time." Mac went upstairs and packed her bag. As soon as the taxi arrived she was on her way to the airport.

~

Once she was back in the States, Mac went straight to her office at the hospital. Sitting down at her desk she called the Director of the Hospital, Martin Fleming. He had personally given her last promotion to her a few years back.

"How are you, Dr. Trotter? I thought you were in Brazil?" The older, white haired man sat back in his desk chair.

"I came back a little early. How are you?"

"I can't complain. I do have a question for you though." He laughed.

"Sure?"

"When are you looking to switch to Geriatrics?"

"Excuse me Sir? I'm not…"

"I'm only joking with you, Trotter. What do I owe the pleasure of this conversation with you? Don't tell me you grew lonely relaxing on a beautiful beach and had to come back to work?"

"No, I actually came home early for other reasons and decided to put in for some personal time."

"Aren't you on vacation?"

"Well not technically, I rearranged my schedule and took a few personal days. I'm actually looking to take my vacation time now." Mac laughed.

"Well I'm sure you have some. Hell, I don't think you have ever taken actual vacation days. I wish more of my staff was like you."

"Thank you," Mac said.

"What are you doing, if you don't mind my asking?"

"Oh...I'm going on a sailing trip. I'm going to sail my boat up to Cape Hatteras and back."

"That sounds like fun. I don't have any problem with you taking a few weeks."

"Thank you, I'm going to catch up with a few things here in the office and leave Sunday, I should be back in two weeks, but I'm going to say three just to be safe."

"No problem. Have a safe trip...and Trotter..."

"Yes?"

"Have fun...enjoy it while you're young." He smiled and hung up.

~

"Come on Stimpy, we have one final stop and we're out of here, I still can't believe I let her talk me into leaving you with the neighbors." Mac grabbed the tiny dog, set her in the Mini Cooper and drove off. They stopped at the pet store up the road from the Marina. "Here's the deal Stimpy, you can pick out a couple of new toys. We also need to get you some food and a new t-shirt. It may be cooler up there. Oh and don't forget shampoo so we can wash your stinky butt." The little dog just looked at her, waiting to be put down so she could have free rein of the store.

An hour later Stimpy and Mac arrived back at the boat and were ready to set sail. Stimpy was happy with her new found furry friends, but he was completely dissatisfied with her mother's taste in clothing and refused to wear the new t-shirt.

"Goodbye, Harry. I'll see you in a few weeks." Mac yelled over to her neighbor as she untied the dock lines.

"Have a safe trip, Mac. I still can't believe you're going to knock the barnacles off of that ol' girl!" He waved.

Mac laughed and waved back. "She's barely six years old!"

~

Twenty four hours at sea and Mac was in no hurry to get to her destination so she sat with Stimpy on the calm water, staring at the flat sails lying against the mast and the sea gulls flying freely. She had decided to save gas and not use the motor unless she had to. Unfortunately, this left her hands tied when the air was calm and she couldn't sail the boat.

"I wish you could play cards, Stimpy, we need to pass the time. At this rate I don't think we'll make Hatteras, we may just stop in Southport for a day or two and come back." The dog looked at her and went below deck to her food dish. "Hey that's a good idea, let's have lunch." She proceeded to make a turkey sandwich, loaded with cheese, mayo, lettuce, and tomato for herself. She dropped hints of turkey and cheese on the galley floor for Stimpy, who nonchalantly grabbed them and took off to eat in private.

"Weird ass dog, I know you have it. I threw it on the floor for you. How else do you think it got there?"

~

The two story house was almost completely engulfed when the Airport Fire Station arrived. The flames were coming out of every available opening. The woman on the grass outside was screaming at the top of her lungs.

"Please! Somebody please get my little girl out of there!"

Captain Smith parked the fire engine as Neil, Harris, and Brown simultaneously jumped out in full turnout gear. Lawson and Vincent pulled up behind them in the ambulance.

"Where's your daughter, Ma'am?" Captain Smith calmly asked the panicking woman.

"She's...oh my god...pleaseee you have to get her..."

"We will, Ma'am...you have to tell me where she is."

"Her bedroom...second...she's upstairs...oh no...pleaseee..."

The older man took Neil and Harris aside. "She has a young child on the second floor, by the looks of it you may not even be able to get to her."

"At least give me a chance at it." Neil was waiting anxiously for the order to go into the burning house.

"Turn your radio on channel two and, Neil, be careful." *God Speed.*

"Come on, Harris, time to get your panties wet." The young rookie followed directly behind her and put his oxygen mask and helmet on as she did. "Can you hear me, Harris?"

"Yes, loud and clear." The entered the first floor through the front door.

"She's on the second floor, watch for the flames, they're getting close to the staircase. Follow me up, I'll go left, you go right."

At the top of the stairs Neil started in the first room, she shined the light around as much as she could, but didn't see anything that resembled a child. She moved to the room next door. She noticed what looked like toys in the corner and a small bed to her left. She shined the light around the room and again didn't see anything, as she turned to exit the room she felt her pant leg move, when she shined the flashlight on the ground she found the tiny girl cradled in the corner under the bed. She had crawled out enough to grab Neil when she saw the light flash. *Oh my god, how is she breathing in here?* Neil grabbed the girl and yelled into her radio that was attached to her helmet.

"I have her! I'm coming out!"

"Copy, Neil, I'm right behind you." The firefighter exited the house first with the limp blond child in her arms. She ran directly to Lawson and Vincent. They tossed the girl in the back of the ambulance and Neil snatched her mask and helmet off and ripped the velcro shedding the yellow jacket that was covering her upper body.

She immediately went to work trying to establish an airway on the child as Vincent started an IV.

"We need to intubate her, now," Kylie said.

"I don't know if I have steady enough hands," Vincent

said. "Her throat is so small."

"I'll do it," Kylie said grabbing the small tube from him. She pressed the girl's jaw down tilting her head back as she pushed the tube down her throat carefully passing her vocal cords. "I'm in," she said attaching the bag to squeeze forcing air into the little girl's lungs. "Go, Lawson, we're ready," she yelled.

The little girl was unconscious and still not breathing on her own when they reached Hilton Head Medical Center. Neil was running next to the stretcher pressing a large bulb methodically.

"What do we have so far?" Lyle said running up to the stretcher as Neil and Vincent pushed the girl inside. Lawson put the girl's mother in a wheelchair and pushed her into the ER behind them.

"Severe smoke inhalation. She was conscious when I found her in her bedroom. The entire house was engulfed. I got her out as quickly as I could. She doesn't appear to have any exterior burns, but she's not breathing on her own." Neil spoke without hesitation. *When she found me, god if she hadn't reached out...*

"Okay let's put her in here." They wheeled the girl into trauma room one. Lyle bent down to listen to hear breathing. "Let's get her hooked to the ventilator and get a pulse oxygen level and take blood for the lab. We also need to get portable x-ray in here as well," he said to the nurse and doctor assisting him.

"Where's Dr. Trotter?" Neil asked quietly, wondering why the Head of Pediatrics wasn't there to assist since her life seemed to revolve around pediatric trauma.

"She's in Brazil with Lor...uh she's on vacation," he corrected himself.

"No she's not. I saw her a few days ago. She took a

sailing trip to Cape Hatteras." The nurse spoke up as she continued to help him with the child.

"When did she get back from Brazil? I thought they were…"

"She came back alone, put in for some vacation time, and took off on her boat."

"How the hell do you know all of the gossip around here, Jennie?"

The nurse smiled. "She only spoke to me for a second. I asked why they were back early. She simply said *I'm* back early and *I'm* taking a vacation trip to Cape Hatteras on my boat. I simply put two and two together, Lyle." He shook his head.

The little girl was stable enough for them to establish a heartbeat finally. Happy that the girl was still alive, Neil decided to head back with Vincent and Lawson. Deep down inside she wondered why Mac had come back alone and taken off again, apparently alone.

~

Three more days at sea and *'Rin'* was moving smoothly through the water, splicing a beautiful line as the wind filled her sails. The salt filled air was breezing by as Stimpy hung on for dear life while Mac mastered the helm. "This is the life, Stimp!" Mac yelled down to the little dog as she followed the parallel line of the horizon.

Late that afternoon they motored into the Southport Marina in Southport, North Carolina. As soon as she had the boat tied up in a slip Mac called information on her phone.

She dialed the number and waited as it rang only twice. An older, male voice answered briskly with a slight southern drawl.

"I'm trying to reach Gordon Trotter."

"This is him. What can I do for you?"

"Uncle Gordy, it's …" She was cut off mid sentence.

"Well my gosh…if it isn't my favorite niece in the whole world. How ya doin,' Mackenzie Leigh?"

She smiled from ear to ear. Her father's brother had always treated her as his child all of her life since he was unable to have children of his own.

"I'm good. I uh…I sailed my boat up here."

"I remember you telling me about your boat. What made you bring her this way? Don't tell me you left the hospital."

"You know that'll never happen, Uncle Gordy, I'm finally on vacation so I decided to see what this money hole of mine was made of."

"Well where are ya? I'm coming to see you if you're in town."

"I just tied up at the Southport Marina."

"I'll be there in twenty minutes."

"Sounds good. I'm at the end of the first dock on the left."

~

Mac took Stimpy with her to stay on the mainland with her uncle for a few days. They caught up on the past few months since she hadn't spoken to him since Christmas. She couldn't believe that he was aging almost identical to her father, if it wasn't for the mustache she almost couldn't tell them apart. Except, her Uncle talked with more of a southern accent than her father ever had. The older man was surprised to hear about Loren and the fiasco that Mac was put through over the past few months.

"I'm so sorry she treated you like that, Munchkin, you deserve so much better. And here I thought she was some big time news person. Ha, what a waste of a beautiful woman."

"Yeah, you're telling me." Mac was happy to be off of the water and sitting in a cozy two story house that her uncle had owned for thirty years. She remembered spending much of her summers up there on the coast with him while her parents traveled for vacation or business.

"So are you seeing anyone new?" He questioned quietly.

Gordon Trotter had always thought of Mackenzie as his daughter. He married only once and was never able to have children of his own. She left him for a man that could give her a child. This left Gordy heartbroken for a few years, until his younger brother's wife had a baby girl. Mackenzie became the light in his eyes. He was an outstanding figure in her life from her first steps, through her brother's death, all the way to her college graduation. She always thought of him as a second father even though her own father was still alive and very much a part of her life.

"Well…" Technically she was single, as single as it gets.

"Cat got your tongue?" He smiled. "Out with it, Mackenzie. I'm not your old man. You can't shy away from me." He smiled once more. She knew he was right, Uncle Gordy could always tell when something was on her mind.

"I was…sort of…uh seeing someone… before Loren's accident."

"Okay…"

"I broke it off and pushed her away to go be with Loren. She needed me and that's all that mattered…"

"Was it serious?"

"I guess…hell I don't know anymore…that was then."

"And now?"

"I realize it was huge mistake, but I broke the other woman's heart. I cut all ties with her practically overnight. I never meant for things to be like that." Mac fought back a tear, but it relentlessly escaped and slid down her cheek.

"Do you love her?" He sipped his tea as he sat back in his oversized and well-worn recliner, slightly chewing his gray mustache.

"Yes…I discovered that a little too late though."

"What do you mean?"

"I never knew how I really felt about her until I was back with Loren and in Brazil."

"Well you're home now, Munchkin. You need to tell that poor girl how you feel."

"It's not that easy, Uncle Gordy."

"Sure it is. Hell you haven't even told me about her…shame on you."

Mac smiled shyly. "Uh…"

"Her name, Mackenzie…what's her name?"

"Kylie…Kylie Neil."

"There ya go, that's a start. She's not another news geek is she?" He grinned.

"No, she's a firefighter, a lieutenant actually."

His eye brows shot up. "My my, that's certainly different. I thought you swore you would never be with someone in your field?"

"Well technically we're not in the same field. I didn't even meet her at the hospital." She laughed thinking about how she met the gregarious woman. "I met her went I went

91

to vote for the new mayor. My voting precinct is at the fire station."

"I see."

"She came after me and I explained my situation with Loren and we became good friends. After I left Loren we …we just sort of slowly got together."

"I bet she's a looker, you always do pick the prettiest girls that I have ever seen."

"She's definitely the complete opposite of Loren that's for sure. She's very tiny, maybe five foot three with her work boots on and a hundred fifteen pounds soaking wet."

"Wow and she's a firefighter?"

"Yeah I know, I could carry her with one arm and I'm not much bigger than she is. Anyway, she has stunning Black Irish good looks. The most amazing blue eyes and long curly black hair that stops just past her shoulders and she's almost as tan as me, but not quite."

"Sounds like she's beautiful, Munchkin." Mac smiled ear to ear. She always felt like she was ten again when he used the pet name for her.

"Yeah…too bad I wrecked everything." The smile quickly faded.

"The hell you did, now listen to yourself. Mackenzie, you're the brightest and most amazing person that I know. She has to see that side of you and know that you made a mistake."

"Yeah but I made a huge mistake and broke her heart."

"Hearts mend, people make mistakes. It's part of being human."

"I…" She let out a long sigh. "I don't think she's into second chances." Mac stared at the old shag looking rug under her feet covering part of the hardwood floor.

"If she loves you she will be."

"I don't know if she loves me, we...we weren't together very long."

"It doesn't take long to love someone, although it may take some people years to realize it."

"Gee thanks..."

"Cheer up, Munchkin, I'm sure everything will work out. You my darlin,' know more about pain than most people ever will."

She knew deep down he was right. Even after all of those years she still missed her brother and could remember everything from his brief childhood through his death. "Do you ever...I mean...I miss him..."

"I know you do, Munchkin..."

"Mom and Dad...they never..."

"It's hard for them to talk about it. It seems like the only time I hear Gregory's name is during the holidays."

"I know, it tears me up...he was my best friend..."

"That little boy admired you so much. He wanted to be just like you. I still remember him running around at Christmas mimicking everything you did with your new toys. He was always more interested in what you had or what you were doing."

"I know it. He drove me nuts, but I always included him no matter what I was doing," she said as a small tear fell from her eye.

"It's good to talk about him and remember. I'm sorry your parents don't do more of that. It's healthy and hell, it keeps you sane. I'll be right back. I have just the thing to cheer you up. You remember when I went to Europe for vacation a few years ago?"

"Yeah, why?" She looked at the old man quizzically.

"I picked this up for us while I was there. I keep

forgetting to bring it with me during the holidays." He returned with a small, ripe, old bottle of brandy and two snifters.

"That looks good! I can't believe you were holding out on me, Uncle Gordy. You know how much I like that stuff." She crossed the room and sat at the kitchen table with him.

They drank most of the bottle and continued to talk about life. Mac crawled into the bed in the spare room downstairs after midnight. She had to literally push the snoring little Chihuahua to the other side of the bed so she could lay down.

The next morning she prepared to motor the large sailboat out of the harbor and back to the open sea. Stimpy walked around the cockpit with her lifejacket on and lanyard that kept her tied to the lifelines for safety. Mac leaned back against the cushion and steered the wheel. She was a little chilly, dressed in khaki colored nylon shorts with a small white and blue windbreaker over her tee shirt. She choose to wear her brown leather boat shoes instead of her sailing sneakers. She threw a white ball cap over her short blond hair and put on her sunglasses before waving goodbye to her uncle who was standing on the dock.

~

Back at sea for the third day in a row, Mac and Stimpy were on their way home. She wasn't sure, but she was beginning to the think the little dog preferred to be on the boat than on land. She quickly set the autopilot and went below deck to make lunch.

"What do you say we share a sandwich, Stimp?" The dog looked on in amusement waiting for her to speak the two of the most powerful words known in the canine world.

"Turkey and cheese?" The dog was practically walking on only her hind legs begging for the all important food to be dropped on the floor for her. Mac thought she semi-resembled a tan colored penguin when she stood in the 'oh my God give me cheese and turkey' stance.

"Here ya go, some for you and the rest for me." The little dog grabbed the small pieces of meat and cheese and took off into the salon. Mac hollered over her shoulder to the little fiend. "You're welcome!" She put the first CD she could find into the stereo system and went back out to the cockpit to take over piloting the boat. She sang along with a mixture of Otis Redding, Aretha Franklin, Percy Sledge, and Howard Tate songs. She found herself singing at the top of her lungs to *You Make Me Feel Like A Natural Woman*.

As the sun went down, the chill of the salty air became very apparent to Mac so she set the autopilot and went to put on her fleece-lined windbreaker pants that matched the jacket that she was already wearing. In addition, the breeze that filled the sails and seemed to be moving the boat rather nicely came to a screeching halt. She decided it was time to motor to a shallow spot and drop the anchor for the night.

Mac decided to lie out on the deck and look at the stars instead of going below deck. She grabbed one of the cockpit cushions for her head and laid back, her mind raced to the woman with the curly dark hair and penetrating blue eyes. The memories of Kylie immediately sent heat to her center, her heart pounded in the pit of her stomach. *I miss you so much, Kylie.*

Mac woke up freezing at four a.m., still lying on the

deck. The middle of May was exceedingly hot during the day and about as cool as you'd ever want it to be at night on the water. She decided now was as good a time as any to continue the trip home. She went below deck to check on Stimpy, who was passed out in the salon on the sofa. Mac could see the small throw-blanket moving up and down in unison with the dog's breathing. *At least she's warm.*

~

"Come on, Neil, let's go get a beer at Dusty's." Kylie cocked her head to the side as one eyebrow disappeared behind her long dark locks.

"Dusty's?" She questioned.

"Whatever the hell the name of that bar is that you guys all go to." Captain Smith seemed agitated.

"Okay? What's up, Smith?"

"Nothing's up, we've had a long day and a hell of a week. I thought you might want to join your old comrade for a cold one."

Kylie wasn't sure what he had up his sleeve. It had been months since she saw him outside of the station. "Sure. Let me go change."

Kylie came back downstairs in jeans and a light blue polo that fit her perfectly. Smith gave her a puzzled look when he saw her feet.

"Flip flops?"

"Yeah, my feet are killing me. I'm still trying to break in my new boots for work. I can't seem to find a comfortable pair at the uniform store since they discontinued my old favorites."

Kylie rode in the passenger seat while the older man

drove his white SUV. They walked into the small bar and sat in a corner booth. The waitress recognized Kylie and nodded when she held up two fingers.

"Heineken okay?" She asked.

"Sure," he said.

The woman came by their table with two bottles of beer and strode off to the next waiting couple. Kylie took a long swallow, nearly emptying the bottle in one shot.

"All right, Smith, out with it." She knew she could be square with him away from the Station house. They had been good friends that watched each other's back since Kylie joined the team four years ago.

"Out with what, Neil?"

"You have something up your sleeve. I know you too well, and you know you can't hide anything from me for shit." Her right eyebrow arched as she glared at him.

"Fine, I was hoping you'd talk to me, Neil. You haven't been yourself lately."

"I'm fine, Smith. You drug me out here to get me shitfaced so I would tell you what was bothering me didn't you?"

He turned away from her and started on his second beer as the waitress dropped off another round.

"Damn it...I'm not that easy."

"Yeah, that much I know. Look, Neil, you're my right hand at that station. We have always been able to anticipate what the other was going to do or say before it was ever thought of, you know that." He took a sip of his beer and sighed. "The past two or three months you've been going in every direction faster than anyone can keep up. I'm worried about you. I've never seen you this high-strung. Even Brown is afraid to go near you. You nearly bit his head off the other day when the truck wasn't clean enough for your standards."

"Well he didn't even clean the chrome, much less polish it." Her voice raised an octave. "When I was a rookie you bet your ass I had to polish the chrome on the fire engine." She finished her second beer.

"Calm down, see what I mean? Something has your jockstrap in a bunch."

"I don't wear a jockstrap, Smith."

"You know what I mean. When I asked you a month ago what was wrong you told me to butt out. You also said you weren't seeing the doctor anymore."

"So." She furled her eyebrows together. *I hate it when he lectures me, get it over with already.*

"It must have been more serious than I thought. I can tell you're still upset about it."

"No I'm not, have you seen me moping around crying? It was hot, heavy, and over just as quick as it started, therefore there's nothing to grieve about. I'm over it."

"No you're not. And you don't have to mope around crying for me to see the sadness. I knew when you fell for her and I knew when she broke your heart."

Loud enough for the bar to hear, Kylie snapped back. "She did not break my heart!"

"Uh huh, I think the entire block heard you. So much rage out of such a little person."

"If you weren't my Captain I'd smack you right in the mouth."

"Okay, you want to go outside and rumble, Neil. Will that make you feel better?"

"Damn it, Smith." She stood up, tossed a ten on the table, and turned to walk out. He replaced the ten with a twenty and went out after her. She was already walking

98

back towards the island.

He quickly caught up to her. "What the hell are you doing, Neil?"

"I'm walking home. I don't live far from here. I'll pick up my Jeep from the station in the morning."

"You're seriously not walking home. Stop," he said. She kept walking.

"Stop! Neil, I mean it goddamn it!"

She turned towards him. It took everything she had to keep from hitting him. "What do you want me to say? It was the one time I finally let go and gave everything to someone. Yes, I was in love with her, I fell too hard too fast and I got my heart broken. There, are you fucking happy now? Leave me the fuck alone!" She felt the tears sting her eyes as she started walking again.

He caught back up to her. "I'm sorry. Let me take you back."

She never looked at him as he drove her back to the station. She climbed into her Jeep and drove home without saying a word.

Chapter 10

Mac was happy to be back in her slip at the Windmill Harbor Marina. She had arrived in the middle of the night and tied the boat up with ease before curling up in her bed. Harry was out and about first thing in the morning welcoming her back and asking hundreds of questions about her trip. She sat on the deck with him drinking coffee. She decided to go ahead and call the Hospital Director to let him know she was back in town if they had any emergencies and she would be in first thing in the morning.

~

Mac parked her dark blue Mini Cooper in the usual spot in the parking garage and headed into Hilton Head Medical Center through the emergency room.

"Well I'll be damned, look it's 'Moby Dick'." Lyle loved jerking Mac's chain.

"Lyle, you want me to slap you now or later?"

"Mmmm it depends…" He laughed.

He followed her into the employee lounge to grab a stale cup of coffee.

"Yuck! It's seven a.m. this can't possibly be last night's coffee," she said.

The man standing next to her in matching scrubs and white sneakers smiled from ear to ear. "I'm sure it is."

"Lyle this is beyond gross!" She tossed it in the trash.

"Hey I kept one of the headlines for you while you were gone. I thought you might want to read it."

"Sure." She never bothered to look at the newspaper; instead, she folded it and tucked it under her arm. "I'm sure I have a hundred messages to tend to and fifty meetings. Not to mention the patients that I have scheduled. I'm sure I'll see you sometime this week if I don't get back down here."

100

"I see how it is, desk jockey." He smiled and she grinned at him. Both of them knew damn well she was no desk jockey. She spent her days juggling her administration meetings between seeing the most severe Pediatric patients and overseeing all of the Pediatricians in the hospital through daily routines of emergencies, traumas, and surgeries. Lyle often wondered how she had time to do all of that in one day and help him out in a pinch in the ER.

Mac sat behind her oak desk and tossed the newspaper to the side. She turned on her computer and began reading the sticky notes attached to the patient charts that needed her signature.

Cardiac Arrhythmia-seen by Dr. Bennett, Cardiology. Ten year old male, put on the donor list for transplant. Signed Dr. Phillips. Mac removed the sticky note and added her signature after reading the chart. She made a mental note to check on this particular patient.

Severe Smoke Inhalation and burnt lungs-seen by Dr. Ferguson, ER. Seven year old female. Kept three days in ICU, released two days later. Mac continued to read the chart. She noticed that the girl was rescued by the fire department. *Hmm.*

An hour later Mac was finished with her email and signing off on the 'Priority' charts that needed to be filed. She sent the secretary down to the cafeteria to find her some fresh coffee. Mac was pleased when she returned with fresh brewed cappuccino.

"It's all they had, sorry."

"No problem, this is better than what I started with today. Thanks." Mac shut her office door and sat back down behind her desk. It was then that she noticed the newspaper sitting on the floor. She picked it up and stared in amazement as she read the headline and saw the picture of Kylie in her fire suit carrying the tiny girl out of the blazing house. *My god!* She sat back and read the entire article. "So you're the one that saved the seven year old little girl. I should've known."

~

Mac stopped in the ER on her way out of the hospital. Lyle was just coming out of the employee lounge and nonchalantly bumped into her.

"And where are you headed?" he asked.

"Is that any of your business?" She grinned. "Home, Lyle. I'm headed home."

"I can't believe you're still here. I pulled a double to cover for one of my sorry ass residents, so I'm finally leaving now. You should've been out of here five or six hours ago."

"Yeah well that's how it is when you're a desk jockey that's been on vacation," she said laughing.

"Speaking of work horse, what are you doing tonight? Any plans?"

"No, I just got back."

"I'm meeting Jennie and a few other people at Daisy's tonight." He looked as his watch. "Actually, I'm supposed to be there now. Damn Residents!"

"You might want to get a move on slacker."

"You should go with me."

"I'm not dressed to go out, Lyle."

"Since when do clothes bother you?" He looked down at the dark blue scrubs that both of them were wearing. Mac's White and blue sneakers stuck out under her pant legs. "I have to go in my scrubs too! We'll be like the

'Double Mint Twins'."

"How cute…"

"C'mon, humor me."

She laughed and shook her head. "Fine, get your ass moving."

Lyle signed his last patient out, tossed his lab coat in his locker, and grabbed his back pack. Mac stood waiting outside of the lounge with her briefcase in her hand. She had left her white lab coat on the coat rack in her office as usual.

Mac drove the short distance to the small waterfront bar. Lyle followed her in his Toyota Camry and parked next to her when they entered the lime rock and dirt covered parking area.

"Hey guys!" A petite brunette yelled to them as Mac and Lyle entered the bar.

"Well, look what the cat drug in…my God, Trotter, do you ever go out anymore?" The woman laughed and called the waitress over to their table. Lyle and Mac ordered a second bucket of beers.

"I'd tell you to kiss my ass, Jennie, but you might just try to do it." Mac grinned.

"I'm surprised to see you, Dr. Trotter." Mac turned to the young, dark haired man sitting next to Jennie.

"Hey, Tony, I almost didn't recognize you, I guess Ferguson and I are the only ones that feel sexy enough in our scrubs to strut around town in them." She laughed and Lyle clinked his beer bottle against hers. Tony Crandall was one of her Pediatric staff members. He was fairly new in pediatrics since he was only a few years out of school. "How did these guys drag you out here?"

He shyly looked her way, not sure how to speak to his boss and still shell shocked to see her in a bar.

"Uh...I'm..."

"Cat got your tongue?" She smiled as her eyebrows shot up waiting for him to spit out whatever it was that he was trying to say to her.

"No, Ma'am, I'm sorry Dr. Tro..."

Lyle and Jennie were laughing so hard they could barely keep their alcohol down. Jennie tried to speak and Mac cut her off. She looked over at Tony who was white as a ghost and sitting rather close to Jennie.

"Crandall, I may be your boss, but I promise I don't bite. I'm a human being and a doctor, not a drill sergeant." She smiled again and sipped her beer.

Jennie couldn't help herself. "She does bite Tony, don't let her fool you!" Everyone at the table was laughing. "He's here with me, we're dating. So you need to behave, Mac, don't scare him!"

"I promise to be on my best behavior." She winked at Jennie.

"How do all of you know each other, and so well?" Tony asked.

Mac was the first to answer. "Well, Lyle and I have known each other since we were both residents in the ER straight out of med school and Jennie joined the hospital as a nurse a year or two later. I moved up to Pediatrics and they stayed in the ER. I guess you can say we've been friends for a while."

"So when did you get home, Mac?" Jennie asked as she ordered a third bucket of beers.

"I pulled into the marina about eight yesterday morning."

"Wow and you turned around and went right to work? You had to be bushed from your trip?"

"I was, but you know how that hospital is."

"So where exactly did you go?" Lyle questioned as he reached for another beer.

"I went to Southport, North Carolina."

"Does your Uncle still live there?" Lyle passed Mac a new beer.

"Thanks. Yeah , I only see him during the holidays now. He keeps asking me to come see him, but I'm always so busy."

"How's he doing?"

"Good, he travels a lot. I guess that's what you do when you're a retired divorcee."

"At least he lives life."

"Oh yeah, I don't think I've ever seen Uncle Gordy not happy." Mac noticed Kylie walking towards her in the crowd; her curly hair was resting on her shoulders. Mac's heart stopped, she never heard another word her colleagues were saying until Kylie made brief eye contact with her and passed by their table.

~

"God damn bathroom." Kylie mumbled. *I just had to walk past that table, just had to look at her. Sure enough she was looking right at you. This is just fabulous!*

Kylie had heard Mac's last name being yelled out when she came in the door and immediately scanned the crowd. She found Mac sitting at a table very close by with a few people from the hospital. Surprisingly she was still in her scrubs. Kylie could hear everything that was being said at their table. Part of her wanted to bolt, but she did miss Mac's voice and her laughter. *At least she's happy.*

"Hey, Harris, I'm going to take off. I have a few errands to run tonight and then I'm back on at the station in the morning." She tossed a twenty on the table and walked out of the bar never looking back.

~

"Excuse me guys." Mac jumped out of the booth and took off out the front door.

"Kylie...Kylie wait." Mac ran up behind her as Kylie went to open the door to Jeep. "Can we talk?"

"Nope." Kylie still hadn't turned around out of fear that she would let herself go.

"Please, I need...we need to talk."

"Our talking days are over. Now if you will excuse me, Dr. Trotter, I'm trying to go home." Kylie opened the door and stepped inside the vehicle.

Mac turned around and walked back into the bar.

Jennie looked surprisingly at Mac. "What the hell was that all about?"

"Nothing."

Lyle was close to the window and could see where Mac ran off to. "Tough luck, huh."

"Yeah you could say that. I think I'm going to head home, I'll see you guys tomorrow."

She stood to walk away. "Crandall, I expect you to be punctual and functioning perfectly in the morning." She looked at Jennie and winked.

<u>Chapter 11</u>

"Who the fuck does she think she is? She can't demand to talk to me," Kylie spat out as she smacked the hell out of the heavy bag hanging in the bay between the ambulance and fire engine. "I'm not a goddamn puppet, I have feelings!" She smacked it a few more times. Captain Smith stood back watching her vent out her frustration.

"Looks like the bag's winning, Neil."

"I'm not in the mood, Smith." She smacked the bag again.

"I'm just saying, hell that thing probably weighs as much as you do." She quickly turned towards him.

"Would you like to be the bag?" she growled. He shooed her back over to the bag.

"Why are you so pissed, Neil? What now?"

"Butt out."

"Oh, the doc must be back in town."

"I'm warning you, Smith." He laughed and shook his head as she continued to smack the bag. As soon as he was out of sight the alarm went off.

"Damn it to hell!" She tossed her gloves on the floor under the bag and grabbed her uniform pants that were hanging on the ladder of the fire engine. She quickly put them on over her tiny gym shorts and threw her uniform shirt on over the sports bra that she had been working out in.

"Lawson is in the shower, Neil I need you to ride on the ambulance."

"Ugh! Great! Let's go Vincent, get your ass moving!"

They pulled up at to a three car pile-up on the bridge leading to the island. The smallest car appeared to have flipped and was lying on its roof, the other two cars were smashed up, but still on their wheels.

"Neil, you and Vincent go assess the overturn. Brown, you and Harris work on that red car, I'll check on the third car."

Kylie bent down and glanced around the car. She could see the driver was banged up pretty bad.

"Are you in the car alone, sir? No, don't move, we'll get you out." He was hanging upside down by his seatbelt.

"My son, he's...back...seat." He was trying to talk between coughs, the airbag had definitely pounded his chest. She was sure he had a few broken ribs, but his airway was open so she left him there.

Kylie crawled through the shattered windshield trying to get to the boy as Vincent worked to free his father. "I got him, he's pretty squished, but he has a pulse." Kylie had to crawl completely inside the crushed up car to stabilize the boy so the she could get him out. Smith worked the 'jaws of life' gas powered clippers to cut part of the car so that they could get the boy free. Since she was the smallest, Kylie was inside of the car holding him still and out of the way. When the cut up doorjamb broke it slipped smacking her in the head. Everything went black.

"Kylie...damn it...Kylie...Harris get over here and pull her out of there, we can get the boy from this side now that the door is loose." Harris ran over and stuck as much of his body into the car as he could.

"She's out cold, Captain."

"Get her out of there." Kylie's head was bleeding just above her right eye.

"Put a collar on her just to be safe. My God, if she wasn't there holding him out of the way that doorjamb would've taken that kid's head off."

*My   head....throbbing...pressure...ouch!   What the...*Kylie opened her eyes as the collar was going around her neck. She sounded pretty groggy as she spoke. Her hand went up to her head. "What the hell! Ouch!"

"Be still!"

"I'm fine, Vincent. Let me up!"

Neil, you got smacked in the head. You need stitches and probably have a concussion."

"Smith, I'm fine, tell this pompous ass to get off of me!"

Captain Smith checked her vitals while Harris and Vincent tended to the boy on the backboard. Her pupils were slightly dilated, but she was okay. "You can sit up."

"My head hurts like hell, what happened? The boy...did you get him..." She looked back at the crumpled car.

"He's over there. Your head saved his life. I always thought you were hardheaded, but you proved it today," Captain Smith joked.

"What?"

"The jam broke and smacked you. If you weren't there holding him away from it, it would've taken his head off."

"Holy shit!"

"Come on, we need to transport him, he's pretty crushed up. Can you walk?"

"Yeah." Kylie felt a little woozy as she stood, but was fine by the time she climbed into the back of the ambulance.

~

"Trotter."

"Hey it's Lyle. I have a pediatric trauma coming in, thought you might want to be down here."

"I'm on the way."

Lyle was already tending to the boy's father when the child came in. Mac ran over to the stretcher to get caught up on his condition and noticed Captain Smith walk in with Kylie. The right side of her face was covered in dirt and blood. *Oh my god...Kylie!*

"Put him in trauma two, her in trauma three," Lyle said.

Mac quickly checked the boy's vitals and began ordering tests. He appeared stable and breathing on his own. His eyes were open and he was trying to talk. She guessed he was probably six or seven. Mac felt for fractures in his face, satisfied that there weren't any, she sutured the large gash on the side of his head. "He's fairly stable. Let me know when the films are back for his arm and leg." She walked out of the room. Lyle was in the hallway heading towards room three.

"How's the boy?"

"Stable, I'll know more when I see his films. He's pretty broken up though, no internal bleeding. Hey, do you mind if I..." She pointed towards Kylie's room.

"Are you sure?"

She shrugged her shoulders.

"Go ahead."

Mac walked into room three. Kylie was laying on the small bed staring at the ceiling.

110

"That bad huh?" Mac walked over to Kylie and felt around her face and head searching for any swelling or fractures.

"Ugh!" Kylie rolled her eyes, flinching at the pain in her head and the warmth she felt everywhere Mac touched her. "Why are you in here anyway?"

"I was called down to tend to the child you saved. He's got a broken arm and leg, maybe more, but stable and breathing on his own."

"That's good."

"They said you blacked out when you got hit, do you remember it?"

"No. I'm fine." Kylie wanted to run out of the room, anything to get away from the blond doctor that drove her crazy.

"I didn't ask."

"Can you please stitch my head so I can go home?"

"Calm down," Mac said. She shot Novocain in two different spots on Kylie's forehead and placed five tiny stitches in her hairline. "There you go, all fixed up." She backed away tossing her rubber gloves in the trash.

"Good." Kylie sat up to leave.

"Oh no you don't, you need to take it easy."

"I'm fine."

"I didn't ask."

"Goddamn it, Mackenzie, I am not a child!"

"I never said you were."

"You can't hold me here. I don't have a concussion."

"True, but you can't leave until I sign this chart and then go have Dr. Ferguson sign it as well since you're not a minor. That could take a while."

"Can you hurry it up please? I'd like to get the hell out of here."

"Can we at least talk?"

"No," Kylie huffed crossing her arms and refusing to look at Mac.

"Come on, Kylie, be civil."

"Civil! Me be civil? You're the one who…ugh! I am not even doing this here!"

Captain Smith walked into the room to check on Kylie. He could hear her yelling all the way down the hall. He was surprised to see Dr. Trotter in there with her.

"My goodness, you'd think they were killing you in here, stitches can't be that bad. It's not like you haven't had them before," he said.

"Nah, she's just trying to choke the life out of me so she can leave," Mac said smiling at him.

"Tell her to let me leave, I'm fine," Kylie said pointing towards the stitches.

"She's free to go as soon as I finish the paperwork." Mac walked out of the room without looking at Kylie again.

"Why on god's green earth are you yelling at the top of your lungs at her?" he asked Kyle.

"Because I can!"

"She's a doctor and was trying to help you."

"You have no idea."

"Then tell me." He asked patiently.

"No!"

"Okay then I'll make you stay in here overnight." He walked over and opened the door. "Doctor?"

"No! Smith, damn it!"

Mac came back in. "Is everything okay?"

"I'm fine!"

"It seems that she may be feeling a little worse than she thought. She might…"

112

"Damn it, Smith, you cannot make me stay here overnight because I won't tell you why I'm mad at her! It's none of your goddamn business!"

Mac's eyebrows shot up. She gave both of them a questioning look. "Maybe I should go finish this chart." She started to walk out the door.

"Good, you do that so I can get the hell out of here." Kylie growled.

"Are you sure that's wise, Doctor? I mean she's in a bit of a rage here. She might need..."

"I'll tell you what I need, Smith! I need to get the fuck out of here!"

"Calm down, Kylie, you are worse than the adolescents that I see every day."

Kylie crossed her arms again and sat there with as much of a pissed off look as she could muster since she had stitches in her head and it was pounding like a bass drum. "I am calm."

"Then why are you so mad?" Smith asked wryly as Mac walked out of the room.

"Stay out of it, please."

"Talk to her, Neil, just talk to the woman for god's sake."

"Fine, I'll talk to her when I'm released," she said. Smith peeked through the door and noticed the doctors and nurses looking in his direction.

Lyle walked up to Mac at the nurse's station.

"What is wrong with her? The entire floor can hear her yelling."

"She's a little pissed off at me."

"A little?" He raised an eyebrow.

Mac smiled. "I'm releasing her now. Here sign this so she can go."

"I'm not use to signing papers for you." He grinned as he signed the forms.

"Well, she's not a minor and she's your patient."

Mac walked back into the small trauma room. Kylie was sitting up with her feet dangling over the edge of the bed. Her blue eyes were sparkling in the bright fluorescent lights.

"Here you go. I gave you a prescription for the pain. It'll help you sleep tonight. Also, you'll need to make an appointment to come back in seven days to have your stitches removed or I can remove them for you if you'd like, just call me."

"Fine." Kylie jumped off of the table and grabbed the papers from the blond doctor. Smith was standing in the corner minding his own business until Kylie tried to leave. He cleared his throat loudly and both women turned towards him. "Ugh!" Kylie was furious that she had to barter a deal to leave the hospital. Mac looked at both of them and cocked her head to the side trying to figure out what the hell was going on. "Can you walk outside?" Kylie spoke so low that Mac barely heard her.

"Huh?"

"Outside, can you go outside?" She growled.

"Oh sure, sorry." Mac quickly left the room. Kylie rolled her eyes and went after her. Mac turned back towards her in the hallway.

"I meant with me."

"Oh yeah…sure. Lyle, I'll be right back, call me if his films come back," She said before walking through the sliding doors behind Kylie.

Mac pushed the sides of her white lab coat back and shoved her hands into the pockets of her scrub pants as she leaned against the pillar. The sky was starting to get dark.

Mac watched Kylie mentally arguing with herself and tapping her foot. *She's so adorable.*

"Look, Smith made me promise to talk to you unless I wanted to stay overnight."

Mac laughed.

"Mackenzie, this isn't funny."

"No, you're right, I'm sorry," Mac said running a hand through her hair.

"So, talk...you're the one that's been trying to talk to me," Kylie said.

"I ...well..." Mac scratched her head and looked away. *Not like this, I didn't want to talk here like this.*

"Spit it out," Kylie growled.

"Are you always this feisty?"

"My head is pounding and sewn shut, plus I'm irate at this moment. I think I have a right to be a little on edge right now." Kylie began tapping her boot on the curb again.

"I can leave here in about an hour, would you mind if I came by to talk to you?"

"Yes I would mind, and I'm not going home anyway."

"Oh." Mac raised an eyebrow.

"I'm on duty until Thursday at the station." Kylie's cell phone rang against her belt.

"Even after tonight?" Mac said. Kylie ignored her and answered the phone.

"Captain, come on. I'm fine...you...ugh! Okay, fine...bye. I guess you win. I'm off tomorrow and picking up a shift on Friday to cover."

"Okay."

"I'll be home, you said an hour?"

"Yeah."

"Mackenzie, don't..." Kylie ran her hands through her

curly black hair that was now down around her shoulders. "Don't think you're going to get anywhere…"

"Kylie I'm not trying to get anything. I just want to talk to you."

~

Mac sat in her Mini Cooper in front of Kylie's apartment. She was still dressed in her dark blue scrubs. *What the hell have I gotten myself into? What are you going to say to her, Trotter? Have you even thought about it?* "Hell no!" she said loudly. Part of her wanted to put the car in reverse; instead she put it in first gear and set the parking brake. "It's all or nothing."

She stepped out and knocked on the door. Kylie answered in tiny cotton shorts and a small t-shirt with what appeared to be nothing under it. She was groggy from taking the pain pill.

"Mackenzie?" Kylie looked puzzled then remembered she wanted to talk. *Shit.* It was too late to go change her clothes and put on a bra. "Uh…come in." Kylie stepped aside.

"How's your head feel?"

"Hurts."

"I won't take up too much of your time. I know you should be resting right now."

Mac sat on one end of the couch and Kylie sat on the other end. Kylie was hesitant, then asked her if she wanted anything to drink, to her dismay Mac asked if she had any whiskey, which of course she didn't. Mac settled for ice water.

She's so damn cute in her scrubs. "What the hell!" Kylie chided herself out loud.

116

"Are you okay?" Mac asked.

Shit...shit...shit! "Uh fine...everything's fine."

Kylie returned with two glasses and sat back in the same spot.

"I should start by saying I'm sorry." Kylie went to speak and Mac put her hand up. "Please, I need to say this to you. I'm sorry. I know I hurt you. Hell, I hurt myself and I didn't even know it. I had a very long history with Loren and history is what it always will be. I made some mistakes and I let history cloud my judgment. I know you hate me right now and you have every right to hate me. I just want you to know that Loren is and always will be my past. I have learned a lot over the past six months, good, bad, pretty, and ugly. I know I have lost every chance of having anything with you, but I really don't want to lose your friendship."

"Mackenzie, what do you want me to say? You tore me apart. I made you promise that you were over her. I didn't want to be your rebound and you used me anyway."

"No, I never used you. Until I received that phone call, you Kylie, you were my life, my world, my everything."

"Well it sure changed overnight."

"My past came back to haunt me. I thought I had to go back to her, to help her, I thought the accident was my fault, that it happened for a reason because I wasn't there to protect her." Mac looked down at her hands folded in her lap. Her knuckles were white from clinching them.

"It wasn't your fault, Mackenzie."

"I know that now. It took a lot for me to see it. I really am sorry."

"I ...don't...can't...what do I say to you? I don't know anymore."

"I'm not asking for anything, Kylie. I just want to try to be friends with you again. I know I ruined my chances with you. Please believe how sorry I am." Mac looked deep into Kylie's eyes. "I hurt myself too, leaving you was the worst thing I have ever done." A small tear fell from the corner of Mac's green eyes. Kylie's hand moved to Mac's face to wipe the tear. "I should go, you need to rest anyway." Mac stood and Kylie walked her to the door. Mac turned back towards her and saw the moonlight shining in Kylie's blue eyes. "Take care of your head."

"Yes, Doctor," she paused. "Goodnight, Mackenzie."

~

Mac poured herself a glass of bourbon over ice. She took the bottle with her as she went to sit in the salon of the boat. Stimpy curled up in her lap and they sat in the moonlight together. Stimpy snored in her sleep while Mac drank and cried. "I'm sorry Kylie, I'm sorry I was too stupid to realize what I had with you until it was gone."

When the alarm went off at five a.m. Mac wanted to toss it in the bay. *My head is splitting. Note to self...no more bourbon nights!* "Come on Stimpy rise and shine!" Mac threw the covers off and the little dog ran back under them. "Big baby! All you do is sleep, it's not like you have a hangover from hell!" She stepped into the hot shower willing her headache to go away.

On her way to the hospital Mac decided to stop and check on Kylie, she wasn't sure of the state she left her in last night, and she wanted to make sure her head was okay. She noticed the Jeep was gone when she turned into the complex. *Hmm.* She turned around and went to the fire station, hoping she wasn't right. Sure enough the black

Jeep was parked on the side of the building. "It's barely six a.m. and she's already here?" *She's so stubborn!* Mac parked next to the Jeep and walked through the open ambulance bay. Harris was standing next to the ambulance repacking one of the emergency bags.

"Can I help you, Ma'am?" He knew exactly who she was and answered himself before she could speak. "Neil, you have a visitor!" He shouted loud enough for the entire station to hear him. All six of the fire station attendees came out, including Neil. Mac was nervous and a little embarrassed. She didn't mean for the guy to wake the neighborhood.

"I'm sorry." Mac titled her head towards the loud mouth. "I didn't mean…I was only checking to see if you…if your head was okay."

"Don't worry about Harris, he's just trying to get washing duty." She said loud enough for him to hear her.

"C'mon, Lieutenant, I had washing duty two days ago."

"Good, then you'll go find something else to do." Her voice rose. "Inside!"

Kylie walked outside of the bay and Mac followed her. "My head's fine. It still hurts like hell."

"I can't believe you're here already. You should be asleep."

"Shift change is at six a.m., besides, I couldn't sleep anyway."

"Me either, I killed a bottle of bourbon and passed out."

"Ouch, I bet you're hung over."

"Yeah, my head hurts, I'm sure I'll feel it about noon. Stimpy tried to get me to go back to sleep, but…" The mentioning of the little dog brought a smile to Kylie's face.

"Aww I miss her, how's she doing?"

"Good, she misses you too."

"Oh really?"

"Yeah, she told me."

"Is that so? Huh, I may have to drop by and say hi to her."

"I'd love that...I mean she'd love that. Of course, I miss you too, but I know you'd be seeing Stimpy." Mac grinned shyly and Kylie smiled. "I need to get going. I have an early meeting today. But, the offer stands, I'm sure Stimpy would love to see you this weekend since I know you're off."

"Don't push it, Dr. Trotter." Kylie smiled again and went back inside.

~

Friday morning arrived before Mac could even figure out where her week had gone. "What a hectic week. I'm never going on vacation again." She said to herself as she took her usual route to her office through the ER. She stopped at the employee lounge to test the coffee, but it looked like sludge in a cup so she decided to skip it. Lyle ran into her as she was leaving the room.

"Hey, long time no see." He chuckled.

"Where have you been?"

"I'm pulling a forty-eight hours on and twenty-four hours off shift for the next two weeks."

Mac wrinkled her nose, "Why? You're the Assistant department head."

"I'm trying to get these new residents trained and we've been really short staffed lately. It seems like everyone either has accidents or goes on vacation in the summer."

"Yeah, my case load always doubles in the summer. You know how to find me if you need me. I'll be tied up in board meetings next week though."

"I'm so glad I don't have to deal with administration. I'd much rather sit here and stitch cuts all day long. But, that's why you make the big bucks."

"Please, you know damn good and well I don't make the big bucks, it's more like the little bucks. But to me it's about making a difference." She winked at him. He was the only one in the hospital that knew why pediatrics meant so much to her.

"Hey by the way, you want to explain what happened the other day?"

"Huh?" She watched him pour a cup of sludge into his cup. "Yuck! Are you actually going to drink that shit?"

"Yeah," he said.

"Gross!"

"Hey, it keeps me going. Want some?"

"Looks like mud in a swamp to me, no thanks."

"So?" he asked.

"What?"

"You and the fire woman. Why was she screaming at you?" He asked.

"Oh that...long story that you already know."

"So she's still pissed at you huh?"

"She's a little passed pissed. But, at least we're trying to work on being friends again...maybe."

"Well that's a start."

"It's anything at this point. I don't know what I'd do without her in my life, everything changed when I met her. I don't know how to go back."

"You two seemed good for each other, at least from

what I saw of you together anyway. I'm sure it'll work itself out."

"A friendship is always better than nothing, at least that's what I keep telling myself," she said.

"Me, Jennie, Tony, and DJ are going to Daisy's tonight, want to go?"

"No thanks. I need to do laundry after work. I haven't washed a thing since I've been back. Thank god we wear scrubs every day. That's all I have left."

He laughed. "Well you know where we'll be if you want to hang out."

She laughed with him. "Yeah, same drinking time, same drinking table."

"Hey, we're not drunks, only doctors and nurses that need a place to vent," he laughed.

~

Saturday afternoon, Mac was in the water changing the zinc plates on the back and bottom of her boat. She never noticed Kylie step aboard. Mac climbed up the step ladder wearing a green and blue string bikini top and tiny little matching board shorts that made her eyes glow brightly. Her tan skin was slick with water and her short blond hair was frazzled from her squishing the water out with her hands. Kylie stood in amazement with her eyebrows in her hairline.

Mac dropped the towel and almost ran right into the smaller woman as she turned to go down into the cabin. "Holy shit! You scared me! What are you doing here? On my boat?"

"You..." Kylie was still mesmerized by the sight of this woman, her blood was pumping and her skin was itching for contact. *Calm down...*

"Kylie?" Mac said waiting for a reply.

"Stimpy," Kylie said.

"Excuse me?"

"You invited me...to see Stimpy." Kylie finally spit the words out.

"Oh yeah...yeah, she's inside you can go see her."

"Are you coming in?"

"As soon as I dry off."

"Were you swimming?"

"No, working on the boat."

"Oh." Kylie went below deck, happy to put some distance between them. The tiny dog ran up to her begging to be picked up, she bent down to get her. "My God she's going to kill me dressed like that Stimpy!" The dog was licking her face. "I know I missed you too!"

"I'm glad to see you two are still in love," Mac said.

"What? Huh?" Kylie heard the word love and turned right into Mac who had been standing behind her. The heat in her body rose again, threatening to come to the surface.

"You and my dog. You guys seem to have a pretty loving relationship."

"What can I say? She's adorable and I do love her."

"That's nice. Your stitches look a lot better." Mac said.

Kylie realized that at her height Mac was probably eye level with the top of her head and the stitches in her hairline. Besides the fact that they were standing less than a foot from each other.

"My head doesn't feel like it's in a vise anymore."

"That's a good sign. Would you like something to drink? I have beer, wine, water, OJ, milk, lemonade...uh...that's it, I finished the strong stuff." Mac was relying on her photographic memory of her refrigerator. She could feel her heart pounding and dared not move away from the adorable woman standing in front of her. Kylie's dark curly hair was down on her shoulders.

"Lemonade sounds good."

Mac was the first one to step way. Kylie silently thanked God that Mac moved before she reached out and grabbed her. She wanted to kiss her so badly. Anything to taste her once again. *What the hell am I thinking? This woman hurt me. She tore me apart and she ditched me for an ex who could care less about her. She walked away from me! Now all I can think about is how good she tastes. Hell no, Neil, not this time, you are not getting your heart broken twice by the same woman!* Kylie sat on the couch in the salon mentally chiding herself. Mac quickly joined her with two tall glasses of lemonade.

"How was your vacation?" Kylie sipped the drink, pleased with the tangy sweet flavor.

"What vacation?"

"Didn't you leave?"

" Oh yeah, you mean Brazil or when I took the boat out?"

"Which one was your vacation?"

"Well, I took some extra time off to go with Loren to Brazil to see her family. That was shot to hell in two days, I wanted to choke her to death. We had a huge fight in front of her family and I told her off. I flew home and decided to call in an old favor in order to take two weeks of vacation time with no notice." She shrugged. "I took Stimpy and sailed up to see my uncle in North Carolina. We spent a few days with him and sailed back."

"Interesting."

"Which part?"

Kylie wasn't really ready to discuss Loren. "You

sailing alone all the way up there."

"I've taken the boat out many times alone. It's not a big deal. It was lonely though, that helped me talk myself through a lot of issues. Then seeing my uncle really helped."

"Are you guys close?"

"Yeah, he's like a second father, more of father than my own father sometimes. My father is not an emotional person. Everything is black and white with him. Uncle Gordy is different. He's like me, he see's color."

Kylie smiled. "Sounds like you had a good time."

"Yeah, he helped me work though my problems and left me to sail home with a clear head. I wish I could see him more, but I'm so busy with work and he's a retired divorcee so he travels a lot." Mac finally went into the bedroom and changed into soft cotton shorts and a t-shirt. When she returned Stimpy was lying in Kylie's lap while she scratched his belly. "You can borrow her if you'd like," Mac joked.

"She's too cute, but no I can't take her from you." Kylie pet Stimpy behind her ears. "Although, she would make a great babe magnet. Maybe I'll borrow her sometime."

"What! You're not using my dog to pick up girls." Mac shook her head and grinned.

"Why not? Is that what you do with her?"

"I wish." Mac laughed sitting down next to Kylie.

"So, what happened with Loren?" Kylie asked still petting the little dog.

"You really want to know?" Mac turned her head to look into Kylie's eyes.

"No. But, if I ever want to be close to you again I need to know."

"When she started recovering I saw the old Loren return, the one I fell in love with. It brought a lot of old memories and feelings back and I stupidly thought she had changed. We went to Brazil to see her family and she started bossing me around again like usual and then brought you up. I didn't know she even knew. She must have been following me or something. I was furious. She never changed. She used the accident as an excuse to reel me back in and control me like she used to do," Mac paused.

"We had a huge screaming match and I told her that taking care of her and coming back to her was the second biggest mistake of my life next to breaking your heart. I thought she was going to slap me when I told her I was in love with you," Mac said.

Kylie's jaw dropped and her eyes bugged out of her head like a cartoon.

"I know there's nothing between us anymore, but I will never stop loving you."

Kylie pushed Stimpy out of her lap and slid closer to Mac.

"Say it again," Kylie said.

"Say what?"

"That you love me," Kylie said placing her hand on Mac's cheek.

"I love you, Kylie. I love you with all of my heart and everything that I am," Mac said as a tear slid down her cheek onto Kylie's hand.

"I love you too, Mackenzie," Kylie smiled pulling Mac against her.

Their lips met softly at first, their mouths opening to claim each other in a passionate kiss. Mac pushed forward slightly and Kylie lay back pulling Mac onto her without

126

breaking the seal of their lips.

Kylie pulled away breathless. "If you ever mention that woman's name again I'm going to beat you to death and if you break my heart again I will leave your beaten body in a burning building," Kylie said seriously.

"Marry me," Mac said.

"What?" Kylie said pushing Mac up off of her.

"I'm serious. I don't want Loren or anyone else ever thinking they can take me away from you. I want to spend the rest of my life showing you how much you mean to me and how much I love you," Mac said.

"I...this...I didn't even come here to get back with you. I figured we would talk and maybe hang out again sometime as friends. I never thought...Mackenzie, are you sure that's what you want? I mean this is pretty sudden."

"You are what I want and I will do anything and everything in the world to have you, Kylie."

"It's not legal here."

"Let's take a trip to New York. It's legal there."

Kylie shook her head trying to get her brain to comprehend what was happening.

"I'll book a flight right now if you say yes," Mac said.

"Let me get this straight, you want to fly to New York and get married this weekend?"

"Yes," Mac said.

"What about a honey moon?" Kylie teased.

"Is that a yes?"

Kylie nodded and smiled as she wrapped her arms around Mac's neck.

"Ever been sailing?" Mac wiggled her eyebrows pushing Kylie back down under her.

The End

Light Reading: One Night

One Night

By

Sydney Canyon

Light Reading: One Night

One

Caylen Jarrett walked into her office slinging her briefcase on top of her dark colored, oak wood desk. The bookcases along the wall matched the large desk. Various awards and degrees filled up one of the walls and three pictures titled *Success*, *Power*, and *Indulgence* hung on the opposite wall. Thick, burgundy wine colored carpet contrasted nicely with the sand colored walls. The office building was two stories high with four large offices on the top floor along with two conference rooms. Four small offices and six cubicles were all located on the bottom floor. The receptionist's desk was the first thing you saw when you walked through the main double doors of the building. Caylen called out to her secretary when she saw her walk by the doorway.

"Sara, can you get me the Culver Management Group file, please? I'll need about an hour to go over their adjustments with them on the phone so hold my calls until..." she paused to look at the platinum Rolex on her left wrist. "Nine, thanks."

"Sure, Ms. Jarrett, anything else? Would you like some coffee? I'm headed that way," Sara asked. She had been with Jarrett Financial Corporation for the past five years and finally worked her way up to the Vice

President's secretary. They developed a great working relationship right from the start.

"No thanks," Caylen smiled thinly before going back into her office. She was thirty-three years old and the VP for the company that her father and uncle had started. Her father passed away four years ago and her uncle Herbert 'Herb' Jarrett took over the President/CEO position and promoted her into the VP position. They had a Director of Sales and a Director of Accounting below them, followed by a few other managers and sales consultants as part of their firm.

Caylen turned on her computer and quickly went to work checking her email and examining the stock market. The black phone on her desk beeped to announce an intercom call so she hit the speaker phone button.

When she heard her uncle's deep voice, Caylen picked up the receiver.

"When you have a minute, I want to see where we stand on the Kent Account," he said.

"I'm about to go into a conference call with the Culver Group, but I'll meet with you when I'm finished," she said scrolling through the new mail in her inbox.

"That's fine," he said ending the call.

Herb Jarrett was like a second father to Caylen and she respected him in the business world. JFC was known as one of the biggest investment banking companies in the United States. Being based out of Santa Barbara, California was a plus. Caylen could hop a direct flight to most of the places she went to meet clients.

~

Caylen ran a hand through her short, light brown hair

133

when she finished her conversation with the Culver Group. She had just finished discussing their decision to spread out another quarter of a million dollars in various mutual fund accounts. Talking people into making business deals was what she was good at which was exactly what her Uncle Herb wanted to talk about. Kent Petroleum Company was an account that they'd been after for years and he was going to send her to schmooze with them deep in the heart of Texas.

Caylen sat in the chair across from his large desk, staring at him. Herbert Jarrett had darker brown hair and a thin mustache. He was just over six feet tall and beginning to get a small gut, but he still appeared much younger than his fifty seven years. In fact, he looked a lot like her father before he died.

"I think three days out there should suffice. Roger Kent is a hard ass and you'll have to take him to a titty bar or he'll never talk to you on his level," Herb said without missing a beat. He knew his niece was a lesbian and seeing a few naked women while throwing around a few thousand dollars wouldn't matter much to her.

"I'll set it up today and leave Monday," She said.

"If anyone can pull the corn cob out of his ass, it's you, C.J. You're just like your old man. I swear he could talk a realtor into buying oceanfront property in Tennessee." He shook his head and smiled. Caylen smiled back. Her father was an amazing man. She missed him, and cursed the day a drunk driver ran him off the road.

"I'm going to Ricardo's for lunch today, want to join me?" She asked before leaving the room

"I can't today I'm meeting your Aunt Vivian at the travel agency to go over Henry's wedding present. We're giving them a honeymoon trip." Henry Robertson was

Vivian's sister's son and had moonlighted over the years as a god child to Herbert and Vivian since they couldn't have children.

"Tell her I said hi. Isn't the wedding in three or four months? I know I saw the invitation in the mail."

"Yeah, I don't remember the exact date but Vivian's going nuts helping Nancy plan the wedding since the bride's mother isn't in the picture much anymore."

"Oh, that's too bad."

"Think you'll ever settle down one day?" He shot a sideways glance at her. The question caught her off guard. She'd dated and had minimal relationships. She was heir to a fortune and already a millionaire just from working there. Most women wanted her for that one reason. Yes, she was attractive at five foot seven with a trim athletic build and intense blue eyes, but none of that mattered when the women learned who she was.

"I don't know. I haven't caught a fish yet worth keeping. I have to toss them back faster than I get them in the boat." She smiled and waved as she went back down the hall to her own office.

Caylen was just about to go into her office when Sara called out to her. She spun around on her heels, facing the shorter woman.

"Yes," Caylen said.

"I have a message for you to call Larry Davis with Eternity Lifeline Company."

"Did he say it was urgent?"

"No, he just asked that you return his call."

"Okay." Caylen took the note. "I need you to book me on a flight to Houston Monday morning, please, and returning Wednesday night."

"Yes, ma'am."

Caylen sat down behind her desk once again. *Thank God it's Friday.*

She spent the rest of the day on and off of the phone with her nose attached to the computer screen. She didn't leave the office until close to seven p.m. and promised her best friend Margo that she'd meet her for dinner at seven. She was already ten minutes late.

~

"I was about to call you," Margo said when Caylen sat down across from her.

Caylen had shed her black suit jacket and the light blue blouse she was wearing made her eyes seem brighter in the low lighting.

"Long day. I'm headed to Texas on Monday, sort of at the last minute, so I needed to have my ducks in a row." Caylen ordered a chicken soup bowl and spring rolls off of the Vietnamese menu.

"C.J., you work too hard." Margo shook her head, her shoulder length auburn hair swinging back and forth. They'd been best friends since they dated once three years ago and realized they'd make perfect friends, but nothing else.

"And you don't?" Caylen asked with a smirk.

"I'm an executive for a mortgage broker firm. I think we both know I put in my fair share of hours, but I don't fly all over the damn country every month either."

"True." Caylen trained her chopsticks on the bowl of chicken and noodles in front of her. "I'm not gone every month though."

"Yes, but you're gone at least every other month and usually for a week at a time."

"I'll only be gone two nights this time," Caylen replied with a mouth full of noodles.

"When do you leave?"

"Monday."

"Let's relax this weekend. I was thinking of going golfing, want to go?"

Caylen raised an eyebrow.

"C.J. golf is a relaxing sport. You should give it a try." Margo rolled her eyes at her impossible friend.

"What the hell," she shrugged. "Sign me up, but I'm only playing nine and make it tomorrow. Not too early though. I need to clean my condo Sunday."

"Really? I should be able to get us into Mallard Cove around ten."

"Okay, it's a date."

Two

Caylen was reading a business magazine in the first class section of the plane while trying to stretch her legs. She had sore muscles that she never knew existed from playing golf with Margo. Surprisingly, she actually had fun and promised to go again when she had time. She used the gym in her condo complex and jogged on the weekends, but playing nine holes of golf kicked her ass.

Spending all of the next day cleaning her two story loft style condo probably didn't help matters. The first floor was cherry hardwood with matching furniture and the upstairs loft, which was her bedroom and bathroom, had crème colored carpet. The condo was oceanfront and cost her close to two million dollars, but it was prime real estate and Margo got her a deal she couldn't pass up. Not that she needed a deal, money wasn't a problem. The location and style was what sold her. Most of the parking was covered and that was an additional selling point. Her Bentley would be kept out of the sun.

The only reason she had the ridiculously expensive car was because her father had just bought it and paid cash for it, a month before he died. He was actually driving his second car, a BMW seven hundred series, the night he died. He left Caylen his black Bentley in his will and she was about to go buy a new car anyway, before he died, so she decided to keep it. It was one more reason for the gold digging lesbians and some straight women to come after her. Other than her car and home, Caylen didn't throw money around. She merely sat on it like a nest egg. Besides, what was she going to buy? She was thirty-three and single with no children.

Caylen met the car service that was there to pick her up and take her straight to the Hilton when her plane landed. She called Roger Kent to announce her arrival and confirm their early afternoon meeting for the following day while on the way to the hotel.

~

By the time the meeting was over, Caylen was worn out. The old-time oil tycoon had drilled her from the minute she presented him with an investment plan. It took four hours for them to come up with a custom plan that suited his needs as well as his ego. After that she took Kent, his VP, and Director of Operations to a five-star restaurant and ate close to a thousand dollar dinner which she paid for.

After dinner, they were on their way to one of Texas' most prominent topless clubs in the company limo. Caylen was glad she pulled a couple thousand dollars from the bank so she'd have cash since these guys were planning on milking her as long as they could.

"I have to say, Ms. Jarrett, this is one of the finest business deals that I've seen in a long time. I believe our companies will work well together," Kent said smiling. He toasted her glass of champagne as the car pulled up in front of the main doors of the club.

"I agree whole-heartedly, Mr. Kent." She finished her glass and got out of the car when the driver opened the door.

They were all dressed in black business suits. The three men had on ties and Caylen was wearing a blue blouse with tiny black pinstripes. She quickly followed Roger Kent as he led them to a table on the upper level in the back corner close to a small stage with a stainless steel pole jutting from the middle. A topless blond was exiting the stage as they took their seats.

The club was upscale. Caylen wondered if you actually had to be in a business suit to even walk through the doors. She'd been in her share of strip clubs, but she'd never seen anything as classy as this place. As soon as the waitress came by, Roger Kent ordered a top shelf scotch, neat. Caylen ordered a glass of Johnnie Walker Blue Label on the rocks and looked around at the various women dancing on the poles as they rotated to each of the fifteen different small pole stages.

Their drinks arrived quickly and Caylen wanted to chug hers, but decided on just a small sip. She didn't have to say anything. She knew the men expected the night to continue on her dime. They wasted no time calling the dancers over immediately for lap dances. She sat back and watched the scenery instead of seeing the old men next to her with semi hard-ons.

"Hi," someone said.

Caylen heard the soft, yet unmistakable voice and looked up to meet the most sensual, smoky gray eyes that she'd ever seen. The dancer smiled and winked as she took her position on the stage. She appeared tall, probably due to the four inch platform shoes she was wearing. Her honey colored hair was wavy and fell just below her shoulders, all in one length. A thin sheen of sweat glistened against her olive skin as her muscular frame flexed in different directions.

Caylen thought she looked like a professional dancer. Her body was perfectly sculpted and her skin looked daringly soft. Caylen couldn't stop the puddle that was forming between her legs as the dancer's pelvis thrust against the floor of the stage, mimicking the missionary position. Her breasts were full and round with light brown areolas. The black thong she was wearing was practically a string of fabric with a thin piece of see-through lace material in the front, indicating that she was completely shaven. Caylen continued to watch as the woman twisted and turned slowly into various positions with the beat of the song that played. Her body formed into exquisite lines over and over again. The beautiful way she moved took Caylen's breath away.

As soon as the song ended, the dancer walked off of the stage and directly up to Caylen. Caylen spread her legs and the dancer stepped between them, sitting in her lap. Caylen had been in enough strip clubs entertaining clients over the years and knew to keep her hands to herself.

"Hi, I'm Candy Coated Rain Drop, Candy for short," She said showing off perfectly straight white teeth when she smiled.

"I'm C.J."

"Where are you from C.J.?"

"California."

"I've always wanted to go there on vacation," Candy said with another gorgeous smile as she wrapped her arms around Caylen's neck and whispered in her ear. The slight brush of her lips sent chills up Caylen's spine. When Candy put her hands in the back of Caylen's hair, Caylen felt her clit stiffen. She knew she was soaking wet.

"I couldn't help noticing you watching me with those sexy blue eyes. Would you like me to dance for you?"

"Sure," Caylen held her composure as Candy slid off of her and began her lap dance routine. She ran her body against Caylen's until her breasts slid across Caylen's face. Caylen couldn't help running her tongue between them. Candy looked down at her.

"It's hard to keep my hands off of you," Caylen whispered huskily, her libido was on overdrive. She'd never been this turned on just by looking at someone.

"I want to feel your hands on me," Candy said as she climbed up on her and straddled Caylen's legs. She took Caylen's hands and ran them all over her body. Neither woman noticed the men watching as Candy ran her hand over Caylen's crotch, forcing direct contact. Then, she spun around to grind her ass against her crotch as she leaned back into Caylen and ran her hands behind her into Caylen's hair once again. The seductive dance continued another minute until the song was finished. Candy leaned over and pressed her lips softly to Caylen's and smiled. Caylen pulled out a hundred dollar bill and tucked it under the thin string on her thong. Candy leaned over whispering in her ear once more.

"Will I see you again?"

Caylen spoke low so only Candy could hear her. "I'm at the Hilton, room seven-sixteen." Caylen didn't usually pick women up when she was traveling, especially strippers, but this woman was too damn beautiful to pass up. Besides, it had been over a year since her last relationship and equally as long since she'd had sex. She didn't spend time chasing women and after the last nightmare, she decided to take some time off from women all together.

"Midnight," Candy whispered before standing up and walking away.

Caylen didn't get another dance from her, nor did she let anyone else dance on her. She politely turned down four or five women as she continued to pay for the men's evening of entertainment.

~

It was eleven-thirty by the time the limo dropped Caylen off at the hotel. She didn't give much thought to seeing Candy Coated Rain Drop, after Caylen saw her spend the next hour dancing all over a few different men. She jumped in the shower to relax before going to bed since she had an early flight back to San Diego. As soon as she stepped from the bathroom wearing an old pair of gym shorts and a t-shirt with nothing under them, she heard a knock at the door.

"Hi," Candy said when Caylen pulled the door open.

"Come in." Caylen was surprised to see the irresistible woman standing in front of her wearing jeans and a black t-shirt style halter top with black leather ankle boots. She was actually close in height to Caylen and maybe only an inch taller in her boots.

Before Caylen could say anything else Candy stepped forward, their bodies touching ever so slightly. She ran her hands up Caylen sides, stopping when she reached her face. The blue eyes looking back at her sparkled when Candy ran her finger over Caylen's soft lips. Caylen's lips parted to take the finger in. She sucked gently, never breaking eye contact with Candy.

Candy slowly pulled her finger away and pressed her

lips to Caylen's. Their tongues jousted for position as they kissed passionately. Caylen heard a faint moan escape Candy's mouth as she wrapped her arms around her, running her hands over her tight ass. Caylen walked Candy backwards until she was against the wall.

"I want you," Candy said running her hands under Caylen's t-shirt to feel the silky smooth skin of her flat stomach, then her breasts. She found two taut nipples begging to be squeezed. Caylen reached between them unbuttoning Candy's jeans and sliding the zipper down. She found the same black thong when she pressed her fingers against Candy's throbbing clit.

"God, that feels good..." Candy breathed into Caylen's ear before meeting her lips once again. Their hunger for each other was barely touched as they began pulling off layers of each other's clothing. Caylen admired the nude body that stood in front of her.

"You're beautiful." She said smiling with lustful eyes.

"I want your hands on me," Candy said as she followed Caylen onto the king-size bed. "I want you inside of me."

Caylen rolled Candy onto her back and began running her tongue across her collar bone, trailing sensual kisses, working her way lower. She stopped at the full breasts demanding her attention. She licked delicately around both areolas, careful not to touch the aching nipples. Candy's hips rose against her. Caylen slid her hand between their bodies, gradually running her fingers around Candy's sensitive hard clit, careful not to touch it as she continued doing the same thing with her tongue on Candy's breasts.

"Baby you're driving me crazy...go inside me..." Candy's voice was altered by her ragged breathing.

Caylen knew she was close, but she wasn't ready to

push her over the edge. She pulled her hand to the side of Candy's thigh and moved up enough to kiss her once more. Candy wrapped her arms around Caylen, running her fingers through her short hair. Candy caressed Caylen's tongue, kissing her tenderly as if she were trying to make herself come from the kiss. Caylen broke the kiss. Looking down into the gray eyes staring up at her she could see the desire burning at the surface. She bent her head to kiss her soft lips once more. Moving her hand back to the slick wet center between Candy's legs, she entered her easily with two fingers.

"Ah..." Candy gasped and held her breath when she felt Caylen move gently in and out of her going deeper with every stroke. Candy thrust her hips up to meet her hand as she tugged lightly on Caylen's hair. "Yes, baby..."

Caylen stroked her fingers in and out of her, mimicking the action with her tongue as she kissed the beautiful woman under her. She felt the rush of warmth as the muscles tightened and began to spasm around her fingers when Candy's body finally gave into the pleasure. Caylen stayed inside of her as she continued kissing her passionately. Their lips stayed in contact as their tongues tasted each other over and over. Caylen could feel the wetness between her own legs as she slid herself over Candy's muscled thigh.

"Mmm..." Candy smiled, rolling Caylen onto her back. "I've wanted my hands on you since the moment I saw you," Candy said, pressing her mouth to one of Caylen's breasts, sucking the hard nipple. She circled Caylen's clit making sure to press down firmly teasing every other stroke.

"That feels good," Caylen rasped, pushing her hips up into Candy's hand urging her further.

"Is this what you want?" Candy teased as she slid two fingers inside of Caylen and quickly pulled them back out to circle her clit a few more times.

"Yes!…Candy don't stop…" Caylen wasn't usually one to beg, but this woman was driving her crazy.

Candy moved up slightly to whisper in her ear. "Tanner. My name's really Tanner."

Caylen barely comprehended what the woman was saying. Her nerves were on fire and her body was hanging over the edge. She looked longingly into the gray eyes staring down at her. "Make me come…Tanner."

They never broke eye contact as Tanner slid her fingers back inside of Caylen, hungrily working them in and out as the walls around them quickly tightened. She pressed her thumb against Caylen's throbbing clit at the same time.

"God yes!" Caylen felt her nails rake up Tanner's back and into the soft hair that was hanging against her face. She was glad she kept her nails really short, otherwise she would've left serious marks on Tanner's back as her body twitched with the end of her orgasm.

Caylen was still extremely aroused. She moved from under Tanner, pushing her onto her stomach as she ran her tongue over the silky smooth skin covering the hard muscles of her back and shoulders. She spread Tanner's legs and entered her from behind when she felt the wetness against her finger tips.

"Mmmm…" Tanner said raising her ass slightly in the air so Caylen could go deeper. "God, you feel so good inside of me."

Caylen slowed her pace and pulled out before Tanner could let go. She rolled her back over so they were facing each other once again. Tanner pushed Caylen down and straddled her stomach, pressing her wet clit against Caylen's warm skin. Caylen quickly put her thumb against the hard mound and began circling it firmly as Tanner rocked against her.

Tanner moved her hand back behind her to reach Caylen's clit, following her motion when she felt Caylen's hips lift off the bed. They rubbed circles of various speeds and firmness in unison until Tanner's body stiffened.

"I'm coming baby...oh God yes!" Tanner spared nothing as she slid her wetness all over Caylen's stomach.

"You feel so good, Tanner." Caylen felt herself shudder and release as a tiny puddle formed underneath her.

They collapsed in each other's arms and fell asleep with no more words spoken. It was the first time Caylen let herself cuddle with someone in close to two years.

~

At five-thirty, Caylen extracted herself from Tanner's warm body to take a shower and head to the airport. She was gone from the hotel by six and her flight took off at eight. She was halfway home by the time Tanner awoke to a cold bed and a hand scribbled note.

Tanner,

I'm sorry I wasn't there to see your beautiful eyes when you woke up. I had a wonderful time with you. Take care of yourself. I'll never forget you.

Always,
C.J.

Tanner showered quickly. It wasn't the first time she'd had a one night stand, and probably not the last. She folded the handwritten note on hotel stationary and shoved it in the pocket of her jeans as she brushed a lone tear off of her cheek. At least there were no bills laying on the nightstand.

Three

Caylen sat at the oval table with her Uncle Herb as they went through a conference call meeting with Roger Kent and his VP. Kent Petroleum Company had been very pleased with their decision to let JFC handle all of their financial investments. Now, they were simply going over a list of stocks and mutual funds that Roger Kent wanted to investment money in on top of the initial list he had already given Caylen two weeks prior when she met with him in Houston.

As soon as the call was over, Herb sat back in his chair with his hands folded in front of him. He looked a lot like her father. She had her father's facial features and light brown hair, but she was blessed with her mother's blue eyes.

"You damn sure made an impression on that man." The corner of Herb's mouth turned up in a smile. "I've been after him for years. How did you do it?"

"It's called tits and ass, Uncle Herb," Caylen said seriously. She laughed when her uncle looked at her with raised eyebrows. "I took him to a strip club and let him burn a hole in my entertainment fund for this month. But, honestly we had the deal finished and signed before we even left for dinner." She shrugged. "Maybe he just likes

149

the way I do business. Plus, I laid everything out in PowerPoint and Excel for him."

"That must've taken a while," he said.

"Yeah, no kidding. Our meeting lasted probably four hours, but in the end he saw what he was looking for and now we have a multi-million dollar investment plan for him." She smiled and wiggled her eyebrows.

"It's Friday, kid, what do you have planned this weekend?"

"Not a whole lot. My condo is a mess and the Bentley needs a bath. It's starting to look gray instead of black." She snickered. "Dad would be pissed if he saw it looking like that."

"That couldn't be a truer statement. Aunt Vivian's making some kind of new dish tomorrow and asked me to invite you since she constantly complains about never seeing you anymore. She actually yelled at me the other day for sending you to Houston." He shook his head. "I swear I think she spends too much time in a kitchen. The heat is starting to get to her or something." He laughed. Vivian, his wife of thirty-five years, was a cookbook writer and had an industrial kitchen in her large house so that she could personally tweak each and every recipe before it was put into a book. So far, she'd published twenty books over the years with various cooking styles and concepts and had been asked numerous times to appear on TV shows to cook her recipes.

"You better never let her hear you say that. She's liable to pull a Sweeny Todd on your ass and bake you," Caylen said. They both laughed. "Tell Aunt Viv I'll be there at six." Caylen gathered her notes and left the room.

~

Late Saturday afternoon, Caylen was going to town cleaning her condo. She'd tossed out two bags of old clothes for Goodwill, on top of that she dusted, vacuumed and swept. She was finishing the downstairs bathroom when she heard the doorbell.

"I'm coming, hold on a second," She yelled out as she put the cleaner and brush down and tore the rubber gloves off of her hands. She didn't bother looking through the peephole before opening the door. The only people that actually knew where she lived were her family and Margo. As well as a couple exes, although none of them ever had the privilege of living with her.

"You shouldn't yell out like that, you're liable to make a girl horny." Margo snickered as she pushed past her in the foyer. "You smell like bleach." She wrinkled her nose up.

Caylen laughed and rolled her eyes at her best friend. "That would be because I'm cleaning, smart ass. What brings you out in the middle of the day on a Saturday?"

"I felt like bothering you," Margo said, helping herself to a beer from the refrigerator and handing another to her friend.

"Uh huh, I don't believe you." Caylen took the offered beer and swallowed a long cold sip.

"I haven't heard this song in forever." She began singing along to *A Horse With No Name*, that was playing semi-loudly on the TV surround sound system.

"You're showing your age and ignoring me." Caylen raised an eyebrow. Margo pursed her lips and squeezing her eyebrows together.

"I beg your pardon. I'll have you know I'm only two years older than your butt, missy." She moved past Caylen

151

and sat down on the couch. "I'm not ignoring you. I'm just trying to find a way to say it, that's all."

"When did she get back into town?" Caylen asked.

"Who?"

"You know who." Caylen sat on the couch next to her.

"Last night." Margo stared at the floor. Her ex-girlfriend Lila was very attractive and the biggest pain-in-the-ass anyone would ever meet. Caylen actually threw a small party when the bitch left town. She not only cheated on Margo during their six month relationship, she actually had the audacity to come onto Caylen knowing they were best friends.

"I thought she ran off to New York with some bimbo?" Caylen asked as she finished her beer. Luckily, it was a light beer since she downed it in two swigs. She was thirstier than she thought. At least the bleach scent was starting to wear off. *Shit.* She remembered she was still cleaning the spare bathroom. She stood up. "I need to go rinse the shower real quick," She said as she walked down the hall. Margo followed her.

"Do you ever go a week without spring cleaning this place? I swear you could eat off of the hardwood floor and brush your teeth in the shine from the tile in the foyer."

"Yeah, yeah, yeah," Caylen said rolling her eyes.

"The bimbo dumped her for someone else and left her broke. She had just enough money to catch a plane back."

"To you."

"No! I'm not taking her sorry ass back." Margo spat.

"Good. I'd have to kick your ass if you took her back." Caylen finished rinsing the glass shower and flushed the toilet cleaner that had been soaking in the bowl.

"I called in a favor and got her a job as a teller at Guardian Credit Union. Maybe that'll keep her out of my hair. The money sucks, but she moved in with her sister so she could save up."

The satellite music station on the TV switched from the seventies to the eighties and a chain of Prince songs began playing.

"Karma is a bitch." Caylen said with a smirk. "Hey, are you up for one of my Aunt Vivian's creations?"

"Why?" Margo had been to a few dinners where Caylen's aunt had cooked something off the wall that she was adding to one of her latest books. She had to admit the woman could cook.

"I got suckered into coming to dinner tonight since she thinks she never sees me anymore."

"I don't have any plans."

"Great, I'll call her and make sure it's okay. I'm sure she'll be excited. You know how she is with food."

"Yes I do." Margo shook her head. "She thinks its art."

~

Three hours later, Caylen and Margo were sitting on the couch in Caylen's Aunt and Uncle's house. They were both stuffed to the gills with lobster and squid quiche, a dish Caylen was sure had never before been attempted, but it turned out to be mouthwatering. They had eaten until they couldn't pick up their forks.

"Aunt Viv, what's the latest book you're working on?" Caylen asked as she sipped the glass of chardonnay.

"This one is all delicacies," Vivian said with an ear to ear grin.

"Well, dinner was wonderful. You're an amazing cook, Vivian." Margo said.

An hour later, Caylen and Margo were in the Bentley on their way back to Caylen's condo when Margo asked her about her trip to Houston. Frankly, Caylen hadn't thought much about it since she arrived back in Santa Barbara. It was actually the most memorable night of her life. She just chose not to think about it.

"Well, uh…it was boring. I met with a rich oil tycoon and basically kissed his ass the entire day, then took him and his upper management staff to a ridiculously expensive dinner and a high class strip club." Caylen shrugged and kept driving.

"A strip club? God, I haven't been to one of those in years."

"You know I have to go to one at least once a year, sometimes more. Most of the time I sit back and let my clients enjoy the entertainment. Sometimes I partake if I'm in the mood."

"And?"

"And what?"

"Were you in the mood?"

"Maybe." Caylen wasn't about to discuss her night of passion with the stripper. *Tanner.* Margo was her best friend, and it wasn't the first time Caylen had a one night stand. What would it hurt telling Margo?

"Was she hot?"

"Absolutely beautiful." Caylen smiled at the mental picture that popped into her mind of the gray-eyed, athletic beauty with honey colored hair. "If there was such a thing as 'love at first sight' she'd definitely be it."

"Wow. Did you get her number?"

"No. Why would I? I live in California."

"You never know. She could be a lot of fun in bed." Margo tossed her hair over her shoulder.

154

"So, you're saying I should've slept with her? Would you sleep with a stripper?" Caylen asked.

"I wouldn't say no. Then again, I guess I've never had the opportunity."

"It was hot when she was dancing on me. She ran her hands all over me and put my hands on her. Her skin was angel soft and she was built like a professional dancer. I swore she was going to kiss me a few times. The look in her eyes said she wanted to. Then, I look over and see her doing the same thing on some guy as I'm headed out the door. That'll sure douse the flames quickly." Caylen let her mind drift back to Tanner lying under her, wet and wanting. She felt her chest tighten as she shook the memory away.

"Eww...yeah I agree. At least you enjoyed your dance. I've had some that either couldn't dance, stunk of sweat and cigarettes, or worse men's cologne, and the best one of all was a woman who tried to impress me by doing some weird flips and shit and she fell off of the stage. I thought I was going to piss my pants from laughing," Margo said.

"Oh my god! That's funny." Both women were laughing hysterically when Caylen pulled into her covered parking space.

"Knock on wood I've never actually had a bad experience in a strip club. Honestly, I rarely get a dance or even give them bills when they're dancing on the stage. Those places don't really do much for me, but my male clients eat it up," Caylen said.

Four

It had been a month since her short trip to Houston. Caylen sat at her desk reading spreadsheets and periodically checking the stock market. She was preparing for her third conference call of the day with a potential client that they couldn't seem to get on the same page with and she had a slight migraine. She rarely flew to meet them in person unless it was absolutely required to close a deal. Caylen hoped this call went well. She didn't have time in her schedule to fly to Seattle to meet with the owner of a small cable broadcasting company. His deal was worth a couple of million dollars, so she'd go if need be.

"I hope we can make Mr. Winthrop agree to a plan here," Herb said as he sat in one of the empty conference room chairs, placing his notebook on the table in front of him. Caylen was already in there laying out her portfolio. Their Director of Sales couldn't close the deal so now Caylen and Herb needed to pull out all of the stops if they wanted to land this account. Kyle Winthrop was an older man that probably still kept most of his money tucked into a sock drawer for all she knew. His business was worth five million dollars and most of that was tied up in debt. Jarrett Financial Company's prime concern was to come up with a deal to get the broadcasting company out of debt and put money back into Mr. Winthrop's pocket as well as their own. If they came to terms, the deal could be beneficial for both companies.

"Me too," Caylen answered her uncle. "I'm not looking forward to a redeye flight to Seattle." The phone buzzed once to announce that their call was set up and ready to begin.

Three hours later, Caylen lay on her couch watching some love story on Lifetime and sipping a glass of chocolate milk. She thanked her lucky stars that she was able to get Kyle Winthrop to agree to let her take a million dollars of his money and use it to get his ass out of debt and put a return in his wallet.

~

"You have a call on line one, Ms. Jarrett," Sara called over the intercom. Caylen grabbed the receiver of the phone.

"Caylen Jarrett."

"Hey, C.J., how's your day going?" Margo asked.

"Busy as usual. Yours?"

"Same. I had to sneak away to call you. I swear my office phone knows when I'm in there. It never stops ringing. Everyone and their brother is trying to buy a house right now with either no credit or horrible credit," She huffed. Her bank account seemed to be the only thing reaping the benefits of her sixty hour work week lately.

"It's a buyer's market all the way around. I thought about moving some of my market shares," Caylen said.

If the stock market crashed again or the president ran the government into a hole then she would surely be hurt by it, but Caylen was smart with her personal investments.

"Let me know if you want to buy another house

157

anytime soon," Margo said.

"Yeah sure, my condo is plenty for me. You know I'm not into giant mansions. I don't know how my aunt and uncle find each other in that house of theirs. I guess I'm more like my Mom. Her house is modest, not small by any means, but a quarter of the size of Aunt Viv and Uncle Herb's."

"How is your Mom, by the way?"

"Good, she just got back from Europe. She and Aunt Cindy, Mom's sister, went and did a three week tour of multiple countries." Aunt Cindy was widowed just before Caylen's father died and ever since the two sisters seemed inseparable.

"Now that sounds like fun!"

"I've never been, but the two of them can't stop talking about it. I think I've seen a thousand pictures of their trip." She laughed.

"Shit, I have another call coming in. Anyway, I was calling to see if you wanted to go out tonight."

"Sure. I'll be in the office until probably seven. I have some loose ends to tie up before next week. I'll meet you at *One Up* around eight-thirty," Caylen said.

"Okay, see you then."

~

True to her word, Caylen walked into the bar at eight-thirty. She was wearing jeans and a tight black polo shirt that showed off a nice amount of cleavage thanks to the underwire bra that gave her the extra lift. She was also wearing black flip flops.

"You know that outfit is nice to look at until you see the flip flops on your feet. I bet everyone standing outside saw you pull up in that outrageously expensive car and their first thought was *Damn! You're cute, but you don't flaunt it.* Then, they see those stupid things you call shoes on your feet and BOOM! Your chances are shot in the ass," Margo said as she took her Gin and Tonic from the bartender.

"Margo, Margo, Margo. You of all people know that I prefer comfort and I wear a god damn business suit sixty hours a week, just as you do. Therefore, I find jeans and flip flops comfortable. Besides, when have you known me to cruise around for companionship? And, what's it to you anyway?" Caylen smiled and rolled her eyes.

She was happy to see the glass of whiskey coming her way. She quickly took a couple of sips and set the glass back on the bar. The two women enjoyed the light banter. It had become a routine for them to pick on each other when they were out at the bar.

"I just can't get over you wearing flip flops like they're going out of style." She shook her head and laughed knowing damn good and well no matter how much money she had or how high class she was by day, comfort was at the top of Caylen's list when she wasn't in that office. Honestly, she probably wore flip flops more than dress shoes.

"You're just jealous. We'll go tomorrow and by you a pair." Caylen winked.

"Wonderful, I can't wait to own yet another pair of flip flops." She grinned. "Seriously, I secretly think they're kind of sexy on you."

"Oh please!" Caylen smacked her arm.

Margo had to admit half of the women in the bar were wearing some kind of sandals. Maybe it was because the bar was a few blocks from the ocean. She wasn't about to join the new trend. She was perfectly happy in her ankle boots. Besides, they gave her an extra inch of height and at five foot three, she needed all she could get.

Karaoke quickly started after nine o'clock. Margo and Caylen usually spent the evening making fun of the singers instead of joining in the chaos.

"I think you should sing tonight," Margo said.

"What? Me? Sing?"

"Yeah, why not?"

"I do not do karaoke, Margo. What the hell is in your drink tonight? First, you grill me about wearing comfortable shoes, then you tell me to sing. Something has gotten into you."

"No, not really. I just thought maybe I could talk you into it." She teased.

"Don't bet me, you know how I am."

"I bet you twenty bucks you won't sing," Margo said with raised eyebrows.

"I told you not to bet me." Caylen didn't like betting because she could never say no. She spent ten thousand dollars one night in Vegas and swore she'd never go back.

"Chicken, bock, bock…" Margo tormented her.

"You're on," Caylen sighed. *Great, now I'll never be able to show my face in this bar again.* Even though it was considered a straight bar, Friday nights were a predominantly lesbian karaoke party. Caylen grabbed the song book and jotted down her selection. She was next, so she finished her drink and quickly ordered another to help calm her nerves. *Damn you, Margo.*

The older woman running the DJ booth called for C.J. to take the stage just before Journey's *Lovin', Touchin', Squeezin'* began playing. Caylen's voice found every note seductively as she sang the words perfectly. Margo noticed a few women turn their heads to see who was singing and wondering who she was singing to.

"Your girl can sing." A brunette sitting next to Margo leaned over to her.

"She's my best friend. We're not together."

"Is she single?" The woman asked. Margo gave her a once over and figured what the hell, Caylen would turn her down anyway.

"Yeah."

The song ended quickly and Caylen made her way back to the table with her hand out. Margo obliged with a crisp Jackson, which Caylen folded and slid into her back pocket.

"C.J., I have to admit you impressed me. All of that singing in the shower has paid off."

"Oh please." Caylen shook her head.

"Excuse me, C.J., is it?" The brunette stuck her hand out.

"Yes." Caylen shook back.

"You have a very sexy voice."

Okay, why don't you just come right out and say it. Caylen thought. "Thank you."

"May I buy you a drink?"

"No thanks." Caylen smiled. "I've had my limit for the night." She really hadn't but she wasn't in the mood to pick anyone up. The brunette smiled and nodded before going back to her own table.

"She was pretty. Why'd you say no?" Margo asked.

"Not in the mood I guess. One night stands are overrated and I don't have time for another gold digger. Hell, I don't have time for any kind of woman at the rate I've been working."

"I hear you. I haven't had sex in six months, but

161

honestly I don't have time for a relationship either." They clinked their glasses together.

Five

Caylen found herself lying on a towel, soaking up the sun rays on the Fourth of July. Her dark blue bikini left little to the imagination, but she hated tan lines and refused to go to the tanning booth like most of the people in Santa Barbara. So she settled for the smallest and most revealing bathing suit that she could find. Her condo building sat right behind her. If she squinted her eyes, she could almost see both of her balconies. The ocean waves crashed against the shore with demanding power lulling her thoughts. She rolled back over and closed her eyes with the tanning oil glistening on her skin.

"I am so glad the banks are closed today, but the traffic is horrendous." Margo plopped down on her own large towel. "All I need now is a frozen Margarita."

Caylen didn't open her eyes. "Yes, that would definitely do the trick."

Neither of them noticed the woman headed their way, chasing a Frisbee. Her blond hair was tucked behind her ears. She was tall and thin, maybe a little taller than Caylen since everyone seemed to be taller than Margo.

"Ouch! God damn it," Caylen yelled when the woman clumsily landed on her with the Frisbee in hand.

"Oh, I'm so sorry," She said as she frantically tried to

regain her ground, flinging sand on Caylen and Margo. "I was running backwards and didn't see you. I'm really sorry." She walked away embarrassed.

"What the fuck!" Margo tried to brush the sand off, but it was useless. "Now they're throwing themselves at you, C.J."

"Oh Please." Caylen smacked her and repositioned herself on the towel. "She scared the shit out of me though." Both of them were laughing about the situation as they replayed it in their heads.

Two hours later, they were packing up to leave. Margo stepped away to shake the sand off of her towel when the Frisbee woman appeared next to C.J. "Hi, I just wanted to apologize again. I didn't mean to hurt you or your girlfriend."

"Thanks. It's fine, neither of us are hurt and she's not my girlfriend. You should ask her out," C.J. said as she finished folding her towel, stuffing it into the backpack she used as a beach bag.

"Actually," The woman took her sunglasses off to reveal golden brown eyes. "I'd like to ask you out."

Hmm…maybe she doesn't know me. This could be fun. She's cute. Caylen usually didn't date women that were much younger than her. She estimated Tanner, the stripper, to be twenty-three at the most, which was by far the youngest person she'd ever been with. This mysterious woman was maybe twenty-seven and still young.

"What's your name?" Caylen asked.

"Jasmine."

"I'm C.J."

"It's nice to meet you."

Margo turned around to see the two women shaking hands. *Oh that's subtle honey. Fall on her in the sand then*

164

apologize and ask her out. Real original. Too bad she's going to shoot you down like she does everyone else. Caylen caught up to her a minute later as the woman walked away.

"Did you tell her to go pound sand?" Margo asked as they walked towards the privacy gate to Caylen's building.

"I gave her my number," Caylen said.

"You what?"

It had been two and a half months since she had sex with Tanner. It was an experience that she'd never forget as long as she lived and she wasn't looking for a relationship now, but it would be nice to go out on a few dates. Caylen knew nothing would come of seeing Jasmine again. She just wasn't ready physically or mentally for another relationship. Who knew if she'd ever be ready again?

~

"I had a great time tonight, Jasmine," Caylen said as she walked towards her Bentley. She had picked Jasmine up from her apartment and took her out for Mexican food. They enjoyed Margaritas and enchiladas as Jasmine curiously asked Caylen what she did for a living. Caylen didn't actually lie; she just gave a very vague answer and said she inherited the car when her father passed away. Jasmine was in retail and worked as the store manager of an upscale boutique in downtown Santa Barbara.

"Me too, C.J. I'm glad I fell on you." She smiled and Caylen laughed.

"Yes well, let's hope that doesn't happen again. I had sand in places I didn't particularly want sand." Caylen spoke seriously but a smile played on the corners of her mouth. It was nice being out with someone who didn't know her and wasn't after her for her money.

"That's a little too much information." Jasmine wiggled her eyebrows. "I'm still sorry about that. It wasn't on purpose. My friend Judy can't throw a Frisbee for shit and I was running backwards. I never saw you guys. Does your friend hate me?"

"No, she was a little surprised and thinks you did it deliberately. But, I don't think you did." *Unless you're lying about knowing who I am. Damn it, Margo, you have me paranoid now. Not everyone reads the business section of the newspaper. Maybe Jasmine really doesn't know.*

"I was so mad at Judy, I refused to go to the beach again with her."

"Wow."

"We're going back this Sunday," Jasmine said sheepishly. Caylen laughed and shook her head. They pulled up in front of Jasmine's apartment. Caylen got out and walked her to her door.

"Will I see you again?" Jasmine asked as she unlocked the door and turned around to face Caylen's blue eyes.

"That depends on you," Caylen said.

Jasmine leaned forward and pressed her lips softly to Caylen's then pulled back. "I'd like to," She said with a smile.

"How about next Wednesday?"

"I can't. I close the store on Wednesday nights. What about Friday again?"

"I think that can be arranged."

~

Caylen sat on her couch reading the newspaper and

drinking a cup of creamy iced coffee. She was planning on spending her Saturday cleaning her condo. That was until Margo called her cell phone.

"How was your date?"

"Not bad," Caylen sipped the cold liquid and swished it around her mouth before swallowing it. "We went to *El Diablo*."

"Ah, Mexican. I was in the mood for a Margarita."

"Margo, you're always in the mood for a Margarita." Caylen rolled her eyes.

"So? What happened?"

"We ate and talked. Then I took her back to her apartment."

"That's it? You make it sound like you're two friends that hung out together. Weren't you on a date?"

"Well, yes, we didn't exactly jump in the backseat of the Bentley and get it on. We had a good time together. She's a lot of fun."

"Are you attracted to her?" Margo asked, trying to get to the point of the conversation.

"Yes, I don't know, maybe. I barely know her and I'm not looking for anything serious."

"What does that have to do with sleeping with her?"

"She's cute and easy to talk to. Who knows where it will lead, Margo. I'm not rushing into sex or anything else with her. Honestly, I'd just like to date her for a while and see what happens," Caylen said. She was definitely not looking for another one night. Besides, she was sure nothing would ever compare to the night she spent with Tanner. But, that was in the past and she pushed herself to let it go.

"Hmm...just don't get in over your head. I'd hate to have to knock her out. She's kind of cute," Margo teased.

"Uh huh."

"So, what are your plans for the day?"

"Not much, finish my coffee and clean the condo. The Bentley needs a bath. I might take it to the car wash later. Why? Do you have any big plans?"

"No, not really. I was going to see if you wanted to do lunch."

"It depends on what time I finish cleaning and since it's already ten and I haven't started, that's probably a no. Unless, you want to drive the vacuum or the feather duster."

Margo smirked. "Not likely, Alice, but do say hi to the Brady Bunch for me when they get home."

"Smartass!" Caylen shot back with a laugh.

"You know it. Anyway, call me if you finish in time for dinner. Maybe we can order a pizza or something."

"Alright, I'll call you." Caylen hung up the phone and forced herself to get off the couch and clean up. What was there to clean really? She was a single woman that worked sixty or more hours a week. Could the two bedroom loft really get that dirty *every* week? She was beginning to wonder if she was just a neat freak with cleaning supplies at her disposal.

Six

Caylen had three messages waiting for her when she walked into her office. Sara had them neatly stacked in the center of her desk. She ran a hand through her hair noting how thick it was. She was overdue for a cut. The intercom on her desk phone buzzed.

"Morning, kiddo."

"Good Morning, Uncle Herb. What can I do for you?" She hated it when he used her childhood pet name at work, but it also made her smile because it reminded her of her father.

"Grab a cup of coffee and come down to my office when you get a second."

Caylen hung up the phone and picked up her second cup of coffee for the day on her way down the hall. She figured she was heading out of town again. When Herb wanted to speak to her in the privacy of his office it was usually to discuss an account that she had to go close because the piss ants below her couldn't close it. In their defense, she only had to do this two or three times a year and it was usually major accounts that they couldn't afford to lose, otherwise she'd just let them do their jobs and get rid of the one's that couldn't pull their own weight. But, Uncle Herb ran the business just as her father had, and just as she would one day when the reins were handed to her. So, Caylen mentally thought about the suits that needed to go to the cleaners before she left town.

"Did you try one of those doughnuts your Aunt made?" Herb asked as Caylen walked into his office and shut the door.

"No, I ate a bowl of cereal before I left this morning. They look good though."

"Oh my god, they're fantastic. Hell on my waist though." He grinned and patted his slightly bulging stomach. His was considered fit for his age, but he had to go to the gym everyday just to keep up with his wife's cooking.

"I don't know how you do it. I'd be as big as a house if I lived with her." Caylen shook her head and smiled.

"My gym membership is my lifeline." He laughed.

She knew he was beating around the bush. He hated sending her out in the field to do someone else's job because they couldn't handle the pressure. But, he also knew how much she loved a challenge. Caylen Jarrett was the best account manager the company had ever had, next to her father. Her numbers were even higher than Herb's.

"How do you feel about New York?" He asked when he leaned back in his chair.

"What account?" She asked in the same gesture.

"Kilpatrick International. It's a shipping company with very large assets."

"When?"

"You'd need to leave Monday, meet with them Tuesday, and come home Wednesday."

"No time to go shopping on Fifth Avenue?" She made a pouting face.

"Oh please," he smirked. "You're not a package

carrying bitch on a mission in high heels."

"No, but I may want to go on a shop-a-thon. How often do I get to the Big Apple?"

"By all means, take a day. Oh hell, take two and shop until your feet fall off. I don't care as long as we close the deal and help Mason Kilpatrick save his business from bad overseas investments."

"That's the easy part. The hard part is finding a pair of shoes to match the new suit I bought so I can wear it." She appeared dead serious before laughing hysterically when her Uncle looked like his niece had been abducted by the department store aliens. Caylen liked to shop and wear nice clothes, but she was a simple patron of the clothing stores. She'd go in and get what she was looking for, and then be on her way. She did in two hours what takes most women two days.

~

Caylen could barely keep her eyes open in the hotel. She'd spent the entire day going over the business plan that she put together for Mason Kilpatrick. The man was by no means stupid, but he made her repeat herself close to twenty times. She was sure he was going deaf, either that or English wasn't his first language. She had simple color coordinated business spreadsheets on her laptop and she plugged in various scenarios to show him all of the different angles of the investment plan to save his business.

By six o'clock that night, the light bulb went off and he finally signed the papers. Then, she had to endure another two hours with him and his business partner Lyle Covington while they ate a six hundred dollar dinner. The jetlag was killing Caylen and she couldn't be happier when the men decided to call it a night after dinner. She was sure they were going to traipse all over New York City until her entertainment funds ran out. Thankfully, they were both older and tired easily.

Her plane was taking off at seven Eastern Time, which meant four Pacific Time. Caylen never could sleep in the air, but she was sure going to try this time. Besides, what else was she going to do for six hours on an overcrowded airplane? At least she was in first class and would have a little more room.

~

"I don't know how you do it," Margo said as she sipped her beer. Caylen sat across from her with bags under her eyes. "You look like hell."

"Gee, thanks. Next time, lay it on thick for me. I want to know how you really feel," Caylen said sarcastically.

"I'm sorry, you just look really tired."

"I am. That stupid ass old man wore me out." She shook her head. Her normally short hair were very unruly, she was starting to look like Rod Stewart with brown hair.

"At least you closed the deal."

"True, but I was starting to think he'd rather lose his business than pay me to put money back in his pocket."

"I know what you mean. I have people all the time that are up to their ears in debt and want to refinance their homes, but they're scared to death to pull equity out of their houses to pay off their debts."

"If I was up to my ass in bills and someone came to me and said for 'X' amount of money I'll make all of that go away, I'd sign on the god damn dotted line. Twice if I

172

had to," Caylen said.

"Uh huh, me too."

Both women ordered another beer when the waitress came by. Their shared plate of chicken wings was long gone, but neither woman was ready to call it a night. Caylen had already called her secretary to tell her she'd be an hour late in the morning because she needed to run an errand. She was actually going to get that mess on the top of her head cut off. She normally wore her hair short enough for a man, but it was cute on her.

"When are you seeing Jasmine again?" Margo asked.

"Probably this Friday night. Why?"

"Just asking. You've been dating for a few weeks now and still haven't slept together." Margo shrugged her shoulders. "It's kind of odd."

"I don't know. It's not like we haven't had the chance. I'm attracted to her and she's let me know a few times that she'd like to go to bed with me."

"Okay? Why don't you then? I'd be all over that."

"Honestly, I guess I don't want a relationship right now and if we start sleeping together we're headed in that direction."

"Hmm..."

"It's too late to sleep with her and then call her a few weeks later and do it again, you know what I mean?"

"Yeah."

"Margo, she doesn't even know what I do for a living, where I live, anything like that. I'm scared to tell her."

"Well, it's not serious so technically she doesn't need to know. Although, I'd find it a little weird if I was dating someone and didn't at least know where they lived or worked."

"She knows I'm in banking and live at the beach, but

173

that's it. She flipped out over the Bentley. I was honest and said my father left it to me when he died, but I'm sure she thinks my family is loaded if I inherited a two hundred thousand dollar car."

"I see your point. I guess you'll know better than anyone when you're ready to settle down again and be truly honest about yourself."

Caylen finished her beer and contemplated ordering another. "I should probably go home and get some sleep."

"Yeah, me too. I have an early meeting tomorrow with my staff of piss ant consultants. I have to put on my bitch hat that goes with my everyday power suit."

"That sounds like fun. I could definitely borrow that hat. I think that's why Uncle Herb doesn't let me head the meetings with our account managers and consultants. I would probably fire half of them."

"No shit. I feel like doing that most of the time."

"Me too, especially when I have to fly all over creation to fix their fuck-ups."

"I hear you."

~

Caylen felt like her usual self on her way to the office. She ran her hands through the recently cut, short hair and felt normal again. She smiled. Sara was waiting with a stack of messages for her when she walked into the office. The pale yellow blouse that Caylen was wearing under her black business suit contrasted nicely with her bright blue eyes.

"Ms. Jarrett, I sent all of your phone calls to your voicemail, except for a few that preferred to leave a message with me." Sara handed her the three pieces of pink paper. "This one was a walk in on Wednesday. Her name is Tanner Bryce. I told her you were in New York on business and asked if she wanted to leave a message with me or on your voicemail, but she said she'd come back."

Caylen wrinkled her eyebrows. Anyone that came to see her had an appointment. She'd never heard of this person before. The only Tanner she knew was the dancer from Texas, and that woman had no idea who Caylen was. "I'm not sure who she is Sara, but if she comes back I'll talk to her. In the meantime, can you check a listing of our accounts and let me know what company she's from? Thanks." Caylen went into her office and closed the door.

She had three backed up days worth of paperwork to take care of. What she really wanted to do was call Margo, or maybe Jasmine, and go lay on the beach. Even with the weather slightly changing to fall, not that it mattered, Santa Barbara had pretty much monolithic temperatures year round. The air was a little cooler, yet still warm enough to lay on the beach.

~

Caylen spent her entire lunch sitting in her uncle's office going over her trip to New York and the deal she closed with Mason Kilpatrick and his business partner. Then, she spent the rest of her afternoon returning voicemails and emails. She thought the day would never come to an end.

It was Friday night and she was sitting in a restaurant with Jasmine enjoying unbelievable lasagna and a bottle of white wine.

"Long week?" Jasmine asked.

"Yeah, too long. What about you?"

"I think everyone is out shopping for a new wardrobe this month. I've been going crazy. I had to fire one girl for stealing. I wanted to choke the life out of her. Here I am heading into the holiday season and I don't have time for interviews and training a new key carrier."

"That sucks."

"You can say that again. After tomorrow I will have put in close to seventy hours this week. That really sucks when you only get paid for forty and the shitty quarterly bonuses don't even equal a single paycheck."

"Is there room for advancement with the company?" Caylen asked. She'd never worked anywhere but JFC.

"Yes, I'm in an advancement program to become a District Manager. I'll be in charge of about fifteen stores, but I'll have to relocate probably when I finish the program in a few months. My boss told me there may be a district opening up in Northern California and his wife really wants to move so if he takes it then I may have a chance to get this district."

"That'll be good for you."

"Yeah, I'm not looking to move. I've thought about getting out of retail all together, but I've been doing this since I was fifteen, so it's close to thirteen years. You'd think I would've left by now." She smiled and shook her head.

"Here's to the future and good luck." Caylen raised her glass for a toast.

An hour later, they were walking along the shopping strip where the restaurant was located. Jasmine grabbed Caylen's hand and squeezed.

"What's going on with you?"

"What do you mean?" Caylen raised an eyebrow. *Oh no.*

"I keep getting the feeling that you don't want us to go any further."

"No, it's not that..."

"Who is she?"

"What?"

"There's another woman isn't there?" Jasmine asked.

"No." Caylen shook her head. There really wasn't anyone else. "I've been through a lot in past relationships and I guess I'm reluctant to get involved again."

"I can't wait forever." Jasmine smiled and kissed her lips softly before pulling away. "I've had blue clit for over a month. I mean I knew it was going to go slow at first, but we've been doing this dating thing for almost two months now."

Caylen laughed. "I know, I'm sorry."

"I don't want to pressure you. Let's do something fun tonight. I'm closing the store tomorrow so I don't have to get up early."

"I'll call Margo and see if she's going to *One Up*. There's usually a pretty good crowd on Friday."

"That sounds like fun. Are you sure she's okay with me?"

"Yeah, she asks about you all the time, actually."

Caylen called Margo and talked her into meeting them at the bar. A half hour later, they were at a small table ordering a round of drinks and watching a guy butcher a song with his horrible karaoke voice. A few couples danced anyway. That was the neat thing about the bar, it was considered straight, but a few gay men and a lot of lesbians usually filled the place up. Caylen sipped her whiskey and watched in amusement.

"Did C.J. tell you she likes to sing karaoke?" Margo asked Jasmine. Caylen shot her an *eat shit* look.

"Really? You do?" Jasmine asked with raised eyebrows.

"No! I do not. Margo thinks it's funny to bet me to do stupid shit and one night she bet me to sing so I sang. But, I do *not* do karaoke! So, don't try it." She finished with a hard tone in her voice but a smile on her face.

"Too bad, I'd like to see you sing." Jasmine shook her head.

"Get her drunk." Margo joked.

"You know, I invited you because I used to think you were my best friend, but right now you're gaining leverage on my shit list." Caylen cocked her head to the side and shot a mocking pissed off look at Margo, but she couldn't stop the smile from tugging at her lips. No matter how hard she tried, she couldn't be mean to Margo.

"Uh huh, you can't even lie to me." Margo shook her head.

The three of them spent the rest of the night drinking and dancing off and on while making fun of the karaoke singers.

Seven

The following Monday morning, Caylen was sitting at her desk replying to emails and going over a business plan for a new account that the Director of Sales sent to her.

"Excuse me, Ms. Jarrett." Sara buzzed the intercom.

"Yes."

"You have a guest in the lobby. Ms. Tanner Bryce is here to see you."

Hmm...the mystery woman from last week. She had to be a referral of some kind from a past client. "Go ahead and send her up." Caylen closed the window on her computer and waited for the visitor. She swore she could hear whistling when the door opened.

Tanner was standing in her doorway wearing a black skirt suit and heels. Her hair was darker, more like rich mocha than honey, and much longer. It hung a few inches past the middle of her back in natural waves. Her gray eyes sparkled when she smiled. The first word Caylen thought of as she looked at her was, stunning.

"Hi," Tanner said stepping further into the room. Caylen flew out of her seat and walked around the large desk. Tanner stood a couple inches taller than Caylen in her high heels, although they were roughly the same height. Tanner stuck her hand out. "Tanner Bryce."

179

"Caylen Jarrett." Caylen felt the spark of electricity as Tanner's warm hand grasped her own. "How...how did you..."

"Those men you were with came back into the club about two months ago and I asked them who you were."

"And they told you, just like that?" Caylen raised an eyebrow.

"No, I had to give both of them a free dance." She shook her head. "But, they finally gave me your first and last name. I Googled you after that."

"Wow. I...What are you doing here?" Caylen was at a loss for words. She never thought she'd see this woman again. And if it were possible, she looked even more beautiful than she had six months ago.

"I guess you could say I'm on vacation." Tanner smiled. Her perfectly white teeth shined under the fluorescent lighting.

"Wow."

"I guess you never thought you'd see me again, huh?"

"Yes, no...hell, I don't even know what to say." Caylen's heart was beating a hundred miles an hour. "You're just as beautiful as I remember you being. You changed your hair."

"Thank you. I went back to my natural color and let it grow out. You look just like I remember you." Tanner held her arms out. "This is a surprise though. I read a lot about you on the computer. I'm impressed."

Oh no, please don't let her be here gold digging. "This..." Caylen spread her arms mockingly, "is my job, my family's company. This office, this place, it's not who I am."

"That's good, because I don't remember you being a stuck up rich bitch." Tanner laughed lightly.

"Please, have a seat." Caylen went back around to her side of the desk. She watched Tanner sit professionally and cross her legs. Her natural olive complexion looked way sexier than any pair of pantyhose. "How long are you in town for?"

"Years, I hope," Tanner said.

"I thought you were on vacation?" Caylen raised an eyebrow.

"Well, I was last week until I went on my second interview Friday. I start my new job in a week."

"What? Here in Santa Barbara? Where?" Caylen was extremely confused.

"I guess we didn't really get a chance to talk much when we were together." Tanner grinned.

Talk much? We didn't talk at all, except for begging each other for pleasure. Somebody pinch me. Am I dreaming? "You're right, we didn't. I still see you as 'Candy' the dancer. And now you sit in front of me as Tanner Bryce, the businesswoman. I guess I'm in shock."

"I kind of expected that. I wasn't sure if you would even see me. I didn't know if you were possibly married or even a lesbian for that matter."

"Well, as you said, we didn't really talk. And no I'm not married and yes I am a lesbian. What about you?"

"No. No relationship at all right now, and I'm a lesbian. Although, I'm not really 'out' to many people."

"I see. So, what brings you to California?"

"Well, I was in my last semester at the University of Houston when I met you. I graduated a few months ago with a B.S. in Computer Science." She let out a deep breath. "I've been through more interviews than I can count. It wasn't until I ran into those guys a while back and asked about you. I guess that made me decide to start

181

looking at companies out of state. One thing led to another and I came here for an in-person interview with Intelitech Communications." When Caylen raised an eyebrow, Tanner continued.

"It's a large software company that was looking for someone on the business side to help install the software remotely and run the help desk information center. After my phone interviews went well, I decided to take a small vacation and go on the face to face interview here. They offered me the job on the second interview and I couldn't pass up a six figure income and an actual career. I was only dancing to pay for college. I called and quit the day I accepted the job here. I've already signed a short lease on an apartment and I sold my car to a friend at the club so I just bought myself a new car too."

"Wow." Caylen was speechless. "I…congratulations. That's a hell of a job you have ahead of you."

"I love computers and I decided to make a career out of working with them when I had to quit my first love." She shrugged. "I got into the University on a gymnastics scholarship with no problem. I graduated high school with honors and was a gymnast all of my childhood. My freshman year I tore my ACL and MCL and went through hell trying to recover. Then, I finally started competing again and broke my ankle in a car accident and after that I gave up on my passion." She paused.

"I took some time off to mourn the loss of my gymnastics career. My family couldn't afford my tuition when I finally changed my major and went back to school. I couldn't live at home and go to school because I'm from Abilene. So, I took a job as a dancer at *Steers*. I was there just over four years. I didn't make six figures obviously, but my tuition and living expenses were easily attainable working four nights a week." She crossed her legs the opposite way. "I feel like I'm rambling."

"No." Caylen shook her head and smiled. "I'm just…well…this is a big surprise. I still can't believe you're here. I'm happy for you."

"Thank you, that means a lot to me coming from you. I had no idea you were this successful. I mean I thought maybe you worked for those guys that you were with. I've seen them in there before and they usually spend some money. Hell, I know you guys spent at least two thousand that night you were there with them."

"Yeah, *I* spent about eighteen hundred in the club. They are clients of ours. I signed a business deal with them that day and they wanted to go out for entertainment afterwards."

"Well, I'm glad you decided to take them. I've thought about you off and on. It's good to see you again."

"It's good to see you too. I can't say I haven't thought of you either. I don't usually do that kind of thing. In fact, I mean I've had one night stands, but never with a stripper."

Tanner laughed. "I hope it hasn't become a regular thing for you then."

"No!" Caylen shook her head with a smile. "That was a first and last for me."

"Ouch! That doesn't sound good on my part."

"No, don't get me wrong. I had a wonderful time with you, Tanner. You're absolutely beautiful and you're obviously a very talented woman. I've heard of Intelitech, they seem to be a well respected company."

"I hope so. It's a bit of a shock coming here from Texas, but I was due for a change."

The intercom buzzed and Caylen picked up the receiver on the phone. Her uncle wanted to know if she got anywhere with the business plan she was going over for the Director of Sales. She informed him that she was in a meeting and she'd get back to him.

"I'm sorry, I know you're busy. I guess I just wanted to say hi and see how you were." Tanner stood to leave.

"Tanner?"

"Yes C.J.?"

Caylen wanted to see her again. She couldn't explain the energy pulling her towards this woman. But, she fought back the urge to jump up and wrap her arms around her. For one, she was sort of dating Jasmine, and two, she was not looking for a relationship. Especially, with a woman that knew all about her, no matter who she was. Caylen guarded her heart and her dignity, not to mention her family's money. None of which she would see until her mother passed away and then her uncle. She wished both of them many years of good health. Losing her father was hard enough. Taking over the family business would be too much for her right now. She squeezed her eyes shut and opened them again to see gray irises staring back at her. "Can I take you to dinner tonight?"

"Sure." Tanner leaned forward and wrote her cell number down on a piece of paper and snatched one of Caylen's business cards from the holder on the front of her desk. "I haven't had the time to get a local cell number. I'm not even in my apartment yet. I'm flying back to Texas on Wednesday to pack and then the movers should be here next week. I'll fly back probably the day before they are scheduled to arrive."

"Sounds like you have everything all planned out. Where are you staying in the meantime?"

"The Hyatt by the interstate."

"That's not far from here. How about I pick you up

around six-thirty?"

"I'll be ready."

"Good, that gives me time to run home and change clothes."

"Jeans?" Tanner asked.

Caylen smiled. "You're catching on quick."

Tanner winked and left the room.

~

Caylen parked the Bentley and waited in the lobby. She was dressed in jeans and a tight black polo shirt with the buttons open revealing a small amount of cleavage. Her feet were once again in a comfortable pair of flip flops. She spotted Tanner walking towards her when she turned around to face the elevator. Tanner was also wearing jeans. Her skin tight white blouse had a V-neck that showed a lot more cleavage. Unlike Caylen, Tanner wore semi-flat ankle boots that gave her less than an inch of height over her. Her long wavy hair hung sexily over her shoulders and down her back with a few strands falling forward. Caylen had the urge to run her hands into the silky strands and pull her into a passionate kiss. *What was it about this woman?* She couldn't figure out why she was so drawn to her.

"You look comfortable," Tanner said. "I like this side of you."

"Good because this is who I am. The power suit only comes out Monday through Friday, eight to five." Caylen grinned. "You look so different. I keep remembering the lighter, shorter hair. But, I do have to say, I like it this way."

Tanner stepped forward grabbing Caylen's hand. Just

185

as before, the electricity passed between them when their skin touched. Caylen interlaced their fingers as they walked outside. Tanner's eyebrows shot up when she saw the lights flash on the Bentley when Caylen hit the keyless entry.

"It was my father's. I inherited it when he passed away," Caylen said as she let go of her hand to open Tanner's door for her.

"I'm sorry about you father," Tanner said as she buckled her seatbelt, admiring the gray leather interior and wood grain trim. "This car is very nice."

"Thanks. I can't bear to part with it. At first I hated driving it and wanted to sell it, but it grew on me I guess." She started the car and turned out of the parking lot. "How do you feel about Sushi?"

"That's fine with me."

Elton John was playing softly in the background on the stereo as Caylen drove them towards the beach. They arrived at the restaurant quickly and found a nice little table in the back. Caylen ordered a bottle of cold Saki and various pieces of sashimi and a few rolls for them to share since Tanner didn't know much about the delicacy.

"So, where do you live?" Tanner asked as she tried to master the chopsticks. Caylen grinned as she reached across the table, grabbing Tanner's hands to help her with the technique.

"I have a loft condo on the beach close to Lighthouse Point. Where is your apartment?"

"Well, the office is downtown, a few blocks from your building. I started there and drove around in my rental car until I reached the beach. It's so beautiful here. I didn't want to spend all of my money renting a place out here so I turned back on Loma Alta and found a nice place that's halfway between work and the beach. You said Lighthouse Point, I think I remember seeing that when I drove down Shoreline."

"You went right by my place then. I'm off of Shoreline but it's private access out where my building is."

"Wow, that must be nice. My apartment is only one bedroom, but it's pretty large and I don't have a lot of stuff. I want to save up to buy a place in a year or two."

"That's the best investment I ever made. Let me know when you're ready. My best friend is one of the Mortgage Directors at a large bank here in town."

"Thanks. I'll keep that in mind." Tanner sipped her saki. "So, what have you been up to for the past six months? Your secretary told me you were in New York when I stopped by the first time."

"I wish I could say I was lying in the sand every day, drinking frozen drinks and sitting on my balcony, staring at the stars while listening to the surf crash against the shore every night, but in all honesty I've been in and out of town a few times and working like a dog over sixty hours a week."

"I like the picture you set before you were honest." Tanner smiled.

"Me, too." Caylen paid the bill and sat back in her chair.

"Thank you for dinner."

"You're very welcome. I still can't believe you're here. It's mind-boggling."

"You keep picturing me on stage, don't you?" Tanner didn't look hurt, but Caylen knew she was trying to get past being a dancer.

"Actually, no. I keep..." Caylen met Tanner's sincere eyes. "I keep picturing you in my hotel bed, shimmering with sweat underneath me."

"Mmm...that's a nice way to remember me." Tanner seductively bit her bottom lip.

"We should probably get out of here before they kick us out. They aren't too keen on people hanging around after they've paid the bill," Caylen said.

Tanner grabbed Caylen's hand as they walked out of the restaurant. Caylen briefly laced their fingers once again before letting go completely.

"What's wrong?" Tanner asked.

"Nothing."

"You've been acting strange all night. I..." Tanner was cut off when Caylen grabbed her hand, tugging her close until their bodies met.

Tanner ran her other hand into Caylen's short hair and Caylen wrapped her arm possessively around her. Their lips parted and tongues tasted each other softly at first. Slowly, the passion between them took over as the kiss deepened. Caylen let go of Tanner's hand wrapping her other arm around her as she held the brunette tightly against her. They drank from each other's mouth like they were part of the only waterfall in the desert sand.

Caylen was so lost in the feeling of being with Tanner again, holding her in her arms and kissing her with unwavering passion that she forgot where they were and what they were doing.

Caylen pulled away first. "I'm sorry...I can't...I shouldn't..."

"You're seeing someone aren't you?" Tanner met Caylen's blue eyes.

"Yes." Caylen squeezed her eyes shut, then opened them to see gray looking back at her. "It's not serious...I mean we're not...sleeping together...but we've been dating a couple months..."

"Okay?"

"My life is so complicated, Tanner. You coming here, this is all too much for me right now." Caylen's body and mind were on overload. She walked around to her side of the car and hit the keyless entry button.

They drove back to the hotel in silence. Caylen was confused. She wasn't sure what to say to the woman sitting next to her, or the woman she had been dating for that matter. *What the hell is going on with me? Why did she have to come here? Everything was fine.* Caylen pulled the car up in front of the hotel and turned to face Tanner.

"I'm sorry."

"No, I shouldn't have expected you to be single and pick up where we left off in a one night stand, six months ago. I'm sure you still can't believe I'm sitting here with you. I was a stripper you slept with on a business trip." Her voice was almost a whisper. "I guess I had hoped it meant more than that," Tanner said as she got out of the car and shut the door, disappearing inside before Caylen could say anything.

Caylen felt a warm tear run down her cheek. She wiped it away as she searched the names in her cell phone and choose the one she was looking for.

"Hey stranger," Margo answered on the second ring.

"Are you busy?"

"No, what's up?"

"Can I come over?"

"Do you have to ask?"

Eight

"Are you kidding me?" Margo almost fell off of the couch. She thought about pouring herself a drink to calm the excitement in her nerves, but she decided she wanted to hear this story stone sober.

"No."

"Why didn't you tell me you slept with her in Texas?"

"I didn't think I'd see her again! Especially, in my god damn office!" Caylen was on the verge of a nervous breakdown.

"This is crazy. So, she moved out here just like that?"

"Yup, just like that."

"Wow."

"I think I've said that about a hundred times over," Caylen said.

"Where is she working?"

"Intelitech. She's a computer programmer."

"Wow."

"Will you stop saying that? Trust me, I've said it enough for both of us," Caylen growled.

"Sorry. So, she quit dancing?"

"Yeah, she graduated from the University of Houston and came here to interview for that job and she took the offer."

"So, how did she find you?"

"The clients I met with in Houston went back to the club a couple months ago and she asked about me. They gave her my name and she Googled me on the computer."

"Ah...you have to love Google. That site can find anything and anyone." Margo shook her head. "How do you feel about her being here?"

"I don't know. My mind's all over the damn place."

"I bet. Personally, I'd be a little freaked out too," Margo said.

"Thanks. You're a big help." Caylen blew out a frustrated breath.

"I'm just being honest."

"She's leaving for about a week to pack and get the movers going with her stuff. I feel bad for panicking on her at the restaurant tonight."

"It sounds like she understood."

"I hurt her and I didn't mean to. I'm so confused."

"Well, C.J., a stripper you had a one night stand with just appeared on your door step basically. God, I'm sure you thought you'd never see her again. Plus, you're kind of seeing someone. If you want to call it that."

"I *am* seeing Jasmine. We're dating."

"What thirty-three year old lesbian do you know that dates someone for two months without ever having sex with the person?"

"I get your point!" Caylen raised her voice but apologized quickly.

"Are you in love with Tanner?"

"What? No! I don't even know her. I literally just met her today."

"I think you better tell Jasmine about this so she doesn't get hurt. Then, you need to take some time for yourself and either figure out what to do about Tanner or at least learn how to be friends with her."

"I know. I feel like I'm in a dream. One night she's a stripper from an erotic dream, the next morning she's a flesh and blood computer programmer sitting in my office."

Margo raised her eyebrows. "It is a little freakish when you put it like that."

Caylen gave her a sideways look. "You think so?!" She said sarcastically.

"Well, the least you could do is tell me what she looks like."

"Which one? Candy, the dancer? Or Tanner, the business woman?"

"Excuse me? Candy?"

Caylen laughed lightly. "Her stage name at the club was Candy Coated Rain Drop."

"No shit! Oh how original." Margo laughed hysterically.

"I'm serious. In the middle of sleeping together she told me her name was Tanner."

"Interesting. Let me ask you this…when you were together that night, did you have sex or make love?"

Caylen didn't have to think, she knew the answer. But, she swallowed and took a minute to calm her nerves. "We made love for hours. It was the first time I had made love to anyone in a very long time. We slept the rest of the night in each other's arms. I haven't done that in so long, Margo."

Margo could see the confusion and pain in her best friend's eyes. It was easy for her to give herself to this woman completely, this stranger that she was never supposed to see again. No wonder she was so scared, the stranger became a real life person a few hours ago.

"That's serious."

"You're telling me." Caylen leaned her head back on the couch and closed her eyes.

"I guess you really want to know what she looks like now don't you?"

"I have to say I'm really curious."

"Well, when I met her in Texas she had honey colored hair that barely touched her shoulders and all the same length, with gorgeous gray eyes. She's very muscular with an amazing body. She was a gymnast all of her life and was actually on a gymnastics scholarship at the university before getting hurt and changing her career. She has very silky smooth, olive complexioned skin. Her body is so soft. Her breasts are larger than average and perfectly round and perky and she also has a tight little ass. I'd say she's my height maybe an inch taller."

"She sounds hot. It's easy to picture her swinging around a pole."

"Well, today when I first saw her, she was in a black skirt suit with a very low cut white top underneath her jacket. Her hair was a lot darker, sort of mocha colored and grown out at least six inches past her shoulders and wavier than I remembered. She said that she went back to her natural color and let it grow out when she stopped straightening it. It's very sexy when it falls around her shoulders, like half in the front and half in the back. Tonight she was in jeans and a tight V-neck top. Her cleavage was practically popping out of it. She's the most naturally beautiful woman I've ever seen. It's hard for me to keep my hands off of her."

"I definitely need to see this girl. She sounds too good to be true."

"She's very young. The youngest woman I've ever been with, that's for sure."

"How old is she?"

"I don't know, but she just graduated from college, so I'm guessing twenty-two or twenty-three maybe."

"Damn, that *is* young."

"No kidding. By the way, I'm not giving you any details so don't ask."

"Aww, you suck."

Caylen wiggled her eyebrows. "If you only knew."

"Pig." Margo laughed and Caylen joined her.

Nine

A little over a week later, Caylen was sitting in her uncle's office when her cell phone rang. She didn't recognize the number, but it was local so she answered it since he was just shooting the shit with her anyway. They were about to head home for the day and put an end to a long week.

"This is C.J."

"Hey, it's Tanner. I was actually just going to leave you a voicemail with my new cell number. I didn't expect you to answer."

"I usually don't during work hours, but I'm about to take off soon and I didn't recognize the number." She felt weird having this conversation with her uncle sitting across from her listening in.

"Well, I won't keep you."

"Tanner...I'm sorry. I owe you an apology."

"It's okay. I've thought about it a lot. I guess I would've been freaked out too."

"I just need a little time to work through some things."

"I understand. Take care of yourself, Caylen."

"You too. I'll talk to you soon." Caylen closed her phone and put it back on the belt clip under her jacket. Her uncle looked puzzled.

195

"Long story." She said with a deep breath.

"I'm here if you need to talk."

"Thanks." *That's all I need, tell my uncle the stripper I had a one night stand with mysteriously moved here, looked me up, and became a business woman all in a matter of weeks.* She chased the thought from her head and smiled at her uncle.

~

Caylen rushed home to change clothes and pick Jasmine up. They had plans for dinner and she was already running late. She arrived at Jasmine's apartment with a few minutes to spare. She planned on telling her about Tanner so her nerves were in a knot. Jasmine heard her at the door and opened it before she had the chance to knock.

"Hey," Jasmine said as she quickly kissed her lips and turned around to lock the door.

"Hi," Caylen said.

"Are you okay? You look pale."

"I'm fine."

"Are you sure? Did you want to come in for a minute?"

"Actually, that would be great."

Jasmine opened the door back up and invited Caylen inside. This was the first time she'd actually seen the complete inside of the apartment. It was small, two bedroom, one bath with light beige carpet and oak colored furniture. Caylen took a seat on the couch. Jasmine sat next to her.

"I need to tell you something."

"Okay?"

"Before I met you…"

"Are you seeing someone else?" Jasmine blurted out.

"No." Caylen met her eyes honestly. "Please listen to what I have to say."

"Go ahead." Jasmine squeezed Caylen's hand and let it go.

"As I said, a little over six months ago and before I met you, I went to Texas on a business trip. I met a woman and had a one night stand with her. We never exchanged more than first names. Wait..." Caylen took a deep breath. "let me start from the beginning. Jasmine have you ever heard of Jarrett Financial Corporation?"

"Yes. What does that have to do with you having a one night stand with a stranger?"

"I'm Jarrett. C.J. stands for Caylen Jarrett. It's my family's company. I'm the Vice President."

"What?!" Jasmine looked baffled.

"I didn't lie to you. I really am in banking and everyone calls me C.J. It's very hard for me to tell people who I am. I've had a lot of women come after me for my money. My father really did pass away and leave me his Bentley. Otherwise, I'd still be driving my BMW which was a third of the price of the Bentley."

"Okay? I'm confused C.J. or Caylen whatever your name is."

"C.J. is still my name, Jasmine. I'm sorry I'm dumping this on you, but I want you to understand where I'm coming from with this." She stopped to back track on her thoughts. "Anyway, I'm very reluctant to let people get to know anything about me."

"That's an understatement," Jasmine huffed.

"I know. So, back to Texas. I had a one night stand with a stranger and to be honest it was one of the best nights of my life. I haven't really given myself to anyone completely like I did that night, in almost two years. A big part of that was the fact that she was a stranger and I knew she would never know anything about me and she wasn't with me at the time because of who I was or what I had."

"C.J. if you think I'm dating you because you have money then you're out of your mind. Apparently, up until this minute, I didn't even know your real god damn name."

"No, I know that. Please let me finish."

"Alright."

"This woman from Texas showed up in my office about two weeks ago..."

"What?!"

"Yeah, I was shocked to say the least. She ran into my clients that I was with the night I met her and they told her my name. She searched for me on the computer because she wanted to see me again. So, to make a long story short, she came to California to interview with a company here and decided to take the job and move here. She came to see me after that."

"Wow."

"I had dinner with her to catch up and actually really meet her for the first time. I'm still freaked out about the whole thing. I don't think she's stalking me or anything like that. She has a great job with a big company. I checked it out just to be sure."

"So, did you rekindle your old flame?"

"No, we were headed down that road when I stopped it and told her about you. The thing is, Jasmine, I haven't wanted a relationship in a long time. That's a big part of the reason I haven't had sex with you. Right now my mind is running in a hundred different directions and I wanted to be straight forward with you."

"Are you in love with her?"

"You know, Margo asked me that same question the other night."

"And?"

"No. But, there is a very powerful connection between me and her. I haven't seen her since that night we went to dinner and I only talked to her once. I kind of hurt her feelings and I didn't mean to. I've just been really confused. I'm thirty-three years old and next in line to take over a multi-million dollar corporation when my uncle retires. Not to mention my bank account or oceanfront condo." She saw the shock on Jasmine's face. "Now, you see why I'm cautious? The gold diggers lurk in the corners. Especially, after they find out I'm a lesbian."

"That's crazy."

"I promise I'm not nuts." Caylen smiled sheepishly.

"I know that. This is a lot to take in though."

"I'm really sorry, Jasmine."

"Let's try being friends for a while and see how all of this plays out."

"I agree. Are you still hungry?"

Jasmine laughed. "Yeah, let's go get Chinese."

"That sounds good."

~

Caylen spent all day Saturday cleaning her condo as usual. She mopped the tile, swept the hardwood floors, and vacuumed the carpet. She washed her bedding and dusted everything. After that, she cleaned both bathrooms.

It was late afternoon when she decided to get the Bentley washed and waxed, something her father did religiously, and she did when she thought about it which was every other month or so. Margo called her just as she was leaving the car wash.

"What can I do for you?" Caylen said when she answered.

"Is that any way to answer a call from your best friend? And what the hell makes you think I want something?" Margo snickered.

"Name it."

"Lila called me today."

"Oh really. Did you tell her to go take a long walk off a short pier?"

"No." Margo laughed.

"What did she want?"

"To have hot sex on the hood of your Bentley."

"Gross!" Caylen slammed on the brakes to keep from running a red light. Margo was laughing hysterically. "Don't crash on account of me."

"Tell me what she really wanted smartass."

"Actually, she just called to shoot the shit, which is really odd for her."

"She wants something and she's bating you."

"Masturbating. That's about all she's doing these days. She says she's single."

"What do you care?"

"I don't."

"Good. Open your front door." Caylen closed her cell phone and walked inside Margo's condo. It was situated further inland instead of beachfront like Caylen's and it was a little smaller and styled more like a townhouse, whereas Caylen's was loft-style.

"Make yourself at home," Margo said as Caylen walked passed her on her way to the kitchen. "There's beer on the bottom shelf."

Caylen came back out with two longnecks and handed

one to Margo. "I told Jasmine about Tanner."

"You did?"

"Yeah, Friday night."

"How did that go?"

"Surprisingly well. I told her all about me and the company, then I told her about Tanner. I did not tell her Tanner was a stripper though. Anyway, we talked for a while and decide we're better off friends right now until we see where all of this goes. Afterward, we went and ate Chinese."

"That's interesting. Have you talked to Tanner lately?"

"She called me Friday to give me her new cell number. I told her I needed some time to sort through all of this. She said she understood."

"Are you going to call her any time soon?"

"No. I don't know. I just decided to be friends with a girl I was dating for two months."

"Wake up, Caylen. You dated a girl for two months and never had sex with her. A complete stranger comes back into your life and you're scared to see her because you can't stop yourself from sleeping with her."

"You make it sound so simple."

"It *is* simple!"

Caylen finished her beer. "Maybe for you."

"I'd call her and see what happens. Just be careful."

"Maybe. I feel like taking a vacation to escape the craziness."

"When and where are we going?"

"Probably sometime next year." Caylen laughed. "I'm entirely too busy right now."

"Yeah, me too, but, the thought was nice."

Sydney Canyon

Ten

It had been close to a month since Tanner walked into Caylen's office. Caylen pushed that thought aside as she stepped into her uncle's office shutting the door. He was sitting behind the desk staring at his laptop screen.

"We have the Annual Santa Barbara Counsel of Business Conference next Friday night," He said without looking up from the computer.

"I saw it on my calendar." She wanted to opt out, but the city put on a large conference for the major businesses in the community every year. Since you had to be invited by the city to attend, it was considered an honor to go to the event. Caylen could care less about schmoozing with the other businesses in the city, but she'd attended every year since she had become VP.

Herb Jarrett closed the screen he was engrossed in and sat back in his chair to get a good look at his niece. Her blue eyes looking back at him seemed paler as he chewed on the corner of his mustache.

"What's bothering you, kiddo?" He sounded like he did when she was six and used to bounce her on his knee when she'd go visit her aunt and uncle with her mom and dad.

Caylen let out a sigh. "Nothing, Uncle Herb, I'm just

tired." She wasn't lying; she hadn't slept much in the past few weeks.

"You look just like your dad when you don't tell the whole truth. He carried his stress lines the same way you do and I could read right through him, so spit it out." He grinned.

"Life is complicated, Uncle Herb. Dad knew it, you know it, and I'm just now figuring it out." She smiled.

"Well, in that case, I'll let you off the hook for now. How's your mom?"

"Good. I never see her anymore, but she loves to travel. She and Aunt Cindy are seeing the world. Or at least that's what they call it."

Herb laughed. "She always was a hard one to keep tied down."

"No kidding, I don't know how dad did it. The woman never slows down. I guess she wasn't this bad when he was alive. Maybe he was the reason she stayed on the ground."

"I can picture her and Cindy traipsing all over the world." He laughed and shook his head.

"Yeah, they have definitely surpassed me in the flyer miles department. I think they've built up enough for a couple of free flights, not to mention hotel points. You know they went to Europe not long ago."

"Yeah."

"They're in Alaska right now and I think they are going to Hawaii in a month or two."

"Viv and I did an Alaskan cruise once. That state is amazing."

"I've always wanted to go there. Hell, I wouldn't mind Hawaii either. Aunt Cindy told me Mom's talking about China or Japan as the next 'big' trip."

"Must be nice to have all of that free time."

204

"No shit." Caylen shook her head.

"You have mountains of vacation time you know."

"Yes, but show me dates when I can take it. My schedule changes from week to week."

"Mine too. Viv is on me about taking some vacation time too. She claims I haven't taken her anywhere in three years and her suitcase is getting antsy."

Caylen laughed. "Ship her off with Mom and Aunt Cindy."

"Hey! That's a good idea. You might be onto something kid!" His face lit up.

"Just don't tell them where you got the idea," she said.

~

Caylen sat on her couch watching TV and drinking a glass of whiskey while checking the email on her laptop. She saw the monthly Alumni letter from UCSB, her alma matter, so she clicked on it first. They announced the posting of the women's basketball schedule as well as a few other sports.

She always tried to make it to a few of the games every season. She scrolled the list of home games, purchasing tickets to the weekend games that she knew she could attend, before closing the link and finishing the rest of her emails. Her mother sent pictures of her and Aunt Cindy in Alaska. Caylen had to laugh at a few of them as she scrolled through. She swished the last of the contents in her glass before swallowing.

Minutes later, she closed the laptop and poured herself another drink before stepping out to the private walkway leading down to the sandy beach. It had been weeks since she last walked on the beach at night. She considered this *her* time. The only time she was able to let her mind free and just listen to the waves crash against the shore as the stars twinkled and the full moon lit up the darkness of the night. The sand was cool between her toes and the glass of bourbon on the rocks was sweating in her hand. Her hair was too short for the wind to blow around, but the sea breeze tickled her skin. She continued to slowly sip the golden liquid and walk along without a care in the world.

For those few minutes, Caylen freed her mind and let her senses peak to their highest potential. The small t-shirt and short shorts that she was wearing were no match for the cool night air. Maybe she would actually get some sleep tonight, more than three or four hours was all she was hoping for. She missed the tranquility of dreamless sleep. It wasn't that she was unhappy or even stressed over the day to day challenges of her job. Caylen had one thing or rather one person on her mind.

Tanner Bryce had been the one person that she allowed herself to be with freely. She let her soul soar to new heights with this stranger, this person that barely had to look at her and she was gone, spent, lost in translation over the gentle way they made love to each other as if they'd been together for years.

Now, this absolutely perfect in every way, shape, or form, *stranger* was much more than an occurrence in her life. Caylen was scared. She ached deep inside for this woman and that alone scared her to death. She'd never ached for anything in her entire life. But, the thought of getting involved again was absurd. She would rather spend the rest of her life in solitary than go through another bad relationship. Not to mention the extreme magnetism between herself and Tanner. It was mysterious and completely inexplicable.

~

"I'm glad I work for a large corporation where I am a peon," Margo said.

"You're not a peon, Margo. You bust your ass and hold an executive position with your company." Caylen reminded her.

"Yes, but we, or rather I, wasn't invited to the Almighty Conference." She raised her voice slightly at the end.

"Would you like to go in my place?" Caylen suggested.

"Hell, no. You go kiss the mayor's ass and get drunk with the rich and famous of the city. Once again, I'm glad I'm not going."

"Suit yourself, I'll deal with a rubber-chicken dinner and free booze all evening. Uncle Herb is my date so it's not like I'll get into any trouble."

"What time is he picking you up?"

"Six thirty. The thing starts at seven."

"Good luck and have fun. Hey, you never know who you'll meet."

"I've been going to this for a few years now and the same lame ass people are always there," Caylen said, rolling her eyes at the cell phone lying on her bed with the speaker button on as she wiggled into the black jacket of her tailored pants suit. The baby blue colored blouse she was wearing made her eyes look like the color of the sky on a clear summer afternoon.

"Was that the doorbell?" Margo said.

"Yeah, gotta go. I'll call you tomorrow. Maybe we can do brunch or something. I'll give you the entire scoop."

"Have fun."

Caylen rolled her shoulders back to relax the tension as she hung up the phone. She hated going to events like this. She'd much rather kiss a client's ass in a stale smoky bar.

~

Herbert Jarrett was standing next to his overly priced car, waiting for his niece. Caylen had only been in the car a few times and honestly couldn't say what the make or model was, but she was sure it cost as much or more than the Bentley she had.

"I figured you'd be in some kind of slinky dress and I'd have to beat them men off of you all night." He grinned.

Caylen usually did dress up for this occasion, but an actual dress was out of the question and tonight she felt like just being comfortable.

"What's wrong with a business suit?" She asked with a raised eyebrow.

"Nothing." He smiled, holding the door for her.

They pulled up at the valet booth a little before seven o'clock and slipped inside without being recognized. They were seated at a round table close to the dance floor with the owner of a large hotel chain and his business partner, along with both of their wives.

An hour later, the mayor said his speech as they picked around their stale dinners. Caylen was glad to see the catering staff picking up the plates which signaled the band to start up and the bar to finally open. She had a few glasses of wine with dinner and now she craved hard liquor to float her through the rest of the night. Why not?

She wasn't driving.

"What are you drinking?" The young woman behind the bar asked Caylen with a lingering smile.

"Whiskey on the rocks. Bourbon if you have it."

"Sounds good. I'll make that two." Herb stepped up next to her.

Caylen took the time to glance around the room as she sipped the smooth liquor. She almost dropped the glass when she saw Tanner headed straight for her with an ear to ear smile. The man next to her was walking rather close and it appeared as if they were there together. Caylen wanted to puke up her cardboard dinner.

"Good evening, you're with Jarrett Financial aren't you?" The tall man asked. His black hair looked like it was wet and possibly slicked back. His dark eyes were barely a shade lighter than his hair.

"Yes, I'm Herbert Jarrett and this is Caylen Jarrett." Herb shook the man's hand first.

"I'm Kevin Lomberto with Intelitech Communications. We've spoken on the phone."

"Oh yes, it's nice to put a face with a voice." Herb smiled. "Caylen, this is the company I was telling you about last week."

"Yes, I remember." She and her uncle decided to update their software and he was in charge of researching companies since she was entirely too busy actually running their company. She knew he was slowly handing the reins over to her. She figured he'd retire in another two or three years so she took every opportunity to handle things on her own. She didn't however, remember him mentioning Intelitech. *Shit.*

"This is Tanner Bryce. She's the head of our technical department," he said, leaning closer to Tanner.

"It's nice to meet you, Ms. Bryce." Herb shook her hand.

"It's good to see you again, C.J." Tanner stuck her hand out. She was wearing a low cut, black silk dress with spaghetti straps. The panic lights lit up in Caylen's head. Tanner was standing there, smiling at her like she was the only woman in the room and still holding her hand out. Caylen shook the thoughts from her head and returned the handshake.

"We're old friends," Caylen said to her uncle when he gave her an odd look. "How are you, Tanner?"

"Good," Tanner said as they shared a secret moment when their skin touched, setting off a tiny bolt of electricity between them.

"So," Caylen tried to play it off. "You'll have to excuse my ignorance, I've been in and out of town a lot lately and Herbert has been taking care of the software upgrade. When are we set to change over?"

"Monday I'll have a tech come in to hook up the links. I'll download and update your software remotely." Tanner said.

"I see."

"Caylen you will be their direct contact during the change over." Herb said. Caylen raised an eyebrow, but didn't say anything.

"May I bring you another round?" Tanner asked when she noticed Caylen was holding an empty glass of ice.

"Oh…uh…sure." Caylen didn't want to walk away with her, out of fear and nervousness, but she did it anyway.

"How have you been?" Tanner asked.

Caylen chanced a look into the gray eyes staring back at her. *God, does she have to look at me like that right here?* "Not bad, working a lot."

"I know how that is. I haven't worked less than sixty hours since I started. Hopefully things will slow down this month though. We're finally getting caught up."

Tanner ordered a dirty martini for herself and the bartender had Caylen's glass of bourbon already waiting for her. Tanner flashed a grin when she saw the exchange between Caylen and the young bartender.

"Well then."

"What?" Caylen asked sipping her drink.

"There are two hundred people in this room and she remembered your drink, plus made sure you noticed her taking inventory of your parts."

"Jealous?" Caylen asked. She wasn't sure going down the road of flirtation was a good idea. Tanner Bryce was dangerous and didn't have to push any buttons. They were permanently held down when she was around.

"Maybe." Tanner winked. "Are you still seeing that girl?" She sipped her martini, never faltering from their shared gaze. Caylen couldn't lie to her no matter how hard she tried.

"No. We were better off friends. I don't think I'm the dating type." *Stop looking at me like you're fucking me with your mind.*

"I see."

The DJ played a good fast song and Caylen felt her foot begin to tap the floor. She was not about to ask Tanner to dance with her. She wouldn't be able to hold it together long enough. She still couldn't understand why this one woman had so much power over her. Besides, Tanner was still 'in the closet', so she wouldn't dance anyway.

"Your boss is coming this way. He looked pretty close

to you earlier."

"Jealous?" Tanner raised an eyebrow.

Caylen never batted an eye. "No. I don't compete with men."

"Good, because I don't sleep with them. As a matter of fact, I don't just sleep with anybody, Caylen."

"I don't either."

"Hello ladies," He said walking up a little too close to Tanner as he slid his hand into the small of her back. "Ms. Jarrett, if you will excuse us, I have a few other clients that I'd like to introduce Ms. Bryce to."

"No, please, have a good night."

Tanner winked at her as she was whisked away. Caylen wanted to rip his hand off and shove it down his throat until he choked on it. *Where the hell did that come from?* She shook her head and downed the rest of her glass. Herb was across the room talking to the mayor so Caylen ordered another drink and made her way over to the two men.

The bartender slipped her a napkin with her drink this time. Caylen winked and slid it into her pocket when she noticed the phone number written in the middle. A night of noncommittal sex with the young bartender was at the top of her list at this point. The fact that she was on her third glass of bourbon after drinking two glasses of wine at dinner probably helped that idea along. Luckily, she had snatched her name tag off early so the bartender had no clue who she was. Her buzz was humming along and her night had taken a decent turn.

"There you are," Herb said as Caylen joined their conversation. She smiled and fell right in step.

An hour and a half later, the party had dwindled and the bar was closing for the night. Caylen was on her way back over to the bar when Tanner caught up to her.

"You're not taking little Miss Teen USA home with you, are you?"

"What's it to you?"

"What happened to 'I don't just sleep with anybody'?"

"Nothing. I don't, but I'm also not looking for a relationship right now. Why the hell am I explaining myself to you? We aren't dating." Caylen walked away from her. She saw the hurt in Tanner's eyes and felt the pain tear through her heart. She took a deep breath and turned around, but Tanner was already gone. *God damn it!* Caylen straightened her shoulders and made her way around the bar.

"Hi." The young woman with light brown eyes and long blond hair smiled.

"When can you get out of here?" Caylen asked.

"Now." She tossed the towel on the bar and led the way towards the door. Caylen didn't see Tanner watching her, but she did catch her uncle staring. She waved at him and kept walking behind the young girl. She could barely take her eyes off of the tight ass in front of her. The woman was about two inches shorter and had a nice athletic build on her petite frame.

"What's your name?" the young woman asked.

"C.J. Yours?"

"Amanda."

"How old are you?" Caylen asked.

"Twenty-one." She smiled stepping closer to Caylen. "Would you like to see my ID?"

"No." Caylen smiled and tilted her head down. Their lips met questioningly at first, then they eagerly explored each other. Caylen pulled away. "Did you drive here?"

"Yeah."

213

"Good. Do you live close by?"

"Uh huh." Amanda linked hands with Caylen and led her to a brand new looking Toyota Camry.

Ten minutes later, they were walking into a small apartment in the middle of the city. Caylen shed her jacket, laying it on the arm of the chair. The small apartment had one bedroom and one bathroom with very eclectic and colorful furniture. Amanda was definitely a college student. Caylen noticed the laptop on the small dining room table next to a couple of text books. Caylen wasn't about to break her rule. She never asked more than a name, except for an age in this circumstance. She was a little nervous. Until now, Tanner was the youngest girl she'd ever been with.

Amanda wasted no time. She began unbuttoning Caylen's blouse as their lips met once again with their tongues exploring the crevices of each other's mouth. Caylen picked the smaller woman up against her. Amanda wrapped her legs around Caylen and threaded her hands into Caylen's hair. Caylen put Amanda against the wall. Her insides were burning and her clit was throbbing. She was soaking wet and ready, but something in the back of her mind said stop. That's when Tanner's face popped into her head along with her hurt filled sad eyes. Caylen squeezed her eyes shut and tried to force the image from her head. *Damn it!* She couldn't take it any longer. Caylen set Amanda back on her feet and pulled away from her.

"What's wrong?"

"I can't do this. I'm sorry." Caylen began buttoning her shirt back up.

"I thought you wanted this?" Amanda asked.

"I did. I'm really sorry. I have to go." Caylen walked out the front door with her shirt half buttoned holding her jacket over her arm. She ran a shaking hand through her hair and dialed a familiar number on her cell phone. The call was answered on the second ring.

"C.J.? What the hell? It's one in the morning. Are you okay?" Margo was half asleep.

"Can you come get me?"

"Uh...what...yeah...where are you? What's going on?" Margo stumbled out of bed towards the dresser.

"I'm at the entrance to Windsor Apartment complex off of North Fairview. Take the 101. I'll explain when you get here. Hurry up." Caylen closed her phone and sat on a bus stop bench. She was still keyed up; her mind was racing a hundred miles an hour in fifty directions. She barely noticed the car pulling to a stop in front of her. She looked completely disheveled. Her shirt was loose and only buttoned halfway and her jacket was laying in a heap next to her.

"What the hell happened to you?" Margo said jumping out of the car.

"Don't ask," Caylen said as she slid into the front seat of the Lexus sedan.

Margo looked at her with raised eyebrows as she pulled away from the curb. Caylen threw her head back against the headrest and sighed.

"I don't even know where to start."

"How about the beginning?"

"Tanner was at the convention."

"Okay? Was that her apartment you were in?"

"No."

"Now I'm really confused. Spit it out, Caylen." Margo handed Caylen the extra cup of coffee that she'd brought with her. Caylen took it and looked at her wide eyed. In all of their years as friends, the only time Margo ever called her by her first name was when she was being straight forward and serious or pissed off at her. Both of which rarely happened. Caylen took a few long swallows of the hot coffee and felt her body relax slightly. That's when she realized the radio was playing Milli Vanilli. She busted out laughing.

"What the fuck are you listening to?" She bobbed her head with the beat.

Margo slammed the radio off quickly. "XM weird ass station. Don't change the subject."

"Fine." Caylen finished the coffee and desperately wished another cup would miraculously appear. "I talked to Tanner. Uncle Herb hired her company to do our software upgrade. I've been so busy that I just agreed to what he was telling me. I had no idea it was Intelitech that he chose. Anyway, her boss was a little too friendly with her. That was odd to watch."

"Hmm…okay so why did I just pick you up from the ghetto?"

"I went home with the hot little bartender, who is a twenty-one year old college student." Caylen hung her head.

"Oh my God, C.J. What the fuck were you thinking?" Margo swerved to make the turn that she just about drove past.

"I don't know. Don't wreck the damn car." She put her head in her hands. "She was cute and flirting with me all night and Tanner was there and I can't get her out of my damn head!"

"Wow, so you decided to fuck a college kid? This isn't like you. I mean random women I understand, but usually they are out of diapers."

"I didn't sleep with her. I stopped myself."

"Well, I guess that's a good thing. What the hell is going on with you and Tanner? Who, by the way, I still haven't met yet."

"Nothing! That's just it. But, she has this power over me. Anytime I'm around her I feel like my insides are going to explode. I'm scared to death of her, Margo. I don't know what the fuck to do."

"I think you're in love with her," Margo said as she pulled up in front of Caylen's condo and cut the engine.

"You're crazy!" Caylen practically fell out of the car, she got out so fast. "I don't, I can't fall in love with anyone. I'm never going through that again. No way." Caylen was shaking her head back and forth and her normally pale blue eyes were dark and large.

"I'm not saying you have to marry the girl, but why don't you try dating her? I seriously doubt she's here to stalk you."

Caylen took a deep breath but it didn't help. She dropped her keys when she fumbled with the door. "Damn it!" She picked them up and finally succeeded in opening the door. "How do you date the one person that you hoped to never see again? Margo, that night with her was the one and only time I have ever really made love to anyone. It was too perfect. How do I compete with that? Dating her will only turn my angel-like dream to dust when reality sets in. Do you know what I mean?" Caylen tossed her jacket on the stair rail and made her way over to the liquor cabinet. *No more alcohol.* She told herself as she kept going into the kitchen to put on a pot of coffee. There was no way in hell she was going to sleep any time soon.

"I think I understand what you're saying. You're afraid that the pedestal that you put that night on will disappear when you move past it? Am I right so far?"

"I think so. The person that I was that night isn't me. I've never felt or even seen that side of myself. It seemed to be the same way for her too. I just don't want to lose that one perfect time in my life."

Margo completely understood why Caylen was so scared. She would never let herself love anyone because of fear that they wouldn't love *her*. That one night stand showed her the passion and love that she dreamed of and now having the woman as a reality in her life made the dream seem fake somehow. No wonder she was confused.

"I'm sure she doesn't even know about the battle you have going on in your head."

"Nope." Caylen padded up the stairs to her loft bedroom to change into a pair of loose pajama pants and a t-shirt. Margo had their coffee waiting when she returned.

"Maybe it's time to let go of flirting and fucking with no strings. I haven't met this girl," Margo reiterated for the tenth time. "But she seems to have abducted my best friend's heart without her even knowing it."

"I can't believe I was going to sleep with some college kid tonight. God, maybe I need help." Caylen leaned against the back of the couch and closed her eyes.

"No, you need to talk to this woman and let yourself be happy for once in your life."

"I have to work with her on Monday and probably Tuesday."

"What?"

"They are installing that new software in our system and Uncle Herb put me in charge. I think he's going to retire in a couple of years. He's been acting weird lately. Plus, I could swear he was pushing me and her together tonight. If he only knew."

"Hmm…at least he got to meet her."

218

"Oh give it a rest already." Caylen smiled.

"So, will she be at your office or…"

"No, but I'll be on the phone with her throughout the entire process."

"Did she see you leave with the teeny bopper?"

"Yeah." Margo smacked her hard on the thigh. "Ouch!"

"You dummy."

"I wasn't thinking clearly. I'd drank way too much. My mind was racing and my libido was on fire. Cut me some slack. Uncle Herb saw me leave with her too. I'm sure he'll be on my ass Monday anyway."

"I suggest you take the rest of this weekend off. Don't think about Tanner or JFC for a whole two days. Monday, you'll be well rested and ready to hit the ground running."

"Uh huh, what the hell did you put in your coffee?" Caylen raised an eyebrow. "I haven't stopped thinking about her since the day she walked into my office. I practically had to beat the men off of her. I don't know how I held it together while I had a regular conversation with her."

"Take it slow. Don't be alone with her for a while. Go to dinner, go to the movies, go to the bar, whatever you have to do. I think you should step back and get to know *her*."

"Easier said than done. I trip over myself around her. I'm thirty-three goddamn years old and I'm scared to have a relationship with a woman I find perfect in every way. What the hell is wrong with me?"

"You have a lot to protect, C.J. Don't beat yourself up over this."

"Could you imagine if Uncle Herb found out she was a dancer? Shit would hit the fan. I'm in line to head up that company in probably a year or two and I don't need some kind of scandal."

"I'm sure she doesn't want the world to know how she paid for college either. It's a secret only the two of you know about, am I right?"

"I think so."

"Then forget about it. She has a great career going for her and she's independent. She sounds like the perfect mate. If I had met her, I could give you more details." Margo ducked when Caylen swatted her with a throw pillow from the couch.

"Hey, I forgot to tell you, I bought the basketball tickets the other day."

"How many games?"

"They're weekend home games, I think two or three."

"Cool. Email me the dates. Nice change of subject by the way."

"I was due for one," Caylen laughed.

Eleven

"Ms. Jarrett, you have a call on line one," Sara's voice announced over the intercom. Caylen saved the spreadsheet she was putting together on her laptop and picked up the receiver to the phone on her desk.

"Caylen Jarrett."

"This is Tanner Bryce with Intelitech Communications. My technician arrived an hour ago and he has your router hooked up. I need to test the line."

Caylen caught onto Tanner's cold voice. *She's clearly upset with me. I'm such a fool.* "That's fine, go ahead and do what you need to do. We have our system off line until two o'clock this afternoon so that we are able to get this upgrade completed smoothly."

Caylen stayed on the line and waited for the line test and the initial start up of the software. A few minutes later, Tanner came back on the line.

"Ms. Jarrett, I'm going to reboot your system remotely so you may see your computer act a little funny for a minute or two."

"Okay." Caylen listened to Tina Turner on the hold music. She was singing along to *Freeway of Love* when Tanner came back on the line.

"Excuse me?" Tanner asked.

221

"Sorry, you caught me singing karaoke to your hold music." Caylen laughed. "Anyway, you were saying?"

"Oh, yes, you should be booted back up and ready to go. The technician left help manuals for everyone in the office with my direct line on all of them. Please have anyone call me if they experience even the smallest problem. This software parallels the one that we upgraded you from so there shouldn't be too many difficulties with it."

"Thanks," Caylen said.

"No problem. You have a good day, Ms. Jarrett."

Caylen heard her about to hang up. "Tanner?"

"Yes?"

"Are you upset with me?" She paused. "No, wait, that's a stupid question. I'm sorry."

"Don't be, it's your life, C.J. and you're free to live it however you choose."

"I didn't sleep with her."

"Who are we talking about? The high school looking bartender that you left with? Or the others that are waiting in line?"

Ouch. "No one. I haven't slept with anyone since I was with you."

"Somehow I doubt that. Look, I'm really busy here. I have two other businesses that I need to get up and running today."

"Are you free for dinner tomorrow night?"

Tanner sighed. "As far as I know I am."

"Do you want to meet me somewhere or may I pick you up?" Caylen held her breath until Tanner said her address.

~

Tuesday afternoon Caylen rushed around trying to finish her day early so that she had enough time to run home and change clothes before picking Tanner up for dinner. Herbert asked her to stop by his office when she had a free minute. None of which she actually had at this point, but she made time to see what he wanted. She was surprised he hadn't bothered her the day before.

Caylen walked in and shut the door. She unbuttoned her dark gray jacket and sat in the soft leather chair in front of his desk. Her uncle was scribbling a few notes in the margins of a report he had lying on his desk.

"How's your day going?" He asked as he tossed the pen on the desk and sat back in his chair.

"Hectic, the new software seems to be holding up to the task, so far."

"That's good. It's about time we updated that old system."

"Yeah, I didn't realize it until I started using the new one. I think I gained an extra hour." She knew he was beating around the bush and she danced the tango right along with him.

"I take it you had a nice time Friday night?" He looked her square in the eyes. She felt goose bumps on her arms. He reminded her so much of her father at that moment.

"Actually, I did have a nice time at the conference. I can't say I did after that. My weekend was spent loathing myself." *At least I'm being honest. I shouldn't have to talk to my uncle about my sex life!*

"And the cause of that would be the very young bartender?"

"She wasn't *that* young."

"Looked to me like she was half your age."

"Geez you make me sound like a dinosaur. And no, I wasn't loathing myself because of her. I called Margo to come get me as soon as we reached her apartment. That was a mistake and I caught myself before I made it worse."

"I see. So why the loathing?"

"It's a very long story and I would rather keep it to myself if you don't mind."

"Well, I respect your privacy as your business partner, but as your uncle you know I have to look out for you."

"I know and I love you for it, Uncle Herb, but I'm fine. I'm thirty-three years old and mom babies me enough." She smiled, hoping she didn't come off as an asshole.

"I'm sure she does. And I know how old you are, that's why it concerned me to see you leaving with such a young girl. You know we all want to see you settle down instead of changing women like you change your underwear."

She wasn't sure what to say to that. Had he really been keeping tabs on her sex life? Just the thought of it grossed her out. Besides, she had really slowed down her dating habits over the last few years. "Trust me, I'm fine. I've just had a lot going on lately. And as I said before, I did not go home with the young woman. Well I did, but I left as soon as I got there." *God, if he only knew how bad I wanted a piece of that, he'd understand how hard it was for me to leave. But, as much as I wanted it, I knew it was wrong, especially when she wasn't even the one I was thinking of.*

"Alright. Go on, get out of here." He smiled. "I'll see you in the morning. And by the way, I didn't tell Aunt Viv anything about last Friday. Just so you know your dirty laundry is your own for the moment."

She smiled. "Thanks."

~

Herbert left Caylen with just enough time to rush into her condo and change. She tossed her suit on her bed and slipped into jeans, a tight white polo shirt, and brown Doc Martens. She was back in the Bentley and heading into town within fifteen minutes. She was praying there wasn't a traffic jam on the 101 when she got on the interstate on ramp. She glanced at herself in the mirror. Her pale blue eyes were staring back at her. Her hair was starting to look unruly since it was two weeks overdue for a cut, but the spiky mess still looked sexy as hell. Or at least that what she was always told when she thought she was in need of a serious haircut.

Fifteen minutes later Caylen pulled up in front of the nicest apartment complex she'd ever seen. There was a colorful waterfall in the large pond on the left and the buildings looked like they belonged in another country. She followed the numbers until she came to building fourteen. Caylen parked next to a convertible Mercedes. She was actually impressed. Most of the cars in the community were expensive. Caylen wondered why the residents were pissing away their money in an apartment when they could have a condo or a house.

"Are you always this punctual?" Tanner asked when she opened the door.

"No, I'm usually early but I was at the office later than usual and I live on the beach so I was stuck in traffic coming and going." Caylen met Tanner's gorgeous gray eyes then gave her a quick once over. Tanner was wearing jeans, a low cut black top that showed off her round breasts and muscular physique, and black leather boots

225

that gave her an extra inch of height which put her even with Caylen. Her thick wavy hair hung down her back and around one of her shoulders.

Their eyes met softly.

"You have the sexiest eyes I have ever seen." Tanner's voice was almost a whisper. "I love the way you look at me."

"You're very beautiful, Tanner. It's hard for me not to look at you." Both women blushed. Caylen cleared her throat and opted for a safer conversation. "So, are you going to make me stand in the doorway or do I get a tour?" She held her breath and smiled. All she wanted to do was gather Tanner in her arms and kiss her slowly until their bodies melted together.

"Well," Tanner turned around and spread her arms wide. "This is the living room." She continued throughout the two bedroom apartment. The carpet was a shade darker than white which matched her beige leather couch and love seat perfectly. The entertainment center and tables were washed oak and glass. The spare bathroom was decorated in mauve and hunter green and was actually more spacious than Caylen thought it would be. The spare bedroom was turned into an office.

"Off limits?" Caylen teased when she saw the master bedroom door closed.

"Only if you want it to be." Tanner smiled opening the door. The queen sized bed and matching dark wood furniture took up most of the room. The bathroom was decorated in various shades of blue. Caylen raised an eyebrow when she noticed every decoration including the towels were all a different shade of blue.

"I tried to match your eyes," Tanner said.

Honesty was all she saw on Tanner's face. Caylen was

flattered. "Did you match it?"

"Yes. Your eyes lighten or darken with the changes of your mood. So, I have seen all of these shades."

"I see." Caylen glanced at the clock on the night stand. "We should probably get going." *Before I lay you down on that bed and kiss every inch of your body until you beg me to make you come.*

~

Tanner was still highly impressed when she saw Caylen's car. Of course, she remembered the reason she drove such a lavish car to begin with. Tanner was equally impressed with the upscale restaurant. She felt underdressed as they walked inside.

"Good evening, Ms. Jarrett, we have your table ready for you." The host who was dressed in a full tuxedo walked them to the back of the room where smaller, more secluded tables were. They were seated in the corner almost completely alone.

"Thank you, Max." Caylen smiled.

"I've heard of this place, but I've never been here. I wish I had known this was where you were taking me," Tanner said as she opened the menu.

"Why?"

"Because I would've worn something different."

"Are you comfortable?"

"Yes."

"Good, because you could be wearing rags held together with duct tape and you'd still be the most naturally beautiful woman in here."

Tanner raised an eyebrow and smiled shyly. "You're too sweet."

"I'm just honest, too damn honest for my own good sometimes." Caylen laughed.

~

Two hours later, Tanner and Caylen were standing outside, waiting for the valet to bring the Bentley around. They'd shared a bottle of wine as well as each other's dinner. Caylen learned more about Tanner's childhood. She was an only child in a middle class family, the only athlete of any kind, and the first person to go to college. Her parents had no idea she moonlighted as a stripper to pay for school. They thought she worked as a bartender and a waitress.

"Dinner was wonderful. We should come back here again sometime," Tanner said as she slid into the gray leather seat of the car.

Caylen agreed with her and smiled. She couldn't get past the never-ending urge to kiss Tanner passionately. It didn't matter where they were or what they were doing. Hell, the conversation they were having didn't even matter. Caylen wanted her and her mind was having a hard time telling her body no.

The rest of the ride back to Tanner's apartment was filled with light conversation about work until Tanner brought up the conference and the bartender. Caylen danced around the subject avoiding confrontation at all costs.

"Hey, are you a basketball fan?" Caylen asked when she parked in front of the stairs leading to Tanner's apartment.

"Uh...I guess. Why?" Tanner turned to face Caylen.

"Well, my best friend and I get together and go to a

few of the UCSB games since we're both Alumni. Anyway, tomorrow night they are playing Houston and I thought maybe you'd like to go since you went there." Caylen watched the smile grow on Tanner's face as her eyes sparkled in the moonlight.

"Oh I see, a rival night huh. Sure, I'd love to go. Is your friend going?"

"Yeah, she's dying to meet you so I figured I'd kill two birds with one stone."

"I'm looking forward to meeting someone close to you." Tanner grabbed Caylen's hand, their fingers interlacing together naturally. "I had a nice time with you tonight."

"So did I. I'll pick you up at five thirty tomorrow if that's okay."

"Sure."

Caylen fought every nerve in her body and leaned closer to press her lips softly against Tanner's. The kiss was short and sweet. Tanner was gone before Caylen let out the breath she was holding. *My god, if I don't get this under control I'm going to explode!* She knew she was left wet and wanting, but it wasn't Tanner's fault. Caylen hadn't tried to go any further. In fact, she was taking things very slow. The change in pace was killing her, especially around this woman who seemed to have every one of her nerve endings on overdrive. Caylen ran a hand through her hair and sighed as she drove off.

Twelve

Caylen spent most of the day Saturday cleaning her condo. It was a little dusty from her working so much, but other than that it looked like a show home that was unoccupied.

By four o'clock she had showered and was listening to Elton John on the radio as she threw on a pair of jeans and a white UCSB t-shirt with the Gaucho logo on the front and back. She bobbed her head and sang along to *Goodbye Yellow Brick Road* as she stepped into a pair of sneakers. She almost missed her cell phone ringing because of the radio blaring and her singing on top of it. Not to mention the phone was downstairs on the island in the kitchen, but in her loft she could look over the rail and see half of the living room and part of the open kitchen. She ran down to answer it.

"Hello?"

"Hey, what time are you picking Tanner up?" Margo asked.

"I'm about to leave, why?"

"Okay, I should be there about the same time then. I had to make a pit stop."

"A good pit stop or a bad pit stop?" Caylen asked as she locked the condo door behind herself and meandered towards her Bentley.

"Good. What station are you listening to?" Margo could hear *Crocodile Rock* playing on the radio when Caylen started the car.

"It's a CD. The funny thing is, I was just listening to Elton John in the house on the TV." Caylen laughed and began singing along as she drove towards Tanner's apartment.

"Hmm…someone's in a good mood."

"My nerves are about to short circuit," Caylen said honestly. She was nervous about Margo and Tanner meeting, but she was even more nervous about spending more time with Tanner.

"Take a deep breath and go pick your date up. I'll see you soon."

~

Caylen wasn't prepared for the sight she saw when the door opened. Tanner was standing in front of her in jeans and a tight white tank top with the Houston logo across her firm round breasts. Her wavy, chocolate brown hair was falling over her shoulders and down her back, as usual. The firm definition in her arms reminded Caylen of how soft that hard body actually felt wrapped around her, she knew she was sweating and hoped it wasn't obvious. Tanner was smiling at her when she looked back at her eyes.

"Close your mouth before you start catching flies." Tanner giggled.

"I…uh…what?" Caylen was embarrassed for being caught looking at her like a deer in the headlights with a hard-on. "I'm sorry. I can't get over how attractive you are.

It's very hard for me to keep my hands off of you." *Shut up before you go way too far.*

Tanner stepped forward and kissed Caylen's lips softly. Their mouths parted easily to allow their tongues to explore each other. Someone moaned into the kiss as it deepened. Caylen finally pulled herself away breathlessly. She could see the desire dancing in Tanner's gray eyes. She fought her body to keep a safe distance.

"We...uh...we'll be late...if we don't leave now."

~

Caylen was still flustered when she saw Margo heading their way. *Please don't let her notice, and dear God, don't let her embarrass me!* Tanner stood next to Caylen in the will call ticket line.

"Hey, I beat you here so I grabbed all of the tickets." Margo said.

"We hit traffic." Caylen lied and Tanner smiled as they stepped out of line. "Margo, this is Tanner Bryce. Tanner, this is Margo Cunni...uh...Cannestopoulis." Caylen chided herself for almost letting Margo's nickname slip out. She had called her Margo 'Cunnilingus' since the day she learned her last name. Margo caught the semi-Freudian slip and rolled her eyes with a half smile.

"It's nice to meet you, Tanner. I've heard a lot about you." Margo shook her hand and mentally took inventory of her gorgeous features when she wasn't looking.

"I hope it was all good." Tanner looked at Caylen and smiled.

~

The game kept them on their toes right up until the final buzzer. The UCSB Gaucho's won by a three point shot during the final seconds. Margo, Tanner and Caylen ate a couple of pretzels and chased them with whatever domestic beer the stadium had on tap. Caylen was glad to see Margo and Tanner getting along and talking during the game. Margo gave her a wink and nod in approval of Tanner; Caylen shook her head and smiled. They were on their way out of the stadium when a young woman stepped in front of Caylen. She was dressed in jeans and a UCSB t-shirt, her blond hair was up in a ponytail making her look even younger.

"Hey stranger," The woman spoke, completely ignoring Tanner and Margo.

Shit! Caylen recognized Amanda the bartender. *What the hell was I thinking? Way too much alcohol was involved in that decision.* "Uh...hi, Amanda, is it? How are you?"

"Good. I'm surprised to see you here," the blond said.

"I'm Gaucho Alumni," Caylen said, smiling proudly. "I try to make it to some of the games when I can." Caylen heard Margo clear her throat in attempt to pull Caylen away. "Oh, I'm sorry. Amanda, this is Tanner," she said as Tanner stepped up, lacing her fingers with Caylen's. "And Margo," Caylen finished.

"It's nice to meet you both," Amanda said, ignoring the brunette holding Caylen's hand.

"We should probably get going," Caylen said.

"It was nice to see you again. Give me a call sometime." Amanda winked.

As soon as they were away from her, Tanner let go of Caylen's hand. Margo raised an eyebrow and gave Caylen a stern look.

"That's the bartender from the convention," Caylen said sheepishly.

"Oh my God! C.J., she's barely eighteen!" Margo shook her head.

"She's twenty-one and I didn't do anything with her, or did you forget?"

"No, I remember coming out here in the middle of the night to rescue your ass." Tanner ignored the conversation as they walked toward the parking lot.

"I think we all need a change of scenery. How about *One Up*?" Margo said.

"What's that?" Tanner asked joining the conversation.

"A straight bar that caters to a lot of lesbians," Caylen answered.

"Hmm...I haven't been to any bars since I moved here. I barely have time to do my laundry and clean my apartment before Monday is here and I'm back at work."

"Tanner, you sound just like C.J. Did you two ride on the same spaceship to Earth or what?" Margo laughed.

"Bite me, Cunni." Caylen grinned raising an eyebrow at Margo. "We can go if you'd like," Caylen said to Tanner.

"Sure," Tanner said with a shrug.

As soon as Tanner and Caylen were in the car, Caylen turned towards her. "I'm sorry we ran into her. I hope you believe me when I say I really made a mistake that night. I couldn't...hell I still can't, get you out of my head and I almost did something really stupid."

"It's okay. I'm not going to say I wasn't upset when I saw you leave with her. I don't know how to compete with a college kid."

"You don't have to, trust me. Tanner, I don't even know how old you are, but I'm sure you are the youngest woman I have ever been with or ever want to be with. Most of the women I have dated have been my age or actually older."

"I'm about to turn twenty-six next week." Tanner said.

"Wow, you are definitely the youngest, by far." Caylen let out a deep breath. "I actually thought you were younger though."

"How old are you, C.J.?" Tanner figured she was maybe twenty-eight.

"Thirty-three."

"Really?"

"I don't like to be referred to as a 'dinosaur' so watch your comments." Caylen teased.

"Ha ha, your one sexy dinosaur!" Tanner leaned across the console and kissed her softly, letting her lips linger before she pulled away. "I like you a lot, Caylen, and I'm willing to do whatever it takes to make you believe that. I felt something the night I was with you, a powerful connection that I have never felt in my entire life. I know you've dated a lot of people and you don't settle down. I won't say I haven't dated a good number of people too, but I'd like to see where this goes. I would be stupid to let the most amazing thing that has ever happened to me get away without fighting for it." Tanner's eyes couldn't tell a lie. Caylen felt like climbing into the backseat with her.

"I'm still getting used to the fact that you are *you*. Do you know what I mean?" Caylen said.

"Yes," Tanner sighed. Sometimes she wished she hadn't met Caylen when she was dancing, maybe things would different between them now.

"You're right, I don't settle down, Tanner. There's a lot about me that you don't know. I'm taking this slow for a number of reasons; the main one being my overpowering attraction to you. I don't think you realize how hard it is for me to sit this close to you and not touch you. Hell, I have a hard time just talking to you on the phone."

Tanner smiled. "I feel the same way."

Caylen breathed a sigh of relief as she started the car and drove towards the bar. "I'm glad we have all of that straightened out." *We barely scraped the surface. What the hell am I saying?*

Thirteen

"It's about time you guys got here. I thought you were leaving right behind me?" Margo said from her position at the high top table she was sitting at.

"We had a slight distraction," Caylen said with a smile. Tanner grinned and turned her head.

"I ordered a bucket of beer," Margo said as the waitress set the bucket on the table.

"That's fine." Caylen looked at Tanner who sat on the stool next to her. "We don't drink draft beer."

Tanner smiled. "Good, me neither, unless I absolutely have to."

"Yeah, that's what sucks about the basketball stadium. They need to invest in those new plastic bottles or something. Draft beer tastes like rusty ass metal pipes." Margo scrunched her nose. "Hey look, C.J., your favorite karaoke singer is here tonight."

"Oh God, please tell me she's not singing." Caylen met Tanner's questioning eyes and raised eyebrow. "That redhead over there can't carry a tune in a fucking bucket and she sings at least five or six songs." Caylen shook her head. "Drives me nuts. Sometimes, I go outside just to keep from putting my fingers in my ears." Tanner laughed hysterically. "I promise I'm not usually a mean person, but

237

come on, someone needs to step up and tell her to listen to herself some time," Caylen said.

"Maybe she has no friends," Margo added.

"Now who's being mean?" Caylen looked at her with a raised eyebrow.

"Touché." Margo raised her beer to her mouth. "Besides, there's no karaoke tonight, just the DJ."

"Thank God," Caylen laughed.

The women listened to the music as the dance floor filled up in front of them. Tanner ran her hand over Caylen's, interlocking their fingers before reaching for a beer.

Caylen felt a tug on her heart strings as she watched the low lighting of the bar play across Tanners eyes when she smiled. Her mind drifted back to that night in the hotel as it often did when she was around Tanner. Walking out of that room was the easiest and hardest thing she'd ever done in her life. A one night stand wasn't supposed to be complicated and it wasn't supposed to repeat itself. It was easy to say goodbye knowing she gave everything to the stranger in that bed and would never see her again, but it was hard knowing, for one small instance, she let herself feel love for the first time. She promised to take the memory of that night and keep it with her for the rest of her life as she kissed the stranger's lips one last time.

Watching Tanner sitting next to her in the crowded bar tapping her foot to the music and smiling at something Margo was saying made Caylen's heart ache. She was scared of losing something as precious as a memory, but she could no longer fight the desire she felt for Tanner. Being in love was uncharted territory for Caylen. She stayed away from relationships because she could never trust someone enough to love them in the first place. She wondered if she was strong enough to trust not only Tanner, but herself as well.

"Are you okay?" Tanner asked. She noticed the shadows in Caylen's eyes.

"Yeah," Caylen smiled.

"You looked deep in thought just now."

"I'm fine," Caylen said.

"Hey, look what the cat dragged in," Margo said across the small table.

Caylen turned her head to see Jasmine walking towards them.

"I wondered if I'd see you two here," Jasmine said.

"Margo can't resist cruising the bar." Caylen shrugged. "How have you been?"

"Good," Jasmine said, noticing how close Tanner and Caylen were sitting. She raised an eyebrow. "You?"

Caylen smiled and introduced them.

"You did the right thing," Jasmine said eyeing the way Tanner looked at Caylen. "Take care of yourself," she said before walking away.

"Do I even want to know what that was about?" Tanner asked.

"Do you remember the woman I was dating when you first came to town?" Caylen said.

"Yeah? Was that her?" Tanner asked.

"Yes. We only dated for a few months and never slept together. The night I told her about you, she told me to go after you if that's what I wanted."

"Wow, that's some girlfriend," Tanner said.

"I wouldn't exactly call her a girlfriend," Margo added. "They were more like friends that barely made it to second base."

Caylen laughed. "It's true."

"I know why she stuck around though." Tanner winked with a grin.

"If a woman made me wait three months for sex she had better be God's gift to the clitoris!" Margo said.

Tanner laughed. "Maybe," she teased as her eyes met Caylen's.

"It can be a few hours or a few months. If it's meant to be it will happen at the exact moment that it's supposed to," Caylen said.

Tanner nodded in agreement.

Margo raised an eyebrow. "Since when do you get philosophical when you drink?"

Caylen laughed. "I don't know. My head's in the clouds tonight, I guess."

"Well, come back down to our level please," Margo joked. She had seen the handful of looks that passed between the two women at her table. She knew her best friend better than anyone in the world, but this was a side of Caylen that she didn't think Caylen had ever seen herself.

"Do you want to dance?" Tanner asked.

Caylen shrugged. She wasn't much of a dancer, but she couldn't resist the temptation of feeling Tanner's body against her. She stood with her hand out. Tanner smiled as Caylen led her to the center of the dance floor.

The song wasn't exactly slow, but it wasn't fast either. Tanner placed her arms around Caylen's neck as she stepped into her arms, moving her body slowly against Caylen's to the beat of the music. Caylen wrapped her arms around Tanner's waist, meeting her hips seductively as they danced. Tanner's jeans were slung low on her hips. Caylen's hands slid along the silky smooth skin on her sides and back where her shirt rode up. She ran her hands up Tanner's back, under her shirt, feeling the hard muscles under the soft skin.

"Let's get out of here." Tanner's breath on her neck caused Caylen's knees to weaken. She nodded grabbing Tanner's hand as they walked back to the table.

"We're going to call it a night," Caylen said to Margo.

Margo grinned behind the beer bottle she was sipping. "I'll call you tomorrow," she said.

~

Caylen drove silently through town. She had never wanted anything so bad and she had never been so frightened in all of her life. She didn't need to ask Tanner is she wanted to come home with her. The lazy circles she was tracing with her thumb on the inside of Caylen's right hand said it all.

Caylen parked the car and led Tanner into her condo building. They rode the elevator up to her floor and stepped off into the wide hallway when it stopped. Caylen fumbled her keys trying to get her door open. Tanner grabbed her hands.

"We don't have to do this, Caylen," she said.

Caylen found the right key and opened the door, pulling Tanner inside with her. "Do you have any idea how bad I want you?" Caylen asked, finding her courage as she backed Tanner up against the door.

"If it's as bad as I want you then we're in for a hell of a night," Tanner said, switching positions. She pushed her thigh between Caylen's legs as she kissed her hard.

Caylen bit her lip, tracing her tongue over the sensitive area as she pulled Tanner's shirt over her head, tossing it on the floor followed by her bra.

Shoes were tossed and jeans were pulled down until they found themselves naked on the floor in the foyer. Caylen wasted no time sliding her fingers through Tanner's wetness pushing them deep inside. Tanner's nails were short, but long enough for Caylen to feel them grip the skin of her back as Tanner's hips arched under her.

"God, Caylen...you feel so good," Tanner breathed huskily against Caylen's face.

Caylen moved her lips to Tanner's, opening her mouth with her own and dipping her tongue inside and back out again, matching the rhythm of her thrusting fingers. Tanner reached between them with one hand, massaging Caylen's wet center in lazy circles.

Caylen was already so close. Tanner applied more pressure to the tender spot until she felt Caylen's entire body stiffen on top of her.

"Come with me, baby..." Tanner growled as the explosion tore through her body. Caylen followed right behind her shuddering until her body relaxed. She rolled half onto her side and realized they were on the cold tile floor.

"That was..."

"Not the end," Tanner finished her sentence with a sexy grin. "I hope you have a bed in here somewhere or we're going to have bruises in unexplainable places in the morning."

Caylen smiled and stood up with her hand out to Tanner. They left their clothes all over the floor at the front door as they walked up the spiral staircase to the loft that doubled as Caylen's bedroom. The vertical blinds were open, allowing the light of the full moon to cast a soft glow over the bed.

Tanner followed Caylen onto the soft sheets,

straddling her hips as she lied back. She ran her hands over Caylen's stomach and up her chest to her breasts, massaging them as she rocked her wet center against Caylen's.

"You're so beautiful," Caylen said huskily. Tanner's nude silhouette in the moonlight was the most breathtaking sight she had ever seen.

Tanner smiled as Caylen sat up meeting her lips in a searing kiss. Caylen ran her hands up Tanner's back, feeling the silky strands of hair falling over her hands and down her arms as she ran her tongue over Tanner's lips, dipping it back inside. Tanner moved against her involuntarily and Caylen slowly rolled her onto her back, careful not to break the kiss until she began moving down her body. She ran her tongue in lazy lines down Tanner's torso to her hips, kissing the tender skin of her breasts along the way.

Tanner spread her legs as Caylen moved further settling between them. She couldn't remember ever wanting something so much or having a sensation pass all the way to her core as Caylen's lips and tongue finally touched her. Every nerve ending in her body was on fire.

Caylen licked and sucked softly, taking her time. Tanner writhed under her pushing her hips up. Caylen continued the languid strokes as she ran her hands over Tanner's stomach up to her breasts and back down again. She could feel Tanner's labored breathing when her hands passed over her. She dipped her tongue lower, sliding it inside of her.

"Oh, Caylen..." Tanner moaned quietly running her hand along the side of Caylen's face and into her hair.

Caylen's blue eyes met gray ones in the moonlight. Caylen quickened her pace, giving in to the pleasurable release Tanner was silently asking for. She moved back up hovering over Tanner as she kissed her. Tasting herself on Caylen's lips fueled the fire burning deep inside of her. Tanner pulled Caylen down, rolling on top of her. She mimicked Caylen, placing delicate kisses on her body as she moved down between her legs.

Caylen's breath hitched and caught in her chest when Tanner's mouth made contact with her. Her body was coiled tightly, like a spring, waiting for the right moment to release. She gripped the sheets for some sort of change in direction, but there was no slowing down. She was racing towards the edge faster than she could breath air into her lungs.

Tanner licked circles, dipping inside, before sucking her into her mouth tenderly stroke after stroke. Caylen's hips bucked gently under her.

Caylen cried out as her body shuttered under Tanner.

"You're amazing," Caylen said breathlessly as Tanner crawled back up to her.

Tanner grinned. "So are you," she said, kissing her.

~

Caylen awoke alone and found Tanner standing at the sliding glass doors, looking out at the ocean glistening below them. She walked over to her running her arms around Tanner from behind as she placed her body against Tanner's back. She moved her long, wavy hair to the side, kissing the tender spot behind her ear as she whispered, "What are you thinking?"

Tanner pulled Caylen's arms tightly around her, leaning her head back. "I'm trying not to wake up if I'm dreaming," she said softly. "I've dreamed of this so often, I can't tell the difference between the dream and reality."

"You're not dreaming. Not this time," Caylen said turning Tanner around to face her. She kissed her softly.

"How did I get lucky enough to find you twice in one lifetime?" Tanner asked.

Caylen pushed Tanner's hair back over her shoulder. "Do you believe in soul mates?" she asked.

"Since I met you I believe in a lot of things I don't understand."

"Me too," Caylen said, wrapping her arms around Tanner as she kissed her again. She pulled away slightly, looking into Tanner's gray eyes. "I fell in love with you the night we met." Caylen put her finger on Tanner's lips when she tried to speak. "I've never been in love with anyone and to have it happen so suddenly, and with a stranger, scared me to death, Tanner. When you showed up in my office, I wanted to run to you and run away from you at the same time. Over the past few weeks, I've realized I can't run anymore. Every direction leads right back to you."

"Something happened to me that night, too. I don't think I really knew what it was until I saw you again. I was drawn to you when I danced for you that night. I've never gone home with someone from the bar before or after you. I had to see you again. That's why I looked you up when I was in town. I had to know if you felt the same way," Tanner placed her hand on Caylen's cheek. "Caylen, I love you so much it scares me."

"Good, then we can be scared together for the rest of our lives because I'm never saying goodbye to you again," Caylen said, kissing her once again.

Fourteen

Monday morning, Caylen walked into her office, stretching her sore muscles as she sat down behind her desk. She had more than a full day of work scheduled with multiple conference calls and other mundane tasks to keep her mind from racing back to the weekend she spent with Tanner in her arms. *I'm never going to get any work done with images of her naked body rolling around in my head.*

The ringing cell phone in her pocket brought her back to reality. She retrieved it, smiling when she saw the name on the caller ID.

"Good morning," Caylen said.

"Good morning to you, too. I was just making sure you made it to the office on time," Tanner teased.

Caylen laughed. "I was punctual as always, but that doesn't mean I'm thrilled to be here."

"I didn't exactly want to get out of bed this morning either. I'm sorry I left you last night. It took me two hours to get my laundry done. I was definitely not prepared to be away from home the entire weekend," Tanner said.

"I need to do laundry too, but it looks like I have a long week ahead of me, so who knows when I will get to it. Maybe we should move in together and hire a maid. Then, we can stay in bed all weekend every weekend and she can clean and do the laundry."

"That sounds too good to be true. Besides, if we lived together the excitement of seeing me would wear off," Tanner teased.

"When is your lease up?" Caylen asked seriously.

"Not for another ten months."

"That's way too long," Caylen yelped.

Tanner laughed. "Maybe I can look into subleasing it in a couple months."

"That sounds a hell of a lot better," Caylen said as the intercom on her desk phone buzzed. "I need to go. I have a meeting with my uncle this morning. If I can find a break in my schedule maybe we can meet for lunch."

"That sounds good. I'm pretty busy today too. Good luck with your uncle. I love you," Tanner said.

"How did you know I was going to tell him about you?"

"Educated guess?"

Caylen laughed. "I love you, too," she said before ending the call and pushing the intercom button.

"Good morning, Uncle Herb. Can we meet in your office instead of the conference room?" she asked.

"Sure."

"I'll see you in a minute," she said.

~

Caylen sat across from her uncle at his massive wooden desk. He reminded her so much of her father.

"You look a little tired. Are you feeling okay?" he asked.

"Yeah. I had a long weekend, so I'm a little tired this morning."

247

He nodded. "I was going over the Olsen Manufacturing file this morning..."

"Actually, before we start talking about that, there's something I need to tell you," Caylen said.

"Okay."

"I'm seeing someone. Wait, let me start from the beginning. Do you remember meeting a woman at the convention that worked for Intelitech, Tanner Bryce?"

"Yes, our software programmer?"

"Correct. I told you we were old friends. Well, we actually met when I was in Houston, meeting with Roger Kent."

"Oh really? Was she working for him?"

"Not exactly," Caylen said, adjusting her position in the chair. "I'm telling you all of this because she and I are together. I want you to know the truth in case it ever comes out."

Herb chewed his mustache. "I knew you were acting strange. Is it safe to say you're in love with this woman?"

"Yes. For the first time in my life I'm head over heels in love. She will probably move in with me sometime in the next few months."

"I'm happy for you and your Aunt Viv will be over the moon. Have you told your mother?"

"No. You're the first person, well besides Margo."

"Why all the secrecy? We are your family, Caylen, and we're all completely fine with your lifestyle. We've been waiting for you to find a woman to settle down with. She's very beautiful, by the way."

Caylen smiled, then sighed. "The secrecy is because she was a topless dancer that I had a one night stand with, Uncle Herb."

"Wha..." he tried to speak as his jaw hit the floor.

Caylen ran her hand through her hair. "We never exchanged names. I flew home the next morning and had no idea who she was until she walked into my office a few months ago. She used to be an elite gymnast until she got hurt and decided to finish her degree in computer programming. She was dancing at night to pay for college after she lost her gymnastics scholarship."

"Wow."

"Yeah, needless to say, I've said the same thing a hundred times. The night I shared with her was something I never forgot. Apparently, she didn't either because she questioned Kent until he gave up my name the next time she saw him. That's how she found me when she moved here."

"Are you sure she's telling you the truth?" he asked.

"Yes. I've checked her out. Tanner's as honest as a day is long. She doesn't talk about that time in her life. I think she'd rather forget it ever existed, but I wanted you to know in case something ever came up."

"Okay. I'm glad you told me," he said. "It's not exactly good for business, but she's not a stripper anymore. If it comes out, it comes out. We will deal with it then. I don't see the need to tell your Aunt Viv or your mother."

"I agree."

"She seems very intelligent and very professional. I talked to her half a dozen times on the phone when we were discussing the software change." He paused, sipping his coffee. "I knew something was up with you the night of the conference going home with that young girl. I also noticed the way Ms. Bryce was looking at you."

"Is that why you made me handle the software change?" Caylen asked.

"She's beautiful and she had an eye on you all night. I

figured why not help you along a little bit." He grinned. "It's good to see you happy and in love."

"I love her more than life, Uncle Herb."

"Are we going to hear wedding bells in the future?" he teased.

"I hope so."

"Well then, I think it's time the rest of the family met Tanner. Don't you?"

"Yes," Caylen said.

"Good. I'll let your aunt know that you're bringing a guest to dinner this Saturday and it's not Margo. That should get her mind racing. She'll put together a dinner party and invite your mom and Aunt Cindy as a surprise."

Caylen laughed. "She's so sneaky."

"Yeah, if that's what you want to call it."

"Hey, maybe they will all get to talking about mom and Aunt Cindy's adventures and they will invite Aunt Viv along on the next one," Caylen said.

"Kid, you're onto something there," he said as his eyes lit up. "We can kill two birds with one stone and they will think everything was their idea." he nodded with a smile.

"If any of this ever comes back to me, I'm going to blame it all on you," Caylen teased.

"Go get some work done so you can take that pretty lady of yours to lunch," he said, shooing her out of his office.

"I was going to ask you to lunch today, but you're right, Tanner is much better looking," Caylen teased before walking out of his office. Checking her watch in the hallway she had a few minutes before her first conference call. Pulling her cell phone out of her pocket she pushed the button to call Tanner.

"Two calls in one morning? You must really miss

me," Tanner teased when she answered.

"You have no idea," Caylen sighed. "You're meeting my family this Saturday at an impromptu dinner party that you and I know nothing about."

Tanner laughed. "Should I be worried?"

"No, they will love you as much as I do," Caylen said, walking into her own office. "You might want to prepare yourself for questions about our wedding and when we are having kids though."

"What?" Tanner screeched. "Are you serious?"

"I need to go. I have a conference call starting. I love you," Caylen said.

"Wait! Caylen...hello?" Tanner said as Caylen hung up.

Caylen smiled at the phone. Her lunch hour wouldn't arrive fast enough and would go by way too soon. She had a feeling she was always going to be anticipating the next time she saw Tanner and dreading the moment she would have to say goodbye to her. She couldn't remember a time when she was ever as happy as she was at that moment. Caylen wasn't the praying type, but she thanked God every day for bringing Tanner back into her life.

"Ms. Jarrett, Olsen Manufacturing is on conference line one," her assistant said.

"Thank you. Sara, can you bring a cup of coffee, please? I forgot to get one after my meeting with Herb," Caylen said, opening the file on her computer and the folder on the desk in front of her. She straightened her posture, smiling at the sore muscles as she joined the call. Monday had officially begun.

The End

Fine

By

Sydney Canyon

Sydney Canyon

Chapter One

"I can't believe this, Mom. Why didn't you tell me you were having health problems?"

"Honey, I never realized it was this bad. I'll be fine. But, I do want you to go get checked out. My doctor says you could be at risk, even at your age."

The blond woman paced the floor of her townhouse overlooking the cliffs of Laguna Beach. "I haven't had any of those type of symptoms in a few years, Mom."

"Yes, Collin, I understand that, but you have had them off and on all of your life just like I have."

"What exactly is going to happen now that you've been diagnosed?"

Clara Anderson ran a hand through her light brown hair and sat comfortably on the couch in her living room. "Well, I'm going to have a hysterectomy, and then they will check my lymph nodes to see if the cancer has spread past my ovaries. They're not sure if I will need chemo or radiation yet."

"Oh my God, Mom. Have you told Dad about any of this?" Collin watched the predawn sun move over the Pacific Ocean. She knew it was close to nine o'clock in Allentown, Pennsylvania where her mother lived and she'd grown up.

"I barely talk to your father, you know that," Clara

answered with a sigh. Since their divorce, close to fifteen years ago, she had kept minimal contact with her ex-husband for the sake of their only child.

"I still think you need to tell him. I would, but then you'd be mad at me for the rest of the year."

"Collin Anderson!" Her mother scolded. "Don't you dare do any such thing. If I want your father to know, I will tell him my damn self."

Knowing her mother never cursed, Collin didn't bother retorting. She knew Clara was mad.

"Fine, I won't say anything."

"Thank you. Now please go see your doctor and get checked out. I'm worried about you, honey."

"I will, Mom, just as soon as things settle down in the office. I promise." Collin stared at the beautiful scene of the ocean basked in an orange glow.

"Don't make me call Lisa," Clara said with authority.

"No, I'll tell her tonight after work. Don't call and freak her out. You know how she is."

"Yes, don't I know. But, she's your wife and you had better let her know. If anything, she'll make you go get checked at least."

"Mom, I will go, I promise. Leave Lisa out of it." Collin let out a long sigh. "I should get going. I'm meeting a client at seven."

"Oh, I always forget the time difference. You're always up though. Sometimes I think you don't sleep, child."

"I do sleep. I love you, Mom. Let me know when they schedule the surgery so I can come out there."

"Aunt Abby will be here with me, you don't need to fly all the way home. I will only be in the hospital a few days."

"Mother, I will not argue with you on this. I am coming home when you have the surgery and that's all there is to it. If I have to call your doctor myself to get the date I will."

"I swear you're as stubborn as a mule. I have no idea where it comes from. Must be your father's side," Clara said, shaking her head. Clear across the country Collin did the same thing, knowing damn good and well she was just like her mother.

"Goodbye, Mom." She said as she closed her cell phone. Minutes later, she let the tears trickle from her blue eyes and roll down her cheeks.

She gave herself a little more time to overcome the devastation of her mother having been diagnosed with a form of cancer that is the number one killer of women. She realized that she'd had similar problems to her mother's most of her life and this meant she may never have children and worse, she was at risk for developing the same form of cancer. Collin wiped the tears from her face and turned away from the beautiful view from her living room.

~

Collin stepped out of her closet dressed in black slacks and a peach colored blouse. Her short, wavy blond hair was cut above her ears and lazily styled. It always looked sexy whether it was tucked under a ball cap, windblown from riding in her convertible Porsche, or styled for work or a night out on the town. Her five foot seven inch frame was lean and muscular, but still held soft feminine curves in the right places.

She walked downstairs, grabbing her black suit jacket

and briefcase as she headed out the door.

Twenty minutes later, Collin arrived in front of Vespera and Anderson, Criminal Defense Attorneys at Law. The two story, glass and steel office building was located in ritzy Newport Beach, California, roughly fifteen miles from her house up in the hills of Laguna Beach.

Chapter Two

"Morning, Collin. How's it going?" Bernard Vespera, her law firm partner of three years, passed her on the way to his office.

She was standing in front of the coffee station pouring a steaming cup of hazelnut flavored coffee for herself. His wine colored tie stood out from the dark gray suit he was wearing and his jet black hair was combed perfectly, as always. Bernie, as he liked to be called, was twelve years her senior and had been a partner with the first firm she'd joined out of law school. When he had wanted to venture out on his own a year later, he offered her a partnership and she had jumped on the opportunity. Now, after three years together, they were quickly becoming established defense attorneys with most of their clients coming from Los Angeles since it was barely thirty miles away from the office.

"Hey, Bernie." She returned his smile and went to her own office.

He quickly popped his head in as she was sitting down.

"You're meeting with Hastings Bennett this morning aren't you?" he asked as he sipped his own coffee.

"Yes, he'll be here in about half an hour. Would you like to sit in?"

"No. I have some calls to make. Let me know how it goes though." He smiled and walked back out of the room. She knew he wouldn't want to sit in, he always let her handle her own cases. He only appeared with her when she needed to go to court, which was generally once a week.

~

Two hours later, Collin had taken three pages of notes from her new client. Hastings Bennett was a young black man, who had been accused of breaking and entering and attempted murder on a Spanish woman in her home in the middle of the night, three weeks ago. Collin had gotten him out on bond for a first time offense and had quickly gone to work conjuring up witnesses and looking at key evidence.

She leaned her blond head against the backrest on her leather chair. The large Chippendale desk in front of her was impeccably kept. Her laptop was sitting in front of her with a few stacks of papers to each side. Two large bookshelves were along the wall to the right and her degree and certifications were framed on the wall behind her. Ivory colored carpet covered the floor of the entire building. Four more attorneys worked in the building under the two partners. Those four shared two legal secretaries and Collin and Bernie each had their own. The firm also had three paralegals and two office assistants who handled various filing and typing duties.

"Ms. Anderson, you have a call on line two." The intercom chirped and a middle aged feminine voice spoke with a slight Spanish accent.

"Thank you, Christine," Collin said to her assistant through the speakerphone.

Christine was a fifty year old woman with as much motherly love for the young lawyer as her thirty years of legal secretary experience could muster. She had also left the same law firm as Bernie and Collin when they'd offered her a position with them.

The blond reached over, picking up the receiver. "Hello, this is Collin Anderson."

"Hey, babe."

"Hey, how's your day going?" Collin continued to lean back in her chair as she talked to Lisa, her wife of close to seven years.

"I'm headed home today, so I should see you before dinner time. Will you be late?"

Lisa ran her hand through her shoulder length black hair, scrutinizing herself in the mirror. She hadn't been to the gym in over a year and as a result had a gain a few pounds and gone up a pant size. Being a real estate agent with her own company for the past six years kept her far busier than she ever thought she'd be in her career. She seemed to spend more time away from home and out of town than she did at home or even in her own city. But, she followed the money and her clients when they wanted something in particular. She was good at what she did.

"I'm meeting my last client around four, so I'll be home after six probably."

"Alright, I'll see you then. Love you."

"Love you too." Collin hung up and closed her eyes.

~

True to her word, Collin's black Porsche pulled into the garage at six o'clock. She parked next to Lisa's dark blue Lexus SUV and quickly grabbed her briefcase. She put the top up on the tiny car before going into the two story townhouse.

Collin smelled food cooking and was happy that she didn't have to slave in front of the stove for a change. Her head was pounding out of control. All she wanted to do was take a hot bath and crawl under the covers.

"I'm home!" Collin called out, setting her briefcase and car keys on the table by the door. She shed her jacket and looked around for her partner as she headed up the stairs. "Lisa?"

She heard the shower running when she walked into the large master bedroom. She ran into the closet, quickly shedding the rest of her clothes, then padded across the room to the large bathroom. Inside, the mirror and glass shower were completely fogged up from the hot steam. Collin smiled and pulled the glass shower door open.

"AGH!!!" Lisa screeched at the top of her lungs.

"It's me, calm down," Collin laughed and ducked under the spray behind her. She slid her arms around the dark-haired woman with golden brown eyes and pulled her close for a passionate kiss.

"Damnit, Collin. Why do you insist on scaring me *all* the time? You constantly sneak up on me on purpose," She growled, pulling away slightly.

"I missed you and wanted to welcome you home. I haven't seen you in three days."

"Well, scaring me isn't the best way to show me that you've missed me." Lisa smirked and went back to washing her hair. "I'm almost done anyway."

Collin ran her hands over Lisa's wet body, feeling the curves as she bent forward to suck on one of the perky breasts beckoning her.

"Collin, I'm really not in the mood for this. I'm tired

and I've had a long week." She sighed. "And it's still not over."

Collin took the hint and stepped out of the shower. She wasn't feeling the least bit sexual anyway, but she was trying to welcome her wife home with loving arms. *So much for that.* She quickly put on a pair of shorts and a T-shirt with nothing underneath and walked back downstairs to see where the food smell was coming from.

"Take out! Again, ugh!" She fumed as she sat at the island in the kitchen, opening the bags from a local Mexican cantina.

Collin was halfway through her dinner when Lisa finally greeted her in the kitchen. "Thanks for waiting for me," she said sarcastically as she sat down.

Thanks for making dinner! Collin thought to herself. She had no idea why they were acting so distant towards each other. Yeah, she was stressed beyond her max and ready to fall apart at any moment, but she still tried to show her partner some attention. What was Lisa's excuse?

"I didn't know how long you'd be and I've had a rough day," Collin said as she finished eating.

"You always have a rough day. You chose that career."

"How was your trip? Did you close the deal?" Collin didn't feel like going down that road. Hell, she'd seen her wife maybe two weeks out of the entire month. The last thing she wanted to do was fight.

"Tiring. We finally came to an agreement yesterday," Lisa said, letting out a long breath. "Two percent less than we wanted originally, but it was either take that or start over with a new buyer so we took it."

"At least you can put it behind you now. I know how much stress that deal has caused you," Collin said sincerely.

"No kidding, I think I woke up with a handful of new grays this week." The corners of her mouth turned into a smile that faded. Although she was only thirty-one, Lisa acted as if she were well into her forties.

"I don't see them." Collin smiled. She was lucky to have such light colored hair, even if she had grays you wouldn't see them.

"Tara called earlier. She wants us to help her this weekend."

"What's she doing?" Collin asked as she finished the last of her chicken enchiladas.

"I don't know, something about painting." Lisa rolled her eyes.

"I'll call her tomorrow when I get to the office." Collin stood up and threw her trash away. "Want to watch a movie?" she asked as she put her hands on Lisa's shoulders and began massaging the knotted muscles.

"No, I have a hundred things to do before tomorrow," she said, reaching up and patting Collin's hand. "That feels good, babe."

Collin continued the soft, circular motion for a few more minutes, then retreated to the couch to watch TV. When they had first got married, it was a cardinal rule not to bring work into the house. Over the past two years, work or better yet, Lisa's work had become the topic of conversation. It seemed as though she spent as much time working at home as she did working in her office. Collin did little to interfere. Her first year out of law school had been hard. She'd struggled with little pay. Then, her first year as a partner in her firm had been horrible. Lisa had supported them until Collin's law firm took off. Now, they both made great money and were living comfortably. Their marriage was slowly becoming the sacrifice for their comfortable lifestyle.

Chapter Three

The weekend passed quickly. Lisa and Collin spent all day Saturday helping their good friend Tara paint her tiny condo in Laguna Nigel, which was only a few miles inland from Laguna Beach.

By Wednesday morning Collin was tired. She had been in court all day Monday and Tuesday, and today she'd already met with three clients. Taking two aspirin to soothe her aching head, she went back to reading dockets and sorting through the bullshit evidence in Mr. Bennett's case. He was obviously innocent. Based on the partial two point fingerprints, the lack of a weapon, or even a motive, the prosecutor barely had a case. All she needed to do was find a way to convince that to the jury in two weeks. The case would bank her a good amount of money, but money wasn't everything. She loved her job. There was nothing like a heated courtroom battle to get her blood moving. Of course, the perks that came with it weren't half bad either, such as meeting celebrities and going to lavish parties.

Her cell phone rang, pulling Collin from the stack of paperwork she was reading. The caller ID flashed, Lisa Wheeler. Just seeing that name still got under her skin. Neither woman would change her last name, leaving another tiny barrier between them.

"Hey," Collin answered happily.

"When were you planning on telling me?" The voice on the other end scowled in a sharp tone.

Uh oh. Collin was trying to think of what she'd done this time to piss off her wife. "What are you talking about, Lisa?"

"I just got off the phone with Clara…"

That was all she needed to hear. *Damnit, Mother!* "Things have been hectic lately. I just found out last Thursday."

"I was home all weekend with you, Collin!" Lisa was just below yelling as she spoke. "Telling me your mother has cancer and you may possibly carry the gene too is not something you forget to tell your wife!"

"I know, I'm sorry. Can we discuss this later please?"

Lisa ignored her. "Have you been to the doctor?"

"No, not yet. I need to find someone to go to."

"I'm calling Mich to see if Kelsey can see you."

Michelle, or Mich for short, and her girlfriend of five years, Kelsey, were friends of Tara's, but they'd only seen them few times over the last two years. Mich owned a construction company and Kelsey was an OB/GYN at Newport Beach Women's Hospital.

"I don't know if I feel comfortable going to someone I know." Collin was nervous as it was. She chided herself for not going to the doctor for close to seven years now. The last thing she needed was to have a friend of a friend poking and prodding her in her nether region or worse, telling her she had cancer.

"I know how freaked out you are about those doctors anyway. You'll be more comfortable with Kelsey." Obviously, Lisa wasn't taking no for an answer.

"Fine." Collin threw her head back against her chair. She desperately wanted to take some more aspirin, but feared she'd overdose since it wasn't helping her pounding headache anyway. "I have a client coming in, Lisa. I need to go."

"I'll call you back when I get you an appointment. I still can't believe you didn't tell me about your mother. Are you planning on going to see her?"

"Yes, she hasn't given me her surgery date yet."

"Well, I'm going with you. It's two weeks from today. I've already made the flight arrangements."

Wonderful. Anything else your hein-ass? Collin wanted to crawl into a dark hole and never come out. She loved her wife, but sometimes she wanted to choke the life out of her.

~

At five-thirty, Collin slid into the soft leather seat of her Porsche and closed the door. She barely had a chance to start the car before her cell phone rang.

"Hey," she answered. She really wasn't prepared to argue.

"I talked to Kelsey's office and made an appointment for you next Tuesday at ten o'clock."

Argh! "Alright. I'm headed home."

"I'll be there shortly. I have to make a few calls before I leave."

Collin hung up the phone and contemplated driving off the cliff as she drove down Pacific Coast Highway. Leave it to her mother to meddle in her business as usual. She desperately wanted a drink. Since Lisa would be running late, she decided to stop at the tiny pub on the corner when she entered the Laguna Beach city limits. She parallel parked and walked inside *Shady's*. Three people were sitting at the bar and one couple was in a corner booth. She slid onto a stool at the end of the long bar.

"What can I get for you?" The young man with a pencil behind his ear and a white towel over the shoulder of his black shirt, smiled as he spoke to her.

"Do you know how to make a Dirty Irishman?"

"Single malt and crème." He winked and came back with a rocks glass full of whiskey and Irish crème. She nodded and chugged the contents on two long sips, before tossing a twenty on the bar and walking back out to her car.

~

Collin turned on her Bluetooth and dialed as she pulled out into the traffic.

"Hello?" The cheery voice answered.

"Hey, Tara. It's Collin."

"Hey, what's up?"

"Have you talked to Lisa lately?"

"No, not since you guys were at my place over the weekend. Why? What's up her butt now?" She snickered.

Collin drew a long breath and sighed.

"That bad huh?"

"My mother's going through some medical problems and I just found out last week…"

"Let me guess, she told Lisa before you did?"

"Oh yeah, not only that, but these problems may be hereditary."

"What's wrong with her?"

"She has to have a hysterectomy. She has Ovarian Cancer."

"Aw, I'm so sorry honey. I'm sure Lisa is just worried

269

about you. That's nothing to play around with."

"I know, but you know how she can be. Tara, she scheduled me an appointment with Kelsey."

"Yikes!"

"No kidding. It's hard enough to go to those kind of doctors, but going to someone that's an acquaintance is worse," Collin said.

"Yeah, and a woman, a *lesbian* woman at that."

"Kelsey lives in the closet."

"She's still a lesbian honey." Tara laughed. "You want me to go with you?"

"No! I'm doing this alone."

"When are you going?"

"Tuesday morning." Collin downshifted and turned to go uphill towards her neighborhood.

"Well, let me know how it goes."

"I hope I don't embarrass myself. God, could you imagine!" Collin sighed.

Tara laughed hysterically. "I seriously doubt you'll get turned on wearing a paper towel with your feet in the stirrups."

"Ugh! Just picturing that makes me want to hurl."

"Relax, Kelsey is a professional. Besides, it's not like you guys are best friends. You know Mich better than you do her. Hell, you guys haven't seen either of them in over a year anyway."

"That's true." She pulled into her garage and cut the engine. Her phone immediately picked up her call when the car radio turned off.

"Is Lisa home yet?"

"No, how did you know I was home?"

"I hear the garage closing."

"Oh. She's running late as usual."

"Hey, I heard about that case you're working on. It's been on the news."

"Which one?" Collin asked, setting her briefcase and keys down in their usual spot before headed upstairs.

"Some murderer or something. I heard your law firm's name."

"Oh, well we seem to have a few of those going on right now. I wasn't aware of the media's interest. It could be one of Bernie's cases."

"I need to run into the grocery store and my piece of shit phone doesn't have coverage in there. Call me when you finish on Tuesday. Maybe we can meet for lunch or something," Tara said.

"Alright."

Collin changed her clothes and made her way downstairs to start dinner. The last thing she wanted to hear was Lisa bitching because she had to cook. *Might as well kill two birds with one stone.* She'd start dinner and have a bottle of wine open and a glass poured for her grumpy, overworked wife.

Chapter Four

Collin hated hospitals, from the stale smell to the cold draft. She sat in the Gynecology Ward in a small maroon colored leather chair with no cushion. The ten or so magazines on the table were over three months old, so she didn't bother picking them up. She'd quickly filled out her paperwork as soon as she had arrived, and was now playing the waiting game. She took a deep breath and sighed. The last thing she wanted to do was be poked and prodded with cold metal instruments. She feared after today she'd never want to have sex again.

"Ms. Anderson?"

The blond nurse, dressed in white and purple scrubs with tiny babies all over the top, called her name from the open door on the left side of the room. Collin jumped up and moved slowly towards her. She felt like a dog on a leash being pulled in the opposite direction as she fought her feet to move forward.

"Doctor Hart will be with you soon. If you'll step over here we'll get you weighed and take your blood pressure," the woman said.

Collin followed her into a small room. She flinched when she saw the number on the scale. *Need to cut back on the ice cream!* She was five foot seven and a hundred and forty-five pounds. She was well built with very toned muscles, but she didn't like being over a hundred and forty pounds. Maybe it was because she was wearing clothes.

She took her suit jacket off so that her blood pressure could be taken. After that she was moved to an examining room complete with the icy cold looking table and metal stirrups. A small chair was on one side and a sink and counter top was on the other. Collin's body stiffened.

"If you will please take all of your clothes off and put this paper gown on, I'll be back to check on you in a few minutes." The nurse smiled and walked out of the room.

"Here we go." Collin whispered to herself as she quickly peeled out of her business suit. She wasn't sure how many minutes a few was, so she hurriedly donned the paper garment, then she laid her clothes out nicely on the chair in the corner, and sat up on the table away from the scary looking stirrups. Just then, the door opened and a petite woman with wavy auburn hair pulled back in a ponytail walked into the room wearing green scrubs that hid her feminine curves. She was staring at the file in her hand.

"Hello, Ms. Anderson, I'm Dr. Hart," she said without looking up.

Collin took inventory as she watched the woman walk further into the room and shut the door. She was maybe five foot four and a hundred ten pounds soaking wet. Collin had always thought she was cute, but this was the first time she'd seen her in scrubs. She looked adorable. Her shoulder length hair had hints of blond highlights from being out in the sun and her skin held a faint tan.

"It's good to see you again, Kelsey." Collin said.

The doctor's head flew up at the mention of her first name. She turned bright green eyes to the half-naked woman on the table and smiled.

"Collin, how are you?" She stuck her hand out. Collin quickly took the offered hand, glad to feel its warmth. Her entire body was ice cold and rigid.

"Well, I'd be a lot better if I wasn't sitting here." She fanned her arms out at her attire and the surroundings. Kelsey smiled, showing off perfect white teeth.

"I saw the problems with your mother in your chart. I'm sorry to hear about her."

"Thanks. She was so adamant about me getting checked out that she called Lisa. Hence my visit here today."

"I see." Kelsey remembered Lisa as being a little pushy. "Well, there's no need to be nervous. I don't bite." She winked and grinned.

Pulling a tiny stool out from between the stirrups, she sat down in front of Collin on the other end of the table.

"I can tell you're nervous, your blood pressure is a little high." She continued to read the chart. "You haven't been to a gynecologist in seven years! Shame on you, Collin. You need to be examined once a year, especially with your family history, not to mention your past problems. After thirty five, you should be having mammograms every few years, too."

Collin grinned sheepishly. "I'm only thirty."

"Wow, you're a baby. I never realized you were that much younger." Kelsey looked up and smiled at the blue eyes looking at her.

"You're not much older than me. Are you?" Collin hadn't ever asked her age, or Mich's age for that matter.

"I'm thirty-seven."

"Wow, you definitely don't look it. Honestly I'd think you were my age or younger if I saw you on the street."

"Thanks. So, how've you been? The last time I saw

you guys you were just starting your own firm, right?"

"Yeah, I left my first firm with a guy that was a partner there and we started our own." She smiled. "Things are going great."

"That's good." Kelsey said as the nurse came back into the room. "Well, let me explain what we're going to do today." She set the chart on top of the counter. "You need a breast exam and a full pelvic exam since it's been so long. We may also do an ultrasound to see if anything looks unusual. Going by your chart, you've had sporadic periods all of your life, so we want to make sure you don't have the complications that may lead to Ovarian Cancer like your mother."

"Okay." Collin's voice shook as she spoke. She followed the directions Kelsey gave her, lying back on the table with her legs towards the stirrups, but didn't put her feet in them.

Kelsey opened the paper gown. Peering down at the left side of Collin's chest, she gently placed her warm hands on her left breast, feeling the soft tissue and working her fingers in small circles. She grabbed Collin's left arm from her side, placing it above her head so she could feel the lymph nodes under her arm. Once again, she pressed her hands against Collin's skin. Collin could feel the warmth of her hands in every place that this woman touched her.

Kelsey slowly closed the left side of the gown and opened the right side. She made brief eye contact with Collin as she followed the same routine of pressing her hands on Collin's soft breast, working her fingers in small circles, massaging the tissue. Once she was finished with her arm pit, she closed the gown and went back to the chart.

Collin noticed the sincere look in the island green eyes staring back at her when Kelsey turned around. "I don't feel any lumps or hard tissue. I may want you to have a mammogram in a year." Collin nodded without breaking eye contact with the beautiful eyes looking back at her.

"Go ahead and slide down to the end of the table and place your feet in the stirrups," Kelsey said as the nurse laid the instruments out on the tray for her. "Now you're going to feel some pressure, but I'll go slow." Collin once again nodded, scared her voice would fail her if she tried to speak.

Collin closed her eyes as she felt the cold metal instrument slip inside of her. Kelsey placed her warm hand on Collin's stomach close to her hairline as she slid her other hand inside. Collin swallowed hard enough for everyone in the room to hear. She felt Kelsey's hand touching the various parts inside of her and cried out when she hit a particularly sensitive spot.

"Does that hurt?" Kelsey asked gently.

"Yes," Collin hissed.

"Your left ovary is enlarged," Kelsey said.

Collin wanted to cry from the pain the exam caused, but Kelsey's gentle touch soothed her slightly as she made small circles with her hand on Collin's stomach.

A few minutes later, she felt the pressure of the tool being removed. Kelsey slipped her gloves off and washed her hands in the sink as Collin slid back up the table and sat up. She wasn't prepared for the look in the green eyes across from her as Kelsey turned around. Her eyes held the same gentle, sincere gaze that she had felt from her touch.

"Let's go ahead and do the ultrasound next week and take a look at that left ovary. I'll know more then, but for now you seem to be pretty healthy." She smiled.

"What happens if it's the same thing?"

"Well, it's probably not cancer. More than likely, it's just an ovarian cyst. As far as what to do, it really depends on whether or not it's hindering you or causing you discomfort. If that's the case we can remove it. Sometimes, a hysterectomy is the only way to be sure you never get cancer or have other problems in the future." Kelsey held Collin's blue eyes as she spoke softly to her.

"I see."

"Go ahead and get dressed, I'll be back in a few minutes." Kelsey said as she and the nurse left the room. Collin quickly tossed the paper towel dress in the trash and put her suit back on. She sat in the chair in the corner of the room.

She stood up when Kelsey entered the room again. She had forgotten she was at least three inches taller than the petite doctor. Collin took a deep breath and let it out slowly. She stuck her hand out. Kelsey met her halfway and smiled as their hands closed together. "Thanks Kelsey."

"You're welcome. I'll see you in a week."

~

Collin felt a tear slide down her face when she got into her Porsche. She squeezed her eyes closed, trying to regain her composure. When she felt semi-normal again she picked up her cell phone and dialed.

"Wheeler and Associates, how may I help you?" The bubbly voice answered on the second ring.

"Hi, may I speak with Lisa please?"

"I'm sorry, she's out at lunch. May I take a message for her?"

"No thanks. This is Collin. I'll call her cell."

"Okay, no problem, Ms. Anderson."

Collin hung up and dialed another number. She waited until the voicemail picked up.

"Hey honey, I just finished with the doctor. I need to have a small test done next week, but everything seems to be fine. I love you. I'm headed back to the office. I'll see you tonight." She ended the call and dialed one more number.

"Hey, how'd it go?" Tara answered, shoving the phone between her ear and her shoulder. Her short brown hair was a mess from running her hands through it all day. She continued to type the presentation she was working on. As a corporate VP she spent most of her time in her office going over business proposals and presentations.

"Surprisingly, not as humiliating as I thought it would be. Kelsey sure has a way of making you feel semi-comfortable as she gently manhandles your body."

Tara laughed. "That's an interesting way to put it. So, were you sexually aroused?"

"Hell no. I mean Kelsey is so damn cute. At first I was worried, but it was too weird to think of anything but the cold instrument stuck up my crotch!"

"HA! You're crazy, girl. So, everything went okay?"

"I'm fine. I have to go have a simple test done next week, but she said I seemed healthy." *Most people with cancer seem healthy too, until it's found.* She thought, remembering how her mother was diagnosed through a routine exam like the one she'd just had.

"Well that's good. Hey, I'm about to duck out of this stale ass office for lunch, want to meet me somewhere?"

"Uh…" Collin cleared her throat, shaking the thoughts from her mind. "Sure, I'm headed back to my office."

Their office buildings were in the same corporate plaza in Newport Beach. "How about Renna's? I could go for a salad."

"Sounds great. I'll see you in a few minutes."

Chapter Five

Collin woke up alone in a cold bed Sunday morning. She didn't bother looking for Lisa. She knew she'd be in their home office typing on her laptop. *God, does the woman ever stop?* She decided to go for a quick run to get warmed up before she met Tara for their weekly racquet ball game. Lisa didn't much care for the sport. She preferred the less aggressive sport of tennis to keep her in shape.

Collin threw on a sports bra and running shorts. She ate a banana and a half bowl of cereal before quickly kissing Lisa goodbye and heading out the front door.

~

"Why do I bother playing this with you? You always kick my ass!" Tara huffed as she packed her racquet bag and changed into flip flops.

"You've won a few times," Collin added. Tara tossed her sweat towel at her.

"Three times in the past four years! We do this just about every weekend!"

Collin grinned.

"How's your mom, by the way?"

"Good, she's having her surgery soon. We're flying

280

out there the day before, and staying for about three days. My Aunt Abby lives with her, so she'll have plenty of company."

"I know how she drives you nuts. I hope she gets better soon."

"Thanks."

"So what kind of test are you having done on Tuesday?" Tara asked as she picked up her bag and followed Collin out of the locker room.

"It's just an ultrasound, but they have to stick this wand thing up in there to look around and get better pictures."

"Ouch!" Tara's face creased and her nose wrinkled.

"Apparently, it's very routine. I'm as nervous as a bug on the interstate though."

Tara laughed at the analogy. "Is Kelsey doing this?"

"Yes."

"Well, at least you're in good hands. She's been doing this for a long time."

"Yeah I never realized how long though. I knew Mich was close to forty, but I had no idea Kelsey was thirty-seven. She doesn't look a day over twenty-five."

"I know, makes you feel young doesn't it?"

"Hell yeah, everyone around me is older. Not that I'm complaining, I love being the youngest." She smiled.

"You're only a few months younger than me," Tara giggled.

~

Tuesday morning, Collin awoke to a quiet bedroom. Lisa was out of town as usual. Collin wondered if it bothered Lisa to sleep away from her in a strange bed so often. She also wondered if Lisa remembered she was having an ultrasound in a few hours. Washing her body and shampooing her hair quickly, she rushed out of the house, leaving her thoughts behind. She had just enough time to stop at the coffee shop near her house.

Collin's day started in the office. She finished reading over depositions and making notes in her files. She was due in court the following week to defend a DUI for one of Hollywood's glamour girls. Those weren't particularly her favorites cases, considering most of the time the person was really driving drunk, but they brought in a good amount of money to the firm so she and Bernie took them when they could.

"Collin, good luck today. I don't expect to see you back here this afternoon." Bernie raised an eyebrow and patted her shoulder.

"It's just an ultrasound," she said.

"I don't care what it is. You're going through a difficult time and you're health is more important than any case on your desk. Have that pretty wife of yours take you out to lunch when your test is finished."

"Thanks, Bernie," she said with a smile. *I can't remember the last time Lisa and I had lunch together simply to spend time with each other.*

Collin drove to the hospital early even though it was only fifteen minutes from her office, but she was always punctual. As soon as she finished the paperwork, she was taken back. This time she was in a completely different type of exam room. It had a large computer and a monitor next to the exam table and another monitor on the far wall for the patient to also see the computer screen.

"Good morning, Ms. Anderson. My name is Gloria, I'm Dr. Hart's assistant. Go ahead and change into the paper gown and lie down. She will be in shortly." The dark-haired woman with Spanish features reminded Collin of Christine, her office assistant.

Collin quickly changed and was laying on the cold sheet when she heard the door open. Kelsey smiled brightly as she walked into the room, towards the bed. Her eyes sparkled in the fluorescent lighting. Collin felt an unfamiliar pull towards her. She had the urge to wrap her arms around the petite woman. *What the hell?* She shook the mental picture from her head.

"Hey, how are you feeling?" Kelsey grabbed Collin's hand and squeezed. Collin felt the warmth of the soft touch from her finger tips all the way to her toes.

"Nervous, but okay." She tried to smile, but her nerves were on overdrive.

"I can tell, your blood pressure is up again. I want you to relax, think of something that will take your mind off of your present surroundings."

"I'll try." She noticed Kelsey still holding her hand and was surprised that they were alone in the small room.

"This will be uncomfortable, but I will try to be quick," she said as she moved away from Collin's side.

Kelsey typed a few key strokes on the computer and prepared the electronic wand with gel lubricant. "Here we go," she said.

Collin's body tightened, rebelling against the foreign object sliding inside of her. Closing her eyes, she concentrated on her own heartbeat and the occasional clicking of the computer keys as Kelsey stopped to make notes and measurements as she moved the wand all around. Collin cried out in pain when she hit a particularly sensitive area.

"I'm sorry, Sweetie. I'm almost done," Kelsey said

softly.

Collin squeezed her eyes tighter, holding back the tears that the sharp pain provoked. A minute later, she felt the invading instrument leave her body and a warm hand caressing her forearm.

"It's over," Kelsey said.

Collin opened her eyes to see Kelsey looking back at her. Collin stared into the depths of her green eyes like they were the oxygen her body needed for survival. She was unsure why she felt so connected to Kelsey at that particular moment, but she was afraid to let go of the eyes holding hers.

"Do you call all of your patients 'Sweetie'?" Collin asked.

"You're more than a patient to me, Collin," Kelsey said as she broke their intense gaze and moved towards the door. "Go ahead and get dressed. I'll come back in a minute to talk to you."

Collin redressed quickly and sat in the small chair against the wall as far away from the table and stirrups as she could get. So far, this entire process had been something she was unprepared for. She wasn't sure it was a journey anyone could really prepare for to begin with. She wondered, too, why she was clinging to Kelsey like a lifeline in the middle of the ocean when she barely knew her and so far everything between them had been completely clinical. Still, her heart beat a millisecond faster when the door opened and Kelsey walked into the room with her eyes shining in the light and a bright smile on her face. *She doesn't know the power that smile has.* Collin thought. She tried to remember the last time a simple smile from Lisa had made her heart skip a beat as she awaited her fate.

"From what I was able to see, you definitely have a cyst on your left ovary that is about the size of a golf ball. To give you some perspective, your ovary is the size of a pea."

"What does this mean?" Collin asked.

"You're obviously in pain on that side. I'm going to suggest a laparoscopy. That's a simple surgical procedure where I make a couple of tiny incisions in your hair line and look inside with a small camera. We will check out the ovary and if we can remove the cyst without compromising the ovary, then we will do that. Otherwise, the ovary will need to come out. With your mother's history, I'd actually suggest we go ahead and remove the entire ovary, but that is your decision."

"Do I have cancer?" Collin asked softly.

Kelsey grabbed her hand, running her thumb over the soft skin on the top of her hand. "I can't be sure until we take that tissue and send it to pathology."

"How soon can we do the procedure?"

"My assistant booked it for next Monday at ten a.m."

"Okay," Collin said, squeezing Kelsey's hand before letting go.

Chapter Six

Monday morning was a blur. Collin arrived at the hospital and was escorted to a pre-op room where she was dressed in a backless gown, signed her life away on a stack of papers, and then hooked up to an IV line. The last thing she remembered was Kelsey's face and her bright smile as she spoke to her just before the anesthesia kicked in.

The surgery lasted three hours. Kelsey removed the entire left ovary and cut a small cyst off of the right ovary near the top of the fallopian tube. She sealed all of the tissue into a surgical bag and sent it off to the pathology department of the hospital as Collin was sent to recovery to wake up.

~

Lisa sat in the waiting room talking on her phone periodically. Tara arrived shortly after Collin was taken back for the surgery.

"Thanks for coming up here," Lisa said.

"It's no problem. I don't mind sitting with her tomorrow and Wednesday either. I know you're in over your head right now with work and I have entirely too many vacation days for a single woman to ever take, so I'll babysit." She smiled.

"I hope this is the end of this mess for her," Lisa said. "Her mother explained to me this morning that she'd had the same procedure. Thankfully, she said it's fairly easy to recover from."

"Yeah, that's what Collin was telling me." Tara shook her head. "She said this was how her mother's cancer was diagnosed. I make it a point to go to my doctor every year. I was adopted. I don't have a clue about my natural parents or their medical history. It's better to be safe than sorry."

"Thankfully, nothing runs in my family. The ones that have died, have pretty much all died of old age."

A nurse in green scrubs interrupted, "Ms. Anderson is out of recovery and has been moved into a private room for now. She's awake. If you'll follow me I'll take you to her."

Lisa and Tara both jumped up, following the nurse.

~

Collin was groggy and in a lot of pain. When she finally did open her eyes, she saw an angel sitting in the chair watching her. After she blinked a few times the angel transformed into Kelsey.

"Hey, you did great," Kelsey said, standing up. She walked closer, grabbing Collin's hand and slowly rubbing her thumb over the back of it.

Collin tried to talk, but her throat hurt and her voice was hoarse.

"Sshhh, don't try to talk just yet. You had a tube in your throat so it'll be sore for a day or so. Here…" Letting go of Collin's hand, she grabbed the cup of ice chips, pulled out a few pieces, and put them in Collin's mouth for her. Her fingers were soft against Collin's lips.

"We removed your left ovary and there was a small cyst growing on the right one near the tube that we were able to extract without removing that ovary. Everything has been sent to the Path Lab, so we should have the results within a week. My office will call you in so we can discuss them."

Collin nodded. Kelsey had gone back to holding Collin's hand and rubbing it with her thumb for comfort. She reached up, wiping away the water running down Collin's chin from the ice chips. She'd always had a small crush on Collin. Hell, most of their friends did, but she was starting to think it was a bad idea allowing Collin to continue as her patient. The intimacy of their clinical connection was beginning to cloud her judgment.

When the door creaked open, Kelsey let go of her hand, backing away to a safe distance. She turned to face Lisa and Tara as they made their way into the gray-colored, brightly lit room.

"Hey guys. Her throat is swollen, sore and hoarse from the intubation, but she's fully awake. We did give her some strong pain medication so she may be in and out of it for an hour or so."

"Hey honey," Lisa said, leaning forward as she kissed her cheek. Collin smiled at her.

"I bet I could kick your butt at racquetball now!" Tara joked and smiled as she patted Collins hand softly.

Collin nodded and smiled. Her eyes fluttered closed.

"We'll get her up and moving around in about two hours. She'll be able to go home after that as long as she can move around and use the bathroom on her own."

"Thanks Kelsey," Lisa and Tara said together.

~

Collin spent the next twenty-four hours in bed. Lisa was thankful they had a spare bedroom so she didn't disturb Collin in her sleep during the night. Wednesday morning Collin was up and moving around, but very slowly.

"Are you sure you will be okay?" Lisa asked, helping Collin to the couch.

"Yes, I'm fine. Go to work. Tara's coming to hang out with me anyway," Collin replied.

Lisa fixed her a glass of water and kissed her cheek before leaving to meet a client. Collin watched her walk out the front door before closing her eyes.

"What do you want for lunch?" Tara asked, waking her up as she got up off of the couch. Collin was sitting on the other end with her feet propped up. She'd taken a pain pill and had completely missed Tara's arrival.

"Whatever you want, it doesn't matter to me," Collin answered, slightly stretching to work the kink out of her back. "When did you get here?"

"A few hours ago. How are you feeling?"

"I'm fine."

"You need any pain medicine?"

"No. Apparently, it knocks me out like a zombie," Collin said. Her head still felt a little fuzzy from the last pain pill.

"I'm on a mini-vacation, so I'm thinking Mac n' Cheese is sounding rather good."

"It's beyond fattening, but I think I won't stop you from making that for lunch," Collin said.

"Good, because you have no choice, gimpy!"

"Hey watch it! I can get off of this couch if I want to. It just takes a few minutes," Collin chided.

They both laughed.

Tara returned a few minutes later with two heaping bowls of Mac n' Cheese. "So where do you go from here?"

"What do you mean?" Collin groaned as she moved a little bit.

"Still hurting badly?" Tara asked.

"God, yes. I feel like they cut me in half and sewed me back together after removing all of my parts."

"Um yeah, that visual was painful enough for me thanks," she grimaced. "Do you go back for check-ups or…"

"Kelsey's office will call as soon as the pathology report is in and I'll have to go to her office to discuss it. If everything looks good, then I go back every year."

"How long until they have the results?"

"No idea," Collin shrugged. "Kelsey said it will take about a week."

"Wow, that's a long time to wait."

"No kidding."

~

The following Wednesday, Collin walked into the hospital once again, and headed towards Kelsey's office. She was alone since Lisa had left that morning to go to San Diego for five days to bid on a piece of property and hopefully close a deal for one of her clients. She knew Collin had a follow up appointment from her surgery and was still waiting for her test results, but closing this deal would be a huge opportunity. *When did work become the most important thing in our lives?*

"Good morning, Ms. Anderson," The nurse said as she led Collin to an exam room. "Go ahead and get changed.

290

Doctor Hart will be in shortly."

Collin replaced her clothes with the paper gown and sat on the exam table. She tried to concentrate on the seascape painting on the wall to the left, but her mind seemed to drift between the warmth she knew she would see in Kelsey's eyes and the tenderness of her touch, to the awaiting results that could be life-threatening. *God Collin, you've got to stop this.*

"Hey, how are you feeling?" Kelsey asked. She patted Collin on the leg as she pulled the rolling stool out and sat in front of her with the chart in her hand. Her auburn semi-wavy hair was up in a ponytail. The long bangs tucked behind her ear easily made her look ten years younger.

"I feel better than I did last week," Collin grinned.

"Are you still sore?" Kelsey cocked her head to the side.

"No, a little tender maybe, but the pain is pretty much gone."

"Good," she said as she opened the chart on her desk and wrote a few notes. "Have you had sex at all, vaginally, since the surgery?"

Collin wanted to crawl into a hole. Discussing her sex life was the last thing she had on her mind. "Uh…"

Kelsey looked up at her waiting for an answer.

"No."

"Well, you should be able to resume a normal sex life after today, just be gentle and if you feel pain, stop."

"Okay." Collin felt very uncomfortable all of a sudden.

"I'm sorry I was late, Dr. Hart. Dr. Sandino needed me longer than she thought," the nurse said as she popped in quickly.

"It's no problem. Collin go ahead and slide down and

place your feet in the stirrups."

Kelsey put on a pair of rubber gloves and positioned herself between Collin's open legs. She slowly inserted the duckbill style tool to open up the vagina, then slipped her hand in while she placed her other hand on Collin's abdomen, pressing gently in various places.

The pressure was more than Collin could stand. She fought herself, but couldn't hold the tiny tears back as a few escaped her eyes.

"I'm sorry, sweetheart. I know it hurts. I'm almost done." Kelsey looked into her eyes and held them for what seemed like minutes, until she was finished.

Then, she removed her hand and the tool from Collin's body. She tossed her gloves in the sink and washed her hands before moving back over to Collin. She ran her hand over Collin's softly, causing knots in Collin's stomach. She knew Kelsey was just a caring person with a passion for making her patients feel comfortable in her office. Still, the terms of endearment were playing nasty tricks on Collin's mind. Allowing Kelsey to be her doctor, knowing she was attracted to her, was turning out to be an irreversible mistake.

"Go ahead and move back up and lay flat. I'll remove the stitches and you'll be out of here soon. Everything seems to have heeled just fine." Kelsey said as she put on another pair of gloves and grabbed a pair of tiny clippers and what looked like tweezers. Collin didn't feel a thing as Kelsey pulled the stitches and cut them loose one at a time. Within a minute it was all over.

"See, not so bad." Kelsey smiled. "Go ahead and get dressed. I'll be back in a few minutes."

Collin was sore when she sat up. It took her longer than expected to get dressed because of the tenderness in her abdomen. She was buttoning her pants when Kelsey walked back into the room.

"Oh I'm sorry," she said, turning to go.

"It's okay, can you help me get back into my jacket?" Collin asked.

"Sure." Kelsey grabbed the jacket and pulled it up over Collin's shoulders, then she reached up around the taller woman's neck, adjusting her collar. "I never pictured myself dressing you." She smiled. "Undressing you maybe," she said softly, avoiding eye contact.

Collin raised an eyebrow, grinning slightly.

Kelsey lingered for an extra second, then backed away. "How's the pain?"

"Hurts," Collin said. She was at a loss for words. The exam had been painful and her mind was racing with thoughts about this woman that she shouldn't have been having. She wasn't sure Kelsey's blatant admission was meant to be heard, but even if it was, what the hell was she supposed to say?

"Go home and take some ibuprofen and lie down. There is still some swelling and I'm sure I just made it worse. You will be fine tomorrow. "

"Good because I have to be in court at eight o'clock in the morning."

"I'll let you know as soon as I get your results. It should be any day."

"Okay," Collin said.

"Here's my card, I wrote my cell number on the back. Call me if you start having sudden bleeding or cramping other than your menstrual cycle, or if the pain persists." Kelsey grinned. "Or if you want to meet for coffee sometime."

"I just might take you up on that, as soon as I get my

case load under control again. I'm leaving in a few days to go to Pennsylvania to be with my mom."

"Don't worry about your results. I'm sure everything is fine. Sometimes it takes a few extra days if something is inconclusive or they get busy with samples to test. Please tell your mom I hope everything goes well for her."

Kelsey stuck her hand out, but Collin pulled the smaller woman into her arms. "I think we know each other well enough to be above the doctor/patient level." She winked and held Kelsey tightly against her before letting go. Both women backed away slowly.

She has to feel this too. Collin thought, trying to calm her racing heart that seemed to gravitate towards Kelsey on its own accord.

Collin slid down into the seat of her car, slamming the door shut. "We're just friends and a little flirtation between friends is normal. Don't get the signals crossed, you idiot. You're married and the last thing you need right now is to make something out of nothing and complicate things," she said to herself as she started the car.

Chapter Seven

"All rise for the Honorable Judge Nielson," the bailiff called out.

Collin stood next to Bernard Vespera and her client, actress Patricia Fogleman.

"You may be seated," the judge said. He was a white haired man with a matching thin beard. He sat down, adjusting his large black robe.

Collin rearranged her notes one last time and waited for the pre-trial hearing to begin.

"Docket number one, four three, two. Los Angeles County versus Patricia Fogleman, one count of reckless driving and one count of driving under the influence. Mr. Johnson, you may begin."

The state prosecutor stood, ruffling the nonexistent wrinkles from his dark blue suit and straightening the yellow tie he wore that stuck out like a beacon in the night. He checked his perfectly styled light brown hair and began talking. Collin wondered if he might just lose his composure if the stick in his butt came loose. *Need to loosen that stick, Anderson!*

"On March sixteenth, the defendant, Patricia Fogleman, was pulled over by LAPD officer Raymond Richmond. I'm going to prove that Ms. Fogleman was not only driving under the influence of alcohol, but she was also driving recklessly down Santa Monica Boulevard," he said before sitting down.

"Ms. Anderson, you may begin."

Collin stood up, buttoning her black suit jacket. She still felt a tiny amount of pain in her lower abdomen that escalated if she moved too fast. Stepping around the table, she tried to hide the grunt that came from her throat when she changed positions.

"Everything okay, Ms. Anderson?" The judge asked.

"Yes your Honor. I'm recovering from minor surgery and I keep forgetting to move slowly. I'm sorry."

"I hope you feel better."

"Thank you." She took a deep breath and smiled at the bleached blond actress sitting at her table next to Bernie. "As the Prosecutor has stated, my client, Ms. Fogleman was pulled over on March sixteenth by an LAPD officer. I'm going to prove that the reckless driving and driving under the influence allegations are merely exaggerations based on Officer Richmond's opinion. My client is innocent, and I will prove it beyond a reasonable doubt." She sat back down, careful not to grunt this time.

"We will reconvene in two weeks to start the proceedings," the Judge said.

'Thank you," both attorneys answered.

"This court is adjourned until April eighteenth at oh nine hundred."

Collin shook her client's hand and her partner's. "Two weeks guys," she said as she packed up her briefcase.

"You're leaving in the morning right?" Bernie asked as they walked out together.

"Yeah, we fly back Tuesday, so I'll be back in the office on Wednesday."

"Okay, no problem." He smiled and patted her

shoulder. "Take care of yourself too while you're there. Don't make me call Lisa on you."

She smiled and shook her head. He knew exactly what calling Lisa meant. He could threaten her with that anytime. It always worked, but lately Lisa had been preoccupied with work and probably wouldn't bother taking his call. Collin didn't bother telling him that.

Chapter Eight

The plane landed with a thud and a small screech, before taxiing to the gate. The terminal in the Harrisburg airport was overly crowded.

"If you get our luggage, I'll take care of the rental car," Collin said.

"Okay. How are you feeling?" Lisa asked.

"Fine." She was tired of lying, but in all honesty she wasn't hurting and had completely recovered from her surgery. On the other hand, being back home with her mother having cancer removal surgery while she waited in limbo for her own test results, seemed to push her nerves to the limit. *I'm fine. If I wasn't, I would've heard from Kelsey by now.*

~

The hour long drive out to her mother's house was moderately quiet. Lisa fell asleep in the passenger seat of the rented four-door Lexus. Collin drove through the rolling hills, listening and humming along to the light Whitney Houston song on the radio. The rural roads from her childhood were now filled with businesses and subdivisions. The miles and miles of pastures had turned into gas stations, McDonald's, Wal-Mart's, and various

298

other places.

She finally made it into Allentown and was surprised to see all that had changed since her last visit. Every time she had come home over the past twelve years, she'd noticed something new. She looked back now on the way her life may have been if she hadn't gone off to law school on a scholarship. The small town life she had grown up in was nothing like the hustle and bustle of living in Southern California. Thinking about how much her life had changed over the years made her smile.

"What are you thinking about, babe?" Lisa rolled her head to the side, noticing her wife smiling.

"Just thinking about how different my life has been since I moved away from here."

"I know we make the trip once a year to see your family, but I swear it looks different every time." Lisa sat up, running her fingers through her hair and adjusting her sunglasses.

"When I was a kid, all of this..." Collin fanned her hands out. "This was cow and horse pastures. I used to go mudding in Roy's old Ford truck out there where that Sam's Club is sitting now."

"I know, honey. I think you tell me that every time we come here." Lisa smiled.

~

They finally pulled up in front of the two-story, ranch-style house with a large front porch, complete with a swing and beautiful flowers growing all around. The cattle fence was still standing at the end of the driveway although, the Anderson family hadn't had livestock in about fifteen years. When Clara and Burk Anderson divorced ten years ago, Clara had kept the house and the twenty acres that came with it, while Burk had gone to live with the woman he'd been having an affair with. Over the years, that woman left him all alone and he and Clara had slowly arrived at the point of speaking to each other again. But, Clara swore she'd never let that man back into her bed or back into her life the way it used to be. He had broken that when he broke their marriage vows. Collin took her marriage vows just as seriously. She never imagined cheating on Lisa. Yes, they had their share of problems, but they still loved each other.

"Hey, honey!" Clara Anderson made her way down the steps of the porch and stopped as her daughter got out of the car. Collin was taller than her mother by a couple of inches and looked so much like her father, sometimes Clara found it hard to believe the child was partly hers. Clara was a slender build like her daughter, but had light brown hair and brown eyes. Burk Anderson, Collin's father, had the blond hair and blue eyes.

"Hi, Mom," Collin said, closing the door and wrapping her mom in a hug.

"Hey, Lisa." Clara went around the car to hug her daughter-in-law while Collin began grabbing their bags. The two story house had three bedrooms upstairs and one downstairs, so there was plenty of room for Lisa and Collin.

"Where's Aunt Abby?" Collin asked as she carried the suitcases up to the house. Lisa followed with their briefcases.

"She's in the kitchen making apple pie. You know how she is." Clara smiled. Collin followed her in and set the bags down as she followed the smell into the kitchen. Her Aunt Abigail Sorenson was standing at the stove adding the finishing touches of her famous homemade apple pie. She was roughly the same height as Collin's mother, with just a couple of extra pounds. Her shoulder length hair was the same wavy style and light brown coloring as her sister's. She was three years older than Clara's age of fifty-two.

"Hey, munchkin!" Abby embraced her niece warmly. She'd never had children and when her husband had died of cancer back in the eighties, she had never remarried.

Abby had always treated Collin as though she were her own daughter and when Clara and Burk divorced she had moved in to help Clara take care of the big house. Both women still worked as writers at the local newspaper. Each of them could've easily been a journalist for any major newspaper if they'd wanted to give up the small-town life.

"Hey, Aunt Abby." Collin smiled.

Lisa walked into the kitchen behind Collin. "It smells wonderful in here," she said.

"Thank you dear." Abby hugged her and went back to her pie.

"How long are you kids here?"

"Five days," Collin said as she peered at the pie one last time. Her mouth watered with anticipation. "How's she doing?" she asked, referring to her mother.

"Good so far. She says she's not in any pain. I think if they hadn't have found the cysts that were causing her pain to begin with, they may have never found the cancer. How are you feeling, honey?"

"Fine."

"Did you get your results yet?" Abby asked as she slid the pie into the oven.

"No. I will probably get them when I get back," she

said, wanting to forget that she was awaiting the results in the first place.

~

The four women spent the rest of the afternoon catching up. They ate a home cooked four course dinner, followed by the apple pie. Collin and Lisa set up their laptops in the study that was used when Collin was home. It had been her father's sanctuary.

"Mom, I'm stuffed. The two of you should be three hundred pounds eating like that every day." Collin curled up in one of the two overstuffed chairs.

Abby and Clara sat on the couch, one working a crossword puzzle and the other watching TV. Lisa was passed out in the loveseat that sat across from the overstuffed chairs in the large living room. The entire house had hardwood floors that creaked when you stepped on them. They had done that for the past twenty five years. Clara and Burk had decided they liked it when they bought the houses, saying it gave the house a voice. It also kept their daughter from sneaking out as she got older.

"Honey, we don't eat such a large meal when it's just us. But, we only get to cook like this once a year since that's about all we see you anymore. So, we have to get it all out of our system while you're here."

"I see, fatten up your daughter when she visits," Collin laughed. "I should wake her before she gets a kink in her neck. I'll hear it for the rest of the night." Collin walked over and shook Lisa's shoulder gently.

"Hmm…" Lisa opened her eyes, already feeling the tightness in her neck.

"Go get in the bed, honey. I know you're worn out."

Collin kissed her cheek.

"I think I'll take a shower first, then lay down." Lisa got up and hugged everyone goodnight.

~

Collin sat up until midnight talking to her mom and aunt. They shared a bowl of popcorn and watched late night TV. Collin told them about the cases that she'd been working on and they updated her on the local news. There seemed to be twice as much gossip these days since the population had grown close to forty thousand in the past twelve years. It was still considered rather small compared to the cities nearby.

Collin had graduated with a class of thirty. She had been the only girl to completely move away. The other three that had left for college, had eventually come back to start their lives in Allentown. Two of the boys that had gone away hadn't come back either. One was a successful doctor in Texas and the other was a stockbroker in New York.

Collin hated begin a part of the local town gossip, but over the years the town had read about Collin slowly becoming a successful defense attorney in the L.A. area and all of Allentown knew about Collin's marriage since her mother and aunt had decided to put their wedding picture and a small caption in the local paper. Lisa and Collin had gone to Canada to get married. Clara had been pissed because for one, she hated flying, but she had also really wanted to have the wedding in Allentown. Collin and Lisa had their closest friends and family there to witness the beautiful wedding in Toronto. Gay-marriage was legal in Canada at the time so it had made sense to go there.

~

Lisa swore she heard a screeching that sounded like a sick rooster crowing before the sun came up. She sat up, looking around. Collin was asleep next to her in the queen-sized bed. She stretched and padded across the room to the bathroom. Collin was standing at the door when she came out. Lisa went to scream but Collin muffled it with a kiss. The kiss was long and lingering, but Collin didn't feel the passion that she was used to when she kissed Lisa. She wondered if Lisa was aware of the growing distance between them.

"What's wrong?" Collin whispered.

"Stop scarring me, God damn it!"

"Sshhh, you'll wake up the house. I'm sorry, I have to pee."

Lisa walked around her, moving back to bed. "What time do we have to get up?"

The crowing noise echoed again in the distance.

"What the fuck is that screeching?" Lisa growled.

"The alarm clock," Collin laughed. "That's probably Oscar. My mom mentioned that an old senile rooster took up residence in the barn. They named him Oscar."

"Ugh!" Lisa sighed and laid her head back on the bed. "Tell that stupid bird the sun isn't even up yet!"

"City girl," Collin said with a shake of her head as she left the room.

"You were a city girl when I met you," Lisa called after her.

~

They arrived in Harrisburg early and the hospital was already waiting to prep Clara her for surgery. Everyone quickly said their goodbyes and Collin, Abby, and Lisa bowed their heads together praying that the cancer had not spread.

Collin paced the floor in the waiting room while Lisa talked on the phone to her office. Abby sat in a stiff chair reading a magazine. Clara had been in the back for close to an hour with at least one more hour, possibly two, to go.

"Want some coffee, honey?" Collin asked Lisa. She quickly waved her off, continuing her phone conversation.

"Aunt Abby, want some coffee?"

"Sure, cream and two sugars. Thanks."

Collin disappeared to the cafeteria, returning just as the doctor was leaving the waiting room.

"What did he say?" Collin asked as she sat down next to her aunt, sipping her coffee.

"Everything went fine. She's being moved to recovery and will probably be able to go home the day after tomorrow."

"That's good. What about the cancer?"

"He said it looked like it was contained to her ovaries. They originally thought it was only the right ovary based on the MRI and the Laparoscopy, but he found a small tumor on the left one as he was removing it. He did biopsy of the stomach lining and other organ tissues just to be certain, but he thinks we're looking at Stage 1B and she will probably be okay with only one round of chemo. "

"That's good news," Collin said, breathing a sigh of relief that the disease hadn't spread further. "Are you sure you'll be able to take care of her by yourself when she comes home?"

"Yes, of course, honey. She'll be sore for a few days but she'll be up and moving around in no time. I remember when I had my hysterectomy. Things were a lot different twenty years ago."

"Yeah." Collin smiled, feeling hopeful that she wouldn't have endure any of the pain and procedures that her mother and aunt had been through.

Chapter Nine

Monday afternoon, Collin was in the kitchen making herself a sandwich when her cell phone rang. It was an L.A. number so she answered.

"Collin, it's Kelsey."

"Hey," Collin said, the smile evident in her voice.

"Are you able to come to my office this afternoon?"

"No, I'm still in Pennsylvania with my family. What's wrong?"

"Your pathology results came in and I wanted to discuss them with you. I'd rather not do it over the phone. When will you be home?" Kelsey asked.

"Just tell me, Kelsey. Do I have cancer?"

"The cyst we removed was actually full of fluid as I had suspected, but they found abnormal epithelial cells on the ovary. These cells tend to mutate into cancer. I'm sorry, Collin."

Collin's mouth went dry. Her heart rate slowed and her eyes barely blinked as she took in the news she had feared she would hear. Nothing could prepare her for that moment. She stared out the window at the fluffy white clouds and beautiful blue sky contrasting with the darkness she was feeling inside.

"Collin? Are you there?" Kelsey asked.

"Yes."

"I said you need to come into my office when you get back so we can discuss the next steps. I've consulted an oncologist friend of mine, so I will be able to give you more information in person."

"Okay. I'll be back tomorrow. Go ahead and schedule me for later in the day and I will see you then."

"Alright. Collin...I really am sorry, sweetie. At least, we found this early and it wasn't cancer."

Collin said a quick goodbye and set her phone on the counter. How early was early enough? She wondered. Kelsey might as well have told her she had cancer. How was having the abnormal cancer type of cells all that much different? She still had something in her body that didn't belong, and gone unnoticed, could easily kill her.

Collin searched the cabinets for something strong to clear her mind of the fog, cursing when all she found was a cheap bottle of wine.

"Fuck," she said, closing the cabinet.

"Oh my...such foul language."

Collin spun around on her heels. "I'm sorry, Aunt Abby. I just received a crappy phone call and I was looking for something stiff to drink."

Abby walked over to her niece and patted her on the shoulder. "Is everything okay?"

"Yeah, it was work related. I'm going to go for a drive. If Lisa asks, tell her you sent me to the store," Collin said, grabbing the keys to her rental car.

Abby watched out the window as the white car disappeared down the long driveway. She knew something was bothering Collin and she hoped it truly was work related. Deciding to keep Collin's distress to herself, she meandered back into the living room to check on her sister.

~

Collin drove a few miles through town and came to stop in front of a small white house in a modest subdivision. A dark blue pickup was parked in the short driveway. She stepped out of the car and began walking up the stone pathway.

"Collin?" a deep voice in the distance grabbed her attention.

She turned to see a stout man walking towards her in jeans and a flannel patterned shirt with short sleeves.

"Hi, Daddy."

"When did you get into town?" he asked, wrapping his arms around her.

"A few days ago," she sighed.

"What's wrong? Where's Lisa?"

"She's at mom's and if you say anything to anyone about me being here I will never speak to you again."

Burk stared at his daughter for a second, then shrugged. "Well, come on in. I have a pot of coffee brewing."

"I was hoping you had something a little stronger," she said as she followed him inside.

Collin sat down on the couch while her father went into the kitchen. He returned a few minutes later with a decanter half filled with brown liquid and two rocks glasses full of ice.

"What's going on?" he asked as he poured the two glasses, handing one to Collin before leaning back against the couch cushions next to her.

"Mom had a hysterectomy a few days ago."

"What? Why didn't she tell me?"

Collin raised her eyebrows as if to say *really?*

"That damn stubborn-ass woman. Well, is she going to be okay? What's wrong with her?"

"She had an ovarian cyst that was abnormal. They removed everything and she's doing better."

"That's good. I will go see her this week."

"Oh no you won't. She has no idea I'm here and doesn't want you to know."

"Goddamn, Collin. I'm a grown man and I was married to that hen for over twenty years. I will always care for her and love her. I don't understand why she hates me so much."

Collin shook her head.

"That stuff is all in the past. We've all moved on from it and I thought your mother and I were getting back on friendly terms."

"Look, I can't speak for her, Dad, but everyone was hurt with that situation and sometimes there can't be enough water under a bridge for some people. Anyway, I will keep you updated on how things are going with her," she said, taking a long swallow from the glass of whiskey in her hand.

"How are things going with you? Somehow, I don't think this is the reason you're here telling me your mother's dirty little secret. Is everything okay with you and Lisa?"

"Everything is fine. I just wanted to see you."

"Well, I'm glad you stopped by to have a drink with your old man. I barely see you anymore as it is. I'm sorry it was under these circumstances though. Your mom is one tough bird. She'll get through this and be right back to cursing me and meddling in your life before you know it," he said with a smile.

Collin masked the tear that slid down her cheek and

finished her drink.

"How long are you here for? Maybe you and Lisa and I can have dinner before you leave."

"I'm sorry, Dad. We're leaving in the morning. We both need to get back to work. I have an asshole judge that scheduled a court hearing today for Thursday morning, so I should have changed my flight to today, but I wanted to come see you and spend a little more time with Mom and Aunt Abby."

"How is the old battle axe?"

Collin laughed. "Aunt Abby is fine and if she ever knew you called her that she would probably beat you to death with a rolling pin."

"Oh, I do miss her pies." He laughed.

"She made apple pie the day we got here."

"Damn you, kid. You should have snuck me a piece!"

Collin laughed and set her glass on the table. "I'd better get going before they send out a search party."

"I'm glad I got to see you for a few minutes at least. Take care of yourself and have a safe flight home."

"I will. I love you, Daddy."

"I love you too. Tell that pretty wife of yours that I said hello."

"I will."

~

Tuesday came quicker than Collin had wanted it to. She'd even contemplated staying, but decided against it since Lisa was chomping at the bit to get home. Collin ran her hand through her short blond hair and finished loading their bags in the car.

"You take care of her and call me," Collin said to her

311

aunt. "I love you."

"I love you too, munchkin."

Collin smiled when her aunt used her childhood pet name and walked over to her mom, who was sitting on the couch. She bent down and wrapped her arms around her. "I love you, Mom. Call me as often as you want so I know you're okay."

"I love you too, honey. I'll be fine. Abby will keep me occupied. Call me when you hear from your doctor."

"I will. I'm sure everything is fine." Collin wiped the lone tear from her face and backed away.

~

Two hours later, Collin and Lisa were sitting on an airplane about to take off from Harrisburg airport. Lisa laid her head against the back of the seat and tried to sleep while Collin opened up a lesbian romance novel that she'd picked up before she left California. She had brought it in case she had any spare time, but as it turned out she had spent all of her waking moments talking with her mom and aunt.

"I'll be glad when we land in California," Lisa said as she drifted off to sleep.

"Me too. But a small part of me always stays back there," Collin whispered.

When the flight attendant came by, Collin ordered two Mimosa's for herself, then went back to reading her book. It had been at least a year since she had read a good book. Especially, one with lesbian characters.

Lisa awoke as the plane bounced through turbulence over Oklahoma. "How much longer?" she asked as she yawned.

"About another two hours I think." Collin was close to finishing the book she was reading. The sex scenes alone were enough to drive her crazy. She hadn't felt that aroused in a while. *Is there such thing as needing a cigarette after reading a good book?* She thought to herself and laughed.

"What's so funny?" Lisa asked.

"Oh, just a part in this book. How was your nap?"

"My neck hurts." Lisa said rubbing the knot in the back of her neck.

~

The plane finally landed in Los Angeles. An hour later, they'd retrieved their bags and driven home. Lisa parked her Lexus SUV into the garage next to Collin's Porsche. She let out a long breath and ran her hands through her shoulder length black hair. "Boy am I glad to be home."

"Honestly, I am too, although I miss my family."

Both women got out and made their way into the house with their luggage. Lisa sat at the desk in their home office as soon as she had put everything away. Collin took a shower and relaxed on the couch watching TV. Her mind was still buzzing with the news of the phone call from the day before and she needed to be at Kelsey's office in two hours to get the rest of the information and find out what the next steps were. She heard a faint beeping noise and wandered around until she found her cell phone. Tara had left her a voicemail.

"Hey, how was your trip?" Tara asked as soon as she answered the phone.

"Good. My mom's surgery went well."

"That's great. I figured you guys would stay a little longer."

"Lisa was dying to come home as soon as we got off the plane in Harrisburg."

"I figured that," Tara laughed lightly.

"Sometimes I think she's married to that damn company, Tara."

"I know it. Anyway, I called to say Jinx is having a Cinco De Mayo party this coming Saturday and she desperately wants you and Lisa there."

Collin laughed. "Yeah she wants eye candy!"

"She knows you're married and have been married forever. Give the girl a break. She likes to look at you. She invited Lisa too!"

"I'm sure we'll be there. It's been a while since we've done anything and you know how Lisa likes to schmooze."

"Good, get there about seven."

"Alright. I'll see you then."

"Call me this week if you want do lunch." Tara said.

"I will. I'm in court pretty much every day."

"Have you heard from Kelsey yet?"

"No, but it should be any day now."

"Keep me posted and tell Lisa I said hey."

"Will do. Bye." Collin closed her cell phone and walked back upstairs, realizing Lisa hadn't once asked about her test results since right after the surgery and her best friend had asked twice in less than a week. *She's burning the candle at both ends.* Collin thought. She loved her wife, but their relationship was past the point of suffering because of Lisa's absurd work ethic.

Lisa was still glued to her computer. Collin rolled her eyes and walked into the office behind her. She swept Lisa's long hair off of her neck and placed tiny kisses on the exposed sensitive skin.

"Mmmm…that feels good, babe, but I'm really busy. I need to get this proposal finished and emailed tonight," Lisa said, leaning back against her wife.

"Bernie just called. One of my case judges has decided to throw out some of our evidence and the damn trial starts in the morning. I need to go into the office and see if I can get this straightened out," Collin said.

"That's ridiculous. Can't someone else do it? Isn't that why you have assistants and all of those other people you pay to work for you?"

"Don't argue with me about working, Lisa, when that is exactly what you've been doing since you walked in the door. In fact, all you ever do anymore is work. I shouldn't be gone too long." *Not that you'll notice.* Collin thought as she left without saying goodbye.

Lisa hadn't seemed the least bit interested in Collin's health since her surgery She'd been so busy working out of town, as well as in their home office when she was actually home, that Collin didn't know where to begin to tell her what was really going on. At a time in her life when Collin needed her wife the most, she seemed more distant than ever, allowing her career to drive a wedge between them.

~

Collin walked into the Women's Hospital, wincing at the stale air that hit her like a board to the face. She never understood why hospitals had to smell like death. Maybe that was just her imagination, either way, she didn't like it. She walked down the hallway towards the private practice Kelsey worked for. There were three different OB/GYN private practices on the second floor, with the first floor acting as the emergency department and the third floor held the surgery wards and the NICU. The fourth and fifth floors were all private delivery rooms.

"Hi, Ms. Anderson. Dr. Hart has been expecting you," the nurse said as she walked Collin to Kelsey's office.

Kelsey looked up when she heard the door to her office open. She stood quickly and walked around the large wooden desk. She wrapped her arms around Collin as soon as the nurse shut the door behind them.

Collin froze when Kelsey touched her, but quickly warmed, melting into the soft curves pressed against her. This was the heartwarming, caring feeling that she should have been getting from her wife. Maybe it was her fault. Maybe she should've told Lisa from the beginning, but she was beginning to wonder if it would've even mattered. The feel of Kelsey in her arms extinguished all thoughts of Lisa.

"I'm so sorry I had to tell you over the phone," Kelsey said, releasing the hold she had on her.

Collin simply nodded. Her mind was still reeling from the warmth she felt in Kelsey's touch.

Kelsey sat down next to Collin, instead of walking back to her chair on the opposite side of the desk. "I figured Lisa would be with you," she said, opening Collin's chart.

"She's working."

"Didn't you two just get back today?" Kelsey asked, raising an eyebrow.

"Yes," Collin replied. Her voice sounded deflated and Kelsey wondered if it was because of the test results or if there was another underlying reason for the lack of motivation in her voice and sparkle in her deep blue eyes.

"As I told you on the phone, I spoke with Dr. Samantha Braxton. She's an oncologist and a good friend of mine. We did a rotation together when we were interns. Anyway, I showed her your results, but kept your name confidential. She gave me a lot of information and said she would be happy to consult with you if wanted her to."

Collin nodded, once again unable to find her voice.

"The abnormal cells that were found are called Epithelial Cells. They are the cells on the outside of everything, many people call them skin cells. Anyway, the ones on the outside of your left ovary were abnormal and this type of abnormality generally begins to mutate after so many abnormal cells grow near each other. This mutation is what grows into tumors that can be either benign or malignant. Yours grew into the form of a benign tumor that resembled a cyst. The difference is, cysts are usually fluid filled sacks and tumors are solid growths with a small amount of fluid in them."

"So, the tumor itself wasn't cancer?" Collin asked.

"No, and many times they aren't. The chance of the abnormal cells mutating into a malignant tumor are low unless you have the risk factors such as family history, positive gene mapping, or previous forms of cancer in other areas of the body."

"Well, we know my mother just had Ovarian Cancer and her sister had a lot of problems and had a hysterectomy in her thirties and may have had cancer if she hadn't had the surgery," Collin said.

"I informed Dr. Braxton of your family history and we both agreed that you need to make a decision. You can either elect to go through with a complete hysterectomy that will remove your uterus, ovaries, fallopian tubes, and cervix, or you can have the genetic testing done to see if you have the mutation gene. The other option is to wait and see if it grows again."

"What would you do if these were your results?" Collin asked.

Kelsey placed her hand on Collin's. "Every situation is different. No one ever wants to get cancer and with today's research and medical testing we are able to prevent it in some people. I guess the biggest question is, do you and Lisa want children?"

Collin took a deep breath. Children? They hadn't talked much about the subject and with their careers keeping them apart so often, Collin wondered if that was even a possibility. She had always wanted a child of her own, but the timing just never seemed right. She realized she didn't even know where Lisa stood with the idea and that thought scared her. They'd been married for nearly four years and this was something they should've discussed and she should've known the answer to.

Kelsey watched the emotion play over Collin's face and wondered if she'd hit a particularly sore spot. She didn't know Lisa all too well and honestly didn't know Collin that much better, but she had always felt drawn to the attractive blond and left it at that, a simple attraction that could easily be referred to as a crush if she were ten or fifteen years younger. Many people occasionally found friends or acquaintances good looking, that didn't mean you had to act on it. Still, she didn't know enough about either woman to say anything about their relationship. Both women had always been friendly towards her at gatherings and had always seemed genuinely interested in each other.

"What are my options either way?" Collin said, derailing Kelsey's train of thought. The litigator in her needed to know the facts on all sides before she could make her case.

"Well, we can schedule the hysterectomy for my next available date, or you can go have the genetic testing done and we can go from there. If you want children, you always have the option of freezing your eggs. That way, you can go through with the surgery if you feel like that is the best solution and still be able to have a biological child. I know this is a lot to think about and I don't expect you to make any decisions right now. I just wanted to give you as much information as I possibly could."

"You still didn't tell me what you would do," Collin said, squeezing the soft hand that was holding hers.

Kelsey looked at the blues eyes staring back at her. "The first thing I would do is go have the testing done to see if I carried the gene."

"Go ahead and schedule that test then," Collin said.

"Okay. I'll make sure you leave today with a lab order. You can call the lab in the morning to make an appointment. It usually takes me about a week to get those results, so let's go ahead and put you on my schedule for next Friday. Does that work for you?" Kelsey asked, letting go of her hand and moving back to the file lying on her desk.

"Yes, but you'd better make it as late in the day as you can. I have a lot of hearings lined up over the next few weeks."

Kelsey wrote a few lines on a sticky note and placed it on the top of the chart for her assistant. "I guess I will see you soon then."

Collin stood and Kelsey hugged her once again, careful not to lean her full body into taller woman this time.

"Please don't say anything to anyone. I haven't told my family yet," Collin said as she opened the door.

"You may be my friend, but you're also my patient, Collin. I can't say anything to anyone unless you allow it." Kelsey smiled softly, wondering why she still hadn't told Lisa. It wasn't her business to get involved in, but the loneliness in Collin's eyes was getting hard to ignore.

~

Wednesday morning and afternoon had quickly come and gone and so had the two days behind it. Collin had spent every waking moment in and out of the courthouse for the past three days. She knew she was in overload and threatening to burn out. At least she had a party to look forward to the next day. The Porsche cruised along in the six o'clock traffic as Collin turned off of Pacific Coast Highway and onto the road the wound up the hills to where her townhouse was located. She was surprised to see Lisa's Lexus SUV in the garage when she pulled in.

"Hey babe," Lisa said when Collin walked into the kitchen. She had an open bottle of wine sitting on the dining room table with two glasses and was in the final processes of cooking their dinner.

Collin walked up behind her, slipping her arms around her waist as she put her chin on the slightly shorter woman's shoulder. It was nice to see her wife at home for a change and able to share a meal with her.

"What are you cooking?"

"Steak with potatoes and crème spinach." She turned her head to the side and met Collin's lips with her own.

"Sounds good. I wasn't expecting you home yet," Collin said, kissing her softly.

320

"I had an early closing this afternoon that gave me time to catch up on my paperwork. Monday I'm headed to Santa Barbara and probably won't be home until Thursday. I also have to go to Pismo Beach the week after that. One of my biggest clients is looking to expand his business and has me out scouting for real estate. I can't complain, if I find the right place at the right price I'm authorized to bid on it without him seeing it."

"Wow, your clients have unbelievable trust in you. I'm happy for you, honey. You're doing what you love and you're very successful at it." Collin kissed her again. "I'll be in court for the next month. I have five cases on the docket at the same time. I think the judges scheduled them on purpose to see if I would crack under the pressure."

"That sucks. I'm surprised you're home then."

"I have the juniors working overtime." She smiled. Honestly, she'd taken the last hour of her regular work day to go have her blood drawn and decided to come home instead of going back to the office. She felt weak and unbelievably tired after the trip to the lab.

Plus, if there was one thing Collin had learned from her parents, it was how to separate work and home. She understood more and more why her parents had divorced. They had both said they fell out of love with each other. It had happened with her father as soon as he met another woman and fell in love with her. And her mother had followed when the devastation of being left for someone else had hit her. She wondered if those reasons were actual choices they had made or a fate that they couldn't control.

"I need to hire a few more office bunnies, but the problem is when my clients want something, they want me to do it. That's why I'm stuck traveling so much."

"Office bunnies, as you call them, will cut back on

321

your working so late at the office and so much at home though."

"Yeah, but I don't have the time or the patience to deal with hiring more people and then making sure they do things punctually."

Collin dropped the subject, wishing Lisa would take a lesson in separating work and home. "Do I have time to shower before we eat?" she asked, letting go of her wife and moving towards the dining room.

"No, it's almost ready."

"Okay, I'll run up and change then."

Chapter Ten

The black Porsche pulled up alongside the curb in front of the house. Tara was standing near the large house holding a beer and talking to two women. Four cars were in the driveway and another four or five were parked along the street. Collin put the top up on the car and got out as Lisa stepped out of the other side.

"Looks like Jinx has all of the lesbians in town coming over tonight," Lisa laughed.

"Yeah, you know how she is." Collin walked beside Lisa as they made their way up the driveway. Tara spotted them coming towards her and excused herself.

"Hey!"she said, throwing her arms around her friends. "I thought I saw the Porsche."

Collin smiled. "Who's here?"

"Uh…Leanne and Stacy, Kelsey and Mich, Patty and her new flame, I don't remember her name. Derrick and David, me, and Jinx. Of course you guys. I think there might be a few people here that you two don't know."

"Hmm…" Lisa said.

"Come on, let's go inside. Everyone's scattered in the house and out back."

Collin and Lisa walked in, following Tara to the kitchen. Lisa poured herself a glass of wine and Collin grabbed a beer.

"Hey, girlies!" Jinx threw her arms around Collin and lingered just a little longer than she should have. Then, she hugged Lisa. Jinx was an inch taller than Collin with short black hair and big brown eyes. Although she was only thirty, she was rich beyond belief thanks to her family trust fund. If she wasn't such a player, she would probably land a decent girl. She was definitely cute and very talented.

"Hey!" Collin smiled. "Good to see you again, Jinxy."

"You too!" She said with a wink and kissed Collin on the cheek. "Make yourselves at home," she said, grabbing another beer for herself and walking back outside.

"Whew! Now that that's over, let's join the party shall we?" Collin laughed and walked with Tara and Lisa outside to the wooden deck that wrapped around the back of the house with a few of the cliffs below.

"Hey, Collin. I haven't seen you in forever. Where's Lisa?" Stacy asked. Her curly red hair was up in a pony tail.

"She's right behind me," Collin said, turning around. "Or she was." Collin saw Lisa walking towards her a minute later.

"Sorry, I stopped at the bathroom. Hey, Stacy." Lisa gave the redhead a hug. "Good to see you again."

Collin made her way over to Tara, who began introducing her and Lisa to the new people at the party. She had seen a few of them at other parties, but had never met them.

"Hello, Collin. How are you?"

Collin heard the familiar voice and felt butterflies quickly form in her stomach as she turned around to meet the green eyes gazing up at her. She smiled from ear to ear. "Hey! I'm fine, thank you."

"That's good. Hey Lisa, how are you?" Kelsey asked

as she sipped her beer.

"Good, thanks."

"There you are. I was looking for you." A woman with short, dark brown hair and extremely tanned skin walked up behind Kelsey, putting her arms around her. She was close to Collin's height and had fine lines on her face from too much sun.

"I saw Collin and Lisa over here and thought I'd come say hello."

"Hey, ladies. How's it going?" Mich smiled at them.

"Not too bad." Collin answered as she swigged her beer. She kept making subtle eye contact with Kelsey.

"How's business, Mich?" Lisa asked.

"Crazy, I'm about to start working on a project down in San Diego. I'm starting to branch out and do more out of town jobs. It brings in a hell of a lot more money."

"Yeah, I've been in and out of town a lot lately too."

"I need another beer. Lisa, do you want me to get you another glass of wine?" Collin asked. Lisa shook her head no. She and Mich were engrossed in a conversation about real estate and construction, as they usually were when they got together. Collin simply shrugged and went into the kitchen.

Michael Jackson's *The Way You Make Me Feel* was playing on the radio and Collin moved her hips to the beat as she bent to get a beer out of the refrigerator. She stood up dancing to the song that had been one of her all time favorites and hadn't noticed Kelsey standing behind her until she spun around.

Kelsey whistled. "You know how to move your hips," she said with a smile.

A light blush crept up Collin's cheeks. "Thanks. I thought I was alone in here."

"I was about to dance with you, but I figured you'd freak out. I know how skittish you are about being touched."

"Only if you leave the cold metal toys at home." Collin winked.

"I promise." Kelsey smiled brightly.

God, she's so adorable and so different outside of the hospital. Collin thought remembering the sincerity in Kelsey's eyes as she had held her in her office. She shook the image from her head. "I should get back outside."

"Yeah, me too." Kelsey grabbed another beer for herself. "How is your mom?"

"She's good, starting to drive my aunt crazy." She smiled again, her blue eyes sparkling in the recessed kitchen lighting.

"I'm glad to hear that she's better."

"Thank you," Collin said, before walking back to the party.

Kelsey watched her walk out of the kitchen. "What the hell am I doing?" she whispered to the empty room, shaking her head and taking a long swallow from the beer in her hand.

~

The party lasted well into the night. Collin saw Kelsey periodically but didn't talk to her again. She did notice Kelsey had been looking her way every time she searched the crowd for her. They'd exchange smiles and go back to whoever they were talking to.

Lisa was ready to go around midnight and Collin was happy since she was tired too. They were getting into the Porsche when they heard a horn honking. Mich's full size truck went whizzing by them as they waved. Collin put the top down on the little sports car before driving off behind them.

~

Sunday was a lazy day for Collin. She cleaned the house from top to bottom, then spent the rest of the day reading another lesbian book, this one being a murder mystery. Reading seemed to soothe her and rile her up all at the same time. Half of the time she wanted to toss the book across the room. There was no way anyone could have that kind of electricity and passionate connection with each other because life wasn't always roses and sunshine. But, most of the time, she was completely drawn into the story line and couldn't put it down.

By Tuesday, Collin was up to her elbows in subpoenas and arguing with prosecutors about questioning her clients without her presence. Her headache was back full force and Lisa was almost too busy to return a simple 'hello, how's it going' phone call, so she only talked to her once at night. She should be used to this. For the past year and half Lisa had been traveling left and right to cater to her high dollar clients. Collin still hadn't told her about the test results and frankly, Lisa hadn't even asked if she'd ever received them. She wasn't sure when or if she wanted to have the children talk with her and that thought stressed her even further.

Collin ran a hand through her short blond hair and leaned her head back against her chair. Her normally bright blue eyes were dark and heavy as they sank behind her lids. The crackling of the intercom startled her. Collin's eyes fluttered open and she jumped to sit up straight in her chair.

"Yes, Christine?"

"Ms. Anderson, you have a phone call on line one."

"Thank you," she said before pressing the button next to the flashing line. "Hello, this is Collin Anderson."

"Hi, Collin. It's Kelsey."

Collin felt the first smile of the day form on her lips. "Hey, how's it going?"

"Good, busy." She paused. "I've delivered five babies in a row today."

"Wow. The day's only half over."

Kelsey laughed lightly. "I've been here since five."

Collin checked her watch, it was a little past three.

"I'd think your day was about over then."

"No, I'll be here until at least five."

"And I thought I was having a long day." Collin laughed. "You definitely have the harder job."

"Some days it's a cake walk, but most of the time it can get a little interesting."

"Yeah, it sounds like it. Hey, I'm leaving my office about five-thirty, would you like to join me for a cup of coffee?" Collin asked. The words came out before she had a chance to think about them. This was something that never happened to her and she wondered if she really was stressed to the point of no return.

Kelsey left the line silent for a second before answering, "Sure. Where did you have in mind?"

"You're not too far from me, so how about Martin's in Fashion Island?"

"That sounds good. I'll be there before six, unless I get an emergency call."

"All right. Just call my cell phone if you can't make it," Collin replied.

"Okay. I'll see you about six."

Collin hung up the phone, unable to hide the grin playing across her face. *Get over it Anderson, you're a married woman and she's just a friend. A friend that understands the level of stress you're under because of your health and your mother's health. Yep, that's all she is, a friend. A friend that you're already leaning on way too hard and a friend that you're attracted to.*

"Attractions are healthy, they remind you that you're still alive in the chaos of the world around you," she whispered to herself, knowing she was making an excuse. She honestly did need a friend she could count on right now because Tara wouldn't understand.

~

Collin pulled into the parking lot of Fashion Island, which was essentially a huge, two-story strip mall in the shape of a circle with all of the stores facing the center and the parking lot on the outside. It was by far one of the main points of interest in Newport Beach. Collin saw Kelsey ride by in a silver BMW and park a few spaces down from her as she put the top up on the tiny convertible.

"Hey." Kelsey was still dressed in light green scrubs and black sneakers. "Hope you don't mind my attire."

"No, I think you look cute in scrubs." Collin grinned.

"Thanks." Kelsey smiled, blushing slightly. *She has the sexiest grin and when those blue eyes lock on you...* She cleared her throat, forcing the thoughts from her head.

They walked through the entrance to the inside circle of shops and took the escalator up to the second floor. Martin's Espresso Café was located across from the

329

escalator upstairs. The inside seating was fairly busy with early evening shoppers, so they carried their drinks to a table outside on the veranda.

Collin sipped from her hazelnut mocha, while Kelsey nursed her green tea. They people watched as the crowd moved along in front of them. Various men and women strutted along carrying bags, some with kids in tow, but most of them were alone.

"Thanks for meeting me. I was in the mood for coffee before I went home to a quiet house." Collin looked over at Kelsey. She felt the corners of her mouth tugging at her to smile.

"I had called to see how you were, but this is even better," Kelsey said, smiling back.

"I'm fine," Collin replied.

"Is Lisa working late?"

"No, she's in Santa Barbara, until Thursday I think."

Kelsey wrinkled her nose. "That sucks. Does she travel much?"

Collin rolled her eyes. "She's gone just about every other week. But, she's making ungodly amounts of money and enjoys what she does."

"Does it bother you?" Kelsey asked quietly.

"At first it didn't. I was so busy with the new law firm, not that I'm not busy now, but I guess I didn't notice as much a year ago, you know." Collin took a long hot sip of her coffee and crossed her legs at her ankles. She honestly didn't remember Lisa traveling anywhere near as much a year ago. "Her business has grown tremendously."

"Yeah, Mich never traveled, then all of a sudden she started taking contracts out of town this year. Sometimes, she's only home on the weekends, but lately there have been many weekends that she's been too busy to come home. I know how frustrating it can be." She sipped her tea. "I'm used to only seeing her on the weekends and maybe once or twice a week nowadays."

"I'm sure you work pretty odd hours at the hospital."

"Yes, I'm on call twenty-four hours a day, seven days a week. I get called out of bed at least once a week, but generally I'm at the hospital seeing patients on a regular basis Monday through Friday. My entire schedule changes when one of my patients goes into labor though."

"I bet." Collin smiled. "I sit in my office behind a desk unless I'm in court, and lately it seems like all I've been doing is talking in a courtroom." She blew out a long breath. "I look forward to Lisa being home at night with me when she's in town."

"Yeah, it's nice to have someone to come home to. Mich and I don't live together, but we try to see each other as much as we can."

Collin raised an eyebrow and looked at the woman sitting across from her. "I didn't know you guys weren't living together."

"Yeah, we're not actually married like you and Lisa are. Sure, we exchanged rings, but privately and we both own our homes so we never moved in together. Besides, I have to be careful because of my job and everything."

"Wow, that sucks. I guess if it's working for you though, why change it?"

"That's how we feel." Kelsey broke the eye contact and looked away at the shoppers passing by.

"As long as you're happy." Collin smiled and Kelsey returned the gesture.

"Have you told Lisa?" Kelsey asked, changing the subject.

Collin sipped her coffee and sighed. "No. There hasn't

been a good time to tell her. She's rarely home and when she is, she's either working in our home office or sleeping."

"Don't you think she should know? She's your wife, Collin. If I was your wife, I'd want to know the minute you found out."

"If you were my wife, you would've been with me and not had to wait for me to tell you," Collin said softly. Without raising her eyes, she felt Kelsey staring at her. "We really have a lot to talk about when the timing is right."

"We do?" Kelsey squeaked. Her heart raced as she tried to swallow the last of her tea around the lump in her throat.

"Lisa and I," Collin corrected.

"Oh, right. Yes, you have a lot going on and she needs to know about it." Kelsey settled her nerves. "This isn't something you have to go through alone, Collin. I'm here if you need someone to talk to."

Collin's eyes fixed on Kelsey.

"Anyway, thanks for inviting me. I needed a break. Besides, Mich's working late tonight so I'm not going to see her."

"Thanks for meeting me. I enjoy talking to you, Kelsey." *More than you will ever know.*

"Me too."

Both women tossed their cups into the trash and made their way back down to the parking lot. Collin stiffened as Kelsey threw her arms around her neck, her hands playing in the short blond hair for a brief second. Collin quickly wrapped her arms around Kelsey, pulling her in and closing the gap between then as she breathed in the sweet scent of soap and light perfume.

Kelsey backed away first, putting light between them.

"It was nice to see you again as always," Kelsey said, smiling, her green eyes dancing playfully across Collin's face.

"I'll see you Friday." Collin smiled and turned back towards her car. *What the hell is wrong with me? She's just a friend. A friend that cares about you. Don't get confused.*

Collin climbed into her car. Aretha Franklin's *Natural Woman* was playing on the radio when she started the car. She found herself singing along as she put the car in first gear and drove off towards her house.

Chapter Eleven

A month had gone by since Collin had walked into Kelsey's office and found out she was positive for the gene that caused abnormal cells to mutate into cancer. She was told, as she already knew, the best form of prevention was a complete hysterectomy. She wasn't even thirty-one years old. She needed to make the biggest decision of her life and she was doing it alone. She hadn't told Lisa anything and even if she'd found the time to tell her, she wasn't sure she wanted to hear her opinion.

Collin had decided to forego the surgery for a little while to decide what was best and finally talk with Lisa since she deserved to know. Kelsey made her promise to come in every three months for a follow up ultrasound to make sure there were no new tumors or cysts growing on her ovaries.

Collin pushed all irrational thoughts aside and went back to concentrating solely on the courtroom drama that was unfolding week by week. She hadn't heard from Kelsey other than to get her tests results and she hadn't bothered contacting her either. Thinking about what was going on inside of her made her think of Kelsey, and thinking of Kelsey made her feel bad for not telling Lisa, and not telling Lisa reminded her of the argument she was avoiding, so it was best to just forget for a little while until she could wrap her head around everything.

~

Collin was sitting in the locker room at the health club, waiting for Tara to finish tying her shoes. Their weekly racquetball ritual was about to begin. Collin contemplated telling Tara about Kelsey. What would she say? What was there to tell? They were only friends and had only had a few friendly conversations. She was making something out of nothing and she knew it, so she kept her mouth shut.

"What's Lisa doing today?" Tara asked, not looking up at her best friend.

"Huh?" Collin tried to clear her head.

"Hello, Earth to Collin. Where are you, girl?" Tara laughed.

"Sorry, I've had a lot on my mind lately. What did you ask me?" Collin chided herself for letting her mind wander towards Kelsey. Something that seemed to happen more and more lately.

"I asked what Lisa was doing today."

"Oh, she's playing golf with a client." Collin didn't bother making eye contact with Tara. She grabbed her racquet and safety glasses and stood up. Tara followed her to the glass door leading to the racquetball court they played on.

"I thought you play golf."

"I do." Collin smacked the ball against the wall to warm up. "I wasn't invited." She whacked the hell out of the ball, it bounced off of the wall in front of them and sailed towards the wall behind them.

"Oh," Tara said as she quickly returned the aggressive

swing.

Both women put the little blue ball through hell, slamming against the wall with sheer force as they played their game. Tara could feel the frustration in Collin every time she hit the ball. She wondered about questioning what was bothering her, but thought better of it. She knew her best friend well enough to know she'd talk when she was ready. *A subject change, that's what we need. Something to calm her down, she's going to kill me out here if she doesn't slow down,* Tara thought.

"I know you've skirted around the subject when I've asked about your test results, but did you ever get them?" Tara asked nonchalantly.

"I'm fine. I have to see her a few more times to make sure the cyst doesn't grow back, but I'm fine." Collin answered without looking at her. She hated lying to her best friend, but she knew Tara would question why she hadn't told Lisa and then that would lead to more questions that she just wasn't ready to deal with.

"Oh, that's good. When do you see her again?"

"Three weeks." Collin said as she hit the ball even harder, if that was possible.

"How's your mom?"

"Much better, she's pretty much back to normal. My aunt said she was a little depressed, but now that all of the pain and discomfort are gone and the chemo is over, she's seems to be back to her old self."

"That's good." Sweat was pouring off of Tara from running around frantically to keep up with Collin as she hit the hell out of the little ball. She had missed it more times than she had hit it. Collin had them playing at a break-neck pace. Tara wanted to crawl into the corner and pant, but she forced herself to try and keep up. "I finished that project I was telling you about."

"Oh really, how did it go over?" Collin played as if she wasn't even winded. She barely had a bead of sweat on her face.

"So far so good. Sometimes I hate working in marketing. The staff under me does a great job, but occasionally I have to take over a project myself when it's a major client that I want to keep happy. That basically puts my schedule in a blender." She laughed.

"I know what you mean. I have the junior associates busting their asses so that I can just keep my own schedule. I wouldn't know where to begin if I didn't have those guys helping. Bernie's case load is just as thick as mine right now, so things are crazy in the office."

Tara desperately wanted to stop for a drink of water, but decided against it. Collin was obviously working out some kind of frustration. Tara found herself feeling sorry for the tiny ball. *What the hell? I should be feeling sorry for myself, I'm the one chasing after the damn thing because 'Babe Ruth' over here thinks she has to hit the damn ball as hard as she can!* "How many junior associates do you guys have now?" she asked.

"Ten, five work for me and five work for Bernie. We could probably use another two, but we make do with what we've got. They might work like dogs, but they're getting paid well, so they never complain."

I wouldn't dream of complaining to her for fear she'd rip my head off and kick it to me and she's my god damn best friend! Tara thought as she ran to the other end of the court to return an out of control ball.

An hour later, Collin finally started wiping the sweat from her eyes. She slowed her returns, but barely enough for Tara to notice. They continued chasing the ball around and whacking it back and forth from one wall to the other.

When Collin was finally getting winded, they stopped playing and sat on the bench outside of the court to rest and replenish their bodies with water.

"I don't know about you, but my ass is worn out." Tara sighed, leaning her back against the wall behind them.

"Yeah." Collin smiled sheepishly. "Sorry if I overworked you. I keep forgetting you're an old lady." She laughed.

"Excuse me!" Tara playfully smacked her arm.

"I should get going anyway. I know Lisa will be tired from being out in the sun all day, so I'm going to make dinner." Collin stood and began gathering her racquet and the extra balls and shoving them into her gym bag.

"Okay, tell her I said hey." Tara stood up and stretched, letting out a groan at the same time. "Don't start." She said when she saw Collin's mouth open to comment. "I'll call you sometime this week. Maybe we can meet for lunch if you're not playing Matlock."

"Ha ha, that's so *not* funny." Collin shook her head and hugged her best friend.

~

Collin was in the kitchen with a small towel draped over her shoulder and three pans going on the flat top stove. One was sautéing mushrooms and onions in olive oil, one was full of steamed white rice, and the last pan had teriyaki chicken strips with snow peas, carrots, and green peppers sautéing. The chilled bottle of white wine on the table hadn't been opened and the candles weren't lit.

Lisa walked into the house with her eyebrow raised

and her head cocked to the side. "Collin?" She called as she made her way to the kitchen.

"I'm in here, honey." Collin called out as she continued stirring the ingredients of the pans.

Lisa looked tired when she walked into the kitchen. She yawned and gave Collin a peck on the cheek. "Smells good. Stir-fry?"

"Yeah." Collin smiled. "How was golf?"

"Fine, we played eighteen holes. I was fighting the wind all day." She stretched as she opened the wine bottle, pouring two glasses.

"You look like you got some sun." Collin pulled Lisa into her arms and kissed her lips. Lisa returned the soft kiss, pulling away to take a sip of her wine.

"How much longer until it's ready?"

"You have time to shower, if that's what you're asking," Collin said.

"Okay, I'll be back down in a few minutes." Lisa turned and headed through the living room and up the stairs.

After dinner Collin joined Lisa in bed. Their lovemaking was quick and passionless. Lisa blamed it on herself being tired from spending the day in the sun playing golf. To Collin, it seemed like their relationship was heading more and more in that direction, everything was becoming quick and passionless. She hoped things would turn around soon. She was happy with Lisa and loved her dearly, but over the past year and a half it had seemed as if they were more like best friends who slept together, versus lovers who were also best friends. Collin closed her eyes and pretended to sleep, but she was still awake long after Lisa began snoring lightly.

Chapter Twelve

Collin waved goodbye to her wife as she backed the black Porsche out of the two car garage. She quickly put it in first gear and drove away. Lisa wasn't far behind her and caught up to her at the stop light. Collin headed north on Pacific Coast Highway to go to her office in Newport Beach, while Lisa went west towards Mission Viejo to look at a house one of her clients was interested in purchasing. She was on her way down to San Diego for the next three days to do an open house on a beachfront villa she was trying to sell for another client.

Collin put her sunglasses on her head as she walked through the front door of her law practice. She smiled and nodded at the receptionist and then the junior associates as she made her way to her large corner office in the rear of the building next to Bernie's.

"Good morning, fearless leader," The dark haired man said, grinning from ear to ear.

Collin shook her head and laughed. "Good morning, Bernie. Must you always be so bright eyed and bushy tailed?"

"If I'm not then who is? It certainly isn't you."

"I'm due in the courthouse in less than an hour, where I presume Judge 'choke on a peppermint' will keep me the entire day. I have a follow up doctor appointment later this afternoon, unless I have to cancel it." *On top of that, my wife left this morning to go out of town, again!* She stopped and thought to herself. "Plus, I'm two days behind on my paperwork because Judge 'ass on his shoulders' thought we should begin closing arguments at six o'clock the other night." She finished, tossing her briefcase on her desk and began going through the messages in her inbox.

"Sounds like you've got your hands full this week, kid." Bernie laughed. "And if you'd stop calling those judges names, they might be nice to you." He snickered again.

One blond eyebrow shot up as she looked at him. "I don't do it to their faces. Although, I'd damn sure like to sometimes!"

"You and me both." He sipped the cup of coffee he was holding. "I'll see you later this afternoon. I'm meeting with a new client this morning, then I'll join you for Judge 'choke on a peppermint' was it?"

Collin smiled. Bernie shook his head and went back to his own office. She was just about to head to the courthouse when her cell phone rang. She debated about sending the call to her voicemail, but didn't know when she'd have the time to return the call anyway, so now was as good a time as any.

"Hey, Daddy." She sat in the chair behind her desk as she answered the call.

"Hey, honey. Why didn't you bother telling me your mother had cancer?" he asked with a bit of tightness in his voice.

Oh shit. "I'm sorry, Dad. She promised she'd tell you herself. She made me swear I wouldn't tell you."

"Damnit, Collin. You know how your mother is. I may not be married to the woman anymore, but I still love her and I care about her. I'm deeply hurt that you didn't tell me the truth when you were here."

"I know and I'm sorry." She paused. "How did you find out?"

"I ran into the Jones' at the grocery store. They asked me if Clara had finished her chemo and wanted to know if I knew when she was returning to bingo! So, I called her."

Damn stupid nosey ass hillbilly neighbors! "Well, you know now."

He huffed. "You also didn't bother telling me you had testing done because it could be hereditary. You're my kid too in case you have forgotten. I deserve to know the truth, Collin."

Here we go. "Dad, I love you just as much as I love Mom. She was having surgery and I went to see her. I'm fine. My results were fine. Everything is fine. That's why I didn't tell you about me." Collin hated dealing with her parents, they seemed to fight over her affection and attention constantly. She wished deep down that they'd just talk and get back together. She'd been pulled in two directions for nearly ten years, eventually they'd have to stop. She hoped. "I need to get going. I'm due in court in a few minutes and I'm still at the office."

"All right, I won't hold you up. Call me soon."

"I will. Love you, Dad." She hung up and raced out of the office towards her Porsche. She prayed the traffic wasn't bad as she sped out of the parking lot.

Collin was saved because the judge was held up on the phone. She squeezed into the large room, sliding into the chair behind the desk that she was suppose to have been sitting at fifteen minutes ago. As soon as her butt hit the leather cushion, the bailiff called the all rise for everyone to stand as the judge made his way from his chambers. *Whew!*

Four hours later, Collin shook her client's hand and walked out of the large stuffy courtroom. Bernie had joined her halfway through the hearing.

"I think we have this one in the barrel." She grinned.

Bernie wrinkled his brow. "What do you know?"

"Nothing. Just something the prosecutor said about the witness." She bit the inside her lip.

"Okay?"

"Did you hear him say something about Mr. Chang's glasses?" She looked up at him slightly since he wasn't much taller.

"He asked him how clear his view was through his window at the nursing home and Mr. Chang said it was usually clear, but the night of the robbery it was storming."

"Right, but he failed to ask him if he was wearing his glasses that night."

"Okay?"

"Bernie! The man's glasses are as thick as bullet proof glass, did you see them when he was on the stand?"

"Now that you mention it, I did see them. What exactly does this have to do with whether or not Leo Vega robbed the bank next to the nursing home?"

"If Chang wasn't wearing his glasses then I guarantee you he couldn't tell one Hispanic man from the next. Without Chang's testimony they have nothing on Vega except a misdemeanor for trespassing."

"I see your point. Call him back to the stand tomorrow and go with that line of questioning. We already know Vega was there, but he wasn't the ring leader and this little tidbit can prove it." Bernie smack her arm and grinned. Collin smiled and looked down at her watch.

"Shit!"

"What?" He cocked his head to the side and looked at his own watch.

"I have to be at my doctor's office in five minutes. I'll never make it in the five o'clock traffic." Collin grabbed her cell phone and dialed the number to Kelsey's office. "I'll see you back here in the morning." She called back to Bernie while the phone rang.

"Hi, this is Collin Anderson. I have an appointment with Dr. Hart at five-fifteen and I was held up in court longer than expected. Can she see me if I'm about a half hour late?"

"Hold on just a minute, ma'am." Collin was switched over to a Fleetwood Mac song as she slid into the leather seat of her car and began driving towards the hospital.

"Yes ma'am. Dr. Hart said she can wait for you. You're her last appointment of the day."

"Thanks, I'll be there soon." She hung up the phone and maneuvered around Newport Beach in the stop and go traffic.

~

Collin ran her hand through her short blond hair. Her body was shivering and she wasn't sure if it was caused by the open back of the paper gown she was wearing, or her nerves knowing what was about to happen. Either way, she swallowed hard and willed herself to calm down.

"Hey, Collin. How are you?" Kelsey asked as she walked into the small exam room. Collin's eyes flew open, landing softly on the green eyes that held hers. She smiled

344

sheepishly.

"Hi, sorry I was late."

"No problem. I had some paperwork to catch up on anyway." Kelsey grinned. "Go ahead and slide down to the end of the table. This won't take long and I'll try to be as gentle as possible."

Collin laid as still as she could and held her breath while Kelsey poked and prodded with the ultrasound wand, taking new pictures of Collin's ovaries and uterus.

After the procedure, Collin dressed quickly and waited for Kelsey to return to the room. Surprisingly, she wasn't as sore as she thought she'd be.

"Everything seems fine. There are no new growths." Kelsey smiled. "I'll need to see you in another three months. We may be able to stretch it to six months between ultrasounds after that if you want. I don't think there is a question of whether or not the tumor will grow back, but rather when it does and we need to be ready to take it out. There is a blood test you can do called a CA125. It looks for markers in your blood that are positive in Ovarian Cancer patients. The downfall is, you can test positive for the markers and not actually have cancer. So, it has positive and negative attributes. Just let me know what you think."

"You're very good at what you do, Kelsey. Thank you for taking care of me." Collin held her eyes.

"You're welcome." Kelsey ran a hand through her shoulder length auburn hair. She looked at least ten years younger standing under the fluorescent lighting in green scrubs and sneakers. The highlights in her hair glistened. "Would you like to grab some dinner with me? Mich's working up in Anaheim until Thursday." Kelsey kept her gaze steady on the deep blue eyes looking back at her.

"I'd love to." Collin grinned. "Lisa's in San Diego again. I think she comes home Thursday too."

"There's a great little Mexican place by my house." Kelsey replied. Collin nodded and walked out into the waiting room while Kelsey wrapped up her day.

~

"I'll have a margarita with no salt," Collin ordered as she opened her menu.

"Make that two," Kelsey added as she scanned the specials. "They have really good enchiladas."

"Hmm…that's actually what I was thinking about ordering." Collin grinned and closed her menu.

"Me too."

The waitress came with their drink order, along with chips and salsa. Both women gave their dinner orders and sipped the margaritas. Kelsey was used to being seen in her scrubs after work so the curious stares didn't affect her. Being seen with another woman used to bother her to no end a few years ago, but she'd done so much to preserve her 'straight' appearance that these days she wasn't as paranoid.

"I don't think I've ever eaten here," Collin said as she looked around at the tiny cantina style restaurant.

"I don't come here much. Mich isn't a big fan of Mexican food."

"Oh, Lisa doesn't eat Japanese and I absolutely love sushi."

"Oh my God, me too." Kelsey smiled. "Mich doesn't eat Japanese either, she's extremely picky when it comes to food. She's more meat and potatoes."

"I know a wonderful place up in Hollywood with a

346

rotating sushi bar," Collin added. "Maybe we can go there for lunch or dinner sometime."

"That would be great."

Their food appeared and disappeared just as quickly. Both women had a second margarita as they watched the sun go down over the ocean.

"I don't think I could live anywhere else. California sunsets are unbelievable," Kelsey said, sipping her drink.

"I agree with you. I grew up in a very small town in Pennsylvania and went to UCLA two weeks after I graduated from high school. I only go back now to see my family a few times a year. Don't get me wrong, small town life isn't bad, but it's day and night compared to living out here."

"I grew up in Seattle and lived there thirty years. I couldn't pass up the job at the women's hospital and I was looking for a change anyway. I met Mich about two months after I moved."

"I met Lisa while I was in law school."

"How long have you two been together?" Kelsey asked.

"Six years total and nearly four years married. What about you guys?" Collin swooshed the ice around in her half empty glass.

"Almost five years."

Collin thought she should toast to their long relationships, but what she really wanted to do was walk along the beach below with Kelsey's soft hand in hers as the sun kissed the ocean. *Whoa, what the hell? This is not the time nor the place for those thoughts. You're a married woman and she practically is too.*

"I always enjoy talking to you." Kelsey broke Collin's radical chain of thought. Collin looked up from the table to meet her eyes warmly.

"There's something about you, I can't quite place it. I feel so comfortable with you," Collin said softly.

"I agree." Kelsey finished her drink. *I feel so much more than comfortable with you, and it's driving me crazy, but I believe our time together with you as my patient is what is driving this absurdity.*

Collin chugged the remainder of her drink and set the glass on the table. The waitress returned with the check and Kelsey snatched it up before Collin could blink her eyes.

"Hey!" Collin's eyebrows rose up.

"I invited you didn't I?" Kelsey smiled and put enough cash in the fold to cover the bill.

"Yes, you did, and I thank you. I definitely have to take you out for sushi now." Collin smiled. "I should probably get going. I'm sure you've had a long day too."

"Yes I did and it starts all over again at five in the morning."

"I have to be in court at seven in front of a judge that is the biggest hard ass in the state."

"I don't envy you," Kelsey replied.

Both women walked out of the restaurant towards their parked cars. They reached Kelsey's silver BMW first. Collin contemplated a hand shake, but pulled Kelsey into her arms for a quick hug instead. Neither woman pulled away. Collin felt Kelsey's fingers in her hair and on the back of her neck as she drew the petite woman tighter into her arms. The heady scent of her perfume mixed with the salt air sent Collin's senses into overdrive. She took a deep breath and closed her eyes, releasing her hold slightly when she felt Kelsey pull back to look up at her. Their eyes met softly in the moonlight and held one another just as easily as their arms did. The muscles in Collin's chest tightened and her heart pounded out of control.

Kelsey shuddered from head to toe. She was on fire from the heated blood racing through her body. They stared at each other for seconds that felt like minutes. Collin opened her mouth to speak and Kelsey closed the distance between them, pressing her lips to Collin's mouth. The kiss was slow and probing at first. The tip of Collin's tongue played on Kelsey's lips until they parted, allowing them to explore each other further. Their mouths moved together, tasting one another over and over. They held each other as if they were scared to let go. The heated passion between them dissolved into tiny ambers threatening to ignite again as Kelsey pulled away. Collin felt frozen in every place that Kelsey's body had been touching her when the cool air passed in the space between them.

"We...Collin..." Kelsey tried to compose herself and catch her breath, but her mind and body were racing and her heart felt like it was about to explode out of her chest. "We can't....what about....Lich I mean Misa..." She tried desperately to make a sentence. Collin grabbed her shaking hands to calm her.

"Ssshhh...it's okay...it's not like we slept together." Collin felt her knees clinking together. She swore she could hear the pounding of her own racing heart in her ears. Her nerves were firing in all directions and her chest felt tight and heavy like she was having a coronary. She hadn't felt that much wetness between her legs in so long she had forgotten what is was like to want something so bad you thought you would die.

"I should go...I'm sorry." Kelsey removed her trembling hands from Collin's hold.

"Don't be. Kelsey, this isn't your fault." Collin tried to calm her down, but she was just as thrown by the situation. "Be careful going home. Call me when you get there…I'm worried about you driving." *I can't breathe. My lips are still tingling and my body is on fire!*

Kelsey didn't say anything else. She slid into her car and was gone before Collin could even get the Porsche started. Collin tried to take a deep breath but her body wouldn't let her. *What the hell have I done?*

Chapter Thirteen

Collin tossed her keys on the table by the front door and padded across the hardwood floor towards the home office that she and Lisa shared. She set her briefcase on top of the desk, unbuttoned her black suit jacket, and took a deep breath as she ran a hand through her hair.

Collin had barely made it up the stairs when her cell phone rang. She didn't recognize the number, but remembered asking Kelsey to call her when she made it home, so she answered the call.

"Hi, I...uh...I'm home." Kelsey's voice was shaky.

"Me too, I just walked in," Collin said.

"Collin..." Kelsey tried to say something, anything, but Collin cut her off, saying the words she was desperately searching for.

"I think we should take some time and let all of this sink in before we try to understand it."

"I agree with you."

Oh thank God. Collin finally let herself breathe, she'd stopped as soon as she heard the other woman's voice on the line. "Goodnight, Kelsey." Collin heard a sniffle on the other end of the phone just before the line went dead.

~

In less than twenty-four hours Collin's entire world had been turned upside down. She was drowning in a sea of confusion, her lungs were burning from literally forgetting to breath, and the rapid flowing blood in her veins was causing her to feel light headed and dizzy. The hustle and bustle of the courthouse and the constraining feeling of the courtroom did nothing to calm her nerves or the ever-present heat between her legs. Her frustration was rising and she feared she'd implode before her case was adjourned for the day.

"Ms. Anderson, you may call your next witness." Collin was almost startled when she heard her name. Bernie looked at her with a raised eyebrow. She shrugged him off, standing poised and ready to attack.

"Thank you, your Honor, the defense calls Lou Chang."

"Objection!" The prosecuting attorney stood from his chair.

"Sustained. Although, I do hope you know where you're going with this, Ms. Anderson."

"Yes, sir." Collin nodded and waited for the man to be sworn in. As soon he was seated Collin met him face to face.

"How long have you been wearing glasses, Mr. Chang?"

"I…don't know, probably forty year." He still spoke with a slight Asian accent.

"How often would you say you wear them?"

"I only take them off when I sleep."

"Okay, so you're saying you wear them constantly, is this correct?"

"Yes."

"The night you say you saw Leo Vega rob the

Community One Bank, what time did you go to sleep?"

"I think ten."

"In your earlier testimony you said you woke up at midnight to use the restroom, is that correct?"

"Yes."

"Do you normally put on your glasses when you go to the restroom in the middle of the night?" she asked.

Mr. Chang thought about the question for a second. "No. I get up and go. The bathroom is close to bed."

"When did you say you heard the bank alarm?"

"After I left bathroom."

"What did you do when you heard the alarm?"

"I went to window and saw that man running with bag." He pointed towards the defendant.

"Mr. Chang, did you walk back over to your bed and put your glasses on before you went to the window?"

He took a second and looked around the room. "No."

"Objection! What does this…"

"Overruled!" The judge snapped and Collin went back to the witness.

"How far away can you see clearly without your glasses?"

"Objection! Mr. Change is not an ophthalmologist." The prosecutor was clinching the brown table in front of him, causing his knuckles to turn white.

"Ms. Anderson, please redirect your questioning." The judge folded his hands together and listened intently.

"Your Honor, I'd like Mr. Chang to remove his glasses while I call up a few members of the courtroom."

The judge nodded and asked the man in the chair next to him to take his glasses off and look at the jury while one light-skinned black man and one Hispanic man, both dressed in the same white collared shirt and black suit

353

jacket as the defendant, walked towards the prosecution and defense tables. Leo Vega got up and stood with them across the room from the witness.

"Okay Mr. Chang, I'd like you to turn towards the three men on your right and tell me which one is Leo Vega, the man you say you saw running from the bank."

He squinted his eyes and stared. "Uh..." He tried leaning as he squinted his eyes, forcing them to focus. "That one." The three men separated a few feet apart.

"Which one?" Collin asked. "Please point him out as he steps forward," she said, asking each man to take a step.

"On the right. Last one, that him."

Collin called the man on the right and asked him to take another step. "Is that the man you saw rob the bank?"

"Objection, your Honor!" The prosecutor was past squeezing the table. Tiny beads of sweat were visible on his forehead.

"Overruled! One more outburst from you, Mr. Watkins, and you'll approach the bench. You may continue, Ms. Anderson."

"Thank you. Now, Mr. Chang, you're aware that your window at the nursing home is twenty yards from the bank entrance, is that correct?"

"Yes, I guess."

"Those men to your right are less than ten yards away, half of the distance that you were looking at the night of the bank robbery." She asked Mr. Chang to put his glasses back on. The witness looked appalled when he saw the black man was on the right and standing ahead of the other two guys.

"You see, ladies and gentlemen of the jury, Mr. Lou Chang made an assumption the night of the robbery. He was unable to see a clear picture of the person that robbed the bank." She turned back towards the judge. "That's all I have for this witness, your Honor."

Collin threw the entire courtroom for a loop with her discovery. She was able to washout the testimony of the prosecution's key witness and send the jury fumbling beyond reasonable doubt. When the judge called an end to the day, Collin couldn't have been happier, she practically ran from the courthouse.

~

Lisa was sitting at the large Oakwood desk in the office finishing some of her paperwork, when Collin walked through the front door of their townhouse. She watched the blond walk by the open office door on her way up the stairs.

Collin marched into the master bedroom's walk-in-closet, shedding her business suit and satin blouse and pulling on a pair of dark blue, loose cotton pants and a white T-shirt. Lisa had come home a day early, maybe it was some kind of sign. Collin knew she needed to calm her nerves and forget about the event that happened twenty-four hours ago. She took a deep breath, walked back downstairs and into the office.

"Hey." Lisa looked up over the top of her lap top sitting in the middle of the desk.

"How was your trip?" Collin smiled and walked around the side of the desk behind her.

Lisa leaned back against Collin's stomach and yawned. "Not bad, I'll be going back in two weeks to finalize the paperwork and close on the property."

Collin bent her head down to meet Lisa's lips with her own. Lisa's mouth was soft and sweet, but not inviting and hungry like Kelsey's had been. Still, Collin kissed her wife with the same love and devotion that she carried in her heart for her. She pushed her thoughts of Kelsey into the back of her mind and their lips parted as quickly as they came together.

"I'm supposed to meet one of my client's for lunch Saturday. He's only in town for the weekend, and I need to go over the details with him on the property that he wants to sell so I can get it listed."

"I'll be playing racquetball with Tara until one."

"I figured you would. I don't understand what the two of you get out of slamming the hell out of that little ball and chasing it around the room," Lisa chided, shaking her head.

"There's a lot more to it. Racquetball takes skill and a certain level of fitness." The corner of Collin's mouth rose up along with one of her eyebrows. She backed away before Lisa could playfully smack her.

"Yeah yeah yeah, go order some take-out for dinner. I don't feel like cooking and I have another hour of shit to do." Lisa moved the wireless mouse to turn the screensaver off. A picture of one of the Beverly Hills Mansions appeared on the screen. Collin peered over her shoulder at the giant home.

"What's that one going for?"

"The owner wants three and a half million, but I have a buyer with an offer of three point two."

"Which one are you representing?" Collin asked as she watched Lisa clicked the mouse to bring up the slideshow with photos of the eight bedroom, six bathroom, two story home.

"The buyer, but in this case, I actually know both of them and have represented both of them in other deals. So,

I'm hoping Roger takes this offer and we close this thing as soon as possible."

"What's your commission on something of this size?" Collin knew Lisa made a very comfortable living, she did too, but neither woman ever spoke about their income. Supposedly, half of their paychecks went into a joint account for the bills and the other half of their paychecks went into separate accounts for personal spending, but Collin had a strong feeling Lisa was keeping a lot more than fifty percent in her personal account. It didn't really bother her since money didn't run her life, but she wondered why there was so much secrecy between them.

Lisa didn't look up as she stopped the slideshow and closed the window before answering Collin. "My rates are adjustable. I cut him a deal on one percent of the buying price since I know them both."

"Hmm..." Collin compared that to her rates as a criminal defense lawyer. Her rates were also adjustable depending on the crime and the notoriety of the client, but she rarely made that kind of money on one client.

~

Collin woke before the alarm Saturday morning. The large king-sized bed was cold and lonely. She wondered where Lisa had gone so early, but didn't bother looking for her as she sauntered into the bathroom to get ready to go to the health club.

Fifteen minutes later, Collin found Lisa in their home office working as usual. *What the hell does that thing have that I don't? I'd rather compete with a woman than a god damn computer!* Collin hid her anger and smiled when she kissed her wife goodbye on her way out the door. She put the top down on the Porsche and drove off without looking back, thinking this car had slowly become the only solid thing in her life over the past two years.

Collin saw Tara talking on her cell phone when she pulled into the parking lot of the health club. She watched as her brown-haired best friend meandered towards the Porsche.

"Hey, how was your week?" Tara asked, closing her cell phone.

Collin got out and grabbed her gym bag. "Long!" she said, as the corner of her mouth turned up. She shut the car door and followed Tara onto the sidewalk heading into the building.

"When are our weeks ever short?" Tara laughed.

"No kidding. I closed one of my cases."

"Which one?" Tara asked as she held the door open to the locker room. Both women sat down and began stretching and removing their gear before they went into the court that they usually played on.

"The bank robbery up in San Pedro."

"Oh, I remember that. It was next to a nursing home or something wasn't it?"

"Yeah."

"Did you win?"

Collin finished stretching, stood up and put her safety glasses on. "I could be conceded and say 'Don't I always?' But, in all reality, there is no such thing as winning. I merely do my best to make the jury think my client isn't guilty." She grinned sheepishly. "And in this case he was found not guilty."

"I don't know how you do what you do. I don't think I could deal with criminals all day long," Tara winced.

"I don't necessarily 'deal' with criminals. I simply

defend the one's that can afford me. I have the authority and the conscience to pick and chose who I defend. Trust me, I read every inch of the case file before I sign my name on the dotted line." Collin hated defending her own job. She loved it because of the thrill of the courtroom as well as the intensity of pushing the truth to its limit.

"I'll stick to marketing thank you." Tara shook her head and smiled. She had more respect for the woman sitting in front of her than she ever had for anyone in her life, or probably ever would for that matter.

~

As usual, Collin won all of the games while Tara ran around frantically chasing the ball in every direction.

"God, are you ever going to let me win one?" Tara scowled with a smile.

"Nope, you must beat me to win a game." Collin smirked with a raised eyebrow.

"Does your head swell this much in the courtroom? You might want to watch that thing, it'll get stuck in the doorway."

"Ha ha ha," Collin said sarcastically as she packed her racquet, balls, and glasses in her gym bag.

"Hey, next Saturday night Leanne and Stacy are going to the beach to play volleyball. David and Derrick and a few other people are going. You and Lisa should come, it'll be fun."

"I'll talk to her. What should we bring, if we go?"

"Whatever you're drinking."

"Okay, I'm not making any promises, I need to see what Lisa has planned."

"Has she been gone a lot lately?"

Collin sighed. "Hell, she's never home. If it wasn't for the pictures on the wall I'd forget what she looked like."

Tara put her arm loosely around Collin's shoulders. "She'll slow down eventually, that or burn herself out."

"I know." Collin patted Tara's hand on her shoulder and forced a smile.

"How are things going with Kelsey?"

At the sound of that name, Collin's body froze and her heart began to pound wildly. She felt the last breath escape her chest as it tightened. "Uh…fine…everything's fine."

"What's wrong?" Tara saw the drastic change in her friend's demeanor.

"Nothing." Collin cursed herself silently.

"You're acting funny, is there something you're not telling me?"

"No, I'm fine. I had my first check up last week. Everything is fine."

"Alright. You scared me for a second there."

"Sorry, I try not to think about Kelsey and those excruciating visits to her office."

"Yeah, I don't envy you at all, but I'm glad you're okay." Tara squeezed Collin's shoulders again and made her promise to be at the beach party the following week. Collin hated agreeing, especially because more than likely, Lisa would be preoccupied so she'd have to go alone.

Chapter Fourteen

Lisa had work to do on Saturday as usual. She was closing on the multimillion dollar estate in Beverly Hills as well as starting a deal on another property in Anaheim, but she managed to finish early enough to go with Collin to the beach.

The Porsche pulled up alongside the curb. Lisa was the first one out of the car. She was wearing short black shorts and a spaghetti strap shirt over her yellow bikini. She grabbed the beach bag. Collin put the top up on the car and carried the cooler full of beer. She was dressed in short orange and black board shorts and a white tank top that left nothing to the imagination, but all you could see was the outline of her bright orange bikini top. Dark sunglasses hid her bright blue eyes as she scanned the beach.

Tara spotted them first as they joined the group in the sand. Various chairs and towels were scattered around. The volleyball and Frisbee were laying close to one of the coolers.

"Hey! You both made it!" Tara threw her arms around Collin, then Lisa.

"What's kickin', Chicken?" Collin grinned from ear to ear, picking Tara up in a bear hug before setting her back down. Both women were roughly the same height and weight, but Collin had more muscle tone.

Tara laughed at the phrase. Obviously, Collin was in a good mood. At least she was until she spotted the woman coming out of the water wearing a pink bikini and dark sunglasses. The highlights in her auburn hair glistened in the sun. Collin felt her breath catch in her throat, causing her to gag and cough embarrassingly.

"Whoa, did you swallow some bugs on the way over? I told you about riding around with the top down on that car of yours," Stacy chided, hugging her friend.

"You okay, babe?" Lisa asked when she set the bag down and pulled their towels out of it.

"Yeah." Collin saw Mich and Derrick playing catch with the football off to the side of the small group.

Lisa spread the two towels out and took her shirt and shorts off before sitting in the middle of her towel to apply her sunscreen. Collin put the cooler behind them and tossed her shirt on top of the bag before she sat on her own towel. Lisa finished her application and handed the bottle of lotion to Collin.

"You look like you've lost weight," Lisa said.

"Yeah, I guess it was the surgery or something," Collin replied, knowing it was all of the stress bubbling at the surface that had caused her to lose the extra ten pounds she'd been carrying around.

"Hey, how's it going?" Kelsey spoke to Lisa and Collin when she rejoined the group.

"Good, how's the water?" Lisa asked. Collin turned to face her wife who was on her left side, then looked back over her shoulder at the auburn haired woman sitting on her right. Kelsey was glad both of their eyes were behind dark glasses. She thought she'd lose all self control if she saw those big blue eyes staring at her.

362

"Cold as hell." Kelsey finished drying off and sat back on her towel which was less than two feet from Collin's. She closed her eyes and willed the butterflies in her stomach to disappear, and her pulse to slow to a normal pace.

"I think I'll pass on swimming." Lisa stretched out, closing her eyes.

"Hey, beach bunnies, who's playing volleyball?" Stacy shouted. Tara was standing next to her. Collin jumped up. She wasn't much of a volleyball player, but she'd do anything to keep a rather large distance between herself and Kelsey. Mich was still playing catch with Derrick, so they moved away from the net. David and Leanne finished their beers before joining Collin, Stacy, and Tara. Everyone grabbed a beer to take with them, even though they weren't actually going very far from the group.

"We need one more." Tara turned to the group. "Come on Kelsey," she shouted.

"I'm too short," Kelsey called back. She was glad Collin had decided to play, now she didn't have to worry about lying next to her.

"Bullshit! Come on!" Tara was walking towards her.

"Alright," Kelsey said, getting up.

"You, me, and Collin against Stacy, David, and Leanne." Tara grinned and tossed the ball in the air.

Wonderful. Collin thought to herself and rolled her eyes, thankful her dark glasses hid her expression.

~

Halfway through the game, Collin's team was losing. She'd face-planted the sand a handful of times and was now covered in it from head to toe. Kelsey had also fallen into the sand a few times.

"I think I've had enough," Collin said. "I'm going to go rinse the sand out of my ass." She laughed and headed down to the water. Kelsey caught up with her as she entered the cold waves. They were roughly waste deep before either of them spoke.

"I didn't know you were going to be here." Kelsey stayed close enough to hold a conversation, but kept her distance.

"I didn't know you would be either." Collin took her sunglasses off and dunked her head. Kelsey saw the sapphire colored eyes lock onto her before Collin put her glasses back on.

"Would you have come if you knew?" Kelsey asked.

Collin raised an eyebrow and let out the breath she was holding. "Probably not."

"We need to talk," Kelsey said softly.

"I thought we were taking some time to sort through this." Collin held her position.

"We are, but I think we need to talk about it."

"We will, when the time is right." Collin headed back towards the shore. Kelsey watched her at first, then thought she'd better get out at the same time or everyone would be suspicious.

~

Collin stayed on her beach towel, avoiding Kelsey for the rest of the afternoon. Various songs played on the IPod docking station that Stacy had brought. Most of the girls snapped their fingers and sang along to the music.

"How much longer do you want to stay?" Lisa reached over, pulling Collin's sunglasses off. She laughed. "You're getting raccoon eyes, babe."

"I know." Collin shielded her eyes with her hand. "We can go whenever you're ready." She closed the distance between them, brushing her lips against Lisa's.

"I'm getting hungry," Lisa said when she pulled away from Collin and handed her glasses back to her. Collin had her back to Kelsey and was happy she didn't have to see the reaction on the other woman's face. *Was there even a reaction?* She tried not to think about it.

"Hey, guys, why don't we pack up and go down to Breezes? They have the best homemade potato soup," Leanne said, covering her light brown hair with a ball cap and pulling her shorts on over her one piece bathing suit.

Collin considered making up an excuse not to go. The intimate kiss that she had shared with Kelsey was still playing on the back of her mind. *It was just a kiss, nothing else. Why can't I just forget about it?* She waited for Lisa to answer for them, thankful she wasn't the one to say yes they were going or no they already had plans for dinner.

"I haven't been there in a while," Lisa replied, looking at Collin. "I could go for soup and a sandwich. Is that okay with you?"

"Sure." Collin heard her stomach growl at the word soup, giving her no excuse for not going to the restaurant.

All of the women packed their belongings up, stowing them in their trunks before walking a few blocks down the street to the deli style restaurant. Everyone inside was dressed as they were, in various shorts and T-shirts or tank tops and flip flops.

Collin found herself sitting between Lisa and Tara at the large rectangular table. Kelsey and Mich wound up sitting on the opposite side of the table, so she had to deal with holding a conversation with them while she ate.

Kelsey seemed to struggle at first, but she quickly fell back into an easy discussion with Lisa about the latest political gossip. Collin and Mich steered clear of that chat, joining Stacy and Tara's conversation about Jinx and her latest fling instead.

~

After a giant bowl of Minestrone soup and a turkey club sandwich, Collin was tired. She was feeling the after effects of sitting in the sun all day and stuffing herself full of carbohydrates hadn't helped. Lisa noticed her wife's drooping eyes and occasional yawns.

"We should get going. I have to meet a client for brunch tomorrow and I know you're tired, babe." Lisa patted her partner's hand. The platinum band that she wore on her left hand, with three large recessed diamonds, matched Collin's.

Everyone hugged each other goodbye, making promises to call and get together again soon. Collin felt her pulse quicken when it came time to hug Kelsey. She quickly shook the nervousness away, wrapping her arms loosely around Kelsey. The hug ended before any other parts of their bodies could touch, but the warm heat between them was electrifying. Collin looked away when Kelsey looked into her eyes.

"Good to see you again," Collin said nonchalantly.

"You too," Kelsey said just before Tara slipped up next to them.

"I hear you're still taking good care of Little Miss Cheater," Tara giggled.

Collin swallowed the lump in her throat.

"Uh?...Excuse me?" Kelsey wasn't quite sure what

they were talking about and hoped to God Collin hadn't mentioned their kiss to Tara.

"Collin and I play racquetball every Saturday. She's told me about some of her doctor visits, but only because I practically beat it out of her." Tara grinned.

Collin watched the blood drain from Kelsey's face as her eyes grew wide. "She's just being nosey about my health, that's all and she thinks I cheat at racquetball, but I'm not sure that is even possible," Collin reassured her.

Kelsey forced a smile, staring back at the captivating deep blue eyes looking at her until Lisa slipped up next to Collin. The intense stare went unnoticed by the group and Collin realized at that moment that she would be much safer away from Kelsey.

Chapter Fifteen

Three weeks later, Collin walked into her friend Stacy's house. She hadn't planned on attending the impromptu party, but when Lisa called to say she'd be staying over an extra night in San Diego and returning in the morning, Collin decided to accept the invite and meet Tara at the Fourth of July party.

"Hey, I was shocked when Tara said you'd be meeting her here. We never see you out on a weeknight," Stacy said, hugging her friend.

"Yeah, Lisa's out of town, so I figured what the hell. I might as well do something."

"Well, I'm glad you came out! Everyone's outback. The coolers are full of beer and Leanne made a huge spread of food, so help yourself."

"Thanks," Collin said as she walked through the house towards the backyard.

Tara was ready with a beer in her hand when Collin walked through the sliding glass doors. Collin smiled at her best friend, taking the offered bottle, and drinking nearly half of it in one swallow. The summer heat was in full swing and the cloudless night was full of stars. Pairs of women were playing horseshoes on one side of the yard and various tables and chairs were set up on the other. Collin noticed a card game going on at one of the tables.

"When's Lisa coming home?" Tara asked as they sat in a pair of teak Adirondack chairs.

"Tomorrow I guess." Collin shrugged.

"Uh oh, trouble in paradise?" Tara teased.

Collin rolled her eyes. "She works too damn much. Other than that, things are fine," she said as her eyes scanned the small crowd of women. Her eyes zeroed in on the one person she never expected to see out on a weeknight. Kelsey must have felt her presence because at the same moment, she turned around, looking directly at Collin across the yard. "Did you say something?" Collin turned back to Tara.

"I asked if you wanted to play horseshoes, but your mind is clearly on another planet," Tara joked.

"I'm just tired. It's been a long week and there is still one more day to go. You can play, I'll cheer you on."

~

Collin spent the next hour avoiding the opposite side of the yard. She felt more than saw Kelsey watching at her in the darkness. She was powerless against the attraction and growing feelings towards the beautiful doctor. She had actually contemplated changing doctors. No matter how hard she tried, she couldn't get that kiss out of her mind and it scared her. She couldn't remember a single kiss with Lisa stirring her so deeply.

Collin finished her second beer and walked inside to get something to eat before her head began buzzing. She changed direction when she saw Kelsey step out of the bathroom in the hallway off of the kitchen.

"We need to talk," Collin said, grabbing Kelsey's hand and pulling her into the spare bedroom.

Kelsey silently followed her. Collin pushed her back against the door as it closed. Their lips met, kissing frantically as they tugged at each other's clothing. Collin found the soft skin under Kelsey's shirt, running her hand across her stomach and up under the swell of her breast as Kelsey's mouth opened, inviting her tongue inside.

Kelsey's hands moved under Collin's shirt, kneading the muscles up and down her back as her hips slid against Collin's in the moonlit room. Their frenzied kissing slowed to teasing bites and seductive licks and thrusts.

Collin's hands were kneading Kelsey's soft breasts with her thumbs, rolling around and pinching her nipples with each drive of her tongue. Kelsey moved her hands under the waistband of Collin's jeans, squeezing her ass and pulling Collin's hips harder against her. Collin slid her hands down Kelsey's smooth stomach and began unbuttoning her jeans.

Noise in the hallway broke their concentration and both women pulled away breathless with their clothes in disarray.

"We can't do this," Kelsey panted, slightly delirious. Her heart was pounding so wildly she was afraid she may pass out if she didn't calm her racing blood pressure.

"I know," Collin replied gently. She was in shock. All she had meant to do was talk to Kelsey. Instead, she'd come very close to putting her hands in her pants and was mere seconds from having sex with her. The desire to feel Kelsey on her fingers was still burning near the surface. "I'm sorry," she whispered.

"Don't be sorry, Collin. I wanted you just as badly." She paused, meeting her eyes in the darkness. Her chest ached and the throbbing between her legs wasn't letting up. "I still do, but this can't happen again."

"I only meant to talk to you."

"I think we're way past talking at this point. Don't you?" Kelsey grinned straightening her clothes before going back to the party. She couldn't remember ever being so wet in her life, so much so, that she was at the point of being uncomfortable and hoping there was no visible spot on her jeans.

Collin walked out the front door without looking back, wondering how the hell she'd let things get so out of hand. One taste of Kelsey had sent her head spinning months ago, igniting a spark deep inside. Tonight, she'd done nothing but pour gas on the fire, when she'd meant to douse the flames of desire.

Chapter Sixteen

Two months later, Collin was laying in the hammock on the back patio of her townhouse with her feet crossed at the ankles, looking at the view of the cliffs hanging over the Pacific Ocean. She was sipping on a cold beer and inhaling the salt air when her cell phone rang on the table next to her.

"Hello, Mom." Collin set her drink down and ran her hand through her hair as the breeze made the hammock sway slightly.

"Hey, honey. How are you?" Clara Anderson was sitting on her back porch watching a blue jay playing in the bird bath. Abby was next to her with the binoculars so she could see the blue and white details of the bird.

"I'm fine, working my butt off. How are you feeling?"

"Great. I had my check up a few days ago and so far I'm cancer free."

"That's great, Mom. You sound like you're outside?"

"Yes, you're Aunt Abby and I are bird watching. You sound like you're in a cave."

Collin shook her head. "I'm sitting outside too, that's probably why."

"Where's Lisa?"

"Working as usual."

"On a Sunday? That woman is going to work herself

372

to death," Clara chided.

"I know, but what can I say that she hasn't already heard? She's here, but sitting in the office surrounded by paperwork with her lap top in front of her." Collin tried not to show the frustration in her voice. She was growing very tired of spending more and more time away from her wife. Their four year wedding anniversary was a week away and when she'd asked Lisa a month ago what she wanted to do, she had simply said let's just go to dinner. Collin had wanted to smack her. From their very first anniversary together they had always made a big deal and planned a weekend getaway. Now, she wanted to *just go to dinner*.

"Make sure you check your mail for the card I sent. What are you doing for your anniversary? Do you have big plans?"

Nothing. Not a god damn thing! "Not much, just going to dinner. I have a few major cases I'm working on and she's entirely too busy to take any time off."

"Hmm, if you ask me, I think you both need a vacation. And leave that damn computer at the house," Clara scolded. Abby smacked her arm and raised an eyebrow at her for meddling.

"Yes, Mom, I know we do. But, we can't just put life on hold so we can run away for a weekend. Lisa practically works seven days a week right now."

Clara huffed. She loved her daughter-in-law, but feared the woman was pushing herself too hard. "So, what did you get her?"

"She's been eyeing this new pendant at Tiffany's. It's sort of heart shaped with an Emerald in the center and tiny diamonds around it. I bought her that and a Herringbone necklace to put it on."

"Wow, that sounds pretty. I can't wait to see it."

"I think she'll like it."

"Hey, Aunt Abby wants to say hi. Hold on."

Collin waited a second for her aunt to get on the phone.

"Hey, kiddo. How are you?" Abby asked as she handed the binoculars to Clara.

"Fine, staying busy with work. How are you?"

"Great. Your Mother and I are having a blast watching the birds out here. How's Lisa?"

"She's good. Working as usual." Collin sipped her beer.

"Tell her I said hi. I love you both. Here's your Mom back."

"Okay. Love you too, Aunt Abby."

"Hey, honey. I'll let you go so you can enjoy your day. Give Lisa my love."

"Alright. I love you, Mom."

"I love you too. Bye."

Collin ended the call and set the phone back on the table. Finishing her beer, she set the empty bottle next to the phone and stared out at the cloudless sky. It wasn't long before she began to yawn, fighting her closing eye lids. She was getting tired of being fine. In all honesty, she was dismal and being under more stress than the human mind could handle at one time was slowly taking a toll on her.

~

"There you are. I was looking for you." Lisa nudged the hammock to wake the sleeping woman. "You're going to be sunburned sleeping out here."

"Huh?" Collin open her eyes and looked around with a

raised eyebrow. "Was I asleep?"

"Yep."

"What time is it?"

"Quarter to three."

"Really? I got off the phone with my mom at one-thirty." Collin yawned and climbed out of the hammock.

"How's she doing?" Lisa asked.

"Good. She and Aunt Abby were bird watching in the backyard." Collin kissed Lisa's lips briefly as she walked passed her on her way in the house. Lisa followed.

"Hmm...I can't wait until I can retire and watch birds all day with not a care in the world." She smiled.

"Yeah, me too. Did you get all of your work finished for the day?"

"Uh huh. I have an early meeting with a new client tomorrow. If everything works out with him I'll be going to San Pedro next week."

"You'll be home Thursday night right?"

"Yes. I'm not going to miss our anniversary. Did you make us reservations somewhere?"

Collin smiled. "Everything is all taken care of. You need to be home by five-thirty. We have reservations for eight."

Lisa raised her eyebrows. "Are we going somewhere in L.A.?"

"It's a surprise. Just be ready to dress up when you get home from work."

~

Tuesday afternoon Collin cut out of the office early. She was thankful that she only had to be in court on Wednesday, that left her in her office the rest of the week to catch up on paperwork. Collin parked her Porsche in the hospital garage and took the elevator to the second floor. She'd meant to change doctors after the fiasco at the Fourth of July party, but she'd been tied up in court and forgot about the impending appointment until the day before when she was called to confirm it.

"Hello, Ms. Anderson. Go ahead and sign in, we'll call you back in just a few minutes." The reception nurse behind the desk gathered Collin's chart and prepared it for her check-up as Collin sat in the uncomfortable leather chair. The one and only reason she was even back in this office was her health. If she didn't need to have the scheduled check-up, she wouldn't be there and at this point it was too late to make any changes. Besides, she didn't really want to start all over with someone new or explain things to Lisa when she found out she'd switched doctors. They were adults and this was a professional doctor/patient setting. What could possibly go wrong?

"Ms. Anderson, I'll take you back now." The blond nurse smiled. Collin followed her to the exam room and changed into the paper gown.

Five minutes later, Kelsey walked in carrying her chart. Collin was sitting on the table with her long legs dangling off the side, as far away from the stirrups as she could get.

"Hi. I honestly wasn't expecting to see you here. I figured you would've changed doctors after everything that happened," Kelsey said.

"I wanted to, but I've been busy and I trust you with my health. If this is a problem for you, then I can reschedule with one of your colleagues." Collin looked up to meet the green eyes passing over her.

"No, it's fine. I'm a doctor and you're a patient. There

is absolutely nothing sexual about this situation. Go ahead and slide down to the end of the table and place your feet in the stirrups." Kelsey said as she prepared the wand and typed a few keys on the computer.

Collin did as she was told, looking into Kelsey's eyes one last time before squeezing her own eyes closed. The routine ultrasounds were becoming a nuisance and they were beyond uncomfortable.

Her eyes drive me crazy. I feel like I can see all the way to her soul when she looks at me like that. Kelsey chided herself for letting the thoughts into her head as she began the procedure.

Minutes later, Collin felt her heart rate increase and her temperature rise as Kelsey placed her hand over Collin's.

"We're all finished," Kelsey said, before quickly leaving the room so that Collin could get dressed and before she noticed the desire burning Kelsey's skin. It was becoming more difficult to be around Collin every time she saw her. She'd never felt anything like the wild, animalistic hunger that was driving her towards Collin. She understood basic need, but this was starting to feel more like Collin was the oxygen her body needed to breathe. A simple touch of skin to skin caused the embers fluttering in her belly to catch flame, threatening to burn right through her if she didn't break contact and cool her heated body. *This is crazy.* She thought as she stepped up to the sink in the restroom, splashing cool water on her face.

Collin put her black pant suit and yellow blouse back on and waited for Kelsey to come back into the room, as per her usual practice. When the door opened, Collin raised an eyebrow, looking quizzically at the nurse who stepped inside.

"Dr. Hart is attending to another patient, so she asked me to brief you." The nurse opened the file. "Everything looks good, there were no new developments. She'll see you back in three months for another follow-up," the nurse said with a smile as she closed the folder.

"Thanks. I'll make my appointment on my way out." Collin stood up and left the room without looking back. She stopped at the receptionist desk long enough to schedule her next ultrasound, then left the building without seeing Dr. Kelsey Hart again.

~

On Wednesday, Collin was sitting outside of the courtroom with Bernie when her cell phone rang. They were waiting to be called back in after a short recess so she answered quickly.

"Hello, this is Collin."

"Hi, Collin. It's Kelsey."

"Hi," Collin said, the surprise evident in her voice.

"I know you're busy, I just wanted to say I'm sorry I didn't get to go over your ultrasound with you yesterday."

"That's okay. The nurse said you had another patient. I know you're busy."

"Yes. I was here until eight with a woman in labor. We finally had to do an emergency cesarean." She hadn't lied, she really had stayed late to deliver a baby, but the woman came into the hospital in labor an hour after Collin had left.

"Wow. Did everything go okay?"

"Yeah, she had a healthy baby boy."

"That's good. Hey, I'm about to go back into court

so…"

"I'll let you go. I just wanted to tell you that I was sorry. It wasn't intentional."

"Don't be sorry and even if it was, I understand. I'll see you again in three months."

Collin's words made Kelsey shed a tiny tear. She hoped she would see her a lot sooner than three months. She couldn't get this woman out of her mind and she couldn't get her kiss off of her lips. Their brief interlude at the Fourth of July party had ignited the flames of desire that were now burning deep inside of her, threatening to claw their way out.

Chapter Seventeen

"You look beautiful, honey," Collin said, crossing the room. She leaned forward slowly, touching her lips to Lisa's. The brunette pulled away before Collin could probe the kiss further.

"Thanks. You look nice too." Lisa smiled. She was wearing a plum colored silk dress with spaghetti straps. Her long dark hair was pulled up off of her shoulders in a loose bun.

Collin turned around, walked into the closet, and came back out with a small black velvet box, deciding to give Lisa her present.

"Here, Happy Anniversary," Collin said, handing the box to Lisa.

She quickly opened it and her jaw dropped when she saw the glistening pendant.

"Oh, Collin! It's beautiful. I can't believe you remembered." She smiled before pressing her lips to Collin's. Their kiss was slightly more intimate this time, but still quick. She turned around, handing her the box. "Will you put it on me?"

"Sure. I'm glad you like it."

"Thank you. I love you, babe," Lisa said, admiring the necklace and pendant in the mirror.

"I love you too."

"Here..." Lisa walked over to her top dresser drawer and grabbed a small silver box, handing it to Collin. "Happy Anniversary," she said.

Collin opened the box to find a Rolex watch with black diamonds around the face and matching black diamond cuff-links. "This is nice, honey. I love it." Collin pulled the watch out of the box and put it on her wrist. She'd been looking for a new watch, but hadn't been able to decide which one to buy. The one Lisa had picked out was perfect.

"Now you can retire that old thing that's falling apart. I knew you were looking for a new one and I kept hoping you didn't find anything you liked. I bought that sucker four months ago."

Collin wrapped her arms around Lisa's waist, pulling her close. She stopped the flash of Kelsey that crossed her mind just before she kissed Lisa. "Are you ready for dinner? Or should we skip to dessert?" Collin wiggled her eyebrows.

Lisa rolled her eyes. "I'm starving, besides I want to see this place you're taking me to."

~

The Porsche pulled up in front of the valet booth at The Blue Room, a very upscale bistro in Santa Monica Shores that was known for its culinary art.

"Have you ever been here?" Lisa asked, scanning the tables and modern décor.

"No. Bernie's nephew, Victor, is a waiter here and he said the food was exquisite. I figured we could give it a try together." Collin smiled. "Hi, we have a reservation under Anderson," Collin said to the man at the small podium.

"Oh yes, right this way." The bald man wearing a tuxedo led the way through the dimly lit room, towards a small room in the back. A woman playing a violin sat in one corner and another was playing a harp across from her. The candlelight and soft music made the small room very romantic.

They sat down as the waiter appeared with the wine menu and a basket of fresh bread bites. Collin couldn't stop the thoughts of Kelsey in the back of her mind. It had been close to two weeks since she had been in her office for the last ultrasound. She briefly wondered if this was the kind of place Kelsey would like, before shaking the thoughts away, concentrating on the nice evening with her wife, instead of the idea of having a torrid love affair.

Lisa ordered a bottle of Chardonnay and buttered a piece of bread as the waiter walked away. "I'm surprised you wanted to come all the way out here," she said.

"Why is that? Do you not like this place? I didn't think you'd ever been here and Bernie gave it great reviews."

"No, I've never been here. I just assumed we were going somewhere close to home, that's all."

Collin asked the waiter to give them a few more minutes after he poured their glasses. She raised her glass, toasting another happy year, before swallowing nearly half of her glass.

"I've been waiting to talk to you about something," Collin said, pausing until Lisa's eyes met hers. "I got my tests results from the surgery while we were in Pennsylvania."

"What? Why didn't you tell me? That was seven or eight months ago!"

"It wasn't the time to talk about it and then we got home and you were busy with work…"

"Collin, that's a poor excuse. We both work a lot. You should have told me as soon as you got them. What did they say?"

"I have abnormal epithelial cells."

"What the hell does that mean?" Lisa asked, refilling their glasses and waving off the waiter. "Do you have cancer?"

"No, I'm fine, but I could potentially get it."

"Oh my God, Collin! Why the hell didn't you tell me any of this?"

"Lisa, you work so much and when you're home, you're still working. The timing was just never right."

"What did Kelsey say?"

Hearing her Kelsey's name made Collin's chest tighten. "She sent me for a genetic test a few months ago and I tested positive for the gene that causes those cells to mutate into cancer."

"Damnit, Collin. I cannot believe you have been keeping all of this from me!" Lisa said, angrily. "I can't believe she knew all along and never said anything when she saw me at the beach. She acted like nothing was wrong with you."

"This has nothing to do with Kelsey. She had to keep things to herself because of patient/doctor confidentiality and I asked her not to say anything to anyone."

"You can't use my job as an excuse. Why the hell didn't you tell me any of this, Collin? I'm your wife! I deserve to know what's going on with you."

"Lisa, I don't want to fight with you about it. I'm telling you now, alright?" Collin sighed.

"Have you scheduled a hysterectomy? Or were you not going to tell me about that either?" Lisa said sarcastically.

"No, I'm fine right now and don't need a hysterectomy. I've been seeing Kelsey to get ultrasounds every three months to make sure there are no new growths."

"How is that fine? You have about a hundred percent chance that you will get cancer. You need to have the surgery, Collin. What the hell are you waiting for?"

"If I have the surgery, then I can't have children," Collin said, meeting her eyes across the table.

"Children? We never talked about having children," Lisa huffed.

"I know and that is why I'm keeping my options open for a little while. I can also have some of my eggs frozen if I want to go ahead with the surgery sooner rather than later. I've actually been thinking about doing that."

Lisa stared blankly at her. "Are you kidding me? When the fuck were you planning on telling me all of this? Why have you been keeping all of these secrets from me?" she growled.

"I'm telling you now and if you'd been home paying attention to what was going on with your wife, instead of traveling all over the damn state you would've known what I was going through," Collin growled.

"I don't want kids, Collin. Freezing your eggs is a waste of time and money. You need to just have a hysterectomy and move on," Lisa said, harshly.

"We..." Collin started, but paused when a tall brunette walked up to their table.

"What's going on?" the woman asked.

"Can I help you?" Collin replied.

"You look surprised to see me, Lisa," the woman said, crossing her arms. "No wonder you said you weren't able to come to town this week."

384

"Excuse me, who are you?" Collin asked.

"This is Miranda. She's a client of mine," Lisa answered. "I'll call you in the morning," she said to her.

The woman raised an eyebrow. "Just a client? Really, that's how you see me after almost a year together?"

"Miranda, you're more than just an important client and you know that," Lisa stated.

Collin watched the woman's face change from a look of confusion to an angry stare as she said, "If I'm so much more then who is this?"

"I'm Collin Anderson, her wife," she said, firmly.

"Wife?" Miranda repeated, slowing turning her head. "You're married!?" she sneered.

"Miranda," Lisa said, shaking her head.

Many of the restaurant patrons had turned in their direction.

"How long have you been married?" Miranda scowled angrily.

"Four years today," Collin replied, her eyes glaring from the woman to her wife.

"Miranda, thank you for stopping to say hi, but as you can see, this is a private dinner. I'll call you in the morning," Lisa said, standing to see her out.

"That won't be necessary," Collin argued, pulling another chair out. "Please sit. I'd like to know how long you've been screwing my wife, because that's obviously what's going on here."

"Collin, this isn't what you think..." Lisa tried to explain, but Collin cut her off.

"A few minutes ago you were pissed at me for not telling you something when clearly you've been keeping larger secrets than I could ever imagine!" she yelled loud enough for the entire restaurant to hear. The manager

385

began hastily making his way towards their table. Collin put her hand up to stop him as she stood. "Don't bother asking me to leave. I left this relationship months ago," she said as she turned to walk away.

Chapter Eighteen

Collin made it to her car before the tears spilled over her eyelids, running down her cheeks. She drove away from the restaurant, unsure where she was heading. She just knew she didn't want to go to home. The wine and emotions mixed together were causing her head to throb like a drum between her ears.

She pushed the call button on the steering wheel as she shifted gears, getting onto the interstate. The line rang three times. She ended the call as the voicemail began and turned the radio up.

A minute later, the song on the radio was interrupted by an incoming call. Collin pushed the button to accept the call.

"Hello," Collin answered.

"Collin? Did you just call me?" Kelsey asked.

"Yes. I probably shouldn't have. That's why I hung up."

Collin's voice sounded deflated and distant, like she was hundreds of miles away.

"What's wrong?"

Collin sighed, not knowing where to begin or even if she should.

"Are you feeling okay?"

"I'm fine," Collin replied.

"Collin, I know you're not fine. You can't fool me. I hear it in your voice and I've been seeing it in your eyes for months. If you need to talk," Kelsey paused. "About anything. Mich is out of town and I'm at home."

Collin changed lanes, watching the exit signs go by as she drove. "That's probably not a good idea."

"Well, do you want me to meet you somewhere? I can tell something's wrong."

"What's your address?"

Kelsey gave her directions and rushed around changing clothes after hanging up. She'd been sitting around in an old t-shirt and shorts since arriving home for the evening.

~

Kelsey's house was modest and slightly smaller than most of the homes in the neighborhood. Collin peered at the various pictures scattered across the mantel of the natural stone fireplace. The single photo of Kelsey and Mich together in the mountains made her chest ache. What was she doing here? Just because her marriage fell apart didn't mean she needed to go and destroy someone else's. Kelsey deserved better than that and so did Mich.

Kelsey walked out of the kitchen with two steaming cups of coffee as Collin was walking out the front door.

"Where are you going?"

"I don't belong here," Collin said, shaking her head and stepping through the doorway.

"Wait a second," Kelsey said, carefully setting the mugs down and hurrying after her. "Come back inside and tell me what the hell is going on with you. I've never seen you like this."

Collin sighed and followed her back into the house. "Today is my four year wedding anniversary."

"Wow, okay," Kelsey replied, slightly shocked as she sat down next to her on the dark brown couch. Collin's deep blue eyes met hers, causing the butterflies to flutter deep in her belly.

"I met Lisa's mistress at our anniversary dinner this evening," Collin said, her eyes never leaving Kelsey's as she spoke.

"What?"

"You heard me. She's been having an affair for close to a year with some woman named Miranda."

"Oh my God," Kelsey grimaced.

"Imagine how I felt when the woman appeared at our table, giving Lisa the third degree about being there with me. Apparently, she had no idea Lisa was married. The entire thing went over like water on a grease fire in the middle of the restaurant," she sighed.

"I'm sorry."

Collin laughed softly.

"What's funny?"

"The irony of me sitting here telling you my marriage is over and you consoling me."

Kelsey thought about it for a second, then smiled brightly. "I guess that is a little strange."

"For the past six months I've been fighting whatever this is between you and I for the sake of my marriage and the vows I took, and the entire time she was fucking someone else like it was nothing. I feel like a goddamn fool."

"You're not a fool, Collin. You obviously have more respect for the vows you took than she ever did. I'm so sorry you're going through this."

Collin reached for the cup of coffee sitting on the side table. "There's nothing to go through. It's over. I'll have my law partner draw the papers up in the morning and file them with the county."

"That's pretty drastic. Are you sure that's what you want to do?" Kelsey asked.

"I've been going through hell with my mother having cancer and my diagnosis. It's not easy to hear someone tell you that you may have cancer. I've aged a few years this year from stress alone, waiting for the shoe to drop and you to tell me the tumor had grown back and I've been doing it all alone. She never asked how I was or what my test results were. I'm not fine. I've never been fine this entire god damn time and she had no clue."

Collin stared at the crème colored carpet below her feet. She wanted to cry, but truthfully, there was nothing left to cry over or be sorry about. Looking back now, she wondered how she'd never seen this coming. The signs were everywhere. Who works that many hours and travels that often? Lisa was obviously working so many hours because she was seeing her lover when she traveled. She needed to make up for the time away from actually working and her time at home with Collin in the evenings and weekends had been the perfect cover. She was so busy covering up her affair that she was completely oblivious to what her wife was going through right in front of her.

"Yes. It's over. It's been over for a year I guess," Collin replied, sarcastically. "I wasted so much time and energy on something that was worth nothing, apparently. In a way, I guess I feel a little bit relieved."

Kelsey held her coffee cup, gazing at its dark contents. She wasn't sure what to say. She and Mich weren't legally married by any means and didn't own anything together. In fact, there was nothing actually tying them together. She'd wanted it that way and Mich seemed content with their arrangement. She thought of her growing feelings for the woman sitting next to her and wondered if Mich had every strayed during their nearly five years together. One thing was certain, Collin hadn't been completely alone. She'd sat up many nights worrying about her and pondering over the feelings she could no longer hide.

"I'm going to go," Collin said. "I shouldn't be sitting here dumping all of this on you. I'm sorry."

"Collin," Kelsey muttered softly, grabbing her wrist before she stood. "Do you think things happen for a reason?"

"What do you mean?" Collin replied, turning towards her.

"This thing between us, your marriage ending…do you think they're connected?"

"Do you want them to be?" Collin asked, turning her eyes to Kelsey.

Kelsey sighed. "I don't know what I want. I've never believed in karma or destiny or any of that, but what I do know is, I can't get you out of my head or off my lips. The more I try not to think about you, the more I want you."

Collin squeezed her eyes closed, opening them when she felt Kelsey's warm hand on her cheek. "I can't be the one to break up your marriage, Kelsey."

"I'm not married."

"You're still in a relationship," Collin said, backing away slightly.

"Mich and I have been going through the motions for so long, I don't think either of us ever bothered to see it for what it really is," she said, meeting her eyes "Yes it's a relationship, but it's a relationship that never got off the ground."

Kelsey put her hand back on Collin's cheek. "Collin, you make me want to fly," she paused, meeting her eyes. "I'm falling in love with you."

Collin closed the distance between them, pressing her lips to Kelsey's, kissing her passionately. Kelsey ran her hands through Collin's hair, pulling her down as she laid back. The feel of Collin's weight on her made Kelsey's stomach flutter as her heart raced and her blood flowed south. She clawed at the clothes between them, needing to feel skin on skin.

Gentle bites and frenzied kisses were traded as Kelsey pushed Collin's jacket off of her shoulders, wadding her blouse. Seconds later, their clothes were scattered around on the floor nearby. Collin ran her hand up Kelsey's body from her waist to her breast, caressing the smooth skin and teasing the nipple with her finger and thumb, while her lips left a trail of soft kisses along Kelsey's neck and collarbone.

"Touch me, Collin." Kelsey whimpered.

Collin pulled back enough to see those eyes gazing up at her. Kelsey's pupils were beginning to dilate as she slid her hand down the front of her body. Kelsey's legs parted further, opening to her. Collin lowered her head slowly, kissing her once more as her fingers glided through the glistening wetness awaiting her.

Kelsey hissed, bucking her hips as Collin moved her fingers in lazy circles. The warm, wet puddle forming on her thigh where Collin straddled her was driving her crazy. She'd seen Collin naked from the waist down many times and even been inside of her a time or two, but she'd never actually felt her.

Kelsey's mouth watered with anticipation as she maneuvered slightly, trying to get her hand between Collin's legs. She succeeded in dumping them both on the floor with Collin now under her.

Both women laughed. Kelsey pressed her mouth to Collin's when she tried to speak, breaking any train of thought that she had formed. Collin's hips bucked as Kelsey's fingers found what they'd been searching for. She couldn't remember ever wanting to touch someone so desperately.

Collin managed to get her hand back to its original place, matching Kelsey stroke for stroke, before pushing her fingers deep inside of her.

"God yes!" Kelsey moaned loudly, riding her hips back and forth on Collin's fingers as she circled Collin's clit with her own, teasing her entrance with every pass.

Beads of sweat formed on Collin's forehead. She ran her free hand through Kelsey's long hair and over her back, settling on her ass as they traded passionate kisses. Kelsey pulled away slightly, lingering to run her tongue teasingly over Collin's lips.

"Please, Kelsey," she panted, needing more.

Kelsey pushed her fingers inside, filling her in one swift motion. Collin groaned, lifting her hips off the floor. She dug her heels into the carpet to get leverage against the woman moving on top of her.

They rode each other, harder and harder as the climax built between them. Collin felt Kelsey's body tighten, squeezing her fingers as she watched the green completely disappear from her eyes. Kelsey panted breathlessly, shuddering over the woman under her, threatening to burst into millions of pieces as the orgasm tore through her.

Collin quickly followed, crying out and grinding her

hips into her as hard as she could, completely oblivious to the carpet scraping the skin on her bare back.

Neither woman moved as they slowly caught their breath. Collin wrapped her free arm around Kelsey, caressing her creamy smooth skin and kissing her forehead softly. Kelsey lifted her head from Collin's shoulder to meet bright blue eyes peering back at her.

Collin grimaced as she rolled over, tucking Kelsey under her, noticing the rug burn for the first time. She watched the green color slowly returning to Kelsey's irises. With her clean hand, she reached up, touching the delicate skin of her cheek and running her finger over the silky, pink lips beckoning her kisses once again.

"I love you," Collin whispered with a smile.

Kelsey smiled back, running her hand through Collin's short hair. "I love you too."

Epilogue

Collin lay on the thin, cold mattress of the gurney. After multiple months of medical testing, exams, ultrasounds and procedures, she should've been used to the stale air and deathly chill of the hospital, but nothing helped take her mind off of her surroundings. She'd finally completed the weeks of hormone stimulation and undergone a successful egg retrieval the previous week, simultaneously freezing eight of her eggs the same day her divorce had finalized.

Now, she was patiently awaiting the end of the year long ordeal. In less than three hours she would be free and clear to move on with her life with a more positive outlook than ever before.

"Hey, sweetheart," Kelsey said, kissing her lips softly. "I just spoke with Dr. Sandino. She's just about ready, so they will be down here shortly to get you. I'm not going to scrub in, but I will be in the room. She should be able to do the hysterectomy vaginally, so it should take a little over an hour and your recovery time will be about three to four weeks."

"Great," Collin teased, "I've already planned a mountain climbing trip for next month."

"Smartass," Kelsey laughed. Grabbing her hand, she said seriously, "You've come a long way with all of this and I'm glad I'm by your side as it comes to an end."

"One ending starts another beginning." Collin grinned.

"Exactly. Our beginning," Kelsey said, wiping a tiny tear from her cheek. "I love you and I will be right beside you when you wake up."

"I love you too," Collin replied. "And don't worry, I'll be fine."

The End

Light Reading: Shadow's Eyes

Shadow's Eyes

By

Sydney Canyon

Light Reading: Shadow's Eyes

One

"Bucky! Houdini!" Tyler McCain called out loudly as she made her way down the back porch steps towards the stables, a hundred yards away from the two story, country style ranch house made of wood and cobblestone. Large oak and maple trees were scattered around the open countryside as far as the eye could see. The ranch house sat five hundred yards off of a side dirt road that connected to the main dirt road, two miles away. The rest of the property consisted of a few rolling hills, surrounded by a lazy meadow and shade trees, with a small stream towards the back and surrounded by thick woods, making up the rest of the thousand acres. The view of the sunrise was breathtaking, like standing on a hillside with the orange and red colors swirling all around you and swallowing you up, along with the rest of the world.

"Come on boys! I guess you guys don't want to eat this morning!" she called again with a thick southern drawl, dropping her g's. She shook her head, straightening her black suede cowboy hat.

Tyler's short blond hair was usually hidden under a hat, but her turquoise blue eyes could be seen from across a crowded room. She finally gave up, pouring the goat feed in one trough and the horse pellets in the other. She tossed a couple of hay bales close by and continued into the stables.

"Morning, Uncle Tucker. Have you seen Bucky or Houdini? You didn't feed them already did you?" she asked.

The older man wasn't much taller than his niece at five foot nine, but he was as strong as an ox. He could still lift her up over his head like he'd done when she was child, even though she was now thirty-two years old and just as muscular as the two young ranch hands they had working for them. If you didn't know anything about Tyler, you'd think she was barely eighteen, and more than likely the baby sister of the young ranch hands. She however, looked nothing like the guys, one with brown hair and brown eyes and the other with red hair and green eyes, but they had the camaraderie of siblings. She'd actually been accused of dating each of them at one time or another.

"No, I haven't seen those fools. They must be playing down by the stream," he said with a slightly thicker accent than hers as he took his brown cowboy hat off, wiping the sweat from his brow with the red bandanna from his back pocket. His hair used to be the same cornflower blond as hers, but over the years it had started graying here and there. Now, his entire head was a combination of white and gray with a little blond and starting to thin out. His eyes were hazel or light brown depending on his mood.

"Hmm...oh well I guess. I put their food out. I didn't have time to play with them this morning and they're probably pissed at me," she snickered, thinking about her self-centered pets as she walked to the other end of the stables.

Twenty five stalls lined each side of the building, creating plenty of room for the forty horses that they'd kept, bred, and sold. Many of their horses were in the American Quarter Horse Breed, and registered in the American Quarter Horse Association, but they'd also had Appaloosas, American Paint Horses, American Saddlebreds, Thoroughbreds and a few ponies.

As soon as she opened the first bay, Tyler heard commotion outside. She closed the bay, walking out of the stables, towards the noise with a raised eyebrow. She smiled when she saw her two best friends playing together.

"Hey guys!" she said loudly.

Tyler's two prized possessions trotted over to her as soon as they heard her voice. The first animal to reach her was Houdini, a Nubian goat, with off-white coloring, brown spots, and long floppy ears like a basset hound. He stood just under three feet tall and weighed about a hundred and seventy pounds. The other animal pawing and stomping around for attention was Bucky, a Sicilian donkey, with slate-gray coloring and a short black mane and tale. He stood only a few inches higher than Houdini. She kissed and patted both of them of their heads, grimacing and wrinkling her nose.

"Where the hell have you two been? You guys stink!"

The goat and donkey were more than just pets, they really were her best friends. She'd raised them both from bottles, weaned them, and broke them in together as brothers. She wasn't quite sure if they even knew they were two different animal breeds.

"Morning, Tyler!" the brown-haired ranch hand called out on his way into the stables with one of the filly horses. He tipped his hat and smiled.

"Hey, Jake." Tyler waved him over. "Do you know where these two have been? They smell like hog mud!" she said.

He laughed heartily. "No, with those two, who knows?!"

"Fine, I guess I'll have to give you both a bath, later," she huffed, shooing them away and walking back into the stables.

Part of her morning routine involved checking on all of the newborn foals, as well as the colts and fillies, which were the young male and female horses. Her Uncle Tucker tended to the stallions, and their two ranch hands handled the mares. Everyone worked together, feeding, bathing, and tending to the horses in the large building.

~

Tyler's dark blue t-shirt and jeans were soaked with sweat and clinging to her muscular figure. The shirt was already tight around her upper arms to begin with. Even with a tomboyish style, she still had very soft skin and adorable feminine features. She looked like Huckleberry Finn and Barbie had conceived a child, with her turquoise blue eyes that resembled Caribbean water, sun-tanned skin, and short, messy blond hair that stood out everywhere when she took her hat off.

Luckily for her, she had kicked the nasty tobacco chewing habitat she'd had about two years ago. Now, she ate sunflower seeds like they were going out of style, sort of like a smoker that quit smoking and started chewing gum. Her Uncle Tucker had told her she'd quit that eventually too. She didn't care since sunflower seeds were a hell of a lot healthier and not quite as gross. She blamed her daddy for getting her started with chewing tobacco. She had been fifteen when he'd first let her try his. The cherry and mint flavors had done wonders to her mouth as she'd chewed and spit almost as a perfectly as her old man.

Her father's brother, Tucker, had smoked cigarettes for about thirty years. He had quit smoking when she had quit chewing. They had done it in her father's memory just after they'd buried him.

Trace McCain, her father, had died in a car accident. He'd been coming home from town late one night when a car from out of town cut him off. His truck had swerved and rolled down into a ditch. Trace had never worn his seatbelt. He was from the old country and didn't believe in wearing one since he had grown up just fine riding and driving in vehicles that didn't have them. Trace had gone through the windshield and died on the scene before the local volunteer firefighters and EMT's could get to the accident. The entire McCain Ranch had been left solely to his daughter, and only child, Tyler. The McCain Equine Ranch bred and raised mainly prized Quarter Horses and some Thoroughbreds. Tyler had moved her Uncle Tucker into the large house with her and hired Rusty and Jake as full-time ranch hands. They'd both worked around the ranch doing odd chores from the time they were thirteen, so it seemed fitting to hire them when she had been looking for full-time help.

"If it gets any hotter, Tyler, I think I'm going to melt," The red-haired ranch hand said as he splashed water on his face and put his straw-style cowboy hat back on.

To any sane woman with a heartbeat and an active libido, the two young, muscular, ranch hands would be hotter than calendar men in g-strings, but to Tyler, they were like her overprotective little brothers.

"Rusty, please don't melt. I don't have time to mop your ass up!" She smacked him playfully. "Let me know when you've finished cleaning these last few stalls. I think

Jake was almost done with the other side."

"Alright. Where are you going?" He asked as he started sweeping, preparing to clean the horse manure and lay down fresh hay. Part of the ranch hand's daily list of duties was to clean all of the stalls while she and Tucker worked with the horses, breaking and training them.

"I gotta go bathe those damn tyrants of mine." She smiled, making sure she had her walkie-talkie in her pocket as she grabbed the scrub brush and bucket.

"Tuck said he was going to let a few of the stallions run."

"Alright." She waved and walked out of the stables. "Bucky! Houdini!" she yelled, then whistled a few times. The gray donkey and spotted goat were galloping over the last small hill towards her. "Come on boys!" She smiled.

She grabbed each animal, putting their harnesses on one at a time and tethering them to the outside wash basin behind the stable building. Houdini was first. She sprayed the goat with the hose, then lathered him up nicely with large animal soap and scrubbed him with the brush until the charcoal colored dirt washed away, showing his creamy colored fur with big brown spots. "Oh you look so much better, Houdini, my handsome boy." She laughed and Bucky, the donkey, made a bunch of squeaky snorting noises. "See, Bucky agrees," she said, squirting the conditioner onto his fur and rubbing it in gently. "Now you smell better." She could swear the goat smiled at her as she untied his tether and took him over to a sunny spot, where she tied him back up so he could finish drying.

"Alright, Buckster. It's your turn." As soon as she sprayed Bucky with the hose, the donkey shook the stinky dirty water from his fur all over her. "Damn it, Bucky!" She took her hat off, setting it at a safe distance, then began lathering the soap in his fur. The donkey hated to get his hooves wet and as soon as the water hit him he shook frantically. She scrubbed him with the brush, then sprayed him again. He shook out his fur, spraying her with water once more. "Ugh!"she huffed, shaking her head. At this point, she pretty much smelled like the donkey had before she'd washed him. His light, slate-gray color came back nicely as the dirt was rinsed away. She rubbed the conditioner into his fur, then took him over by the goat and tied him back up.

She hated tying them up, but it was much easier to bathe them this way. It was the only time they ever saw a tether. Once in a while, if there was a child around, Bucky could give them a short ride since he could carry about a hundred pounds.

Tyler cleaned up the brush and bucket and took them back into the stables. As soon as the animals were dry, she grabbed Houdini, checking his hooves, and brushing his fur out nicely. Then, she did her best to clean his teeth. "There you go," she said, untying him. The goat rubbed his chin on her hand as she pet him. "I love you too, buddy. Try to stay clean longer than two days this time. I have my work cut out for me with those horses in there. They make me money and you too tend to spend up my time *and* my money."

She went to work, checking Bucky's hooves, cleaning his teeth, then brushing his fur. "Alright, go play guys." She patted Bucky on the head.

Two

Jake was at the other end of the stable, finishing up the last stall, when he heard honking in the distance. Squinting his eyes, he saw a car, some six-hundred yards away. He shook his head, wondering who the hell it was since no one owned an actual car anywhere near this side of Amarillo. The Ranch was located fifty-five miles north east of the city in a small town called Dusken. Technically, it wasn't even a town since it had no stop lights and barely two stop signs.

Jake decided he had better go on up to the gate and check this car out, figuring they were lost. They would've had to have been seriously lost to be way the hell out in the middle of nowhere. They had to have gone down miles and miles of dirt roads to even get to the ranch. When he made his way down to the locked gate, Jake could smell the rich cologne of the salt and pepper haired man before he ever saw him. His obviously rented Mercedes was covered in clay dust from the dirt road.

"Can I help you?"

"Hi, are you Tyler McCain?" the man asked, with a semi-deep voice.

"Uh, no sir." Jake stared at the man. Maybe he'd come about a horse. Rich folks visited the ranch often to pick out

407

a prize winning Quarter Horse or Thoroughbred. Those particular horses, when ready, were sold for anywhere from fifty to a hundred thousand dollars. One Thoroughbred that had been sold a few years ago, had gone on to place in the Kentucky Derby. A few others had won races as well and many of the Quarter Horses had won various awards over the years. Tyler, her father, and her uncle were occasionally invited to watch when one of their horses had been a favorite in a big race or participating in a big show. Most of the people that came to the ranch inquiring about a sale knew who Tyler was or at least knew Tyler was a woman.

"Do you know where I can find him?" he asked impatiently.

"Well..." Jake paused and grabbed his walkie-talkie. "Tyler?" he said, pushing the button.

"Yeah?" The radio crackled with a muffled voice.

"There's a man here to see you. He's at the gate."

"Alright." She started the four-wheeler and rode up towards the house. A few minutes later, she noticed the dusty car sitting at the gate a few hundred yards away.

"Can I help you, sir?" she asked, as she came to a stop and cut off the engine.

"I'm looking for Tyler McCain. I was told this is the McCain Equine Ranch and this is his property."

She smiled. "Well, yes sir, the sign on the gate says McCain Equine Ranch. You're at the right place and I'm Tyler McCain, by the way." She stuck her hand over the top of the gate.

The man wasn't sure which person smelled, but one of the two of them smelled worse than a wet dog. He met her handshake firmly.

"What can I do for you, mister..." she paused.

"Wright, Donald Wright." He smiled. "I'm from Los Angeles, California. I tried to get in touch with you a few weeks ago."

"Oh yeah, the movie guy. You sent me a couple emails about our website didn't you?"

"Yeah." He tried not to mock her southern drawl, but it came out that way anyway. He mentally chastised himself. He had been expecting a man, but the young woman standing in front of him was appealing, even if she was a country bumpkin. He wondered what she looked like under the jeans, cowboy boots, and a Stetson hat. "I'm about to start shooting a movie and I'd like to talk to you about it. I know you're very busy, do you think you could give me a half hour of your time?"

Her blue eyes twinkled. There wasn't a mean bone in her body. She was almost too nice for her own good, maybe that's why Jake and Rusty were always protective of her. But, they'd also seen her kick a foreigner's ass one night at the local bar when he had squeezed her breast. She wasn't a big girl by any means, but she had a lot of muscle on that slender frame and she'd used every pound of it to nail him in the jaw. Anyone nearby had heard the loud 'crack' when she'd connected. He had screamed like a girl and she'd stepped over him to get another beer.

"Sure, I'm about done anyway. Come on in." She pushed the code to open the large iron gate and he walked inside. "It's a long walk. You can drive in if you want or you can ride with me." She nodded towards Jake. "Tell Uncle Tucker I'll be in the office for a little bit, if he needs me."

The salt and pepper haired man hopped onto the quad behind her, sliding very close to her before turning his nose up and moving away slightly as she drove away. He grabbed her shirt to keep from falling off as the force of the quad slung him back. She laughed. *City boy.*

~

As soon as they walked into the large two story house, Donald Wright took in the scenery. It wasn't full of animal skin rugs with heads mounted on the wall like he'd pictured. Instead, it had light colored, stained teakwood floors with beautiful throw rugs. The L-shaped couch and Lazy Boy chair were both tan colored, suede leather. The coffee table and end tables were hickory wood, stained with a dark cherry color and the walls were the color of beach sand. A medium-sized TV sat across from the couch in a built-in entertainment center that looked like it had never been used. A large mantled fireplace was on the other side.

He noticed the white tile floors, pewter colored counter tops and white appliances as they walked past the kitchen towards the office. This room had a large mahogany desk with a matching book case behind it. Mr. Wright was impressed to see the state of the art computer system sitting on the desk. A regular high back chair sat behind the desk, and two uncomfortable looking leather chairs were in front of it. Pictures of horses covered all of the walls.

"Have a seat, Mr. Wright," she snickered to herself as she said it, then went around to her side of the desk. She laid her hat on the corner of the desk. Her blond hair was in disarray and she did nothing to fix it. "So tell me more about why you're here. I don't think I quite understand what it is you want." She folded her hands together and leaned back, just as her father had done when he'd been making a deal. She had learned his style right there in that very same room when she had been a child.

"Well, Miss McCain, like I said. I'm with Bravado Pictures and we're about to begin shooting a movie called 'Shadow's Eyes'. It's about a woman who trains this horse named Shadow. He's very small when he's born and no one thinks he'll amount to much. This ranch hand woman buys him cheap and decides to work with him. The movie continues as she breaks him and trains him to be a racer. She's in need of money and can't afford to keep him so she sells him to a man that will race him. The horse wins a few races, then gets hurt. She rescues him and nurses him back to health when they try to put him down. She gets him healthy again, but lies to the owner and decides to buy him back and keep him as a pet. You see it's almost like a love story. She loves this horse and he loves her. They get separated but reunited."

"Okay, so why are you here telling me this story?" she asked.

"We'd like to film the movie here on your ranch."

"Why here?"

"From what I saw on your website, this place is beautiful. It's what I pictured when I read the script. You see, I'm the director and I always see a place in my mind when reading a script. I knew this was the place as soon as I saw it. It's even more stunning in person."

"Hmm..."

"I would also need your help and your input on handling the animals and so on. There's a nice amount of money in this for you as well."

She arched an eyebrow. This man had no idea what kind of money she had, therefore, he had no clue she didn't need his 'nice amount'. "Money's not an issue with me, Mr.

Wright. I'm more concerned about my animals and their safety."

"Yes, ma'am, that's why we would like you to be right there involved in everything we do to ensure the safety of the animals and our crew."

"So you'd need to use my foals, colts, and stallions too, am I right?"

"Yes, ma'am."

She sat back in the chair. Her aqua colored eyes darkened slightly in the bright light of the room. "I'd need to think about it. This is a family ranch that is well known in the equine community around the country. I sell top-notch quarter horses as well as prize winning thoroughbreds. I have a lot at stake here."

"Miss McCain, we definitely understand that and it's part of the reason we chose you. You're a pillar in the community, if you will."

She stood, putting her hat back on. He also stood and handed her a business card. "This is my cell number. I'm flying back tomorrow. Please call me as soon as you have had time to think about it."

She smiled thinly. Whether or not she wanted to submit her home to this mayhem, she was still a decent human being so she showed him as much courtesy as she would anyone else in her home.

~

Tyler pondered over the idea for a few days. She'd told her uncle why the man had come and what his intentions were. Uncle Tucker wasn't sure what to tell her. He gave his opinion and what he believed her father would do, and left her to make the decision. It was *her* ranch after all. She paced the floor of the office, until she was tired enough to go to bed. She'd need to hire a few temporary ranch hands to help out if she was going to supervise the movie. The extra money coming in from it would surely cover their salaries. *Okay Daddy, it's up to you, give me some kind of sign. Would you do it if you were still here?*

She woke up at two in the morning, swearing that her father had just spoken to her in her dreams. *Tyler, the ranch is yours now. I left it to you because you'd always do right by it. This time is no different from any other time. Your my kid, but most of all you're a McCain. I trust you, so will everyone else.* She felt a chill in her bones as his words replayed in her head. Her father had always taught her to stand up and be strong. Her mother had died giving birth to her and he had been left to raise her alone. Sure, Tucker had helped. His wife had even been around for a while, until she'd left him for some two-bit wannabe country singer that had amounted to nothing. Being raised by her father was part of the reason she was such a tomboy, but she'd showed more of her feminine side when he died. She had held herself together in public to get through his funeral, but after that, she'd lost it for two weeks, sitting at his desk in his office and crying all day every day.

Rusty, Jake, and her Uncle Tucker had been the only people to witness her in that state. After she'd cried her last tear, she'd taken a shower and gone back to work on the ranch. No one ever spoke about her grieving, only about her father's memory. So, she literally had no tears left to cry at times like this when her father gave her advice from beyond the grave. In a way, she was thankful she'd cried her last tear. It had made her stronger.

Three

"Bucky! Houdini!" Tyler called, tossing a couple of bales of hay out and some pellets in the trough. The two animals came frolicking up to her, making noise. She smiled and rubbed each of their heads, before walking into the stables to start her morning routine.

"Morning, Tyler," Rusty called from a few feet away.

"Hi, Rusty. Have you seen my uncle?"

"Yeah, Tuck's out back with a stallion." He continued putting the pellets in each trough and preparing to sweep and re-hay each stall.

"Thanks." She walked to the end of the building and opened the door. Her uncle was watching one of the stallions run around the pen.

"Morning," he said to her.

"What have you got them out for?" she asked, walking up next to him.

"I put some new shoes on them yesterday. Just making sure they set okay."

"Are they doing alright?"

"Yeah, looks like it anyhow." He rubbed the nose of the large brown horse when it trotted up to them. "So today's the big day huh?"

"Yep." she kicked the grass with her worn roper-style

boot. She'd replaced the laces at least three times, but never could fathom tossing out the old boots that fit her feet like a glove.

"Nervous?" he asked.

"A little."

"Second thoughts?"

"Nah. Just not quite sure how all this is going to affect life around here, that's all. I guess we'll see."

"I reckon we will. Tyler, you did the right thing. I'm sure your daddy would have done it too." He smiled. "Hell, he'd have done it just to make sure the animals were safe during the filming."

She laughed. "I know." Her walkie-talkie crackled to life in her pocket. "Yeah?" she answered.

"Tyler, that Mercedes is back with the city boy."

"Thanks, Jake. Let them in. I'll be right there." She turned towards her uncle. "Come up there with me so I can introduce you to them. I'm going to need your help with this, so it's best you meet each other now."

~

"So, as per our agreement, we'll set up everything in the morning. The trailers should be here before noon. I'm assuming, if all goes well, we'll be out of here in less than three months. We'll have to film completely out of sequence so that we can keep up with the weather. It's semi-hot now, but it'll be snowing soon so we need to have the horse at the right age for that time in the movie. It may be a little confusing for you."

"I'll be fine. I may talk with an accent, Mr. Wright, but I'm sure I can keep up with your movie."

He laughed. "Yeah, I guess everyone sounds funny to

415

someone else."

"How many people will actually be here?"

"Uh..." he mentally counted. "Well, there's the lead actress, Reegan Delsol, and then eight or ten other actors and actresses, plus the film crew. This is a low-budget picture so our crew is a lot smaller than you would see on a regular film set."

"You're using our training track for the race scenes, am I right?"

"Yes, we will shoot those with a green screen behind them and cut and paste those into actual derby footage."

"Sounds like a plan. I hired two temporary ranch hands to help out while I'm working with you. I doubt you'll see them much, but you'll see Rusty and Jake. They're great handlers. Of course, Uncle Tucker will be with me too."

"Good. I'm sure you guys will make this a lot smoother for all of us."

"Would you like a tour of the property today, before everyone gets here?" She asked politely.

"Sure!" He couldn't help his excitement.

"Come on." She pointed towards the four-wheeler. She rode her four-wheeler more than a horse most of the time. She was all over the place on most days, moving supplies like oats and hay and that wasn't easy to do on horseback. She did ride at least one horse daily though, everyone on the ranch had to ride them to keep the horses exercised and moved from pasture to pasture.

~

Tyler had been a little put off by the closeness of the man behind her as she drove around, showing him the

416

meadow areas, which happened to be Bucky and Houdini's favorite hang out. Both animals ran along next to the quad for a few yards before going back to frolicking and eating the grass. She continued driving through the different areas of the large pasture, intentionally staying away from the stream. That was considered her secret spot, very few people even knew it was back there.

She'd been happy to have her space back when she dropped Mr. Wright off at the front gate. She wasn't sure if he had sat literally against her because he thought he would fall off or if he had been trying to be fresh with her. Either way, one of the guys could take him around next time. She'd had her fill of having a man on her back.

~

"Morning, Tyler."

She stretched her arms out, watching the sun come up. The air was starting to cool down more at night, causing her to start the day in long sleeves. She'd strip her flannel shirt off about midday.

"Hey, Jake. Did you get Dewy and Will started on the bays?"

"Yeah, Tuck told them what he wanted done. They both went right to work."

"Good. Good." She walked towards the stable with Jake next to her. "Bucky! Houdini!" she yelled for her pets.

"I think I saw them out by the meadow."

"They're always out there." She shook her head, going through the routine of putting the hay bales out and pouring food pellets in the trough. "I don't have time to go find them today." Just as she said that, the goat and donkey walked around the corner making noise. "There you guys are. Go eat," she said, petting them. "Ugh! Phew! Oh my God, you stink!" she screeched, backing away.

"Eww, they do stink!"

"Yeah, like something dead. Damn it, you guys!" She went into the stable and came out with both harnesses. "Come on." She walked them to the other end of the stable, tethering them to the basin while she went to get the soap, bucket, and brush.

"I'll be out back if you need me. Bucky and Houdini smell like something rotten. I need to bathe them before the sun makes it worse." She shook her head.

"They're just like having kids." Her uncle laughed. "We'll call you when the city folks get here."

~

Bucky got her wet with stinky water as usual when she washed him and Houdini had actually splashed her too. The crew had begun to arrive shortly after she finished and she'd had no time to change and was already starting to stink.

Tyler had the four motor homes park on the other side of the house away from the stables so that the generators and noise wouldn't bother the animals. By the end of the day, she stunk like a rotten animal, her property was beginning to look like a parking lot, and she was way behind schedule.

"Tyler, the city folk are looking for you," Rusty's voice crackled over the walkie-talkie. He was about to head home for the night.

"Alright. I'll be there in a minute." She walked from the stables, past the house to where the group was gathered.

Donald Wright was the first person she recognized. "Hey, Miss McCain. I have someone I want you to meet. She had a late flight and the car bringing her here got lost, so she's just arrived." He knocked on the motor home. Tyler was not expecting what she saw when the door opened.

The woman that stepped out was wearing thin, black dress slacks and a crème colored, sleeveless blouse. Her straight black hair hung a little past her shoulders, all in one length and her eyes were the color of melted caramel. She smiled, extending her hand as she walked down the stairs. The sun was beginning to set, causing her olive complexion to contrast nicely against the orange sky. The woman looked like a Brazilian swimsuit model that had stepped off the cover of a magazine.

"Reegan, this is the owner of the ranch, Tyler McCain. Miss McCain, this is Reegan Delsol, the lead actress for 'Shadow's Eyes'."

Tyler's breath caught as she started to speak. She quickly cleared her throat. "Welcome to the McCain Ranch. It's nice to meet you, ma'am." She tipped her hat and smiled.

"Thank you." Reegan gave a half-hearted smile and walked back inside. Once she was gone, Donald turned to Tyler.

"She's not used to this kind of lifestyle. She'll come around in a few days," he said, hoping he was right, otherwise his movie was going to backfire in his face.

"She's definitely a city girl." She replied, shaking her head. "I'll see you in the morning, Mr. Wright."

"Please, call me Donald."

"Alright. You can call me Tyler if you'd like." She

419

walked away staring at the stars as they filled the sky. The moonlight danced along the rolling hills, casting shadows behind the trees. She pondered the idea of going down to the stream, but decided to go up to the house instead. Houdini and Bucky found her on her way up the path.

"Hey boys." She scratched them both behind the ears and walked them over to the stables. They weren't locked away at night like the horses, but they had an open bay that they shared to sleep in. Most of the time, they came and went as they pleased around the property.

~

"What's with your attitude?" Donald asked as he sat on the small couch in the motor coach.

"I don't have an attitude. Where did you find the hillbilly? She smells like something dead!" Reegan rolled her eyes.

"Reegan, you'd better make nice with that woman. She owns this place and if it wasn't for her, who knows where we'd be shooting this movie. These people have a lot of knowledge and will be an asset to us. Play nice."

"She's barely a teenager, Donald." She shook her head and huffed. "Fine. Can you go so I can get some sleep please? I'm sure these hillbillies will be up before the sun and I have jet lag." She shut the door behind him and sat back on the couch.

Reegan wasn't exactly sure why, but something about this young woman seemed to get under her skin. She'd never seen eyes that particular shade of blue-green and wondered if the cowgirl wore colored contacts. *Who gives a shit?* She thought.

420

Four

Tyler was up before the sun rose, as usual. She glanced out the window at the old worn-out, green Army Jeep with no doors or top that had been in her family since before she was born. She usually drove it down to the stream to watch the sunrise or sunset every chance she got. But, lately she seemed busier than ever and she hadn't been to the stream in close to a month. She'd hoped to get one more swim in before the cold weather set in. As it was, the temperature was already dipping into the fifties at night, but it was staying in the eighties during the day. The rainy season had just ended and the snow season was about to begin. September was an interesting month and sort of an in between, being hot as hell during the day and cool in the evening.

She put a blue and gray flannel shirt on over her tight fitting black t-shirt and tucked it into her jeans as usual, figuring this wasn't going to be a morning to go down to the stream. She'd had too much on her plate lately for any free time of her own. Her roper-style lace up boots were already on her feet. She looked out the window one last time, grabbing her big black hat on the way out the door.

Rusty and Jake were already in the stables with Dewy and Will. She nodded and walked to the other end of the building where her uncle was filing the hooves of one of the mares, getting ready to put some new shoes on her.

"Morning," he said, smiling brightly.

She hoped it would be a good morning, after all she hadn't heard any noise coming from the film crew. Yet. "Hey, I brought you some more coffee." She handed his mug to him.

"Thanks. I checked that new batch of strawberry mash this morning. It looks like it's going to be ready to run off in the next day or two. The blueberry mash is about ready too" he said.

"Alright. I'll prep the still later," she replied, referring to the nearly fifty year old moonshine operation that had been passed down through generations in her family from her great-grandfather all the way to her. She still used the old style copper pots, thump kegs, and barrel worms that her family had used and she hand-pumped cool, freshwater from the stream, just as they had.

Making moonshine had been illegal since backwoods people had first began making it, but it had been a long-standing tradition in her family. When her father had first taken over his father's still, he'd began making fruit mashes with the secret family recipe and had bootleggers all over the surrounding counties, selling hundreds of gallons a year. He had stopped the distribution when she'd started college.

Tyler had taken over the still and family recipes when her father died. She'd occasionally sold moonshine jars to the folks around town when they'd ask, and a few gallons to people needing it for special event like a wedding or something of that nature, like her father had done, but that had been only a few times a year. She wasn't running a bootlegging operation or supplying regular customers.

Most of the time, she didn't even use the large one-hundred gallon still, instead relying on the much smaller twenty gallon one that her father had used to perfect the fruit recipes before making large quantities to sell. The smaller still made enough for her and Tucker and a few close friends. She preferred to make smaller batches of different flavors, over one large batch of a single flavor.

"When is the party again?" she asked. They'd been asked to make ten gallons of strawberry shine for Jake's parents' twenty-fifth anniversary.

"Next weekend, I think."

"Okay. Tell Jake he'll need to take it with him as soon as it's jarred. I don't need those city folks finding it," she said.

"Speaking of them, have you run into the group yet?" Tucker asked as he sipped his coffee.

"No. I figured I'd give them time to wake up and get situated. I met the actress last night. Boy is she a piece of work."

"What do you mean?"

Tyler turned a bucket over and sat down on top of it. "For one thing she has an attitude. She's as mean as a rattlesnake with no rattle and she's definitely high-maintenance. Have you seen her yet?"

He laughed. "Nope. Is she a looker?"

"Ha." she snickered, shaking her head. "She's as beautiful as a day is long. Looks like she stepped off the cover of a magazine."

"I bet she has no sense when it comes to animals." He rolled his eyes.

"Yeah, I guess we'll see." She flipped the bucket back over when she stood up. "The sun's up. I'd better go check on them before they tear something up." She walked out of the stables towards the house and noticed a few people heading her way, including the unsociable brunette.

"Morning," she said with her usual southern drawl as she tipped her hat.

"Hello, Miss McCain, ready to get started?" Donald looked awkward dressed in jeans and a polo shirt with a thin windbreaker. Tyler shook her head when she saw the loafers on his feet. *City boy.*

"Sure," she said, merely glancing at Reegan as she led them towards the stables. She introduced the crew to all of the ranch hands and her uncle. He winked behind Reegan's back and Tyler shook her head and smiled at him.

"So, I figured we'd start today out with some horseback riding so Miss Delsol and the stallion can get used to each other," she said, stopping in front of one of the bays. A large black horse stood in the back of the stall staring at them. "This is Madagascar. We call him Maddy. He's still a colt, but he's going to be very large when he matures. He's a registered Quarter Horse and he's well broken and friendly." Tyler made a clicking noise with her mouth and called Maddy over. He walked right up to her and she rubbed his head as Donald stepped forward, petting him as well.

"I think he'll make the perfect 'Shadow' for us," he said, looking back at Reegan.

"Good, now we have some others to choose from for the foal and colt parts, and Maddy can pose as the thoroughbred for the racing part also." Tyler turned towards Reegan. "I'll grab the saddle so we can get you on them."

"I…Uh…Wha…" Reegan's eyes grew large and she turned to Donald.

"Is there a problem?" Tyler asked.

"No, Reegan has never been on a horse, that's all." He tried not to look embarrassed for hiring an actress without asking her specific questions. In fact, he'd gone through her agent and hadn't actually spoken to her until the day she'd read for the part and blew him out of the water. Tyler looked like she wanted to smack him.

"Alright. Well, you're making a movie about a horse. I'd suggest you give it a try." She mused.

"I think we'll start with the opening shots of the movie, then go into Reegan working as a stable hand."

"It's up to you. You should let your actors work in the stable for a day so they can learn what goes on. Miss Delsol should probably work in here too, since she's supposed to be a stable hand."

"I agree," he said.

"Good, I'll leave my uncle in charge and let you guys get started."

~

Tucker paired the actors with Rusty, Jake, Dewy, and Will. He suggested Reegan work with Tyler, and his niece gave him a dirty look as Reegan left to change into the jeans and boots that were part of her costumes. Tyler walked around the back of the stable building and over the first hill. Her goat and donkey were out in the meadow. Both animals came running when they saw her.

"Hey, boys." She pet them vigorously. "I know, Buckster, she's definitely a high maintenance city girl." She shook her head as he sniffed her hand and made a noise. Houdini agreed, nuzzling up to her hand and making noises of his own. They followed Tyler around the meadow and over to the motor coach.

"What the hell?" Reegan stepped back when she rounded the corner.

"Oh." Tyler turned around. "These are my two best friends, Houdini and Bucky. They're harmless. Actually they're more friendly than some people I've met lately," she said half under her breath.

"They smell." Reegan turned her nose up.

"Well they *are* animals, Miss Delsol." Tyler held back the urge to sling a handful of mud at her. The brunette walked away, towards the path to the stable building. Tyler fell instep next to her with the animals on her heels.

"Ugh! Do they go everywhere you go?"

"Yes ma'am, unless they're occupied with something else. If I'm working in the stables they're usually playing in the meadow on the other side of that hill out there." She pointed off in the distance. "Right now, they're just curious with all of these people around." Bucky got a little close and sniffed Reegan's back. She screamed and the donkey made a loud noise. Tyler laughed and pet him on his nose.

"He just wants you to pet him," Tyler said.

"UGH!" Reegan moved to storm off and Tyler grabbed her arm, her hand slipping down to Reegan's. Reegan snatched hers away quickly, after feeling Tyler's touch.

"Miss Delsol, you'll have to get familiar with animals if you're making this movie. I promise I won't let Houdini or Bucky hurt you. If you can't even pet them, how are you going to go work in that stable?"

Reegan let out a deep breath. "Fine." She stuck practically stuck her hand in Bucky's face. If he'd been any other donkey, she probably would've been bitten. He sniffed and simply turned his nose up.

"Nah, you're doing it all wrong. Come here, Bucky."

Tyler called him back over and pet his nose. She grabbed Reegan's hand, holding it in her own as she stroked the course fur on the donkey's head. Bucky showed his teeth and Reegan snatched her hand away.

"It's okay, he's smiling," Tyler said. Reegan stuck her hand out, cautiously petting him again.

I'll be damned, Bucky likes her. "Houdini!" Tyler called and the goat walked up to them.

"He's a little different. He likes you to scratch his ears...like this." Tyler did it first, then grabbed Reegan's hand and helped her. Reegan was surprised at how soft and gentle Tyler's touch was. She'd expected hard, callused man hands.

"See, they're not so bad."

"No, I guess not, but they do stink." She curled her nose.

"I know. I just gave them a bath yesterday." She smiled, her eyes sparkling in the sunlight, reminding Reegan of the shallow reef water in the islands. "Come on, let's go work with some horses," Tyler said, breaking her concentration.

~

Tyler spent half of the day showing Reegan what goes on in the day to day life of a ranch hand. She started with the feeding process. Different sized horses were given different portions, although everyone was given a fresh bale of hay to chew on. After that, they moved on to sweeping and shoveling the hay nest full of manure and placing new hay on the floor in every one of the bays. Then, there was a schedule for bathing the horses, filing their shoes, checking their teeth, as well as many other daily duties. Not to mention checking the pregnant mares and preparing them for birthing. Tyler knew Reegan couldn't get the life of a ranch hand down in one afternoon, so she'd have to work with her for a few days on each area until she had the lingo and mannerisms down. Otherwise, she'd come off as a phony.

~

The next evening, Tyler was glad to be away from the movie crew. They'd been on her ranch less than seventy-two hours and she was already second guessing her decision. She rode her four-wheeler down to the backside of her property, near the freshwater stream. Tucker had already poured the blueberry mash into the smaller still and the strawberry mash into the large copper still. He had both fires going and was mudding the joints with flour paste when she'd arrived. Their moonshine operation sat in the middle of an overgrown thicket in the woods, near the bend in the stream that ran for miles through the twists and turns along the backside of her property.

"Did you get the city folks to bed?" he asked.

Tyler laughed. "I'll be ready when this is finished. I could drink a couple of jars right now," she said, checking the temperature gauges on each pot. Each still was sitting up on cinderblocks with a small, stone furnace under it to keep the heat in. She'd kept the tradition of heating her stills with firewood the way her father and grandfather had done, simply because driving all over, trying to refill multiple propane tanks had been more tedious than chopping up a few tree limbs.

"It won't be long now and we'll have plenty to drink," Tucker replied, sitting down in a folding chair and pulling a harmonica from his pocket.

Tyler placed glass mason jars where each cooling worm exited the barrel in order to catch the alcohol as it ran off. The sky above her was dark and the stars were shining brightly as Tucker began a rhythm. Sitting by the still under the stars, tapping her foot and listening to her uncle play always reminded her of her father.

It wasn't long before the first drops of clear liquid dripped into the jars. She watched as the drips quickly turned into a steady flow, then she carefully replaced the first filled jars. The foreshot, or first batch of moonshine to come out of a traditional copper still, could be laced with methanol that hadn't cooked off and be deadly if ingested. So, she'd followed the same routine handed down to her, dumping it in the woods away from the stream.

As soon as the next two jars were filled, Tyler replaced them with empty ones. She then poured half of the strawberry shine into an empty jar and filled it up with blueberry shine from the other jar. Tucker took the original jars, taking a sip from each one.

"Not bad." He said, nodding his head and taking another drink. "Your old man would be proud."

Tyler took a long swallow from the mixture in her jar and grinned. "Damn, that's good."

"Maybe you should take some of this over to that city girl," Tucker smiled. "It might loosen her up a bit."

"Yeah, she is wound a little tight," Tyler replied, shaking her head and taking another sip.

~

Close to a month had gone by since the movie crew had arrived and the ranch was bustling with noise. Reegan hated doing the stable work, even if it was only a small portion of a scene. They'd shoot it over and over until it was perfect and eventually move on. Tyler gave her input when and where it was needed, but spent a lot of time checking the animals and doing her daily routine. She did keep a very close eye on them, however.

"This place smells, I smell! Come on Donald, this is ridiculous. How many takes do you need for this God damn scene?!" Reegan let her frustration show.

Tyler heard the yelling from a few stalls down and walked over to see what was going on. In this particular scene, Reegan was supposed to be brushing the horse's teeth after she'd bathed him. She looked like she'd had muddy water poured on her, then let it dry. Reegan was right, she did stink. Tyler laughed and went back to what she was doing.

"Those city folks sure are loud, aren't they?" Rusty called over his shoulder.

"Yeah. I'm sure it's about to get worse too."

"What do you mean?"

"She's never been on a horse."

"What?" His voice rose up. "You're shitting me, Tyler!"

Tyler took her hat off to scratch her head and put it back on. "Nope." She grinned.

"This gets funnier every day, I swear." He shook his head, laughing and walked back over to where he'd been working.

Five

"Damn it Reegan, we've done all of the shots that we can without you on a horse. This is it, you need to get over this shit and get on a horse so we can get on with the filming. I can't afford to run over budget here." Donald was in the motor coach, yelling at Reegan.

"Why can't we use a body double?" She huffed, crossing her arms.

"A body double? For what? It's a God damn horse. You agreed to this!" He fumed.

"I've put up with this hillbilly charade for a month now!" she yelled back.

"Excuse me, you signed on to star in this movie. I suggest you suck it up and get on that fucking horse!" He stormed out of the coach, slamming the door and heading towards the hills.

Tyler was out in the meadow with Houdini and Bucky, watching the stars and feeding them alfalfa hay, which was considered a treat.

"Evening," she said as Donald walked up to her.

"I wish we had a clear sky like this in Los Angeles. With the city lights it's hard to tell it's even dark outside sometimes."

"Yeah, I spent some time in Dallas going to college. I

431

hated the city."

Donald had a feeling when he first met her that this young woman was no hillbilly, but he was still surprised that she had a college degree. He blew out his frustration in a long deep breath. Tyler looked at him, then turned back towards her animals.

"She needs to ride a horse starting Monday or this picture is cancelled." He kicked some grass with his loafer.

"Ah." Tyler nodded. "Miss Delsol is definitely a handful. That's going to be a hell of a time."

"I was hoping you'd help her out. She seems to get by when you help her with this ranch stuff."

"I don't know." Tyler sent Bucky and Houdini up to the stables. "I guess there's always Bucky. He seems to enjoy her company."

"Yeah, I saw her petting them. See, that's what I mean, you know how to talk to her."

It won't hurt to try I guess. "Let me see what I can do," she said as the gears began turning in her head. The sooner she got this woman on a horse, the sooner these people would be off of her ranch and out of her hair.

"Thank you, Tyler." He smiled, shaking her hand.

~

Tucker was sitting on the couch with a mason jar half-filled with shine in his hand, when Tyler walked into the house. She hung her hat on the post by the door and tossed her flannel shirt in the dirty laundry. Tucker had already showered and was relaxing comfortably. She on the other hand, was dirty and sweaty, so she sat on the floor in her jeans and t-shirt.

"Cat got your tongue?" he asked, passing her the jar.

"Nah, just thinking." She stretched her back, taking a

432

long sip. "I told you Reegan's never ridden a horse right?"

"No, but I could tell. Kind of hard to make a horse movie if you can't ride one isn't it?"

"Yep. She has until Monday to learn how. I was just talking to Donald. He's asked me to work with her on it," she said, handing the jar back to him.

He scratched his head. Uncle Tucker reminded her so much of her own father. "Sounds like you got yourself a hell of a situation then. What are you going to do?"

"Since tomorrow's Friday, I figured I'd go on over before the sun comes up and have a talk with her. Either she'll do things my way, or she can pack her shit because their movie will be in the can if she won't get on a horse."

"You have a point there."

~

Tyler was up way before the sun. She put on a pair of jeans and a blue t-shirt under a black and gray flannel shirt. She laced up her boots, grabbed the black cowboy hat she always wore, and moseyed on over to the motor coaches. Reegan's was the first one of the group.

Here goes. Tyler took a deep breath and knocked on the door, waiting patiently. Most people living on a ranch were already up before the sun and ready to start their day. When there was no answer, she knocked again. Louder this time.

Finally, the door flew open and Reegan stood there poised in shorts and a tight little tank top. Her hair was hanging loosely around her shoulders and she looked like she was about to slap Tyler across the face for waking her. Tyler simply stared at the beautiful woman. *Say something, you dipshit!* "I'm sorry to wake you, but we

433

need to talk."

"Excuse me? What the hell do you want? And where the hell do you get off barging in here at four o'clock in the God damn morning?!" She yelled.

"Calm down, Miss Delsol. Invite me in and I'll explain everything."

"UGH!" She stomped across the room. "Come in!" She bellowed. "Hillbilly idiot." she said, sneering under her breath. Tyler walked inside and shut the door.

"You might want put on some clothes."

"I'm fine. What the hell is so important?" Reegan said, sitting on the couch. She couldn't believe how simply looking at Tyler had stirred her. She had been ready to leave the day she'd arrived, realizing she may have made the biggest mistake of her life.

Tyler searched the room for an object to stare at, instead of the beautiful, half naked woman in front of her. *Don't stare. Don't stare. Don't stare. She's absolutely beautiful. Why does she have to be so damn mean?* "You really don't like me much do you?"

"Are you just now figuring that out?" Reegan huffed, afraid to look at her.

Tyler ignored the jab. "I'm here because you're having trouble with the horses and I've been asked to help you."

"What do you mean?" Her frustration clearly visible.

"You're shooting a movie about a horse and you can't even ride one. I'd say that's a start," Tyler said flatly.

"That's none of your business." Reegan's voice rose again.

Feisty little thing aren't you? "Listen to me, Miss Delsol. I'm trying to help you."

"Help me? Are you kidding? What the hell is this? Did Donald put you up to this?"

434

"Damn it, Reegan!" Tyler shouted. The stunned brunette looked up, staring at her in disbelief. "Now that I have your attention, I'm sorry for cursing. If you'd just listen to me, I can help you ride the horses."

"How?" Reegan muttered, still shocked that the cowgirl had just yelled and cussed at her.

"It's not hard. You have to trust me and you have to trust the animal."

"It's not that easy," Reegan snapped.

"I came over here to talk to you, but you obviously don't need my help." Tyler said, leaving the motor coach.

~

Reegan waited a few minutes, then slung the door open. Tyler was nowhere in sight.

"Tyler?" Reegan called. "Damn it, what do you want me to do?" she said to the open air.

Tyler smiled, deciding right then to give it all of her effort. She stepped out of the shadow a foot away, taking her large black cowboy hat off and holding it in her hand. Her short hair was messy from her putting her hat on when it was still wet from her morning shower. "If you'll agree to put all of your trust in me, I promise I won't let you get hurt." Tyler's eyes twinkled in the early morning dawn. Reegan noticed the deep swirls of blue and green in them, realizing they were natural and not contacts. They were the most gorgeous eyes that she'd ever seen, although she'd never admit it.

"I don't know if I can do that. I don't even know you." *And you drive me nuts, but for some ungodly reason I'm drawn to you. You smell like a wet, rotten animal, I don't think I've ever heard you pronounce the letter 'g', and you*

435

dress like Paul Bunyan. Why do you keep getting under my skin so easily and why do I keep allowing it? Reegan squeezed her eyes closed, then opened them again. Turquoise eyes continued to stare back at her beneath tousled blond hair. Tyler had heard what she'd said, but waited silently. "Okay, what do you have in mind?"

Tyler smiled. "Well, for starters, I'm going to talk to Donald and send the crew out of here this morning. That'll give us three full days with no one around, except my ranch hands and my uncle. Then, I'm going to get you out of this tin can and help you loosen up. You're wound tighter than a rubber band on the space shuttle."

Reegan arched an eyebrow, but held the laughter and the smile inside.

"Put some clothes on, preferably jeans and boots. You'll need a jacket or sweater since it'll be cool out until about noon. I'll be right back."

Tyler turned around, walking over to the motor coach next door. She knocked on the door a few times. Donald finally answered, wearing only shorts, very small shorts to say the least.

"Good God!" Tyler yelped. "Put your clothes on!" She turned around shaking her head. He scrambled for a shirt and a pair of pants and came back to the door.

"Okay, okay, come in."

Tyler walked inside and sat on the couch. His motor coach was set up the same as Reegan's with a small living area with a satellite TV, and a kitchenette with a stove, refrigerator, microwave, and sink. A decent sized bathroom, and a large bedroom with a big closet were in the back. The other two motor coaches housed the rest of the actors and the crew so they were bigger with staterooms like you'd see on a large boat. Everyone seemed to be comfortable.

"It's all settled. I need you and your crew to leave for the weekend, starting as soon as everyone gets up. I don't want to see any of you until Monday morning."

"Why?" he asked.

"Have you met that woman?" she asked, raising her voice slightly. "She needs to relax. I'm going to spend the weekend teaching her about life on a ranch. She has to learn to respect the animals. Trust me, Mr. Wright, she'll be riding by Monday."

"If you think this will work, I guess it's my only shot," he sighed.

"The more you pressure her, the harder this is going to be. Why you're doing a movie about a horse with a woman that's never been on one, I'll never understand," she said, shaking her head.

"Tyler, to be honest, I had no idea she couldn't ride a God damn horse. If I had, I wouldn't be over budget and behind production right now wondering if I will even be able to finish this picture. You can call me a stupid man, this is definitely one stupid mistake. Good luck with her. I don't know much about her, but beneath that diva, bitch exterior has to be the person I thought I saw when she read her lines."

"Everyone has a soft spot somewhere. Besides, like I said, she needs to learn the country life. Once she does, she'll calm down." Tyler smiled and walked out of the coach. She saw Donald walk over to Reegan's motor coach as she headed towards the stables.

~

"I can't believe you're making me spend the weekend

with the hillbilly kid, Donald," Reegan barked.

"Hey, you're the one who agreed to it. I found out after you did. Look, I need you to ride a God damn horse and she thinks she can help you. Besides, it might do you some good to calm down."

"I don't need to calm down, I'm fine!"

"A little fresh country air might benefit you too."

"You mean the fresh air that smells like horse shit and wet dog?" Reegan huffed.

He laughed. "By the way, I'm sure you know she's not a kid. Although, she looks younger than those guys she has working for her. I think she's close to your age and she's most definitely not a hillbilly."

"Whatever."

"Have a good time this weekend. Loosen that stick that's up your ass and let her teach you to ride a horse. That's all I'm asking."

"Fine. I said I'd do it. Get the hell away from me so I can get ready. I feel like I stepped onto the fucking set of Hee Haw. I'm firing my agent when this is over."

"What if you win an Oscar?"

"She's still fired!" Reegan slammed the door behind him. *Ugh!* She needed to pull it together to get through the next two months. Spending more time with the charming ranch owner was not what she'd had in mind.

~

Reegan met Tyler over by the back porch of the house. She wasn't thrilled about their venture and it hadn't even begun. Tyler climbed onto the four-wheeler and nodded for Reegan to climb on behind her. Reegan simply stared at her.

Lord have mercy, she's worse than Bucky and Houdini with this stubbornness. Speaking of which, I should wake them up. I'm sure they'd like to tag along. "Bucky! Houdini! Come on boys!" she yelled loudly. Both animals came out of the stables and trotted over to her. She'd already put their food and hay out in case they decided to stay behind. Tyler turned back towards Reegan. She'd opted for a tan baseball cap since she was going to have a passenger that probably didn't want a hat brim in her face.

"Alright. From this moment on, you have to let yourself go. I promise I'm not going to hurt you or let you get hurt."

"Tyler, I'm not..." Before she could finish Tyler cut her off.

"Just get your butt on this quad, Reegan, and stop arguing with me."

Reegan rolled her eyes and climbed on behind her.

"You'd better scoot closer and hold on."

Reegan did everything she could do to keep from touching Tyler, but as soon as the quad was started and Tyler gunned the throttle, Reegan almost fell back. Wrapping her arms around the blond, she held on tightly.

Tyler smiled and continued over the hills. *Trust me.*

"Where are we going?" Reegan yelled over the roar of the motor. Tyler slowed so they could talk to each other.

"I'm going to show you the McCain Ranch. You've only seen the business side of it. This place has so much more to offer."

"How big is it?"

Tyler stopped in the meadow, killing the engine, and turned slightly in the seat so that she was eye to eye with Reegan with their faces less than a foot apart.

"Well, we have a little over five-hundred acres of land

that is semi-cleared, but it's closer to a thousand when you count the other side of those rolling hills and all of the wooded area behind them."

"What's back there?"

"We'll go out that way tomorrow. I'll drive my Jeep. Today, I wanted to show you part of the countryside. I was hoping Houdini and Bucky..." Just as she said their names, they came strolling up. "There you guys are. This is their favorite spot since this entire pasture is one big meadow. They both eat the grass, but Bucky eats a lot more of it."

"They act like dogs. Are they always this loyal?"

"Yeah, but they can be a pain in the butt too. In fact, that's how he got his name." She pointed at the crème colored goat with the brown spots and long floppy ears. "When I first got him, he'd sneak out every day. I must have chased his butt for miles. He was climbing through the boards of the fence, so Uncle Tucker and my dad and I put chicken wire all around the fence. We hired Rusty and Jake to help. At the time they were ranch hands here and only did odd jobs as stable boys.

That entire project took us two weeks. I don't think I even slept during those weeks. I was up at four a.m. doing my ranch chores until four in the afternoon, then we'd eat a quick dinner and start working on the fence. We'd work until midnight, sometimes later. So, that's why he's named Houdini." She smiled. "He's five years old now, so is Bucky as a matter of fact. I got him a few weeks after we'd finished the fence. I named him Bucky because he had big bucked teeth when he was a foal. Over the years, his teeth have straightened out nicely. Uncle Tucker tells everyone he used to wear braces." She shook her head and Reegan laughed. *Progress.* Tyler started the quad and continued to ride along the different trails. Bucky and Houdini stayed close by.

"I want you to drive. Think you can manage?" Tyler turned a little further, her lips were close to brushing Reegan's because they were sitting so close together. Reegan felt her breath catch. She cleared her throat, shrugging off whatever feeling was starting to stir inside of her.

"I've never really driven one of these."

"It's easy. I'll help you."

They switched places and Tyler turned her hat around backwards. "Okay, this thumb lever here on your right is like the gas pedal." she said, reaching around Reegan and putting her hand on the handlebar. "You pull the lever on that same bar for the front brakes and the back brake is the lever down here in front of your foot." She put her hand on Reegan's thigh, pushing down. "Okay, now this one is an automatic, so you don't need to change gears. It's also four-wheel-drive and has reverse. Think you got it?"

Reegan shook her head, unable to speak as her heart raced.

Tyler laughed. "Slide as far forward as you can. I'm going to reach around and help you until you get the feel for it, alright?"

"Uh...okay." Reegan tried to hide her smile, but the corners of her mouth turned up. She noticed for the first time, with Tyler's warm body against her back, that the blond didn't smell like stale animal carcass. Reegan sniffed the air again, liking the soapy smell with a hint of musky vanilla cologne.

Tyler started the four-wheeler and pressed the thumb tab as they took off. Slowly, she let Reegan take over until she was fully in charge. "See, you got it. I'll make a country girl out of you before you know it."

Reegan laughed loudly.

"Keep going down this trail here," Tyler said, without sliding back. The smaller woman felt good against her and she couldn't remember the last time she'd had another woman this close to her. Bucky and Houdini had stayed back at the meadow as the quad rode off in the distance.

~

They rode around the upper part of the property for a few more hours and returned to the stables around noon. "Do you want to see the rest of Duskin, then go down to Amarillo?" Tyler asked when she parked the quad and shut it off.

"Sure." Reegan couldn't explain it, but for some reason she wanted to do whatever Tyler was doing.

Tyler traded her ball cap for her black cowboy hat and tossed her flannel shirt in the console compartment of the old Jeep. Her blue t-shirt clung to her muscular frame nicely. Her perky round breasts were small, but in perfect proportion to the rest of her body. Reegan left her sweater laying on the quad and climbed into the open Jeep. She was glad she had worn part of her movie wardrobe. At least now she wouldn't look so much like an outcast.

Tyler started up the Jeep and wrenched the gearshift down into first gear. They drove off, waving at Rusty as they passed by the stable. She reached into the console pressing the remote control for the gate. Tyler shifted the gears and reached over to turn the stereo on as they pulled out onto the main dirt road. Seconds later, country music was blaring from the speakers and she sang along with just about every song as they bounced along the dirt road with a dust cloud behind them. It felt like they were going at least fifty, but in actuality, there were only going about thirty. The roads were rough and washed out from the rain over the summer. Tyler turned the radio down when she saw Reegan's lips moving.

"What was that?"

"I was just asking how much of the town was dirt roads."

"Oh. Well, with a town of only a hundred or so people, there really isn't much of a need for paved roads I guess."

"The entire town is dirt roads?"

"Yeah." They pulled up next to a small building that looked like a rundown shack. Tyler turned the Jeep off. "Welcome to the other side of town, and to the Duskin Post Office." She smiled. Reegan's eyes grew large.

"You're kidding me?"

"Nope. Come on." They got out and walked into the building. Tyler found her box, which was about the size of a regular Post Office Box. It was empty when she opened it. "Huh. I usually have something in there. Anyway, this is it." She held her arms out and spun around. The little building had a concrete floor, covered in dusty dirt. It was a small, one-room shack, full of rows of mailbox squares. Everyone had the same sized box, then there were about two dozen larger boxes to house different size packages.

"This is crazy. I can't believe this is your post office." Reegan was amazed at how small the town really was.

"Do you want to have an early dinner?" Tyler asked.

"Uh...sure." Reegan shrugged.

They got back into the Jeep and drove off. Just up the road from the Post Office Reegan saw a small Mom and Pop store which carried groceries and essentials and a small gas station with one pump was sitting next to it. Reegan wondered how she'd missed all of that on her way to the ranch the day she'd arrived. She kept waiting to see a horse drawn carriage and buggy.

~

They ate a quick dinner at a small Mexican restaurant on the edge of town. After that, they stopped at a few shops nearby where Reegan bought a bottle of wine and Tyler picked up two hundred pound bags of corn. She'd told the salesman that it was for all of the deer feeders on her property and he never gave her a second glance. The moonshine mash called for cracked corn and buying that in bulk would look suspicious, so she always bought whole kernel corn when she was in town and ran in through the corn grinder in the old barn.

The sun had finally set and the stars were beginning to come out when they headed through the back roads once more. Reegan talked about her life in L.A. She'd never been married and had broken up with her latest boyfriend a few months earlier. Her father lived in Brazil, where he was from and her mother lived in Costa Mesa, California, where she'd grown up. She was an only child and had gone to college for a little while in southern California, and had modeled on the side. Then, she'd given it all up for an acting career. She'd been working on three straight movies back to back to back and had barely seen the million dollar apartment she owned. Reegan was shocked at how easily she was able to talk to Tyler. She was usually a very shy person with a quiet social life.

They pulled up next to the gate in front of the ranch and Tyler pushed the button in the console to open it.

"So, you've seen the entire area. What do you think?" she asked with a grin.

"It's different, definitely different." Reegan smiled. Tyler drove through when the gates opened and parked close to the house in her usual spot. The moon lit up the night sky above them as she walked with Reegan back to the motor coach.

"You didn't have to walk with me, thank you, though." Reegan couldn't understand why she felt so comfortable around Tyler. "I had a nice time today. What's your big plan for tomorrow?"

"Well, I'm hoping to get you on a horse."

"I doubt it." Reegan opened her door. "Let me guess, we'll be up and at it before the sun rises, am I right?" she said, sarcastically.

"Yes, I'm always up before the sun. Watching the sun rise and set are my two favorite times of day." She smiled. "I'll see you in the morning. Get a good night's sleep, you're going to need it." Tyler turned, walking away.

~

Reegan felt like she'd just fallen asleep when she heard the knocking. Luckily, she was already up and dressed, for what, she had no clue. With a half empty coffee cup in her hand, she answered the door.

"Morning." Tyler stood in front of the steps with a solid gray flannel shirt on with the collar of her white t-shirt visible underneath. She had on her usual jeans, boots, and cowboy hat.

"It's not morning yet," Reegan said, with an attitude as she invited the blond inside. "Want some coffee?"

"No thank you, my uncle and I just finished a pot in

445

the house," Tyler said as she switched her weight back and forth from foot to foot. She wasn't sure why she was so nervous around this woman who seemed to annoy her to no end. *I'll be glad when this is over with and these city folks are out of here.*

"Does he live with you?"

"Yes. He moved in after my father died. That house is way too big for just me and he's all alone anyway," Tyler said, waiting for Reegan to finish her coffee.

They walked towards the stables together in silence. By this time, the sun was already rising and basking the meadow and rolling hills in an orange glow. Tucker was working with the ranch hands on their morning chores.

"Morning, Tyler..." Rusty tipped his hat. "And Miss Delsol." He made sure to give her a once over.

"Hey, Rus." Tyler walked past him towards one of the stalls, stopping in front a smaller chocolate brown mare.

"Reegan, this is Galaxy. She's very gentle, you'll like her." Tyler opened the stall and walked inside. She rubbed the horse's head a few times and motioned for Reegan to join her.

"I...no...I can't...I'm not ready." Reegan turned away and walked out of the stable.

"What's her problem?" Jake asked as Tyler walked past him in the direction Reegan was headed in.

"I don't know." Tyler quickened her pace and made her way out of the building. Reegan was heading back towards the motor coach.

"Reegan!" Tyler yelled. The brunette never turned around, so Tyler jogged until she was walking next to her. "What's wrong?" She could see the tears on Reegan's cheek.

"Nothing." Reegan kept walking, trying to hide her

face. Tyler grabbed her arm to stop her.

"At least tell me why you're crying."

Reegan turned her head and looked into the beautiful eyes staring at her. "Leave it alone, Tyler. Please."

"Alright, come on." Tyler laced her fingers with Reegan's and held her soft hand tightly. Reegan didn't say anything as her chest burned and her stomach tightened from the innocent contact.

"Where are we going?" Reegan asked as they walked towards the Jeep.

"I have something I want to show you," Tyler said, starting the vehicle. She drove down the dirt path along the fence, past the meadow and over the rolling hills. Minutes later, they were on the other side of the property. She parked in a small, natural clearing.

"This is my quiet place. I come down here to escape the world when something's on my mind." *I've been coming down here a lot more since you've interrupted my life.* Tyler hopped out and walked over by the edge of the fresh water stream.

"Oh my God, Tyler. This is beautiful." Reegan bent down next to her, sticking her hand in the water, surprised at how warm it was. "It's so clear!" She could see the large river rocks sitting on the bottom.

"Want to take a walk?" Tyler asked.

"Uh…sure."

Six

"If you don't mind my asking, where's your mother?" Reegan questioned as they walked along the bank of the stream.

Neither woman was in a hurry as they slowly moved along. Tyler kicked rocks out of her way with her boots as she led her in the opposite direction of the hidden still shed a hundred yards upstream. "Well, my mom died giving birth to me. Her blood pressure got really high and she had a stroke. It was an at home natural birth. There aren't any hospitals near here, so that's the way it's done. The local doctor was called, but it was too late."

"Aww, I'm sorry." Reegan wrapped her fingers around Tyler's hand.

Tyler felt the warmth in the soft hand immediately penetrating her body. *How is she able to do that to me? No one's ever done that before.*

"I'm scared to ask about your father."

Tyler smiled. "Don't ever be scared to ask me anything." She moved her hand so that their fingers were laced together. "My daddy, Trace McCain, was a well-known man around the equestrian world for a very long time." Tyler took a deep breath. "Two years ago he was on Route Two, coming home from Amarillo when someone

448

from out of state who was lost and not paying attention, ran him off the road."

"Oh my God." Reegan squeezed her hand.

"He was an old town guy that didn't believe in seat belts or air bags. He'd had a newer model pickup truck, but he'd turned the air bag off and wasn't wearing his seat belt. He died on the scene before the volunteer rescue and firefighters could get to him."

Reegan stopped walking. She turned towards Tyler, placing her hand on the blonde's face. She saw the tears welling up in the sea green eyes, threatening to fall.

"Tyler...I...I'm so sorry. I didn't mean to upset you." *Damn it, Reegan, you always know how to ask the wrong questions.*

"It's alright. I'm fine...I never...I haven't cried about it in a while." Tyler took a deep breath, drying her eyes. She squeezed the soft hand that she was holding. "Reegan?"

"Yeah?"

Tyler stopped walking and turned, waiting for Reegan's golden eyes to meet hers. "Tell me why you won't ride a horse. I know you're scared, but why?"

"I...Tyler, I can't..."

"You can trust me. What happens out here, stays out here."

Reegan ran a hand through her long hair, looking up at Tyler. "When I was ten my parents sent me to camp for the summer. I was miserable at first, but it was actually a great time. One of our activities was horseback riding. I loved feeding and caring for the animals, and was so excited when it was my turn to ride the big black horse. One of the camp counselors helped me get up into the saddle and as soon as I grabbed the reins, a small animal like a squirrel or raccoon, scurried nearby and spooked the horse. He took off at full gallop with me on his back."

Tyler saw the fear in Reegan's eyes as she let the tears fall.

"I don't know how far the horse ran before they were able to get control of him, but I was hanging halfway out of the saddle, being dragged next to the animal as he ran. I finally fell off, breaking my arm and my leg. It was the most horrifying experience I have ever faced. I was traumatized, Tyler. It took almost two years for me to be able to be near any kind of animal."

"Wow, that's terrible. I'm sorry that happened to you." Tyler pulled Reegan close, wrapping her arms around the smaller woman. She held her tightly, breathing in her scent and feeling Reegan's warm body against her. Reegan let Tyler hold her as she cried.

"I would never let anything like that happen to you," Tyler whispered. "I know how to help you. We can do this together."

"What are we doing?" Reegan asked, pulling away from and wiping the remaining tears from her face.

"You're riding an animal." Tyler grinned.

Reegan shook her head. "I don't know, Tyler. I don't think I can."

Tyler began whistling loudly and yelling at the top of her lungs. "Bucky! Houdini!" All of a sudden, Reegan saw them galloping over the hill in the distance.

"Wow, how the hell did they hear you all the way out here?"

"They have unbelievable hearing. They're just stubborn and do what they feel like doing sometimes, but when they hear me whistle they come running to me like obedient dogs. It's actually really cool."

Both animals walked right up to Tyler, sniffing her

and making sure that she was okay. Tyler rubbed Bucky's nose and scratched Houdini's ears. "Come on, you've touched them once already. These two are the most trustworthy animals I've ever met. Reegan, they won't hurt you. I promise my life on it."

Reegan stuck her hand out, petting Bucky's head, then Houdini's long ears.

"How much do you weigh?" Tyler asked, nonchalantly.

Reegan shot her sideways look. "Excuse me?"

Tyler raised her eyebrows in confusion. "I asked how much you weighed."

"I know. Why?"

"Because Bucky has a weight limit." Tyler waited patiently for the answer to her question while Reegan continued to pet the animals.

"What does that have to do with me?" Reegan sounded agitated.

"Do you always have to answer me with a question?"

"No, only when you ask me something that's none of your business. How much do you weigh?" Reegan cocked her head to the side and raised an eyebrow.

"'About one thirty, one thirty-five." Tyler answered, easily.

"First of all, I can't believe you answered me, and second, there is no way you weigh that much."

"Why? It's only your weight. It's not like I asked your bra size or something, you don't have to freak out on me. And why would I lie to you?"

"Fine, I'm one fifteen, and you're not much bigger than me so there's no way you weigh that much more."

"I'm a few inches taller than you and most of my weight is muscle from working on the ranch. Anyhow, you're a little more than his limit but he can handle you."

Tyler walked over to the embankment, calling Bucky to her. He meandered over and stopped, waiting for her to pet him.

"I want you to stand up here and climb onto Bucky. I don't have a saddle for him so you'll have to go bareback, but I'll hold him and go slow."

"You want me to ride the donkey?" Reegan laughed, shaking her head.

"Yeah. He's a lot smaller than a horse and this is a good start," Tyler said, seriously.

"This is crazy."

"Reegan, trust me. You'll be fine."

Reegan walked over to Tyler and her donkey. Following Tyler's instructions, she put one leg over the animal's back and hopped up onto him. Bucky wobbled for a second then gained his grip, standing still.

"Alright. See it's not so bad. Now, I'm going to walk him around, just hold on and keep your balance centered."

"Don't let go of him, Tyler." Reegan demanded.

"I've got him."

Tyler walked the donkey around for a few minutes along the path of the stream, then turned him around to go in the opposite direction. The goat walked next to her on the opposite side. She helped Reegan down when they arrived back at their original spot.

"Wow, I...I'm still shaking." Reegan's body was trembling from her frayed nerves.

Tyler smiled. *Next step complete. She's so beautiful, if only she wasn't a city girl!* "Are you ready to go back?" Tyler asked.

"Yeah. I wish the sun was setting. I bet this place is just as beautiful at night under the stars."

"Yes, I can't describe it."

"So, what's your next plan?" Reegan questioned as she climbed up into the Jeep.

~

"This isn't going to work. Riding a donkey is nothing like riding a horse, Tyler." Reegan said as they parked the Jeep and walked into the stable.

"Trust me." Tyler looked at her, grinning. The colorful swirls in her eyes sparkled in the fluorescent lighting.

That silly grin was starting to tug at Reegan's heart. *What is going on with me lately?* She thought, stepping a little closer to Tyler.

"What are you up to?" Tucker asked, noticing them as he walked out of a stall.

Reegan moved away from Tyler's side, walking to a stall a few feet away to pet the small white horse.

"Reegan rode Bucky a little while ago," Tyler beamed.

"Really?" He nodded in surprise.

"Yep. How's Guardian doing?" she asked as she walked into the stall, petting the large brown horse.

"He's fine. Are you going to take him out?" Tucker questioned.

"Yeah, he's big enough to hold us both. Maybe if she rides around with me for a little while she will get more comfortable on a horse's back."

"She's awfully scared of these horses, Tyler. You ought to be telling that movie guy to take a flying leap," Tucker said, shaking his head.

"She'll ride again. It's a long story. Besides, if anyone can help her, it's me."

"That I know," he said, helping her get the big horse saddled up.

Reegan stared at the large beast, thinking that she may pee her pants out of nervousness if she wasn't careful. The horse looked nearly twice the size of the one she had fallen off of.

Tyler put the large step stool next to the wall and climbed up into the saddle, putting her feet in the stirrups. As soon as she was situated, she held a hand out towards Reegan.

"Trust me." Tyler's voice was full of compassion as the bright light of the stable danced across her eyes.

Reegan took a deep breath and climbed up behind her with a little help from Tucker. She wrapped her arms tightly around Tyler's waist and slid forward until she was practically sitting on her back. They molded perfectly together.

"Don't let go," Tyler said.

"I don't plan on it," Reegan replied, shakily.

"Be careful, Tyler," her uncle muttered as he watched the horse move away slowly.

Tyler pulled the reins and made a soft clicking noise. The horse began trotting. They went down into the meadow first, then headed towards the hills.

"Doing alright?"

"Yeah." Reegan continued holding onto her with a death grip. Tyler had kept the horse trotting at a very slow pace.

"I'm going to let him gallop, hold on tight. I promise I'll never let anything happen to you, Reegan."

The brunette couldn't possibly hold on any tighter if her life depended on it and Tyler enjoyed the closeness, although she'd never admit it. She'd given up on ever feeling the warmth of a woman again after her heart had been broken. She'd been having a fleeting affair with a bull rider's lonely wife while her husband was away on the tour. Her uncle had been the only person that had known what she was doing. When the woman's husband finally came home, she broke all of her promises to leave him. She pushed Tyler away like quitting a bad habit, breaking her heart and shattering the dreams they'd built together. A couple of months later, Tyler's father passed away and she threw herself into running the ranch, never looking back.

Thinking about the old memories drove Tyler to push the horse from a simple trot into a fully fledged gallop as they reached the other side of the hills. Reegan was amazed at how easily Tyler controlled the large animal racing through the pasture. Reegan squeezed her firmly, praying she didn't fall off as Tyler came back to reality, slowing the horse to a light jog.

"I think it's your turn to drive," Tyler said.

"Oh, I don't know," Reegan replied shakily.

"Reegan, you know how to ride a horse. You just needed me to help you get over the fear caused by your accident. I'll be right here." Tyler slid off the horse and Reegan moved forward, putting her feet into the stirrups.

"Now, I'm sure you've noticed we don't use bits with our horses, so the reins are attached to the harness around his head. Just give a slight tug in the direction you want him to go and he will move. If you shake the reins and give him a little soft kick with your heel, he'll pick up speed and you simply pull back on the reins to slow him or stop him," Tyler said, climbing up behind her. "Is any of this coming back to you?" she asked as she inched forward until she was against Reegan's back and able to reach around and help her with the reins.

"A little," Reegan could barely think, much less form a sentence. She prayed she didn't screw up and fall off. She wasn't sure what made her more nervous, riding the horse or the way her body felt with Tyler against her.

~

They rode all around the property and returned to the stables an hour later. Tyler jumped down and Tucker helped Reegan use the step stool. He had been surprised to see the brunette in the saddle, but said nothing.

"It'll be dark soon," Tyler murmured, turning towards Reegan. "Would you like to have dinner up at the house?"

"I don't know," Reegan hesitated.

"Well, I was thinking maybe we could have an early dinner together and go watch the sunset at the stream."

"I'd love to see that, but you guys usually work until after dark, don't you?"

"Yes. It'll just be you and I for dinner. I'll leave the leftovers for Uncle Tucker."

"Oh." Reegan smiled. "Sure."

"Is there anything you don't eat?" Tyler asked.

"Uh…I don't care for beets or radishes, but I pretty much eat everything else."

"Well, I've never had a radish or a beet, so I wouldn't even know how to cook them." Tyler grinned.

~

Tyler had made a lemon-pepper chicken dish with steamed vegetables for dinner. Reegan brought the bottle of Chardonnay that she'd bought while they were in Amarillo the day before.

"This is amazing," Reegan said, finishing the last of her meal.

Tyler smiled and walked into the kitchen. She returned with a cold mason jar. Reegan watched as she unscrewed the cap, handing the jar to her. She sniffed it, raising an eyebrow.

"Take a sip," Tyler urged.

Reegan took a tentative taste, then a long swig, opening her senses as the sweet, smooth alcohol burned a cool path down her throat. "What is this?"

"Do you like it?" Tyler asked.

Reegan took another drink before handing the jar back to her. "Yes. It's strong, but it's very good."

Tyler grinned. "It's strawberry and blueberry moonshine."

"Moonshine?" Reegan questioned. "Like the hillbillies make?"

Tyler laughed loudly. "I guess you could say that. The recipe has been in my family for a few generations and it's been perfected over the years. We use a fruit in our mash to get the strong, sweet fruity flavors."

"Isn't this illegal?"

"Yep, but we stopped distributing it nearly ten years ago."

"Oh my God, you were bootleggers?"

Tyler laughed again, taking a long swallow of shine before recapping the jar. "We were moonshiners on the side. Horses have always been our top priority and our love. Bootleggers are the people that transport the illegal liquor."

"Wow." Reegan reached for the jar, opening it and taking another sip. "It's very good. I'd drink this over any fruity cocktail in Hollywood any day of the week. It puts that bottle of wine that I brought to shame."

Tyler smiled. "Come on, we better go before we miss the sunset."

~

The sun was just about to fall below the mountains in the distance. Tyler drove as fast as she could without tossing them both out. She parked near an old oak tree when she reached the stream. Reegan climbed out and walked towards the water as Tyler grabbed an old wool blanket from the back of the Jeep, spreading it out on the embankment. She was glad she'd decided to leave the jar of shine back at the house. She'd wanted to enjoy this moment sober.

"This is so amazing. I've seen beautiful sunsets in many different parts of the world, but none of them ever looked like this." Reegan murmured as she sat down, stretching her legs out in front of her.

Tyler sat next to her, stretching her own legs. The sun cast a bright orange glow over the land, glimmering across the clear water in front of them. As the last of the orange cleared the mountains, the full moon lit up the darkness, casting shadows as far as the eye could see. Millions of stars began glowing above them. Tyler tipped her head back, looking up since she had her cowboy hat on.

"Do you ever take that thing off?" Reegan asked, the sarcasm in her voice went unnoticed.

"Uh...yeah. I don't wear it to bed or in the shower." She grinned, removing the hat and setting it in the grass next to the blanket. Reegan had only seen Tyler's short blond hair once or twice the entire time she'd been there.

"You didn't have to take it off on my account."

"I felt like taking it off. It's not glued to my head," Tyler laughed playfully and leaned back on her arms to stare at the sky. This was the first time she had ever shared a sunset at her special place with someone other than her two furry pals. Of course, her family and ranch hands knew about the stream, but no one bothered going near the area. Somehow, it felt right having Reegan there next to her.

"I'm so glad you brought me here, Tyler. This place is so beautiful," Reegan said as she leaned over, kissing Tyler's cheek. She wasn't sure if it was the slightly warm evening, the gorgeous view of the night sky, or simply the fluttering in her stomach that enticed her to make such a bold move. Reegan's lips tingled as she chastised herself. *What the hell was that for?*

Tyler turned her head to face the honey colored eyes staring at her. Without hesitation, she closed the tiny distance between them, pressing her lips against Reegan's. Tyler kissed her softly at first, tasting the sweetness of her lips and hearing the moan escape her mouth as their lips parted.

Reegan ran her hands through Tyler's short hair, tugging lightly as she lay back, pulling Tyler on top of her. Tyler placed tender kisses along Reegan's neck to her collar bone, moving under the top of Reegan's shirt. Reegan reached between them, unbuttoning the gray flannel shirt Tyler was wearing. Tyler sat up slightly so that Reegan could pull the shirt free and toss it next to them. Reegan slid her hands under the back of the t-shirt Tyler still wore, feeling her silky smooth skin. Their lips met once again, parting to allow their tongues to glide together passionately.

Tyler rolled over, pulling Reegan on top of her.

Reegan leaned back so that she was straddling her and Tyler sat up, pulling Reegan's shirt off and tossing it aside. Bending her head down, Tyler ran her lips lightly over Reegan's naked chest. Reegan tossed her head back arching into the mouth kissing her breasts. Reegan's hands trembled as she moved back, pulling Tyler's shirt and bra over her head. She leaned forward once more, pressing her breasts to Tyler's.

Slowly they worked together, removing the rest of their clothing and Reegan pulled Tyler back on top of her. Tyler ran her hand leisurely across Reegan's stomach and down her thigh, continuing back up the other side, and stopping when she reached the soft folds in the center. She moved her fingers lazily around the edges, careful not to touch the sensitive middle.

Reegan moved into her touches helping to set the pace. Her hips rose up, urging Tyler to go inside. Tyler slid her body down Reegan's until she was able to run her tongue along the throbbing mound her fingers had just been circling. She pushed two fingers inside of her, continuing to tease her with large circles of her tongue, then smaller ones as her fingers moved deeper and faster.

The glowing moon above cast them in a shadow next to the stream. Tiny beads of sweat dripped from Tyler's brow. Reegan reached down and locked her fingers with Tyler's free hand and tugged gently on her short hair as her hips bucked against the tongue circling her clit and the fingers probing deep inside of her. No words were spoken, only faint moans escaped from both women, echoing softly in the darkness. Reegan was breathless, shuddering and clawing at the woman between her legs, holding nothing back as she climaxed. Tyler kissed her way back up Reegan's body until she met the warm eyes glistening in the pale light.

Reegan rolled Tyler onto her back and straddled her. Grabbing Tyler's hands, she pushed them above her head as she bent down, teasing Tyler's lips with her tongue first, then tasting herself on Tyler's mouth as the kiss probed deeper. Tyler rocked her hips against Reegan's, searching for contact.

Reegan let go of her hands and Tyler wrapped her arms around Reegan, running her hands up and down her silky smooth skin. Their bodies molded together into one shadow next to the flowing stream. Reegan ran her hand along Tyler's body, caressing her small round breasts and massaging her muscular stomach, inching lower until she found the wetness awaiting her. She moved her fingers through the wet folds, dipping the tips inside of her with each pass. Tyler's hips rose, meeting each teasing thrust, pushing her further inside. Reegan kissed Tyler's lips as her fingers slid deep, filling her for the first time. She pulled them out teasingly, then pushed them back in for more as Tyler's body bucked against her. Tyler moaned as Reegan slowly continued sliding her fingers in and out of the wetness. She covered Tyler's chest in kisses as she worked her mouth lower.

Tyler tried desperately to hold back. She wanted to experience every part of this woman that had her body on fire, pulsating and begging to let go. She felt the first surge of orgasm throttle her as Reegan's tongue raked across her swollen clit. Tyler jerked her hips and Reegan probed further, pulling her fingers out long enough to slide her tongue inside. She felt the muscles tighten around her tongue as Tyler's hips thrust one last time. Tyler felt like she'd died of pure pleasure next to the stream as the waves of orgasm washed over her.

Tyler caught her breath and pulled Reegan back up to her. Their lips met once more, mixing the taste of each other in the passionate kiss. Tyler caressed Reegan's face softly, tracing her jaw with one finger. Reegan gently placed tiny kisses along Tyler's collarbone and back up her neck. The undeniable passion they'd shared was raw and powerful.

Reegan looked deeply into the bluish-green eyes admiring her. "Tyler," she whispered. "I've...never..."

"Sshh..." Tyler murmured. She saw the tears in Reegan's eyes, threatening to fall.

Reegan lay her head on Tyler's shoulder, tucking her forehead under her chin and Tyler wrapped her arms protectively around her. They lay there under the stars, listening to the rolling stream nearby and the cadence of their soft breathing until sleep claimed them.

Seven

Tyler cracked her eyes when she felt Reegan stir against her. The memory of their lovemaking came rushing back. Her eyes flew open, focusing in the darkness. The moon and stars were covered by thick heavy clouds. *How long have we been asleep? What time is it?* The cool air stung her skin as Reegan peeled herself off of her.

"Hey," Tyler whispered.

"Hi. I'm sorry, did I wake you?"

Tyler's smile quickly faded when she noticed the sadness in Reegan's eyes. "Are you okay?" she questioned.

Reegan felt around the grass next to them, searching for her clothes. Tyler sat up, putting her hand on the brunette's shoulder. "Reegan?"

"Tyler...I'm sorry...I..." She choked back the tears and took a deep breath. "I need to get back."

Tyler's chest burned as the painful realization passed through her. She wasn't sure what to say or do, so she did the next best thing. She stood up, quickly dressed in silence and drove Reegan back to her motor coach. After that, she took a long walk around the property trying to make sense of her evening. Her heart ached and her head pounded. It had been years since she had been serious with anyone and she was too old fashioned to have a one night stand. If Tyler was involved with someone she was looking at forever. The impromptu lovemaking and abrupt dismissal scared her. She feared she'd made a huge mistake.

~

Tyler had spent the rest of the late night and early morning walking around, unable to sleep. When she finally decided she had no answers and couldn't come up with a rational explanation for Reegan's erratic behavior, she took a shower and dressed for the day. She was in the stables at four a.m. By the time her Uncle Tucker joined her at five, she'd already fed Bucky and Houdini, and was a quarter of the way through her chores for the day.

"What's bothering you, kiddo?" he asked, without looking her way. He knew her moods as if she were his own child.

She took a deep breath and sighed. There was no way she could lie to her uncle. It wasn't in her to lie anyway. Hell, she wasn't even sure if she knew how.

"Come on...spill it. You got at least a half hour before them boys get here," he said, referring to Jake and Rusty as he turned a bucket over and sat down. He began filing the hooves of the smallest mare. Tyler stood nearby, watching him work.

"I think I made a big mistake, Uncle Tucker." She hung her head.

"Well, what did you do?" he asked, looking up at her.

She didn't have to answer him, he could tell by the look on her face. Her beautiful island colored eyes were dark and hollow.

"Hmm...that city girl break your heart?" he questioned as he switched legs on the horse.

She was tougher than this. Why the hell had she been letting it get to her so badly?

"You're strong, Tyler McCain, just like your old man had been. But, you wear your heart on your sleeve just like your momma did." He stood up and squeezed her shoulder as he moved around to the other side of the horse.

A loud clap of thunder echoed across the sky, startling Tyler. Lightning flashed, illuminating the ranch in the darkness as large drops of rain fell from the low hanging clouds.

Tucker looked up at her with a raised eyebrow as the rain poured down heavily. Lightning and thunder alternated back and forth across the sky as if they were battling each other. The late Fall thunderstorms could be some of the worst of the year, often flooding the land and forming tornadoes.

~

The brutal storm moved slowly across the sky over the next few days, turning the ranch into a muddy mess. Regular ranch chores continued, making everyone miserable. Tyler worked dusk to dawn each day, drenched from head to toe and covered in sticky mud, wondering if the dark, dreary weather had been somehow caused by her indiscretion. She didn't need anyone to point out her mistake, her own heartache was enough of a reminder. The rain had barely let up on the end of the third day, when she decided to take Hercules out for a muddy run. She'd drank enough moonshine to kill a small animal over the past few nights, and wasn't in the mood for anymore.

"Be careful out there," Tucker said, watching her saddle up the large stallion.

"I'll be fine. Don't hold dinner for me. I'll make a sandwich or something later," she replied, climbing into the saddle.

Tyler walked the horse into a trot as she left the stable. The early evening sun was hidden behind the dark stormy clouds. Rain fell in lazy drops, running off the brim of her cowboy hat. Her jeans and thin flannel shirt were pasted to her like a second skin. She dug her heels into the horse, urging him to pick up the pace. She hadn't given the horse any direction, choosing to let him run free while she held on for the ride. Hercules galloped, racing across the meadow, splashing through the mud. They reached the stream in no time. She slowed him to a walk, moving past the narrow clearing, before pushing him to run at his full gait. She'd nearly fallen out of the wet saddle as he weaved through the woods, striding as if she weren't on his back.

Tyler saw the light coming from the other side of the property as they crossed one of the hills in the meadow. She slowed Hercules once again, trotting close enough to see the motor coaches, but too far away to be seen though the windows, under the darkened sky in the pouring rain. She didn't need to be any closer to see what was inside the nearest bus, Reegan's face was a mental picture burned in her memory. She closed her eyes, letting a few loose tears mix with the wind pelting her face. Lightning flashed across the sky, illuminating her briefly, like a ghost in the night. She quickly turned the horse, working him into a gallop as the thunder clapped loudly in the distance.

~

The movie shooting had been postponed for most of the week because of the bad weather. On Thursday, the sun finally rose high in the sky. Tyler decided to wash the gritty mud from her pets and put them in a stall until all of the puddles had dried up. The rain had come in so quickly, she hadn't had time to put them in the stable like she usually did. As a result, they'd taken the opportunity to run wild, splashing through the muck until they were covered in thick Texas mud.

"Damn it Bucky!" she shouted as he shook, covering her in nasty, soapy water. "Do you always have to wet me?" Luckily, she'd traded her cowboy hat for a ball cap when she'd decided to clean them up.

Rusty walked around the corner laughing. He stopped when he took in the sight of her tight wet t-shirt and jeans. Even though her shirt was black, it clung to every womanly curve of her sexy muscular body. He quickly turned away. Tyler was like a sister to him.

"They kicking your ass, Tyler?" he asked.

She slung the soapy wet sponge at him, but he ducked as it went sailing past him, hitting Reegan square in the face, soaking her.

Tyler froze. Rusty laughed hysterically before leaving when he saw the anger in Tyler's eyes. Tyler grabbed the dry towel she'd been saving for herself and walked towards Reegan.

"I'm so sorry. I didn't see you standing there," Tyler said shyly, handing her the towel as she bit back the smile forming on the corners of her mouth. She knew that the filming had resumed that morning, but she'd sent her uncle to the set in her place.

Reegan tried to towel off her face and hair. "Can we talk?" she growled through clenched teeth.

"Uh...yeah. Yeah sure. I just need to take care of these guys really quick."

"I'll be in my motor coach. I need to go change and I have to be back on set in a half hour." Reegan turned and walked away.

~

Tyler finished scrubbing her stubborn pets, towel dried them as best she could, then closed them in a stall to hopefully keep them clean. She checked the watch on her wrist. *Damn.* Reegan needed to be back on set in fifteen minutes. She was still damp from the animals shaking soapy water on her, but that would have to wait. Tyler's brisk walk towards the motor coaches turned into a jog.

Reegan opened the door as soon as she heard the knock. Tyler searched her eyes, but saw nothing. The beautiful honey colored glow that she'd seen the night they were together was gone.

"I'm sorry it took so long. Houdini wasn't very cooperative." She shrugged, removing her ball cap. Her hair was pasted to her head from wearing the hat all day.

Reegan turned her nose up, sniffing. "You stink," Reegan stated as she waved Tyler over to the couch.

"I know, it's par for the course I guess. I probably shouldn't sit down though," Tyler replied. She wanted to pull Reegan against her and kiss her lips, kiss away her pain, kiss her until she could no longer breathe. Instead, she put her hands in the front pockets of her jeans to keep them from trembling.

"Tyler..." she faltered. "God, I had this whole speech memorized." Reegan took a deep breath, running her hand nervously through her long hair.

"I'm not sorry," Tyler said, finding Reegan's eyes with her own.

Reegan felt like she was going to drown in the shallow pools gazing at her. "We're starting the last section of scenes tomorrow," she paused. "It's time for the riding portion." She broke their eye contact, staring at the floor, before looking back at Tyler's eyes. "I..."

Tyler heard the shakiness in her own voice. "I'll be there."

"Thank you," Reegan whispered. Her two-way radio crackled to life. "I need to get back over there."

They walked out of the motor coach together, then went their separate ways. Tyler put her ball cap back on and walked up to the house. As soon as she stepped inside, she let one lonely tear roll down her cheek. She then wiped her face and drank a few sips of shine from the glass in the refrigerator, before heading back to work. She didn't want to be near Reegan. In fact, if she ever saw her again it would be too soon, but in order for her to ride the horse alone and finish the movie, she needed to give Reegan the comfort of knowing Tyler was right there. So, she'd suck it up and be there if that's what it took to get those people off of her ranch and that woman out of her life.

~

The next morning, Tyler had already been in the stable for an hour when her uncle caught up to her.

"You look tired," he said, handing her a travel mug full of coffee.

"What gave it away?" She smiled, drinking a long swallow.

"You yawned, and I don't think I have ever seen you

yawn." He raised an eyebrow quizzically at her, before starting his daily routine of chores.

"Not sleeping much I guess," she muttered as she finished sweeping the stall she'd been cleaning. "They're starting to film the riding scenes today, so I'll be over there most of the day."

"You think she's ready?" he asked from the next stall.

"As ready as she's going to get, I suppose."

Tyler walked to the last bay and slung the door open. She made a clicking sound, calling the large black horse over to her.

"Hey Maddy. How you doing buddy?" She ran her hand over his silky mane and he sniffed her. "You'd better be nice to her today." She smiled and started to saddle him up.

~

By noon they'd gotten through more scenes than they'd expected. Reegan was handling the horse surprisingly well, despite the fact that Tyler had to be so close that she was going to have to be cut out of at least five or ten minutes of film and Reegan had a body double do the long distance and fast riding. Everything seemed to be running smoothly. At this rate the movie would over within a week or two. Luckily, the love scenes had already been taped during the previous month. Tyler hadn't been around for any of those shots.

Unfortunately, Tyler did have to witness a few more kissing and heavy petting scenes that took place on the horse while Reegan's character rode around with the lead male, Brandon Macey, supposedly falling in love. Tyler didn't have a mean bone in her body, but as soon as that man had put his hands on Reegan she had wanted to kill him. She didn't realize she'd bitten her bottom lip until the taste of metal coated her tongue. Tyler turned her head and spat the warm red liquid on the ground like a pool of tobacco spit, slowly choking back the anger that had been boiling inside of her. She wasn't sure why a simple fake movie scene had made her so mad, but she was glad when the director cut the day.

~

A week later, all of the riding scenes that Reegan had to shoot were over and Tyler disappeared from the movie set. She even made herself unavailable for the wrap-up party. Reegan gave up the hope of seeing her again.

"Please tell Tyler...tell her, I said goodbye." Reegan tried to hide the sadness as her voice cracked.

"I'm not getting involved, but I will tell you this..." Tucker took his cowboy hat off and leaned against the gate at the main entrance to the ranch. The car that had been sent for the actress was waiting patiently for her. He pursed his lips. "Tyler's not a one-night-rodeo kind of girl. She's a lot like her old man. When Tyler McCain loves something, it becomes her whole life, the very air she breathes." He looked into Reegan's tear-filled eyes. "You just remember that." He stood back up and put his hat back on. Reegan got into the black sedan and rode away.

~

Tyler sat on the bank next to the stream, almost in the exact spot where she and Reegan had made love. It seemed like a lifetime had passed. The small stones that she tossed

471

in the water made a 'ka-thunk' sound as they splashed into the clear water flowing in front of her. Tyler had laid her cowboy hat down on the ground next to her and opened the last of her jars of strawberry and blueberry mixed shine. The air had finally starting getting cooler, but the midday sun still shined bright and hot. She was glad the shine was still ice cold from the refrigerator. She didn't feel the bead of sweat running between her shoulder blades and down her back. She'd already rolled the sleeves of her flannel shirt up a few hours ago. She didn't have to look at her watch to know Reegan was physically gone, she'd mentally left a long time ago.

Bucky and Houdini were playing in the meadow close to the stream. Tyler cracked a smile and sipped from the jar as she watched them chasing each other. "When I die, I want to come back as a donkey or a goat," she said to the emptiness around her, then tossed another rock into the water. Even though she knew her heart wouldn't stop hurting for a while, the tears had long dried up.

Eight

Four months later, *Shadow's Eyes* premiered and had been a box office hit. Millions of people had flocked to the theater to see it. Tyler decided to wait for it to come out on DVD, but even then, she wasn't sure if she'd watch it, and she most definitely wasn't going to go see it with a bunch of other people.

~

"Did you see it, Tyler?" Rusty asked as he helped her feed the horses.

"Nope. You?" She didn't have to ask what he was referring to. She'd decided to keep Will and Dewy on staff part time to give Rusty and Jake two days off a week like a normal job and the four them had done nothing but talk about the movie the entire week.

"Yeah, Jake and I saw it in Amarillo a few nights ago. It was good, damn good. I really liked the part where they showed her half-naked in one of the stalls."

Tyler spun around to face him. "Excuse me?"

"She's damn hot...whew!" He whistled.

Tyler reared her fist back to knock his teeth out of his mouth, then reality caught up with her. He didn't know, no one knew. Her uncle suspected, but even he didn't *know*.

She settled for a stern talking to instead of killing poor Rusty, the red-headed, horny little brother she never had. "Do me a favor, Rusty, don't ever talk about a woman like that in front of me again. It's disrespectful and vulgar and if you ever refer to Reegan Delsol like that again, I'll hang you on a meat hook by your gonads."

He blushed. "I...geez I'm sorry, Tyler. I didn't mean to upset or offend you. I know you two kind of got to be friends." He smiled apologetically.

"It's okay, I forgive you this time." She laughed and smacked his ball cap down over his eyes to break the intensity between them. Jake snuck up behind her, picking her up in the air from behind and swinging her around.

"Holy shit!" she screamed. "Put me down!" She knew who it was when she heard his squeaky laugh. "Damn it, Jacob Denton, you had better put me down if you know what's good for you!" she yelled.

"Jake, you might want to put her down before she kicks your ass, son." Tucker stood next to Rusty chuckling.

Jake finally set the kicking and thrashing woman back on the ground. Tyler turned around and nailed him in the stomach with her fist. She knew better than to hit his face, she was strong enough to knock his teeth out. Jake doubled over, coughing and trying to catch his breath.

"You're a weakling. I was holding back on you." She laughed.

All three of the guys began singing Happy Birthday to her. When they finished she looked at Jake. "Why did you grab me? You pain in the neck."

"It was getting serious in here. Rusty looked like he was about to cry. I had to come up with something quick."

Jake was still coughing from the blow to his mid-section. She shook her head and gave him a pouting face.

~

After they finished their work, they ate cake and ice cream together in the house. Will and Dewy had joined them later in the day. Everyone knew Tyler didn't like a big fuss for her birthday, and she definitely didn't want gifts. She did however, get a call that evening from a client that she'd sold a thoroughbred to a few months back. The horse was racing in the Buenos Vista Derby and the new owner invited Tyler to fly to Arcadia, California to watch the horse's first race. Every so often she'd been given invitations like this to see one of the horses that she'd bred perform either in a show or on the track. The thought of going to California did not appeal to her, but she'd said yes to the offer for business purposes since the man was possibly interested in another horse.

"I can't believe you're going to California. You'd better bring us back some pictures of the California babes," Rusty teased.

Tyler raised an eyebrow and grinned. "I'm not exactly going to cruise the beach or the bars, but I'll see what I can scare up for you." she said with a wink.

~

The plane landed on time with a hard thud. Tyler stretched her back and stood. She'd felt uncomfortable without her jeans, boots, and some kind of hat on her head as she exited the plane, carrying a small briefcase and carryon bag. The flight attendant smiled as she gave Tyler a once over at the door. Tyler looked at her with a raised eyebrow and kept walking. She noticed a young man standing in the baggage claim area of her terminal, holding a sign that read: T. McCain, as she came down the escalator.

"Hi, I'm Tyler McCain," she said.

"I'm Robert, your driver. Do you have any checked baggage?"

"No."

"If you will please follow me, the car is right outside," he said.

Tyler followed him to a black limo parked alongside the curb. She watched the scenery go by as he drove them through L.A. towards her destination since that had been the airport that she'd flown into.

Tyler couldn't believe her eyes when she stepped out of the limo in front of the luxury, high-rise hotel. The building was eggshell white with polished gold trim around the revolving door. A man dressed in a tuxedo with tails, stood with his hands behind his back, waiting for the limo driver to hand over her luggage. Tyler followed him inside, where another man dressed in similar attire met her.

"Good evening. My name is Malcolm. I'm the concierge here at the Grand Palisade." He smiled. "My job is to make sure you have everything you need for your stay here in Arcadia."

"It's nice to meet you. I'm Tyler McCain."

"You can check in right over there and your bag will be brought up to your room," he said. Malcolm had been expecting her, but he was taken aback by the thick southern accent. He knew she was an important guest since she'd been put in one of the two master suites just below the presidential suite. He glanced at her once more, watching her tight butt move under the dress slacks she wore as she walked towards the desk to check in.

Robert 'Bobby' Gillis, was the owner of the horse he'd renamed Wonder Bred. He'd made thousands and turned those into hundreds of thousands over the years in the horse racing world. His latest colt was out of the McCain Equine Ranch and had come highly recommended. He'd paid a pretty penny for the light brown horse and was betting a lot of money at the Buena Vista race. If his horse placed in the race, he'd come away with half a million dollars and if the horse happened to win he'd receive something near a million dollars since his horse was a favorite. The jockey who he had chosen to ride Wonder Bred, would get twenty percent and the trainer/handler would get twenty percent. The other sixty percent was pure profit for him. That's why he'd invited the horse breeder. If everything went well, he'd hoped to hand pick another colt or filly within the year. So, he'd put Tyler McCain in one of the classiest rooms at the most prestigious hotel nearby and prepaid for her to have full amenities.

Tyler walked into the enormous suite, surprised at the size. She moved from room to room noticing two bedrooms, two bathrooms, and a kitchen with a dining area. She stopped in the living room when she saw the gorgeous view of the city lights below her. The ringing phone on the table, next to the sofa, pulled her attention from the large floor to ceiling windows.

"Hello?" Tyler answered.

"Good evening, Ms. McCain. This is Bobby Gillis. I hope you were able to get settled in."

"Yes, thank you."

"Good, I hope you like your room."

"It's perfect, yes."

"Excellent, I hope you enjoy your stay in Arcadia. I was calling to let you know that there is a private party after the race tomorrow and I'd like you to accompany me."

"Sure," she replied. Tyler wasn't sure what to wear to the race, much less some kind of fancy private party.

"Wonderful, if you need anything at all, please don't hesitate to ask Malcolm. He's been instructed to be at your beck and call while you're here."

"Thank you again. I'm looking forward to tomorrow."

"The limo will be there to get you at eight. The race starts at ten, but I thought you might like to see Wonder Bred before he races and meet his jockey, Hans Lescher."

"That would be great," she said as she finished the call and hung up. She made one quick call home to her uncle to see how the ranch was doing and to tell him she'd made it. Then, she called Malcolm and asked if there was a shopping center nearby.

~

At eight o'clock the next morning, the phone in Tyler's room rang to announce the limo had arrived to pick her up. She'd been dressed and ready since seven, pacing the floor of the large suite trying to get comfortable in the new clothes that she'd purchased. She'd been taken to four stores and each store had a sales person waiting for her arrival, thanks to Malcolm. It wasn't Rodeo Drive, but she'd felt like the girl in Pretty Woman, which made her laugh.

Tyler was wearing dark slacks with a yellow silk blouse that buttoned down the front. It was snug, but not

478

too tight, with three quarter sleeves. She'd left the first three buttons open. She was also wearing a pair of low-heeled, leather dress boots. Her hair was styled slightly messy, like she'd just run her fingers through it. She thought she looked even younger when she glanced at herself in the mirror.

Normally, when she'd attended a race or show, she'd worn black jeans and a nice button down blouse and her shiny black cowboy boots. But, she was attending this private party and it had been fairly obvious that Bobby Gillis did everything flashy, so she pushed her cowgirl roots to the side.

"Good morning, Ms. McCain. You look superb," Malcolm said with a smile as he walked her out to the waiting limo.

Tyler smiled and thanked him for his help. She couldn't wait to get home and tell her uncle about having to get all gussied up for Mr. Gillis and his dog and pony show. He'd get a good laugh out of it. Tyler's idea of dressing up was literally a nice pair of jeans, a button down collared shirt and her black boots. She was born a cowgirl and would die a cowgirl. City life had been neat to experience each time she traveled, but it was definitely not her.

~

Tyler arrived at the Equestrian Village and had been escorted by security to the air conditioned stalls where the owners, jockeys, and handlers were gathered around their horses, preparing for the race. Tyler walked around until she found the stall for Wonder Bred. Bobby Gillis hadn't changed much since the last time she'd seen him. He was

479

still short and fat, with balding hair and had a large cigar hanging from his mouth. He was dressed in an expensive looking business suit.

"Tyler McCain," he said, sticking his hand out to her. "It's good to see you again."

The handler and trainer for the horse was a tall skinny man that looked to be about forty and the jockey had been at least six inches shorter than her and definitely less than a hundred pounds. He looked like she could pick him up and throw him over her shoulder with one hand. She was always amazed at how someone built that little could handle such a large animal.

After the introductions, Tyler walked into the stall and rubbed Wonder Bred's head between his ears like she did when he had been a colt. He sniffed her and seemed to look into her eyes as she ran her hand down his long snout. "Hey buddy, remember me?" she said softly, smiling at him. "I'm so proud of you. Win or lose I'll always be proud of you." She kissed her fingers and placed her hand back on his head, petting him a little more before joining the rest of the group that had left to go place their race bets.

"Are you going to bet?" Bobby asked when he saw Tyler standing off to the side. Tyler never bet on any of her horses. She wasn't a gambler and didn't care to start. She shook her head no. "Are you sure? He has unbelievable odds." Bobby enticed once again. Tyler simply smiled and shook her head.

~

It was close to noon by the time the festivities had ended and the race had actually begun. Tyler was sitting in a private box with Bobby Gillis and a few of his business partners. Wonder Bred had been third out of the gate and held his line going into the first turn. Coming out of the second turn he moved into second place. Everyone in the stadium was on their feet. Bobby was screaming and jumping up and down. Tyler felt her heartbeat pick up as the horses rounded the last corner. Wonder Bred slowly challenged for the lead coming down the straightaway. When they crossed the finish line, Wonder Bred had nudged slightly ahead.

They'd called a photo finish and everyone waited, holding their breath. Bobby was ecstatic, he'd won a chunk of money already and was only waiting to hear how much when they showed the photo on the big screen. Wonder Bred had won by a quarter of a snout and seemed to have had a smile on his face.

Bobby jumped up and down screaming, "That's my horse, that's my horse!"

Tyler smiled and cheered with the rest of the group as they walked down to the track for the trophy and check presentation. Bobby introduced Tyler as the breeder as he answered the questions from the press.

An hour later, they walked into the private party. Tyler had been told earlier in the day by one of the businessmen in Bobby's group, that a few actors and actresses, prominent businessmen from around the state and California politicians would be attending the event. The crowd wasn't very large, but Tyler wished she'd found an excuse not to go. Schmoozing with California's royalty wasn't her idea of a good time, but she was there on business, so she smiled and passed out business cards as she shook hands, making her way around the room with Bobby.

So far, the swanky reception hadn't been as stuffy as

she'd expected. The hors d'oeuvres had been edible and the high-dollar champagne in her glass tasted okay, although she wished she had a jar of shine in her hand instead of the bubbly and bitter sparkling wine. Tyler had actually found herself enjoying the party when she felt the hair on the back of her neck stand up. She looked up to see the golden eyes that she'd thought she'd never see again, staring back at her. Tyler dropped the glass of champagne that she'd been holding. It spilled as the crystal glass bounced on the plush carpet. Tyler's hand shook as she bent to pick it up, but the waitress shrugged it off, handing her another full glass. *Talk about ghosts from the abyss.* Tyler shook her head. *My God, she's beautiful.*

Reegan Delsol was standing fifteen feet away, wearing a slim black dress with thin spaghetti straps and a low cut V in the front and back. The thin material stopped a couple of inches above her knees and fit her slender figure like a second skin. Her long black hair had been pulled up in a bun at the nape of her neck. Tyler felt her breath catch in her throat. Her hands quivered, threatening to drop the second glass of champagne. She'd been nursing the first and had had no intentions of picking up a second.

Tyler wanted to down the glass in one sip and pray that it would have the power to make her vanish. She was scared to blink, afraid that if she did, the image would disappear. She fought the urge to turn away, but Reegan hadn't made a move either. They stood quietly, staring at each other for what seemed like forever.

Reegan hadn't been sure what to do or say. She'd been just as shocked to see the woman standing across the room. Even if her mind had somehow conjured up the nerve to say hello, it was too late. Bobby had pulled Tyler away, ushering her towards the president of Capital Bank.

He was an avid fan of horse racing and looking at purchasing his first horse. He'd mentioned to Bobby that he may be interested in Wonder Bred's bloodline. Tyler hadn't been hurting for money, but now that one of her horses was a large purse winner, this was a great opportunity to raise her prices. It'd be very easy to accomplish since she owned the dam and sire of Wonder Bred.

Tyler hadn't forgotten about Reegan, but she had been asked to attend the party for business purposes and she'd planned on taking advantage of each opportunity as it arose throughout the afternoon. By the time the party was ending, she'd had four meetings set up for the following week that could potentially bank her nearly half a million dollars in horse sales.

Tyler's flight was leaving the next morning, so she had one more night in Arcadia and even though she didn't want to, she wondered if she could leave without speaking to the woman that had invaded her world and broken her heart in the same night.

Nine

Tyler walked out onto the balcony. The smokers were huddled at one end of the large patio area, so she went to the other end, leaning over the rail and looking down at the empty stands and freshly raked track. It was five o'clock, so the California sun was starting to set in the distance. The temperature was cool, but not as cold as Texas. Fall had come and gone and winter would be rolling into spring before long. Tyler breathed in the clean air at her end of the balcony, sipping the lingering glass of champagne and sloshing the bubbly liquid around her mouth before swallowing. She'd tried to clear her mind, but it kept coming back to Reegan. She was reminded of all of the sleepless nights she'd had as her heart and mind fought like the thunder and lightning in a Texas thunderstorm, over the abrupt dismissal and heartache caused by the beautiful brunette.

Tyler was lost in thought when Reegan stepped out onto the balcony. Her scent gave her away in the cool breeze.

"I'm surprised to see you here," Tyler said, without turning around.

"I'm here as a guest of my agent. She's a huge gambler. I guess you could say I'm surprised to see you too. I didn't realize your ranch bred and sold race horses," Reegan replied, sliding up to the rail next to her.

"We didn't really talk about the ranch much."

"Yeah, I guess you're right."

"Thoroughbreds bring in good money, but we don't sell them often. Quarter horses are show horses and they can sell for three or four times the price of a thoroughbred sometimes and are generally our bread and butter."

"Wow, I had no idea. So, the horse that won today was one of yours?"

"Yes. I sold him to Bobby Gillis last year."

Both women had been skirting around the main subject, each other. Tyler hadn't cared to see her and would never have come to the race at all if she'd known Reegan would be there. It had been hard enough coming to the same state and nearly the same city, but having the woman stand beside her, a mere foot away, was killing her.

"Did you see *Shadow's Eyes*?" Reegan whispered.

"No," Tyler said flatly. She still hadn't turned to face the woman next to her, out of fear she'd fall all over again. She'd tried so hard to get over everything that had happened and move past Reegan. The past five months had been hell.

"I'm sorry you haven't seen it. It received great reviews and may even win some awards this year."

"That's good." Tyler finally faced her. "I need to go find Bobby and say goodbye."

"How long are you here?"

"I leave in the morning."

"Have dinner with me," Reegan blurted out. She wasn't sure where that had come from, but then again, when it came to this woman she couldn't hold anything back and that had scared the hell out of her.

"I, Wha–"

"Please, Tyler. I didn't get to say goodbye to you and I need to explain why." Reegan's voice was pleading.

Tyler squeezed her eyes closed. This had been the last thing she'd had in mind. She just wanted to go home, but she found herself saying, "Okay."

"Where are you staying?"

"The Grand Palisade. Do you live close by?"

"No, I live in Beverly Hills."

"Where's that at?"

"Outside of Hollywood."

"Oh, well, you can come back with me and order room service if you want. I'm staying in a huge suite and the food's decent."

"That's probably a good idea since I rode with my agent. I guess I didn't really plan this out before I asked you to dinner." Reegan smiled softly.

~

The limo pulled alongside the curb in front of the high-rise hotel. Malcolm opened the door, greeting Tyler as she walked inside.

"Malcolm, this is a friend of mine." She nodded towards Reegan. "When she's ready to go, can you please have a car take her home?"

"Yes ma'am, Ms. McCain. You have a pleasant evening."

Tyler smiled and led Reegan towards the elevator. She didn't think she could ever get used to the attention from the hotel staff, not to mention the enormous suite she had been staying in. She was looking forward to going back to her ranch with sweat on her forehead and dirt on her boots.

"This view is amazing," Reegan said, looking through the large windows in the living room.

"Yes it is. I think Bobby may have been trying to impress me."

"Did it work?" Reegan asked.

"If you have to ask, then you don't know me very well," Tyler said, turning her eyes away from Reegan and the view behind her.

She walked into the master bedroom, pulling the tight leather dress boots off of her feet and massaging her aching toes. She wasn't sure how anyone could squish their feet into those things and call it comfortable. "The room service menu is on the desk. Get whatever you want," she yelled through the open doorway as she removed her jacket.

Reegan had been too nervous to eat, but ordered the food anyway. She sat on the couch, realizing Tyler was right. She didn't know her, not at all. But, for some reason she wanted to know everything about her. Tyler McCain had intrigued her in ways she'd never imagined. She'd steered clear of the word love so many times in her life that she wasn't even sure if that was what this was. She never imagined how much a simple script would change her life when she'd read *Shadow's Eyes* over a year ago. Donald Wright had been correct about one thing, Tyler McCain was definitely not a hillbilly.

"I had to get those shoes off of my feet," Tyler said, walking back into the room and breaking Reegan's concentration. "Did you order anything?"

"Uh...yeah. I wasn't sure what you wanted," *Because I don't know you.*

"I'm not very hungry, but everything I've had from the

restaurant here has been good so far," she replied, sitting down next to Reegan, careful not to touch her.

The electricity in the small space between them was surging powerfully, making the hair on Tyler's arms stand up. She fought off the pulsing beat of her own heart and tried to focus on having a normal conversation with this woman sitting next to her. But, God how she ached to touch her.

Reegan peered down at Tyler's bare feet and grinned. She had been surprised to see Tyler at the track, but the shock of seeing her dressed in something other than dust covered jeans, old cowboy boots, and a sweaty flannel shirt still hadn't worn off. Tyler looked like she'd been given a wardrobe makeover courtesy of Armani.

Reegan glanced at her again. Tyler resembled the kind of enigmatic, powerful woman, exuding sex appeal, that straight women threw themselves at behind closed doors and behind their husband's backs, but as soon as she'd spoken, that thick southern accent had sent Reegan's mind right back to the gritty dirt and animal smell of the ranch.

Reegan smiled. *You can take the girl out of the cowgirl, but you can't take the cowgirl out of the girl.* She thought to herself, realizing for the first time how out of place Tyler actually looked. She much preferred that sweet country girl in her memory over the aloof city girl sitting next to her, miles away.

Over the past few months, Reegan had tried to rationalize what had happened between them, but she'd failed over and over. She'd been attracted to a few women over the years, but there'd been no logical reasoning behind her attraction to this one in particular, and she had absolutely no sensible explanation for allowing herself to go as far as sleeping with her. They had nothing in common and lived hundreds of miles apart. Their worlds were literally day and night. Maybe that's why it had been so appealing. Tyler was safe. No one in Reegan's circle knew her. Yet, here she was sitting on the couch inches away from her. Reegan was scared to death, but all she could think about was being in Tyler's arms and feeling that smoldering passion burn her from head to toe once again. She wanted her.

"That fancy champagne turned my stomach, but I think there's wine and liquor in the wet bar. Help yourself, if you want anything," Tyler said, breaking Reegan's erratic train of thought.

"I'm fine. I'm not a fan of champagne either. I'd actually rather have some moonshine," she smiled thinly.

"Me too. Tyler agreed. "Well, I guess we should talk. That is what you're here for, isn't it?"

Reegan sighed. "Yes, I guess it is." She looked out at the city lights in the window across from them, avoiding the beautiful eyes questioning her. *I could get lost in your eyes all over again. I don't have the courage to tell you the truth.* Reegan thought about the words that had played over and over in her mind. *When Tyler McCain loves something, it becomes her whole life, the very air she breathes.*

"How about we start with why you left things the way you did?" Tyler said.

Reegan sighed. "We shouldn't have slept together and I'm sorry for allowing it to happen."

"Why did you? Allow it to happen, I mean."

"I don't know. We'd shared an emotional day and I'd been caught up in everything." Reegan met her eyes. "I care for you, Tyler, but that woman on the ranch and out there by the stream, she's not me."

489

Tyler clenched her teeth, turning cold eyes towards her. *I knew you were trouble the moment I laid eyes on you and I let myself fall head first. It's my own damn fault.* "Well, I guess that's it then," she said, pursing her lips.

"That's it? You don't have anything to say?" Reegan asked.

Tyler was not a confrontational person. She lived her life simply in black and white. "There's nothing else to say, Reegan. You basically said you made a mistake. I'm not going to sit here and call you a liar. You have a right to your own feelings, just as I have a right to mine. If they aren't the same, then we're sitting here wasting our time."

"How can you be so damn rational?" Reegan growled.

There's that feisty, hot mess that drove me crazy for three months. Tyler shook her head. Saying goodbye to Reegan wouldn't be easy and she had a feeling Reegan was going to make it twice as hard. "Reegan, you said it yourself, you're sorry we slept together. I'm not. Therefore, we have a difference of opinion and obviously very different feelings. Uncle Tucker has a saying, 'don't beat a dead horse'. You care for me and I care for you, a lot more I guess. Let's just leave it at that. Your life is here in the city with the bright lights and fancy clothes and mine's in the woods under the stars with sweat on my brow and dirt on my boots."

Reegan tried to stop the tears from slipping from her eyes, but she was too late. *How do you know me so damn well?*

Tyler reached up, wiping some of the tears from her cheek. "You'll always have a place in my heart, city girl," Tyler whispered.

Reegan kissed Tyler's cheek, then she stood and walked out of the suite with as much dignity as she could muster. She'd barely made it into the elevator before she began sobbing. When the elevator landed on the lobby floor, Reegan bowed her head, sneaking out without being seen by the concierge as she hopped into a waiting taxi.

~

Tyler waited until she heard the bell of the elevator before letting out the breath that she'd been holding. She knew Reegan felt more for her than she was letting on, but she couldn't make the woman love her no matter how hard she'd wanted to try. A light knock on the door made her heart skip a beat. Tyler snatched the door open, revealing the cart of food Reegan had ordered. The man in the tuxedo stood patiently. Tyler chided herself for getting her hopes up as she opened the door further, waving him inside. She tipped him with the cash she'd kept in her pocket and sat back down on the couch, wishing she'd had a jar of shine in her hand to wash away the pain. She'd finally fallen asleep, never looking at the contents under the stainless steel lids on the cart.

Ten

Three months later, Tyler was sitting on a bucket in one of the stalls of the stable, rubbing the swollen belly of a pregnant mare that had been in labor all day. She'd given all of the ranch hands the weekend off and her uncle was up at the house, making another pot of coffee. The snow on the ground had finally thawed and the meadow had slowly begun sprouting the purple and yellow weeds of spring.

"Settle down, Daisy-Bell. It's okay," Tyler murmured, soothing the animal.

"Tucker said you've been out here all day with her."

Tyler spun around wide eyed, falling off of the bucket into a pile of hay, knocking her black Stetson off.

"Easy, cowgirl," Reegan grinned. "You look like you've seen a ghost."

Tyler stared blankly at the woman leaning over the door of the stall. "What are you doing here?" she muttered, clearing her throat.

"Can we talk?" Reegan asked.

Tyler stood, slowly regaining her composure. "I don't think there's anything left to say."

"Cappy needs to be ridden," Tucker shrugged, walking by them. "I can keep an eye on Daisy-Bell," he called over his shoulder.

Tyler blew out a frustrating breath, knowing her uncle could have easily taken the horse out for a stroll around the pasture himself. She walked out of the stall, raising an eyebrow when she noticed Reegan's attire. The brunette was wearing faded jeans, worn boots, and a white t-shirt. Tyler's heart skipped a beat as she nodded towards Reegan and walked down to the end of the stable.

"You can ride Snowflake. She and Cappy are both Pintos. They are gentle and about as laidback as it gets," Tyler said, saddling up both of the horses.

Reegan was nervous about riding a horse again, but she trusted Tyler. She stepped closer, noticing the large bright white patch of fur on the side of the light brown horse and realized the pattern had probably been the reason she was named Snowflake. Tyler finished tightening the straps and led her out of the stall, tying her to the rail along the top, before going into the stall next door. Cappy's fur was a mixture of light and dark brown with a few off-white patches and her mane was black.

"She's beautiful," Reegan exclaimed.

"Yeah. When she was born, Uncle Tucker said she reminded him of coffee. So, we named her Cappuccino, Cappy for short," Tyler replied, pulling the horse out of the stall and handing the reins to Reegan.

Both horses were only about fourteen and a half hands, which wasn't very tall and just above pony size, but Tyler pulled the step stool over for Reegan to use as she climbed up on Snowflake's back. As soon as she was situated in the saddle, Tyler walked over to Cappy, hopping up on her like it was nothing.

Tyler led Cappy down the path that ran through the meadow, where Bucky and Houdini were frolicking, and back towards the other side of the property, near the stream. Snowflake trotted along beside her, obediently.

"Are you okay?" Tyler asked.

"Yes." Reegan smiled.

Tyler enjoyed the silence as they wound through trails. The backside of her land was the most peaceful place that she'd ever seen. As they neared the stream, she wondered why Reegan had returned. She wasn't sure she wanted to know. Her mind kept telling her to think rationally, but her body was more drawn to Reegan than ever before.

"We need to stop and let them rest for a bit," Tyler said, hopping down.

She walked over to Snowflake, holding her hand up. Reegan took the offered hand, climbing down with a slight wobble. Tyler grabbed the reins of both horse and led them over to the stream to drink. Reegan stood next to her, petting Snowflake's side.

"Are you about ready to tell me why you're here?" Tyler asked.

"I won the Best Actress Golden Globe Award last month for *Shadow's Eyes*. I brought it to you because without you, I would've never won it. Hell, I probably would've never finished the movie."

"Is that why you're here? I don't want your award, Reegan."

Reegan looked up. Nearly half a dozen months had gone by since they had lain on a blanket in the that very same spot, making love under the stars. No matter how hard she'd tried, Reegan had never been able to get Tyler's eyes off her mind. They'd followed her like a shadow, appearing when she least expected it. Reegan's heart ached as the sea-green eyes locked onto hers. She didn't think it was possible to fall any further than she already had, but the burning in her chest and fluttering in her belly told her otherwise.

"I made huge mistake," Reegan muttered.

"We've already been over that."

"Tyler, there's so much you don't know," Reegan sighed.

"What do you mean?"

"When I said I made a mistake sleeping with you, I was telling you the truth, but not because we shouldn't have made love. That was the most beautiful night of my life. It was a mistake because I wasn't honest with you and that wasn't fair to you."

"So, you lied to me?"

"No. I never lied to you, but I didn't exactly tell you the truth either."

Tyler moved the horses up the embankment to graze in the fresh spring grass and walked back down to Reegan, who had leaned back against a nearby tree. She squatted, picking up a few rocks and tossing them into the water one by one as she stood back up.

"What am I missing?" Tyler asked, tossing another stone.

"Where do I start?" Reegan asked, mostly to herself. She'd memorized a speech, but it no longer made sense.

"How about the beginning," Tyler said, meeting her eyes.

Reegan exhaled slowly. "I've never trusted anyone enough to let them inside. I come off as a cold bitch because of that very reason. I worked hard to build the walls around me. Everything changed the moment I met you," Reegan paused.

"Is that why you hated me? I had no idea what I'd

done to you, but you acted like you wanted to scratch my eyes out," Tyler stated.

"I saw my soul in your eyes and my walls crumbled. I did my best to stay away from you because I was powerless. I've been attracted to and dated many people, but in all my life, I've never met someone who stirred me so deeply. I knew you were the one and I didn't want you to be. I wasn't ready. I still don't know if I'm ready, but I can't take being away from you anymore."

"What does all of this mean, exactly?"

"I'd never slept with another woman. It wasn't because I didn't want to. I'd found women attractive here and there, but I always dated men. I wasn't ready to come to terms with what was hiding behind those walls," she sighed.

"Tyler, I'm telling you that you were the first woman I ever made love with because it was meant to be. You were the one I'd been waiting on. I've known all along that I was a lesbian, I just didn't want to believe it. You opened my eyes. My physical reaction to you made it painstakingly obvious and I fought the desire as long as I could. We are so very different, as you willingly pointed out in Arcadia. That's why I brushed you off and never looked back. I was so mad at myself for giving into my feelings for you and I'm tired of fighting this. I can't do it anymore."

Tyler stepped closer, wiping the tears that had escaped Reegan's golden eyes. "Where does this leave us?" she whispered. The sun had begun setting, casting an orange glow around them.

The radio on Tyler's belt crackled before Reegan could answer.

"Tyler, Daisy-Bell's close to crowning," Tucker called.

"Be right there," Tyler called back. She quickly untied

496

the horses and helped Reegan get back on Snowflake's back, before jumping up on Cappy.

~

They rode back as quickly as they could, despite the fact that they were on lazy horses that weren't much bigger than ponies. Reegan was still uneasy in the saddle and it was just about completely dark. Daisy-Bell was on the ground, rolling around in the hay next to a large pail of water, when Tyler and Reegan walked up to the open stall. Tyler took her hat off, setting it on the rail post.

"Is she going to be okay?" Reegan asked, cautiously.

"Yeah, she's fine. It won't be long now," Tucker said, removing his hat. He and Tyler dressed in yellow rubber aprons and donned clear gloves that went up to their elbows.

Daisy-Bell got up and walked around once more before laying down on her side. She snorted a few times and Tyler walked over to her, lifting her tail to the side as the milky white sack appeared. Reegan stood back out of the way watching in awe as Tyler and Tucker opened the sack, revealing two skinny little legs and tiny hoofs. Daisy-Bell continued breathing deeply and making grunting noises as Tyler and Tucker moved from a squatting position to their knees, pulling on the legs.

Seconds later, a small grey head with a black stripe down the middle, slid out. Reegan gasped. Tyler had sweat rolling into her eyes and no place to wipe it. She and Tucker appeared as if they were working harder than the horse giving birth, yanking and tugging on the foal.

The horse tried to roll to her feet, but Tucker stopped her, freeing up a hand to rub her side. "Don't do that now, you'll break his back," he said to the horse.

Tyler pulled a little harder and the rest of the small foal slid out onto the hay, followed by golden brown liquid. The foal took a bunch of quick, shallow breaths as Tyler began removing the rest of the birthing sack. Reegan smiled and grimaced at the same time. She'd never seen anything as beautiful in all of her life.

"It's a colt," Tyler said, revealing the sex of the little foal before standing and moving to the side.

The foal was solid grey, except for the black stripe down the center of his head. He rocked around back and forth trying to get his bearings, before laying his head back down to catch his breath.

"He's beautiful," Reegan exclaimed.

Tyler cleaned his naval with a medicated solution.

"What are we going to name him?" Tucker asked, giving the mare some alfalfa hay when she finally stood.

Tyler looked up at Reegan, smiling like a new mom. "Let's name him Shadow."

"Aww, Tyler. I think that's a perfect name for him."

"Uncle Tucker," Tyler turned back towards him. "This one's not for sale. I'm going to keep him for myself."

"Sounds good to me," he replied, checking the mare to make sure she wasn't showing signs of complication. "You did real good, Daisy-Bell," he murmured to the horse, petting her head.

"Pretty neat, huh?" Tyler said, taking her apron and gloves off.

"Yes. It's amazing. You're amazing." Reegan smiled brightly.

"I'm going to head on up to the house and call Doc Edwards and let him know she gave birth. Do you want anything to eat?" Tucker asked, removing his apron and gloves.

"I'm not hungry. Reegan?" Tyler questioned.

"No, thank you. I'm good."

"Call me on the radio if you need anything." Tucker put his hat back on and walked out into the darkness.

Reegan checked the time on her phone, surprised to see how late it had gotten. "When will he get up and walk around?"

"When he's ready," Tyler replied, watching the foal as he rolled around again, trying to get his feet under him. It had been close to an hour since his birth. Daisy-Bell walked over to her foal, sniffing him and rubbing her head on his. "That's a good sign," Tyler said.

Shadow finally got his legs under him enough to push up. He stood shakily with his skinny legs spread out as far as they would go, taking tiny steps all around to keep his balance. Daisy-Bell moved next to him, rubbing her head on his and encouraging him to follow her.

"That's incredible," Reegan said, watching the animals bond in front of her. She wiped the few tears that fell from her eyes.

"They're extremely smart animals," Tyler exclaimed as the foal found his mother's milk.

She stepped out of the stall, closing the door as she walked to the mudroom at the end of the hall to wash her hands and arms. She dimmed the overhead lights in the stables, leaving the light slightly brighter over the mare and her foal. Reegan was still standing outside of the stall, peering over the top of the gate at the new equine family.

Tyler cleared her throat and Reegan spun around to face her.

"I'd say I'm impressed, but it's so much more than that. You're smart and caring and the most genuine person that

I've ever met," Reegan grinned. "And sexy as hell with that natural southern charm."

Tyler smiled. "I don't know what to do about you," she said, leaning against the door of the empty stall next to the mare and foal and crossing her boots at her ankles.

"What do you want to do about me?" Reegan teased, stepping closer.

Tyler grinned. "I think I'm still trying to swallow everything you told me down by the stream. We've kind of hit a roadblock," she replied, nodding towards the horses nearby.

"The night we spent together next to the stream was the best night of my life. I should've told you the truth, instead of running away like I did. I was so scared. What felt so right also felt so wrong. I'd fallen for someone hundreds of miles away, physically and literally. I never thought I'd see you again. I spent months trying to get over you and then you appeared right in front of me like a slap in the face."

"If I'd known you were going to be there, I wouldn't have gone."

"I'm glad you were there. Seeing you made me realize that I'd made the biggest mistake of my life pushing you away. Tyler, I'm in love with you."

Tyler raised her eyebrows, the breath catching in her throat. She'd never heard anyone say those words to her.

"You asked me why I was here. I'm here because I'm so damn tired of making myself miserable. I had to know if you felt the same way," Reegan said.

Tyler closed the distance between them, and putting her hands on Reegan's hips, she kissed her with everything she had. Months of pain washed away as desire filled her heart. Tyler lifted Reegan off the ground, backing her up against the stall door as she drank from the passion overflowing between them, like a vampire feasting on life. Reegan wrapped her legs around Tyler's waist, desperate for contact and Tyler rocked her hips into her. Their kissing was unrestrained and raw, as if their lives had depended on it.

The foal in the stall next door neighed loudly, playing with his mother and breaking Tyler's concentration. Her head snapped back, reality slapping her across the face like a two-by-four. She backed away breathlessly, setting Reegan back on her feet.

"Tyler..." Reegan panted, licking the last of Tyler's kiss from her lips.

The arrant hunger in her voice cut through Tyler like a razor, splitting her to the core. The flames of desire burned deep in her chest with an unbearable pain. She felt like she might die if she didn't touch Reegan. Reaching out, she grabbed Reegan's hand, leading her inside the empty stall and closing the door. Reegan trembled as Tyler tugged a thin blanket down that had been draped over the wall, laying it on the thick bed of hay covering the floor.

Reegan stepped close to Tyler, yanking her shirt out of her jeans and over her head in one swift motion. Tyler followed until there were no clothes left. Reegan moved to the blanket, pulling Tyler down on top of her. Their lips met in a fierce kiss, igniting the embers that were still burning below the surface. Tyler ran her hand over Reegan's silky smooth skin, massaging her breasts and teasing her nipples with her thumb. The dim lighting above cast a faint glow over them.

Reegan pushed Tyler onto her back, straddling her as she slid back and forth over her hips, while running her hands over the compact muscles in Tyler's upper body and stomach.

Tyler sat up, kissing Reegan tenderly as she ran her hands through the hair dancing across the middle of her back, before rolling over and tucking Reegan under her. Tyler watched the light dance across Reegan's golden eyes. She stuck her tongue out, licking the edge of her open mouth and across her bottom lip.

"Tyler, please...I need to feel you," Reegan sighed, hungrily.

Tyler moved her hand lower, sliding her fingers through the wetness, easing slowly inside of her. Reegan gasped, bucking her hips against Tyler, pushing her deeper as she tangled one hand in her short hair and pushed the other one between them. Tyler was equally as wet and wanting as she had been.

Tyler groaned as Reegan teased her, sliding her fingers in lazy circles around her throbbing center. She slowed the fingers thrusting in and out of Reegan, matching her stroke for stroke. The balmy spring air of the evening did nothing to cool their heated bodies as a light sheen of sweat covered them, glistening in the dim light. Tyler circled Reegan's center with the pad of her thumb as her fingers pushed deep inside of her, then almost all the way out and back again.

Reegan had never felt arousal anywhere near the animalistic craving driving her body. The closer she felt Tyler get to climax, the deeper the hunger inside of her. She moved her fingers back and forth, milking her and teasing her entrance with each pass, causing Tyler to pant heavily. She could no longer hold back, pushing her fingers deep inside of Tyler and nearly howling like a rabid animal as her own climax ripped through her body. Tyler groaned loudly as the fingers plunged inside of her, releasing the tension like the snap of a rubber band. She shuddered uncontrollably, collapsing on top of Reegan and sliding off to the side.

Neither woman spoke as they fought to catch their breath, staring up at the dim light above them. Tyler felt like she'd died and gone to heaven. She'd never felt her body so constrained, and yet it easily relaxed into a puddle of tender mush in a blink of an eye.

No wonder people smoke after sex. Reegan thought, stretching her aching muscles. She'd never done drugs, but her body felt as if she'd just flown to the moon in two seconds and was floating back to earth. She took in her surroundings, the heady scent of sex mixed with the smell of fresh hay, horse and leather, tickled her nose. The soft yellow glow of the overhead light cast everything in a golden hue. Reegan kissed Tyler gently, tasting the brine saltiness from sweat on her lips.

Finally finding her voice, Reegan said, "I guess I can scratch 'a roll in the hay' off of my bucket list."

"What's a bucket list?" Tyler asked, still trying to get her bearings. Her mind had never been more tranquil and her body had never felt so incapacitated. She didn't think she could muster the strength to move if the stable was on fire.

Reegan rolled her head to the side, smiling at Tyler's innocence. "I love you."

"I love you too," Tyler grinned, using the last of her energy as she pulled Reegan into her arms and closed her eyes.

~

The sun was a half hour away from rising when

Tucker walked into the stable with two steaming cups of coffee. Tyler was checking the mare and foal when he found her. Reegan was standing off to the side. He raised an eyebrow, peering from one woman to the other, noticing that they were in the same clothes from the day before, albeit slightly askew, and Reegan had stray pieces of hay in her hair.

He grinned. Handing Reegan a mug, he said, "Looks like you're staying to me."

Tyler turned around, taking the second cup from him. "What's that supposed to mean?"

Tucker shrugged, and walked away to begin his work day.

"When I arrived yesterday, I told him I wasn't sure if I'd be staying. I figured you'd toss me out of the gate onto my ass."

Tyler laughed, sipping her coffee. "How long *are* you planning to stay?" she asked.

"Forever if you'll let me," Reegan answered.

"What about California?"

"Hollywood can wait. Besides, I can live anywhere and still have my career." Reegan stepped closer, kissing Tyler's lips. "I love you, Tyler McCain and I'm never saying goodbye to you again. Plus, this ranch thing is kind of fun," smiled.

"City girl," Tyler grinned, shaking her head.

The End

About the Author

Sydney enjoys reading everything from magazines to historical books and boasts about her massive collection of paperbacks and hardbacks in her personal library. She's also a huge fan of multiple TV shows, which she says take up too much of her time.

You can message her and like her fan page at facebook.com/sydneycanyon

Go to www.tri-pub.com to get information about Triplicity Publishing or to submit your manuscript.

Other Titles Available From Triplicity Publishing

Cypress Lake by Graysen Morgen. The small town of Cypress Lake is rocked when one murder after another happens. Dani Ricketts, the Chief Deputy for the Cypress Lake Sheriff's Office, realizes the murders are linked. She's surprised when the girl that broke her heart in high school has not only returned home, but she's also Dani's only suspect. Kristen Malone has come back to Cypress Lake to put the past behind her so that she can move on with her life. Seeing Dani Ricketts again throws her off-guard, nearly derailing her plans to finally rid herself and her family of Cypress Lake.

Crashing Waves by Graysen Morgen. After a tragic accident, Pro Surfer, Rory Eden, spends her days hiding in the surf and snowboard manufacturing company that she built from the ground up, while living her life as a shell of the person that she once was. Rory's world is turned upside down when a young surfer pursues her, asking for the one thing she can't do. Adler Troy and Dr. Cason Macauley from Graysen Morgen's best seller, *Falling Snow,* make an appearance in this romantic adventure about life, love, and letting go.

Bridesmaid of Honor by Graysen Morgen. Britton Prescott's best friend is getting married and she's the maid of honor. As if that isn't enough to deal with, Britton's sister announces she's getting married in the same month and her maid of honor is her best friend Daphne, the same woman who has tormented Britton for years. Britton has to suck it up and play nice, instead of scratching her eyes out, because she and Daphne are in both weddings. Everyone is counting on them to behave like adults.

Falling Snow by Graysen Morgen. Dr. Cason Macauley, a high-speed trauma surgeon from Denver meets Adler Troy, a professional snowboarder and sparks fly. The last thing Cason wants is a relationship and Adler doesn't realize what's right in front of her until it's gone, but will it be too late?

Fate vs. Destiny by Graysen Morgen. Logan Greer devotes her life to investigating plane crashes for the National Transportation Safety Board. Brooke McCabe is an investigator with the Federal Aviation Association who literally flies by the seat of her pants. When Logan gets tangled in head games with both women will she choose fate or destiny?

Just Me by Graysen Morgen. Wild child Ian Wiley has to grow up and take the reins of the hundred year old family business when tragedy strikes. Cassidy Harland is a little surprised that she came within an inch of picking up a gorgeous stranger in a bar and is shocked to find out that stranger is the new head of her company.

Love Loss Revenge by Graysen Morgen. Rian Casey is an FBI Agent working the biggest case of her career and madly in love with her girlfriend. Her world is turned upside when tragedy strikes. Heartbroken, she tries to rebuild her life. When she discovers the truth behind what really happened that awful night she decides justice isn't good enough, and vows revenge on everyone involved.

Natural Instinct by Graysen Morgen. Chandler Scott is a Marine Biologist who keeps her private life private. Corey Joslen is intrigued by Chandler from the moment she meets her. Chandler is forced to finally open her life up to Corey. It backfires in Corey's face and sends her running. Will either woman learn to trust her natural instinct?

Secluded Heart by Graysen Morgen. Chase Leery is an overworked cardiac surgeon with a group of best friends that have an opinion and a reason for everything. When she meets a new artist named Remy Sheridan at her best friend's art gallery she is captivated by the reclusive woman. When Chase finds out why Remy is so sheltered will she put her career on the line to help her or is it too difficult to love someone with a secluded heart?

In Love, at War by Graysen Morgen. Charley Hayes is in the Army Air Force and stationed at Ford Island in Pearl Harbor. She is the commanding officer of her own female-only service squadron and doing the one thing she loves most, repairing airplanes. Life is good for Charley, until the day she finds herself falling in love while fighting for her life as her country is thrown haphazardly into World War II. Can she survive being in love and at war?

Fast Pitch by Graysen Morgen. Graham Cahill is a senior in college and the catcher and captain of the softball team. Despite being an all-star pitcher, Bailey Michaels is young and arrogant. Graham and Bailey are forced to get to know each other off the field in order to learn to work together on the field. Will the extra time pay off or will it drive a nail through the team?

Submerged by Graysen Morgen. Assistant District Attorney Layne Carmichael had no idea that the sexy woman she took home from a local bar for a one night stand would turn out to be someone she would be prosecuting months later. Scooter is a Naval Officer on a submarine who changes women like she changes uniforms. When she is accused of a heinous crime she is shocked to see her latest conquest sitting across from her as the prosecuting attorney.

Vow of Solitude by Austen Thorne. Detective Jordan Denali is in a fight for her life against the ghosts from her past and a Serial Killer taunting her with his every move. She lives a life of solitude and plans to keep it that way. When Callie Marceau, a curious Medical Examiner, decides she wants in on the biggest case of her career, as well as, Jordan's life, Jordan is powerless to stop her.